FIVE
DAYS
OF
FOG

Anna Freeman is a lecturer in Creative Writing at Bath Spa University as well as a multiple slam-winning performance poet who has appeared at festivals across Britain including Latitude and Glastonbury. She lives in Bristol. Her first novel, *The Fair Fight*, was short-listed for the Authors' Club Best First Novel award.

Also by Anna Freeman

The Fair Fight

FIVE
DAYS
OF
FOG

Anna Freeman

WEIDENFELD & NICOLSON

First published in Great Britain in 2018
by Weidenfeld & Nicolson
an imprint of The Orion Publishing Group Ltd
Carmelite House, 50 Victoria Embankment
London EC4Y 0DZ

An Hachette UK Company

1 3 5 7 9 10 8 6 4 2

A CIP catalogue record for this book is
available from the British Library.

ISBN (Hardback) 978 0 297 87199 6
ISBN (Export Trade Paperback) 978 0 297 87200 9
ISBN (eBook) 978 0 297 87202 3

Typeset by Input Data Services Ltd, Somerset

Printed in Great Britain by Clays Ltd, Elcograf S.p.A.

MIX
Paper from
responsible sources
FSC
www.fsc.org   FSC® C104740

www.orionbooks.co.uk

For Norman, who has always given me books
And in memory of Cora.

The First Day of the Fog:
Thursday, 4 December 1952

Florrie comes up from the Tube at Kennington to find that the afternoon is frozen into stillness, the air holding its breath. Cigarette ends and dead leaves lie just where they fell. The movement on the shabby, familiar street is all human, the hunched and hurrying people, the buses and bicycles.

Unseen and unimagined above her, up past the leafless fists of trees and the brick chimneys, and further still, beyond the hanging clouds, something rare and powerful is beginning to form: an anticyclone. If there were clear skies, tomorrow might be an eerily windless day, dry and bracing, tingling the lungs. If this were the countryside, there might come a clean white fog, the clouds fallen to the earth.

But this is an anticyclone over London, and in December. Before morning comes, the clouds will drop and as they do, they'll catch everything that they can; the fumes from millions of coal fires, the smoke from the chimneys of factories, the exhausts of motor cars, every scrap of airborne dirt.

London is well used to fogs. But this will be something

else entirely, toxic, impenetrable and unmoving. It will bring the city to a halt, will poison the lungs of the old, the very young and the sick. This won't be a peasouper, or a London particular, or a dreary day. It will be the sky's smothering hand, and before it lifts, thousands of London's most vulnerable will be dead.

Beneath the waiting sky, Florrie is looking down. She's watching her own legs move, her skirt pushing at the fabric of her swing coat. No one would guess how tightly she's packed herself, that the clothes she's tucked into her bloomers shift with every step, the cardboard label of something scratching at her inner thigh.

Her lungs ache as though she's been breathing peppermint, her toes are numb. But right in her centre, burning where no cold can touch it, is the knowledge that tomorrow her mum will be home.

When Ruby went away, two years ago, clothes were only just off the ration and most of the women in England were still competing to see how dutiful and drab they could make themselves. Today Florrie saw it all through her mum's eyes, the new and extravagant availability of good cloth, the full skirts and thick coats. She wants to get home, spread her haul out on the bed, and imagine Ruby's face when she sees it.

She turns the corner onto Kennington Lane. A couple of blokes in sharp suits are standing outside the pawn shop, rolling cigarettes. One of them looks her up and down and gives a whistle. 'Will you look at those legs.'

When she doesn't reply, he calls, louder, 'Alright, sweetheart? Lovely pair of pins.'

The other fellow whispers to him, and she can guess from his urgent manner that he's saying, *That's Florrie Palmer, you idiot*, or something like it. And next second the first bloke's calling out, 'No offence, miss. No offence.'

She doesn't spare him so much as a glance. But that's another thing that's changed since Ruby went away: Florrie herself. There's a world of difference between fifteen and seventeen, and she hopes her mum will see it and treat her like a woman, not a little kid.

And now, unexpectedly, here comes Ted walking towards her, in his work clothes of heavy boots and an old corduroy suit that's fit for dusters. The very opposite of those blokes, and thank God for it. He has his hands pushed deep into his pockets. He's grown up too, and now, at nineteen, his face has lost its soft edges. He's far too thin, looks stretched, rather than grown. But it's there, in his big hands and feet and solid jaw, the outline of the man he'll be.

'Hello, there,' he says. 'I was just thinking about you.' He puts one hand on her elbow.

'I should hope so, too.' She can hear her voice grow less common, matching itself to his. She can't help it. Her second cousin has a lovely way of talking. He went to a much better school than she did.

'Give us a smile, then,' he says, and she realises she hasn't, and makes herself. She's not always good at remembering to smile.

'That's better. I'll walk you home, shall I? Will you take my arm? I know I'm filthy. You needn't,' but she's already giving him her hand and letting him tuck it into the crook of his elbow.

She says, 'Ain't you a gent, to walk me two steps?' The moment they turn the corner they'll be on Aunt Nell's street.

He walks her anyway, past the terrace of narrow houses,

Florrie holding herself a little apart so that she won't bump his leg with her own, secretly padded ones.

Aunt Nell's is just beyond a blank stretch of rusty fence, bordered all along its length by weeds. One of the corrugated panels has been kicked inwards, where kids or tramps have pushed their way in. Half London is like this even now, seven years on from the end of the war, the terraces of houses broken, like a crowded mouth with teeth knocked out.

He stops at the gate and seems to be deciding whether to kiss her, right here in the street. She tips her chin up at him to say, *Go on, then.*

He looks serious. His cheeks have gone pink in the way they do.

'Look here,' he says, 'it'll be alright,' and she knows he's thinking about her mum coming back.

She's almost as shy as Ted. 'It's going to be a bleeding awful row, more like. But they have to find out sometime, don't they?'

Then he does lean down and kiss her on the cheek, very fast, the first time he's kissed her in public. He smells of coal smoke and tar.

'We'll stick together,' he says. 'It'll be alright. You'll see. You go on. I'll be in, in a minute,' and he walks off, back down the street the way they came.

She doesn't ask where he's off to, because she's glad he isn't coming in just yet.

Aunt Nell calls out, 'Which one of you is that?' from the kitchen as Florrie opens the front door.

'Me,' she calls back, and Nell replies, 'Nearly tea time, alright?' but she doesn't come out of the kitchen, and Florrie's glad of that, too.

She takes off her shoes without bending down, the toe of one foot on the heel of the other to prise the shoes off, and a shove to get her feet into her blue pompom slippers. Then, still wearing her coat, she goes quickly up the stairs.

This is Ted's bedroom, but for the last eight months, since Florrie and her gran came to stay, he's made himself a bed up in the attic. That's what a decent man he is. And now Grandma Dolly's gone – God rest her – it will be Florrie and her mum in here together.

The room isn't pretty. The wardrobe is old and heavy, the chest of drawers is plain utility. The bed is brass and creaks whenever anyone moves so much as a toe. But there's a brand-new dressing table, already crowded with bottles of scent and hair tonic. It's a welcome-home present for Ruby, big enough for the two of them to sit side by side on the cushioned bench. Too big for the little room, really. In the gloom, the mirror's scalloped edge makes it look like it's wearing a crown. Fit for a queen, just right for her mum.

She lifts her skirt and looks down at the swollen legs of the hoisting bloomers, her shins like pale twigs. The knickers are of pink silk, with ribbons at the knee; she reminds herself of chicken drumsticks. Thank God Ted didn't put his hands on her waist. He'd have felt how tightly she's stuffed.

And now she begins to pull out her carefully rolled treasures, and unroll them just as carefully. An indigo cardigan with a white collar. A floral blouse. A pair of woollen stockings, tiny zigzags running through the knit. And prettiest of all, a pair of pyjamas in butter yellow with embroidery at the collar and cuffs. They seem to glow against the faded candlewick bedspread.

She puts the new things away in the wardrobe and then

just stands, stroking the arms of the jumpers, the skirts of the dresses. She's been at it for months, getting a bit here and a bit there. It's been like bringing her mum home piece by piece. And tomorrow she and Ruby will stand in front of the wardrobe together.

It's more than a welcome-home present, it's a peace offering. Although that feels hopeless, really, like seeing the roof about to give over your head and putting a hand up to catch it.

She's never talked back to her mum, never disobeyed her at all. No one would, with Ruby for a mother. It really is going to be a god-awful row. But only imagine if it works, if she's allowed to leave the gang, set free to marry Ted, to learn how to be a decent person. She won't be big bananas in the neighbourhood anymore. No one will nudge anyone quiet and say, *That's Florrie Palmer*, ever again. She'll miss that. But she won't miss anything else.

And surely, she thinks, stroking the sleeve of a green wool dress, surely they can still go out together, Florrie and her mum; a little shopping trip now and then will be alright, even when she's straight as an arrow. Ted needn't know. And nobody gets hurt at the shops.

Ted walks past Fisher's Pawn and Loan every day – it's just around the corner from their house, after all – but he hasn't been inside since he was a little boy, after his father was killed.

The shop feels pretty much the same, is still crowded with unwanted things, the smell of dust and the ancient sweat of strangers. He catches a whisper of himself at seven, clutching his mum's brooch, bringing the money home wrapped in the pawn shop ticket. The weight of it all.

6

His dad gone, his mum alone in the world, a war on.

But this is a different man at the till, middle-aged and thin, in a shirt with a sweat-stained collar.

'Mr Fisher?'

'What can I do for you?' the younger Mr Fisher says.

'I wondered if you might have a ring.' He steels himself for whatever teasing might come next. 'A ring for a girl.'

The fellow doesn't blink at him, just rummages under his counter. It's almost a disappointment. There's the clink of keys and the man reappears, holding a jeweller's tray.

The rings are all different, a mess of styles and stones. Mr Fisher moves an electric lamp over and the tray bursts into glittering life.

Ted gazes at them, imagining how each one would look on her finger. He doesn't know the size. How do other fellows manage to find such things out?

He puts his own index finger to one with a dark red stone. It might pass as brand new, it's that clean and shining.

'Twenty-two nicker.'

Ted draws back his finger.

Mr Fisher laughs. 'Oh ho, a bit dear for you? Not to worry, son. Have a butchers at this one. I can let this one go for thirteen.'

It's a thin gold band with a flat stone of pearly white. Mr Fisher picks it up carefully, between finger and thumb. His hands are big for such a thin man, and the ring looks tiny in his fingers. But then he holds it right under the lamplight and the stone is suddenly made of pink and blue sparks, full of depth and movement.

'Opal,' he says. 'And fourteen-carat gold.'

Ted holds out his own hand and Mr Fisher puts the ring into it.

7

'Fit for a princess, that one,' Mr Fisher says. 'Like a ring for a fairy, ain't it? That pretty.'

'Thirteen quid,' Ted says, doubtfully.

'I'll knock off ten bob if you take it now. How's that?' Mr Fisher says, and Ted closes his fist over the ring. It's picked up the heat from the lamp and is warm against his palm.

He hands over his savings with a little wrench, and Mr Fisher gives him a tiny cloth bag in exchange. He opens the drawstring and peers inside. The fairy ring lies at the bottom, only a hint of shine in the dark.

Behind him, a voice says, 'Unlock the back for us, Davey boy,' and Mr Fisher comes out from behind his counter so fast he might have been pulled on a string.

Ted turns. There are three blokes standing among the tea sets and vases, the younger two in draped jackets and brightly coloured ties. The old man is Harry Godden. He's dressed so smartly he'd not look out of place in the Savoy. The loose skin of his neck sags against his starched collar and his cheeks droop, but even so, he's more wolf than bloodhound. Half the neighbourhood is ready to come when he calls, and the other half ready to run.

Harry nods at him, and Ted raises a hand in reply.

Mr Fisher looks at Ted in surprise, no doubt wondering how a scruffy kid like him knows Harry Godden to say hello to.

Looking past Harry at the younger blokes, a fist of loathing curls in Ted's belly. He knows one of them, or knows of him, which is more than enough. Don's not much older than Ted but he's broader in the shoulder, with a big meaty head. His moustache is greased into a neat line along his upper lip. Don looks right at Ted and he looks back, trying not to blink.

Harry nods at him again as they go by, following Mr Fisher. Ted stares at Don's back in its pricey jacket until it disappears into the corridor at the back of the shop. There's the creak of feet as they climb a set of unseen stairs.

That greasy spiv. Ted still can't understand why Florrie ever went about with him; it must have been like kissing a side of ham. Well, she's told him to hop it now and Ted's got a ring for her finger in his pocket. He's going to lift her from the filth she was dragged up in like a man plucking a flower from the soil.

It can't be done by halves. Only look at his mum, trying so hard to be respectable and still always with cousins and aunts bringing God knows what into her house. And now Harry and his hangers-on have set themselves up at the top of her road.

Even so, he can't help imagining what he, Ted, might look like with a neat little moustache. What it might be like to wear handmade shoes and drive an American car. He can't help wondering, just a little bit, whether Florrie might rather that he did.

The tea isn't going to be up to Nell's usual standards. She's got to make a cake for Ruby coming home tomorrow, so the eggs and sugar must be kept, and she'd better hang onto the last of the jam as well.

She slices the bread, counting one piece for each of them, and the rest for breakfast. There's an art to slicing National Loaf. You have to hold it up at the same time you press down, or it crumbles. But they do say it's better for you than the white stuff.

There's a tin of tomatoes, so tomatoes on toast might do. But that's hardly enough tea for three, and Florrie and Ted eat so much, both of them still growing.

To make up for it, she puts her second-best oilcloth on the table, the one with a pattern of cherries and twining leaves. She puts out the red teapot to match. If they can't be well fed, they can at least have something cheerful to look at.

When Florrie and Aunt Dolly first came to stay they brought in so many little extras. Shameful though it is, Nell did get used to it. Since Aunt Dolly died that's all dried up.

So they'll have to apply for Ruby's ration book the minute she gets back. Her cousin's homecoming has been tugging at the edges of Nell's mind all morning. It's not as though she's sorry they're letting Ruby out early, not after she's been so ill, it's just that it would be nice if her cousin had somewhere else to go.

She hasn't seen Ruby for ages. They wouldn't let her have visitors once they sent her to the prison hospital, and however much Nell had hated going to Holloway, that was still a terrible thing. *They'll let me see you when it's too late, I suppose*, Nell had written. She'd regretted sending that one.

But it's not too late after all. Fingers crossed, Ruby will make a full recovery. That would be too much, to have first Aunt Dolly, then Cousin Ruby come to stay here, only to go and die.

She can hear Florrie rattling about upstairs, but Ted's not in yet, so she doesn't call the girl down. Florrie has a steady, cool way of looking at Nell that can make her feel quite unsettled. When Nell was seventeen she'd been scared to say boo to anyone, still wearing pinafores and lisle stockings.

She goes out into the hall and touches up her lipstick, taking her time, making sure it doesn't spread into any of the lines that have sprung up around her mouth in the last couple of years. She looks alright for forty-four. Her hair, which used to be a sandy red, is fading into mousy blonde. But some women try for this very colour from a bottle, and never get it.

She's still peering at herself when there's a knock at the front door and her cousin Maggie calls, 'Cooee, only me,' as if she comes round every day.

Nell doesn't reply, but only waits where she is, just inside the door. And just as she'd expected, Maggie comes waltzing in without being asked. If she's going to start coming around uninvited, perhaps Nell should keep the door locked, even while they're in.

'God alive, you nearly gave me a heart attack, Ellen. What are you doing, hiding behind the door?' Maggie stops with her hand to her chest.

She steps forward, far too close, but Nell has the mirror at her back and only waits for her cousin to move.

Maggie's a bit shorter than Nell, but she carries herself as though she's big and somehow you believe it. They're almost the same age, too, but the blasted woman hardly looks older than thirty, as smooth as if the war never touched her. Which, of course, it didn't. Here it is, not quite five o'clock, and Maggie's all dolled up like she's going to a party, her hair dyed a vivid red, her nails and lips done in scarlet. Nell, who had been so satisfied with her own looks just a moment before, feels dowdy and frumpish and smoothes down her apron.

'I don't think I've seen you since the funeral,' Nell says.

'Bloody hell, Ellen, I've only just stepped in the door and you're griping at me,' Maggie says. 'Some of us have things to do.'

'I didn't mean that,' Nell says. Although she hasn't had a penny off Maggie to help with feeding Florrie. She knows Maggie takes the girl out to cafes and all sorts. You'd think she'd spare a thought for the daily cost of getting dinner on the table.

'Well, you want to say what you do mean, that's all. Course I've come round. Need to make sure you're all ready for my sister coming out, don't I? Here.' Maggie holds out two flat tins and when Nell doesn't move, she grasps Nell's arm by the elbow, lifts her arm for her and pushes them into her hand. 'You're welcome, I must say.'

Nell looks down. Corned beef. It's exactly what's needed.

'Very nice,' she says, because she can't bring herself to thank her cousin. 'I suppose you'll want to stay for tea.'

'Not if you're going to look like that about it,' Maggie says. 'Honestly, Nellie, no wonder you can't find a fellow.' She laughs and jabs Nell's upper arm with one polished nail.

'Don't.'

'You look sour enough to curdle milk. That why you've taken to hiding behind doors? Face like that, I don't wonder.'

She jabs again. It hurts, and finally Nell makes herself step sideways, along the hall. Maggie steps right along with her. She's so close that Nell can see crumbs of face powder caught in Maggie's eyelashes.

'Don't,' Nell says, again. She stops at the foot of the stairs.

Maggie sighs, and pushes Nell's shoulder with the flat of her hand. 'Love of God, Ellen, learn to take a joke. Are you making tea, or what? I'll stay, if you're offering. And then I'll get Florrie out from under your feet. I'm sure you've things to do. There must be a speck of dust left somewhere.'

Nell turns and calls up the stairs, 'Florrie! Come down at once. Your aunt's here.'

In the kitchen Maggie goes straight for the best seat, Dolly's old chair, and plonks herself down on the cushion.

'So. My sister's coming home at last. You got everything you need, Nellie?' Maggie lights up a cigarette.

'I suppose so.' Nell pushes the ashtray over to her cousin.

'This house is quite the place for poorly queens. It's getting to be a habit of yours.'

'So she will be . . . that. Will she?' Nell can't bring herself to say the word *queen*.

Maggie winks. 'Oh, well, ain't you Miss Innocent. If you don't know, I'm sure it's not for me to say. You being so clean and decent.'

The kettle begins to wheeze and whistle. Nell takes it off before it shrieks, pours the water into the pot and brings it all to the table. She doesn't sit down; she'll only have to stand up again. She goes to the larder and gets the tin of tomatoes, digs about for the tin opener. It's one of the army kind, and Nell's always afraid she'll cut her hand open.

Maggie's leaning back in her chair, watching her.

'Give me that.' She holds her hands out, and Nell puts the tin and the opener into them.

Maggie pushes up the sleeves of her silk blouse, show-ing strong arms, the inky blue blobs of her tattoos. She punctures the tin with no more trouble than cutting into an apple.

'You look like Popeye,' Nell says.

Maggie laughs.

Nell gets the bread from the crock so that she won't have to look at her cousin. 'I have missed your mum ever so much, I'll have you know.'

She has, more than she'd ever have expected. And the little treats. But she hasn't missed the endless visitors, the shifty types hanging about the street, the boxes of black-market rubbish being carried in and out of her house. She supposes all that's about to start again.

'Here, did you ever find anything else of my mum's?' Maggie asks, as though she hadn't carried off armloads of Dolly's belongings before they'd even had the funeral. But Nell's saved from replying by the sound of feet on the stairs.

'Here she is, look,' Maggie says. She stands and holds her hands out.

'Alright, Auntie Maggie?'

If only the girl would smile a bit.

Maggie says, 'Don't you look a picture? And here's me come to take you out. I'll have to fight the blokes off you.'

From the hall there comes the click of the front door opening and the shuffle of boots on the mat.

Maggie says, 'And that's our Ted coming in now. Good. We'll all have tea.'

The kitchen table isn't a big one, and Florrie is very aware of Ted sitting next to her, of the older women opposite, watching them both.

She's managed to keep Maggie away from Ted for months, going out to meet her aunt at pubs or at the shops. Now she doesn't know how to talk, how to move her body, which voice to use. She's a different person around Ted, or she's trying to be. And any minute Auntie Maggie's going to say something to shame her.

Nell and Maggie look very alike in the face. Nell is paler, but they have just the same round chins, the same small mouths, the same way of pursing their lips and drawing their pencilled eyebrows in. In dress they're worlds apart. Maggie has on a blue silk blouse with a ribbon at the throat. Florrie would be afraid to eat tomatoes on toast in a get-up like that. Nell's still wearing her apron. Maggie's probably never worn an apron in her life.

The two of them look absurdly like incarnations of Florrie's own possible futures, one brassy red and wild, the other fair and good. Like having an angel and a devil on your shoulders. But Florrie would hate to be like either of them. Nell isn't really out of the life, not the way Florrie wants to be. She's just at the bottom of the heap, where everyone can walk on her.

Maggie pushes her empty plate away and immediately fetches out a cigarette, without waiting for the others to finish.

'Here, Teddy,' she says, 'be a love and light me.' She'll have her own light. She's just doing it so that Ted will jump up patting his pockets.

Now she's leaning over the table, the cigarette between polished nails, her fistful of gold rings flashing as they pass underneath the kitchen light. The edge of the tattoo shows a curve of blue ink at her cuff.

'It looks like the weather's turning,' Nell says, looking over at the darkening window.

'Just a bit of fog.' Maggie widens her eyes at Florrie. 'You ain't afraid of a bit of fog, are you, Flo? You'll come out with me tonight?' It's not really a question.

Florrie hates fog. Has always hated it. The claustrophobic damp of it, the feeling of the world made hidden and dim. 'Course I will.'

Maggie says, 'Course you will. A bit of fog never hurt anyone.' She laughs, and Florrie knows that hurting someone is just what she means to do in it.

From the corner of her eye she can see that Ted is watching her, wanting to know where they're going. She asks, 'Where are we off to?' There. Let Maggie tell the lie, if someone must.

'Round Hazel's, is all.' Maggie winks at her. 'She's got some things for us to try on, won't half suit you. And some bits of make-up, I think.'

That's actually rather a good joke, and Maggie knows it. Florrie has to look down at her teacup so as not to smile. That's the trouble with her aunt: she keeps you laughing even while she's making you feel sick to the stomach.

'Fog can be quite nasty,' Nell says, taking the butter dish, and by her tone, Florrie wonders if she's guessed. You never know with Nell, who's sharper than she looks.

'Don't fuss, Ellen,' is all Maggie says.

Ted seems to have stopped listening, anyway. He's draining his cup and lighting his own cigarette, watching his mum bustling about.

Florrie and Maggie leave Nell still fussing around in the kitchen. Ted sees them off at the door with a cheerfulness that makes Florrie's chest ache at how good he is, how good he imagines her to be.

Or perhaps it's the fog, which is coming in properly now, bringing with it a sulphurous smell that's unusually foul, even for a London peasouper. The darkening sky is hazed, the distances blurring. It's awful the way it shrinks the world, robs her of her ability to judge what's coming.

But Maggie is growing more and more cheery. 'This weather's just what we need,' she keeps saying. She sways as they walk, in order to bump Florrie with one shoulder. 'Ruby's back tomorrow, and just in time for Christmas.'

'Counting the minutes,' Florrie says.

'Another queen in the family, hey? When Mum died I thought, you watch, those Godden bitches will be coming over here, trying to take the crown off us, but here we are.'

'Hazel Godden says they don't want it.'

'Know what's good for them, right enough. The gang would fall to bits without the Palmers. And if you play your cards right, it'll be you crowned after Ruby.'

'Or you,' Florrie says.

Maggie laughs. 'No fear. Too much for me. I'm the muscle, not the brains.'

'Maybe it's too much for me, and all.'

'Don't be daft. We're training you up. Don't you say that sort of soft rubbish to your mum. She's got her heart set on you taking after her. She's said so often enough.'

'Who's coming tonight?' Florrie asks, so that she won't have to think about that.

'Cissy. Thought she could be the bait. Now, don't look at me like that. Cissy's alright. Does what she's told. I'm teaching her all I know.'

'God help her,' Florrie says, because she can see Maggie's in a good enough mood to take the joke.

Maggie does grin, and then pokes Florrie in the shoulder with one gloved finger. 'Don's driving us to the club.'

'Leave it out.'

'I'm just saying. You could do worse than Don. He's well in with Harry. The Godden Boys have always been a good choice for a Cutter girl. A lot of family ties, there.'

Florrie thinks of Don, right after her gran's funeral. A bright, heart-breaking spring day. Don grabbing at her waist, calling her a cold bitch. She shakes her head involuntarily.

'Well,' Maggie says, 'I'm just telling you. You want to remember. You can't just choose any old boy. Don's alright.'

They're almost at the end of Nell's road. Florrie can feel the shape of the thing she wants to ask sitting in her mouth, but she should wait. Surely. Wait and ask her mum.

It spills out. 'Hazel went off with a greengrocer for a bit, though.'

She can feel Maggie turn to look at her, but she keeps her eyes on her own feet, the damp pavement.

Maggie says, slowly, 'She did. A greengrocer. Only imagine. Course, it didn't last.'

Florrie wants to ask why not, but she's afraid to.

Maggie huffs through her nose, and tells her anyway. 'I should think she got bored. I know I would.'

'But Gran let her go off with him.'

They're at the corner. A few more steps and they'll be at the pawn shop.

Maggie is looking at Florrie with a half smile she doesn't like at all.

'Here, you ever hear about Ivy Richards? Before your time. Ada's cousin. Hazel's great-aunt.' She puts a hand on Florrie's arm and stops her walking.

'No. What about her?'

'She was a Cutter girl. Your age, too, I'd say. Went off with a boy from over the river, didn't she? A bloke from the old Green Gate gang. Got herself in the family way. Just after your gran was crowned queen, this was.'

'I never even heard of Green Gate.'

'Well, they ain't about now. Your gran told her no, but off she went. What do you think happened to her?'

Florrie shrugs.

'Well. The fellow had a nasty accident. Ran into a lead

pipe, didn't he? Careless. Don't know what became of Ivy after that. A girl all on her own, and a bun in the oven.'

They walk on, Florrie still quiet, her fists clenched in the pockets of her coat. No one would do that to Ted. Ted's family.

Now they can see Don's car, waiting outside the pawn shop.

Maggie says, 'Don't you bother your mum about this when she gets home. I won't have it. She was right to do it.'

'Do what?' Florrie's watching Don's car, the bulky shape of him behind the wheel. Cissy's leaning over from the back seat to talk to him, one elbow on the back of the seat in front, the other hand playing with her hair.

'What do you think, Miss? Leave your dad and come home. Didn't want to be another Ivy Richards, did she? Ain't that what you was asking about?'

'Yeah,' Florrie says. 'Course.' But it's given her a jolt. She's never been allowed to ask about her dad, hasn't thought about him much since she was a kid. All she knows about him is that he was called Robert, he was killed by a train, and he was a lazy good for nothing.

'Your dad died not long after,' Maggie says. 'So it turned out for the best. I mean it: don't you bother your mum with that old story. It don't do to dwell on what can't be helped.'

Florrie wants to ask if he really did run into a train or if it was another lead pipe but she doesn't dare. Maggie's mood can switch so fast. But if her mum had to decide whether to leave the gang for love, had to make the same choice Florrie does, as Ivy Richards had to, as Hazel did with her greengrocer—

Faintly, through the car's window glass, Florrie hears Cissy say, 'Here they are. About time.'

Don gets out and opens the doors for them. First the front passenger side for Maggie, who winks at him and says, 'Good boy,' as she gets in, then the back door for Florrie. He gazes over her head, like a butler.

She says, 'Evening, Donnie,' just to annoy him.

Cissy, next to her, says, 'There you are. Weren't you ages.' She's done up about as cheaply as she can be, bottle-blonde hair and too much lipstick.

Maggie leans over from the front seat to slap her on the shoulder. 'You want to be quiet.'

Cissy gives a little smirk as though she's done something clever. She's not even family. The joke of it is that when Maggie first brought Cissy around, Florrie had a moment's hope that they might be friends, being the same age, and she'd felt sorry for Cissy, growing up in a children's home. But the girl's an idiot and catty with it. Florrie's not that lonely. Not by a long shot.

She watches London go past through the windows and tries to steel her nerve for what they have to do. The fog smokes the glass, blurs the world into something softer than it is.

Don drives so fast that before she feels halfway ready, he's dropping them off in Soho.

The Golden Palm looks shabby when it's empty. It smells of floor polish and old beer. The brass edging on the bar still gleams, the crystal chandelier is as sparkling as ever, but the scuffs show up on the dance floor, the stage looks forlorn without the band. There's no one here but the two hostesses, putting candles out on the little tables.

Maggie leads them across the club, Cissy following and Florrie trailing behind, wishing she could go home.

'Know why this place is called the Golden Palm?' Maggie

says, to Cissy. 'Named after my mum, ain't it? Palm, for Palmer. You never met my mum, did you?'

It's named for Ada Godden and her granddaughter, Hazel, as well. Trust Maggie not to mention that.

'No,' Cissy says. 'But I've heard a lot about her.'

'She'd have loved you,' Maggie says.

Florrie can almost see her gran, sitting in one of the chairs she's edging past now, drinking gin and bitter lemon, smoking black cigarettes. If she'd have paid any attention at all to Cissy, it would have been to tell the girl to go home. It would have been good advice, too.

Maggie gives a knock at the door beside the bar, the one marked *Private*. She gives two quick raps, two slower ones and then two more fast: the Cutters' knock.

After a few moments Hazel opens the door.

Florrie's a bit shy of Hazel, who is twenty-five and seems so sure of herself that she might be ten years older. She's quite striking to look at, with the same big bones as the rest of the Goddens, a perfectly straight nose and long, dark lashes. And, of course, she's Ada and Harry's only grandchild. She's not someone to mess about with. She looks about, checking over the empty club, and then nods at them all to come in.

Cissy looks around herself. Perhaps she's imitating Hazel, or maybe she's checking to see if the hostesses have noticed she's special enough to be allowed through the private door and then into a poky storeroom full of boxes and stacks of chairs. Either way, Florrie thinks she's a berk.

'You'll have to be quick,' Hazel says. 'My gran will be back in a bit and you know she won't like it.' She tugs, distractedly, at the drop of gold hanging from her ear.

Maggie, who has to tilt her head up to look at Hazel, says, 'This ain't just your gran's club, is it? My sister's back tomorrow, and she's got a half share. And we're only changing our clothes. What's the crime in that?'

For a moment Florrie thinks Hazel might be about to tell them to go, and there won't half be a scene if she does. But then she says, 'Just be quick. And you want to be careful bringing these kids in, Maggie. We've had the coppers crawling all over us the last few weeks. Do what you came to do and shove off.' If Florrie talked to Maggie like that she'd get her eye blacked, but Hazel can get away with it, somehow.

'I'm nearly seventeen,' Cissy says. 'And Florrie is already.'

Florrie can tell Hazel doesn't think much of Cissy. She wrinkles her nose and says, 'Even so. Hurry up. I'm off as soon as I can get this paperwork done. It's my night for the pictures.'

Maggie winks at Florrie and says, to Hazel, 'Going to meet a fancy man, are you? Got yourself another greengrocer? Just you bring us back a couple of oranges.'

If Hazel minds, she doesn't show it. She just says, 'If I am, that's my affair,' in her ordinary voice. She has to edge around Cissy to get out, and does it without looking at the girl at all.

Maggie's already pulling the men's suits from the holdall, shaking out the creases.

Florrie takes the dark grey one, the one she thinks of as hers. She'd rather not undress in front of Cissy, but there's nowhere else to go, and Maggie has no patience with modesty.

Cissy goes over to a stack of three chairs in the corner and sits on top of them.

'Ruby was nicked in this very room.' Maggie is already unbuttoning her blouse.

Florrie doesn't reply. She pulls off her stockings.

'I thought she was nicked at the shops,' Cissy says.

'You don't think even Ruby would get two years for that, do you? Use your head. She done over a nice big house. Just like the one I got you set up in as a housemaid. She gets back here with the stuff, and next thing you know the place is crawling with the old bill. Some bastard grassed. Oh, for the love of God, don't look at me like that.'

'I never meant to,' Cissy says.

'You won't get nicked. You're only going in to sweep the blooming floors.'

Florrie gets herself into the trousers and finds a bandage to strap down her breasts. Behind her she can hear the rustling and shifting of Maggie doing the same.

There's something comforting about the feeling of the bandages, like being wrapped in strong arms. But she doesn't like the look of it. She waited long enough to grow a figure; it's a wrench to hide it.

None of the shoes fit Florrie quite right. She wraps another bandage around her feet to bulk them out, and pulls on a pair of black socks. The socks have been worn before, and don't feel clean in her fingers. She laces the shoes as tightly as they'll go.

'Don't you have the shoulders for it, Flo,' Maggie says, as Florrie puts the jacket on. 'I say so every time, don't I?'

Cissy looks at Florrie with a bit of spite in her smile. 'Oh, Maggie, ain't you mean? Florrie's got a lovely figure.' She smoothes down her skirt, which is rather a cheap one in gaudy pink.

Florrie ignores her, which is all she deserves.

Maggie fetches out an eyebrow pencil and she and Florrie darken each other's eyebrows, and draw on moustaches with careful, downward strokes.

'Oh,' Cissy says. 'It ain't half good.' She sounds surprised, even a little nervous.

Florrie, looking at her aunt, can see why. It's not just that Maggie looks like a bloke in the half-light, with her hair pushed back into her hat, the smudge of kohl along her upper lip. It's that she looks like a man you'd cross the street to avoid.

It all makes Florrie feel the way she often does around her aunt, a poisonous cocktail of strength and fear, bravado and cowardice. With Maggie behind her, Florrie could do anything. Anything, that is, except disobey her aunt.

Maggie pulls her shoulders back and sticks her hands in her trouser pockets. 'Right then.' She pitches her voice low. 'Let's go and get ourselves a bit of pocket money.'

'Let's,' Cissy says, far more eagerly than she would if she'd done this before.

Nell goes into the patchy fog of the garden, closing the back door behind her with hardly a sound. Here, behind her potted rosemary, is the gap in the fence, where two panels have lost their rivets and can be pushed apart with a bit of effort. She squeezes into the bombsite next door, feeling the water run off the damp fence and down her neck.

The remaining pieces of the O'Briens' house – part of the hall and a bit of the back wall – stand up dark and jagged-edged. She stays well clear of them. What's left of the floor could cave in at any time, and below it is a long drop into the cellar. Anyone wandering carelessly might be pitched down, buried alongside all the things that had made up the lives of Mr and Mrs O'Brien.

After Edward died and Aunt Dolly and Ruby came to stay for the first of what would turn out to be many times, she used to imagine letting her leg break through into nothingness, the fall into darkness. Just walking out into the middle of the wreckage and jumping up and down. She might really have done it, if it hadn't been for Teddy. She feels a shameful sort of sadness now, when she remembers that.

She picks her way, watching her feet, feeling the damp rubble move about under her shoes. In no time her stockings and shoes are clogged with a pale mud as dense and grainy as mortar. But here, towards the O'Briens' back fence, is Nell's secret: the old Anderson bomb shelter, swamped in brambles, like the thorns growing over sleeping beauty's palace.

The Anderson always had been an inconspicuous one, buried in the garden and its roof covered with turf. Now, after all this time, the hump of its back is just a swell in the middle of the tangle. If you didn't know where to look, you'd never see it at all.

She pulls aside the brambles that hang like a bead curtain over the steps. Every strand tries to shower her with droplets of dirty water but it feels good to rip and tear and pant, to feel the thorns crinkle against her pigskin gloves.

Inside, by the faint, greenish light, she finds the shape of the hurricane lamp and the waterproof tin of matches, and the shelter unfolds itself. Here it is, her retreat, and almost as she left it. She's always afraid that she'll come in to find that tramps or kids have found the place, but the only intruders have been the snails, who have left their shining silver tracks across the floor. The corrugated walls glisten with damp.

But she's made the shelter quite a little home over the last eleven years. The floor has a rag rug, the table has a dark red oilcloth. The bunks are made up with patchwork blankets, knitted by Nell herself, over the hours she's sat here. She has a new gas bottle for the little stove. She's brought in tea and powdered milk. She even has a couple of tins of food, hidden in here for a rainy day, and one of Edward's bottled ships. She'd given away so many of his things, after he died. But it's nice to have something to remember him by, tucked away where Teddy can't be upset by it.

Other things about the place are left from the nights spent sharing the shelter with Mrs O'Brien, and then, after their neighbour left for Shropshire, with just little Teddy. The old gas masks are still here, although they're probably rotted through. All those leaflets they used to hand out, warning against getting gas masks wet.

She lights the paraffin heater and sits on the bed, still in her hat and coat. She hasn't been here for months, not since just after Aunt Dolly died. But she needs a bit of time away from the house this evening, with the idea of Ruby coming home hanging over her head.

She looks, as she always does, at the two framed photographs on the corner shelf, one of herself and Edward, and the other of her mother, Lillian. This place has been her shelter from the family, as much as it ever was from the Blitz. But more than that, it's a place to think about Edward, her mother, all the friends lost. And now there's Aunt Dolly to think about, too. Without the shelter she might have cracked and gone off weeping in public. It's astonishing that everyone else in England seems to have come through the war and be managing without a place to hide themselves.

Edward would have disapproved when Ruby and Dolly came to stay, and Lillian, God rest her soul, would have been horrified. Even in her photograph Lillian looks stern, her mouth set. She might be about to say, *You behave, Ellen, or you'll end up like that sister of mine.* She could make the word 'sister' sound dreadful, a hissing spit.

When Nell was little she hadn't understood what all the fuss was about. Aunt Dolly had lovely clothes, and sometimes she had more money than she could spend, even if she was penniless the rest of the time. She kept her hands soft, while Lillian took in laundry on top of her factory work, screwing endless lids onto jars of pickled onions.

Even all those years ago Aunt Dolly would turn up at their door, Ruby and Maggie trailing behind her. Sometimes Lillian would let Dolly in, and sometimes she wouldn't. It didn't matter whether they came begging or, as they occasionally did, bearing heaps of presents. It depended only on Lillian's mood. *I worked my socks off to get out of this sort of life, and here you are, trying to drag me down,* Lillian would say, whether she was taking a bag of oranges from her sister's hands or shutting the door in her face.

But Lillian is dead, along with Edward and half of England. They hadn't been there when Nell had to find a way to get Teddy's school uniforms with only Edward's pension, never mind the cost of food. And alright, it wasn't a really good school, not a private preparatory, which was what she'd always wanted for him, but it was the best she could do. And even if Ted hasn't made the most of the opportunity, she can't be sorry she kept him out of the sort of school she'd had to go to herself, half the children crawling with lice and impetigo. She made the best decisions she could, just as everyone did during wartime, and Ruby and Dolly kept them all from going hungry, whatever else there was to say about them.

Nell, who spends far too much of her life on her knees scrubbing at the floor, who has to scrimp over every penny of Edward's pension, could almost admire all those Cutter girls making their own way, rather than letting life grind them down. They know they'll spend half their time in prison and they do it anyway, so that they can live it up while they're free.

She tells her mother's picture, 'Dolly always said the world's unfair, and she was just evening things up for herself.'

But it doesn't sound convincing. And now Teddy's got a little crush on his second cousin; Nell isn't keen on that, not at all. Of course, she has only herself to blame, since she's the one who let the Palmers into their home. She understands now why Lillian wept with relief on Nell's wedding day and said, *There, you're out of it, at last.* Edward, an engineer at a printworks, had been a coup for a girl like Nell. And, though Nell hadn't realised it at the time, his presence did keep the Palmers away. They came back quickly enough, as soon as he was gone.

'Well,' she tells her mother, 'Ruby never does stay too long, and she'll take Florrie with her when she goes. It might all blow over.'

Lillian stares back at her, her lips drawn tight. She might be about to shake her head.

From where Florrie's standing, Cissy's pale face and hair seem to be floating in the dark. It's only when she paces into the lamppost's light that the whole of her becomes visible, her shoulders hunched against the cold, her head sticking forward like a chicken's. Her coat is too tight for the full skirt and shows a clumped ruffle at the hem. She walks a few paces and retreats back into blackness. Then here she comes again, back into the light.

The fog is hanging about the glow from the lamppost, smudging the outline of the pillar box, the corner of the building, Cissy's silhouette.

Beside Florrie, in the shadow of the doorway, Maggie tuts and whispers, 'Straighten up, you daft bint,' under her breath. She slaps her life preserver against her palm. It's a bit of lead pipe, cheap enough to throw in the river if needs be.

The doorway they're standing in smells of piss. The fog is beginning to settle on the back of Florrie's neck, dampening the collar of the suit, and her hands, in the pockets of the overcoat, are growing numb. She takes her right hand from her pocket, draws off the knuckleduster, flexes her fingers, slips the foul thing back on. In the moment the metal has been away from her skin it's already grown cold.

And there's a fellow coming now, a black shape in trench coat and trilby, the spark of a cigarette at his lip.

'Here we go,' Maggie murmurs.

The man is speaking to Cissy, who tilts her chin up to look at him, runs her fingers down his lapel.

Florrie finds herself willing them on. *Come on, come on. Hurry up.* She thinks this, even while she's wishing she could be somewhere – almost anywhere – else.

The couple are moving nearer, though they're out of the light now and Florrie can see them less clearly. The slap of their footsteps on the damp pavement grows louder. Then they're lit by the lamppost at the alley's mouth, hardly two yards away from where she and Maggie wait.

She hears Cissy giggle and say, 'You're a hot one, ain't you?' as they turn into the alley.

Maggie's eyes are shadowed by the brim of her hat. The kohl moustache makes a black slash across her face. She holds up a finger. *Wait.*

Maggie always waits too long. It's not fair on Cissy, who'll be starting now, trying not to go too far before they come, listening out for them. But Florrie doesn't speak up. She just stands, waiting, a coward with a knuckleduster.

At last Maggie whispers, 'Alright.'

As soon as they're moving, Florrie feels a familiar calm come over her. It's a flat, pale feeling, and pushes everything down. She follows Maggie without a thought in her head. Anything might happen. Anything, almost without her meaning it to at all. It's not really her fault, if she doesn't even think.

They go as quietly as they can to the mouth of the alley. Through the descending fog they can see the shape of the bloke, and poor old Cissy, up against the wall.

'Alright, alright,' Cissy's saying. Then she stops, and stares over his shoulder to where Florrie and Maggie stand. The bloke turns to look, but what can he see? The lamppost is behind them. They're two silhouettes in hats and coats just like his own. And again there comes the slap of the preserver against Maggie's palm.

'Alright, lovebirds?' Maggie sounds as much like a bloke as any woman could. 'Let's see you empty your pockets.'

Florrie stands as straight as she can behind her aunt, her shoulders square.

'I should think not,' the bloke says. He sounds afraid.

Don't blame me, Florrie wants to tell him. *I don't want this to be happening either.*

Cissy's stepped off to the side, her arms wrapped around herself.

Have something good, Florrie wills the fellow. *Have something good, so we can go home.*

But there's not a lot, just couple of quid and a cheap watch. And Maggie doesn't like to waste a fog.

Ted sits in the windowless attic, cross-legged on the camp bed and wrapped in the quilt his mum made him when he was just a little boy. The camp bed's iron frame digs into his thighs, but he's used to it and hardly notices. In one hand he has the torch, and in the other, between finger and thumb, he holds the opal ring.

In the beam he's finding new colours, green and turquoise, flecks of violet. He's staring at it as though it were a crystal ball and could show him his future with Florrie. But it's better than that. It's going to give him, what? Not authority, exactly, but something like. Let's see Maggie try to carry Florrie off for the evening once she's got Ted's ring on her finger.

He wonders what they're doing. Almost ten o'clock: they're probably at some bloody drinking club. Perhaps Maggie's pushing Florrie to talk to other fellows, he wouldn't put it past her. But Florrie won't do that. He hopes to God she won't.

He hears his mum coming out of the kitchen, the creak of her climbing the stairs.

He puts the ring back in its little bag, unfolds his legs and lies back with his hands behind his head, looking up at the roof. There's something soothing about the crisscross of the beams, the solid thoughtfulness of the structure. He quite likes it up here. Or at least, the feeling that he's doing something gentlemanly and self-sacrificing by giving up his room to the ladies.

It's what his dad would have done. Edward was decent. That's the word everyone uses, when they talk about him. When he went off to fight, Edward had made Ted shake his hand and give his word that he'd look after Nell. He'd told him that a good man looks after the ladies in his life.

Of course, Ted hadn't been able to look after his mum in any way that mattered. He was still a child. Instead the Palmers came, just when Ted and his mum were wondering how to make ends meet, and put food on the table that most people in London hadn't a hope of getting their hands on. Ted was too little to have an inkling of where it all came from, had thought Ruby and Dolly really were like queens, with their furs and jewels and boxes of chocolates. Now just the thought of Ruby coming home makes him feel suffocated.

England is emptied of half its men, Ted's house is full of women, and none of them listen to him much. It can't have been what his dad was hoping for, when he marched off to give his life so that Ted could go on. He wonders what Edward would say if he knew that the main thing Ted needs to protect his women from is other women, and half of them his own bloody family.

He lies still, in a discontented restless way, and listens to his mum singing quietly below him. He holds the little cloth bag in his hand and turns it over and over, feeling the shape of the ring through the cloth, just waiting for the sound of his girl coming home.

*

Florrie is back in the club and back in her own dress. They got changed in the alley by the back door and wiped their faces with their hankies. Now she's in the lavs, jostling for a bit of space at the mirror. The air is heavy with the smell of girls out on the town; hair tonic, perfume, sweat. On either side of her they're primping their hair, spritzing themselves with scent. Behind her there's a queue for the lavs, and everyone in it chatting. Some of them are smoking or holding drinks, even in here.

Florrie has a pink smudge under her nose, the skin irritated where she's wiped the kohl away. It looks as though she's smeared her lipstick right over her top lip. She's doing her best to cover it with powder.

'Budge up,' someone says, and Hazel's face appears in the mirror beside her own. Florrie shifts a little closer to the girl on her other side, who's adjusting the neckline of her dress. Hazel gives Florrie a smile in the mirror and fetches a comb out of her handbag.

'Where's Maggie?' Hazel asks.

Florrie just jerks her head at the door. Maggie hadn't even bothered to check what she looked like, past a peep into her compact mirror. Florrie has the feeling her aunt enjoys looking a bit rough around the edges. She'll be out there talking to all the people she knows, and they'll nudge her and ask what she's been up to, to get herself so tumbled about.

'Get anything good? Where did you go?' Hazel asks.

Florrie huffs through her nose. 'Wherever Maggie said. Like always.' She tries not to sound bitter.

'Ah, well. You're back now.' Hazel gives her a wink and there's something so understanding in her look that Florrie feels a wash of relief. She wishes, not for the first time, that

Hazel were her sister. Hazel's mum's in prison. She must know how Florrie feels, must be thinking about her own mum, with Ruby coming back.

This thought, and the bit of kindness on Hazel's face, makes Florrie brave enough to ask, 'You weren't really out with a greengrocer?'

'Him!' Hazel wrinkles her nose and leans too close to the mirror. She bares her teeth at herself, looking them over. 'That was ages ago. A hundred bloody years ago. Your aunt just likes to mess about.'

Florrie gives up on the powder, fetches out her lipstick instead. 'But you,' she swallows, and leans in close to look at her own nose, so that she won't have to look at Hazel's face, 'you came back?'

Hazel's drunk, or close to it. She's got both hands on the edge of the counter now, the comb still in one fist, as if she might fall without something to hold her up.

'He wanted me to work in the shop. Do I look like a greengrocer's wife?' She gives a hard, barking laugh and looks down at her hands, with their rings and polished nails, the soft white skin. 'He weren't that good looking. Not enough for that.'

'But they let you go? My gran. She let you go off.'

Hazel looks hard at her now. 'You're soft on some boy.'

Florrie shrugs again. Hazel grabs her by the elbow and pulls her into the corner, by the roller towel. Florrie has to fumble her handbag off the counter top by its strap so as not to lose it.

'They let me go alright,' Hazel says, so quietly that Florrie has to lean right in to hear her. Hazel's breath is sickly sweet and alcoholic. 'They cut me right out. Didn't let me into meetings. Wouldn't talk to me, if they could help it.

And then the bastard starts knocking me about. I ask my gran – and your gran – to give me a hand. I fucking beg them. And you know what they say?' Hazel shakes Florrie's arm by the elbow, banging her upper arm against the roller towel's metal case.

'No.'

'They say, "Oh, well, if he don't beat you, he don't love you." So I go to my granddad. Mr Harry Godden, got half the world in his pocket, can do anything he likes. You know what he says?'

'No.' Florrie feels slightly sick.

'He says it ain't his place to meddle in lovers' tiffs. And he sends me back. Not one of them lifts a finger to help me till he breaks my jaw.'

'Pardon me.' A girl is standing in front of them holding her hands out, limp wristed and wet.

'Push off,' Hazel tells her.

'Well!' the girl says, but she does step back. 'I only wanted to dry my hands.'

'Some people have no manners,' her friend says. She has wet hands, too. Hazel gives her a look that makes her wipe them on her skirt.

'And then what?' Florrie's almost whispering.

'You know what,' Hazel says. 'They see I've learned my lesson and they help me teach him his. I'll say we fucking teach him. And then they set me up with this place. I only thank God I never had a baby by him.'

Florrie says, 'My fellow ain't like that.'

Hazel gives an unhappy laugh. 'They none of them seem like that at first. But it don't matter. Even if he's nice as pie, you'll be all on your own, scraping for pennies and working your hands to the bone. What can a girl like you or me do, out there? You'll end up working in a factory and thinking you're lucky to have it.'

Florrie looks at her own shoes standing on the grubby lino, silk-covered, with a pointed toe. Lovely shoes. Expensive shoes. But she can get shoes anytime she likes, all by herself. She won't be in any old factory. Not a chance.

Hazel says, 'You have a bit of fun with this bloke, whoever he is. Just don't you marry him. Mark my words. It ain't worth it. Now. Let's go and get ourselves a drink.'

Outside the lavs, the club is back to its rightful self. The light from the crystal chandelier catches in glossy hair and raised glasses, glints off the brass. All about the walls echoes of it shine from the mirrors.

Hazel gets them both a gin and Florrie knocks it back, and goes off to dance. She feels full of blazing hope. She's sorry for Hazel, of course she is, but the Cutters just let Hazel go. It wasn't even a row. Florrie couldn't care less about going to meetings. She'll still see her mum; her mum would never cut her out completely. She doesn't care about the rest of it. And maybe, if her mum really did have to make that same choice over Florrie's dad, she'll know how it feels. Her belly is hot with gin. All around her girls are swirling their skirts, their hands held by blokes who have shed their jackets and hats. She's wild with relief and exhaustion and the sway of the music, warmed right through with the drink and the crowds and being here, in a Cutter club, a Palmer club. They'll still let her come in here. Of course they will.

And now Cissy's dancing too, holding her skirts above her knees like a French girl in the pictures. You'd never know she cried her eyes out most of the way here, till Maggie gave her a smack.

And when Maggie finally pushes through the dancing couples and hooks her thumb at Florrie and Cissy to say, *come on*, Florrie's so buoyed up she doesn't even bother to feel silly for following after her aunt like a duckling.

As they pass a table of women, all done up to the nines and shrieking with laughter, half off their heads with booze, Maggie leans over and picks up a fox-fur coat from the back of one of the chairs and slings it over her own shoulders, bold as brass.

Florrie looks back, but none of the people at the table seem to have noticed, caught up as they are in their own good times.

It seems someone does, though, because as they leave the band leader says, 'And here's a song for the lovely ladies just on their way out,' and launches into another tune. It's 'Lady Be Good'.

Maggie turns and waves at him. The lilt of it follows them up the steps and into the cold.

The Second Day of the Fog:
Friday, 5 December 1952

All through the night, the fog comes in. In some parts of London it's a drifting haze, in others it's impenetrably dense. By the early hours of Friday it seems that the Thames has the worst of it, and the shipping port has to be closed. As the sunless morning breaks, it spreads out across the city, creeps through cracks in windows, comes softly down chimneys and into the lungs of sleeping people. It has no trouble at all in breaking into Holloway, notorious as it is for draughts and damp.

Ruby lies on the thin mattress, fully clothed. The blankets, coarse and smelling of sour salt, are clammy beneath her and the ghost of the TB is scratching at her chest.

It's barely dawn; the high window is sliced into neat rectangles of grey. Through the thick glass, the shape of a pigeon shuffles around on the windowsill. The electric bulb, which sits overhead in a metal cage of its own, casts a plain and unfriendly light onto the distempered walls, the stone floor. The ancient pipes groan and clank in the walls like storybook ghosts.

But none of this matters anymore.

For the first time since she got the news of her early release, she's letting herself imagine the outside. It still feels reckless, in case they change their minds and whip her freedom out from under her feet. She's thinking of her daughter, her sister. The feeling she gets when the Cutters are together, the whole rowdy, laughing lot of them. That she belongs to something powerful. Something worth having.

And she'll have to jump straight in and do whatever needs to be done, no matter if it's overwhelming coming out, no matter if she's tired. She has to go home a queen. She knows, from the vague hints in the girls' letters, that there's some sort of trouble she'll have to deal with. Aunt Frannie arrived at the prison last week, swearing someone grassed her up. And there's Florrie to think about: the girl will need taking in hand. There'll be all sorts of choices to be made on the outside, rather than having every little thing decided for her. And that's always a rather difficult thing to get used to, just at the beginning.

She can hear the ring of the screw's footsteps on the iron stairs, coming up to unlock the cells so that the women can slop out their pots.

Now there's the clonk and grind of the locks, the burst of voices as each woman comes out onto the landing. A few times there comes the sound of knuckles on her cell door – some of the women knocking her a goodbye as they're chivvied past. Twice the knock is the Cutters' special one. But no one comes to let her out.

Prison teaches a person how to wait, and Ruby is very good at it. She stares at nothing. There's nothing to look at, and what there is she's seen every day for two years.

A bit of a fog has snaked its way past the badly fitting

window glass to haze the ceiling. But let it come in. She, Ruby, is going out.

Outside Florrie's window, faintly, someone says, 'Oh, will you look at this weather. And I've gone and left the washing on the line.'

She can feel the icy air on her cheek, though the rest of her is warm and weighted by layers of blankets. She lies very still; the moment she moves, the cold will find her.

Her mum's coming home. She pulls that thought to her and holds it. The memory of last night is trying to get at her, tugging at the edges of her mind. Her Aunt Maggie, panting. *Now you, Florrie. Give the soft prat a remembrance.* Although the poor bastard had been past remembering, and it was Florrie who was soft, not to say no. She can still feel the rubbery give of his stomach against the toe of her shoe.

But Florrie's good at not thinking about things that bother her, and a lot of the things she's not thinking about will be alright, once Ruby comes back. She might very well be about to be set free, along with her mum. If she can just get Ruby to understand.

She turns over, towards what was Dolly's side of the bed. Dolly died on this very mattress, this very spot. Ever since, she's been keeping her limbs tucked in so as not to touch the place, but now she puts her hand out and lets it slide across the cold sheet. Tonight Ruby will be here, warm and real and alive, and thank God.

Nell is cleaning the kitchen, although it's barely light outside. The wireless is turned low so as not to disturb Florrie and Ted. *London has been caught in an overnight fog,* the newsreader murmurs, as though she might not have noticed. *Delays on many major bus routes. Visibility low. Take care when driving or crossing the road.*

It certainly does seem like the filthiest kind of day. There are wisps of fog creeping in through the crack where the window doesn't quite close. It's like a swarm of minuscule flies gathering up by the ceiling.

It's silly to be doing the floor now, when Ted and Florrie will be down for breakfast and will be bound to walk on it, but she can't stay still, not with Ruby coming home. The thought of it is running through her arms, pushing the brush back and forth. The posture, kneeling, arms outstretched, is a little like praying, though she couldn't say what she hopes for exactly.

What she should do, of course, is go out in the horrible weather – taking care while crossing the road – and see what she can get to help feed Ruby up.

She's left an unwashed strip of lino from the kitchen door to the scullery, so that they can all go out to the garden to use the WC. It's satisfying to see the clean floor on either side.

Swish, swish, the brush pushes itself back and forth. It doesn't matter how she feels about it. It's happening. There's no need even to look at the tangle of her own thoughts. Just let them swish away with the grime.

She goes to the back door to tip out the bucket but the moment the door is opened the smell of the fog, sharp as flaring matches, catches at her throat. She's never smelled a fog like that in her life. She slams the door on it and the water goes down the scullery sink instead, leaving a scattering of grime all over the enamel, a grey flower with a plughole at its centre.

When she comes back to the kitchen Ted is at the table,

eating bread and butter, twiddling with the dial on the wire-less. Static whooshes in and out, scattered with snatches of voice and song. She sits opposite him and pulls her teacup towards her. Ted chews and looks about at the kitchen as though he's not sat in it every day since he was born.

Nell says, 'Well. Your Auntie Ruby will be home today.'

'I don't suppose I still have to call her Auntie. She's not my aunt.'

'You don't have to, I'm sure. But it is polite, Teddy. Or perhaps you could call her Cousin Ruby. You might rather that.' She smiles, but he doesn't even look at her.

At last he says, 'And I suppose she'll stay for a while, will she?'

'I'm sure I couldn't say.' Nell puts her cup down with a little chink against the saucer. 'I expect they'll want to be off before too long. They like a faster life.'

Ted's mouth twitches into a half smile, though there's nothing funny about it. 'What's that supposed to mean?'

'I don't suppose it means anything much at all.' She taps her own fingers on the table and looks away. 'But don't be in a hurry. For anything. You're only nineteen. You've got your whole life ahead of you.'

'I should just think I'm old enough to know what I want.'

Nell sighs. 'A baby knows what it wants. A dog knows what it wants. But neither knows what's good or bad for them.'

And now he has the strained smile he uses when he's upset. She's made a complete mess of talking to him.

'Well,' she says, at last, 'I left your lunch in the larder.'

'I told you, you needn't bother,' he says, but he gets up and goes to the larder anyway.

She takes one of his cigarettes from the packet on the table, although it makes her a bit sick to smoke first thing.

He hasn't a clue. She's always managed to keep the worst of it from coming into the house. But if she were to tell Teddy what she knows about the Cutters, what then? He's always liked playing at being the white knight. It might just make him more set on the girl.

Ted is standing among the jars and packets, hiding like a coward. He'd come downstairs meaning to tell his mum about the ring, about his plans. And then she goes and looks at him like that, so bright and spiky, and he feels like a child.

She's left him sandwiches wrapped in brown paper. He sniffs at them. Fish paste. She's pencilled 'Teddy', onto the top of the wrapper. And that's another thing, he doesn't like to be called Teddy anymore. He's Ted, a grown up.

He pours tea into his thermos, listening out to see if she's going to make it easy on him and leave the kitchen. No such luck.

The milk bottle is standing in a bowl of water to keep it cool, as if it needs it, cold as it is in the house. He takes his time adding a couple of inches of milk, holding the bottle up to check that he's left enough for the others, watching the milk make clouds against the glass as it moves.

And then he has to go back out and smile at his mother. She's still sitting at the table, smoking one of his cigs, which isn't like her. Neither of them mentions it.

'Rotten day,' she says, instead. 'I don't like to think of you out in it.'

'It's only a bit of fog.'

'Good luck to you, then, Ted,' she says, and he thinks she might be sorry.

As soon as he's out in the street he feels better, although

his mum's right, it's a rotten day. London is darker and quieter than it should be at eight in the morning. The fog makes all the noises flattened and muffled. There are a few faint sounds of buses and delivery vans and, once, a bicycle bell, streets and streets away. Nearby there's nothing but his own footsteps, no wind at all, no rustling of leaves. It's still so dark that the houses are a black cliff to his left-hand side.

He walks with his shoulders hunched and his cap pulled low. But in the inside pocket of his coat he has the little cloth bag and inside that sits the ring. It'll be easier to tell his mum when it's all settled.

Out on the Kennington Road the streetlights have been left on. The feeble glow passes in patches over his head, the fog like a grey army blanket strung above the street.

Florrie comes down the stairs in her dressing gown. She can hear Nell rattling around in the kitchen. She's only come down to use the WC, but the post is already lying on the doormat, and her own name, *Miss Florence Palmer,* catches her eye.

She sits on the stairs, the envelope in both hands. She looks at her own name again, so neatly typed, and then she slides her finger under the flap and tears it open.

> *We are writing to confirm that we have received your application for the post of telephonist. We request that you present yourself at the address above at eleven o'clock on Monday morning for interview.*
>
> *Please bring with you a reference from a profession-al person of respectable standing attesting to your good character and your Matriculation Certificate or Matricu-lation Exemption.*

She'd been so sure of a rejection, and the wording is so dry, that it takes her a moment to understand.

They'll never want her. They'll rule her out the minute they clap eyes on her. The lovely clear voices saying, 'Hold the line, caller,' are from good homes, have bothered to finish school, have never been to borstal. Girls who become telephonists have Matriculation Certificates and references attesting to their good character. Telephonists don't stand at the sink with their aunts, washing blood from their knuckles.

But this is her chance; this is how she can get out without being a housewife or a factory girl. And she can get around the business of the certificate: one of the Godden Boys spent the war printing medical Grade Four cards for men who didn't fancy dying. He still has hold of his printing press and can run off all sorts of papers, for a price. He might even be able to knock her up a reference.

The sound of the Cutters' knock makes her stuff the letter into the pocket of her dressing gown, but there's no time to answer the door. Maggie comes straight in, calling out, 'It's only us,' before Florrie's had a chance to do more than put her hands up to feel the fuzz of her hair coming out of its pins.

Behind her is Harry Godden. Maggie's family, but Harry's not a bloke she wants to bump into in her night things. A billow of fog comes in with them, like they're the baddies in a pantomime.

Maggie's wearing the fox-fur coat she took from the club. She laughs in surprise when she sees Florrie.

'Ooh, look at this. Having a slutty morning, are you, dear? I don't know. This family. Every time I come round, here's one of you lot hanging about in the hall.'

She laughs again and Florrie tries not to look bothered, even while she feels like running away up the stairs with her hands over her face.

Harry says, 'I always say, you don't know a girl till you've seen her in the morning. You're still a looker, sweetheart. You don't need all that slap you girls put on.'

'Oh, you are terrible, Harry.' Maggie taps at his arm with two fingers, like a Georgian lady coquetting with a closed fan.

Florrie says, 'Nell's in the kitchen. I'll just go and get dressed.'

'Don't be a prat,' Maggie says. 'You don't need to do yourself up for us, we're family. I want a word. Come on.'

Harry's bad enough, but any minute his boys might be bursting in, or one of the other girls. Maggie and Harry are hardly ever by themselves.

Florrie makes herself say, 'I won't be two ticks.'

Maggie shrugs off the fox-fur coat and hangs it on the pegs by the door. She seems to be considering whether to insist that Florrie come into the kitchen with them just as she is.

But then, thankfully, she winks. 'Go on, then. But if you make us hang about for you too long, I'll come and drag you down in your knickers.'

'And wouldn't that be a sight to see,' Harry says.

And then Florrie does run up the stairs, their laughter snapping at her heels.

Nell jumps at the sound of Maggie's voice and puts the last plates back into the dresser before they are properly dry. She's glad, now, that she started cleaning so early. The kitchen looks bright and respectable. She leans to collect a few missed crumbs from the tablecloth with a damp fingertip.

Maggie comes into the kitchen, dirty shoes on Nell's clean floor. And worse, Harry's behind her. Nell tries not to look at him overlong.

Maggie says, 'Morning, Nellie. Look at you, still in your curlers. And here I've always thought you was so proper. We just got an eyeful of Florrie in her nightie, and all.' She shows all her teeth when she laughs.

Harry winks at Nell, who has to force herself to smile.

'We weren't expecting callers.'

'Listen to you, callers,' Maggie says. 'We ain't callers, are we, Harry?'

'You're a nuisance, is what you are,' Nell says, 'But if you sit down I'll get the tea on.'

Maggie, who was just about to draw back Dolly's chair, stops where she is and juts her chin at Nell. 'Nuisance, are we? You want to be grateful. Here we are coming out on a filthy day to save you a trip.'

Nell says, 'Oh, hush, you know I'm joking,' although heaven only knows why Maggie thinks it's Nell's job to fetch Ruby from the prison. Ruby is Maggie's sister, not Nell's. And you don't see Maggie offering Florrie and Ruby houseroom in her fancy little flat on the other side of Kennington Park.

Harry sits down at the table but Maggie is still standing, her hand on the back of her mother's old chair. It's just like Maggie to take the best seat, when by rights it should be offered to Harry.

Nell says, because it's so much easier to back down than to quarrel, 'It's very good of you to go. Alright?'

'Sit down, firecracker.' Harry leans to pat the cushion.

'Harry's the good one.' Maggie scrapes back the chair and sits down. 'It's him doing the driving.'

'This?' Harry gestures vaguely at the air. 'This is nothing to driving in blackout.'

'They say it will clear up.' Nell brings the pot to the table.

'Most things do,' Harry replies, and his hand slides under the hem of Nell's skirt. His thumb strokes the back of her knee. She twitches and steps away. She should know better than to get near enough to let him.

Maggie, thank God, doesn't notice a thing. Now she's lighting a fag and looking around for an ashtray, without asking. Nell puts the cheaper of the two ashtrays at Maggie's elbow, the blue pottery one with *A Gift From Wales* painted across it.

'And tonight we'll have a little do, shall we? Get some of the girls? I thought you might get us some things.' Maggie puts her hand on Harry's arm. She's actually batting her eyelashes, tilting her head like a bird.

Harry puts his own hand over hers and says, 'I know a fellow got a load of choc boxes. Something like that?'

'And gin.' Maggie gives a laugh full of breath and smoke. Then she seems to notice the way that Harry's watching Nell, who's standing at the sideboard, not even pretending to clean the kitchen anymore, and says, 'What? Nellie won't mind a few of the girls round for Ruby's homecoming. Her own cousin.'

'No, I'm sure,' Nell says, 'if Ruby's up to it.'

'Ruby loves a party. Do you good and all, I'd say. You look like you need cheering up a bit. Don't she, Harry? I always say, our Nellie's so stiff she might've been starched.'

'She looks alright to me.' Harry leans back so that

Maggie can't see him, and blows Nell a kiss. She turns her head away, as though it really might land on her face.

Maggie says, 'Oh, don't look like that, Nellie. I'm only teasing. Let's have another drop of that tea.' She looks up at Nell's cat clock. 'We've got time. Unless it's a bother. Don't want to impose, do we, Harry? I'd hate to stop you scrubbing.'

Nell puts the kettle on to refill the pot. She thinks of Harry's hand on her leg and wonders if she's glad. It serves Maggie right, anyway. Her cousin can have more hot water, but there's not a chance Nell's sparing her another tealeaf.

Ted is almost at his yard, walking past the shop on the corner. He can hear Mr Griffith, the ironmonger, coughing and rattling about, unlocking the padlocks on his door. Next moment it opens and Mr Griffith calls out, 'Morning, sonny.' He's a big man in late middle age. His left cheek is spattered with tiny scars and most of that ear is missing.

'Morning,' Ted says, hoping he won't have to stop long. He likes Mr Griffith – who's taken a chance on Ted, after all, by renting him the yard at the back of the shop – but it's too cold and miserable to stand in the street.

'Pongs, don't it?' Mr Griffith waves a hand in front of his nose. 'Haven't had a stinker like this for years. Got deliveries coming today, supposing they come out in this muck. And a fellow coming to see the flat above the shop. It'll be a wonder if he finds the place.' A cough comes rumbling up through his huge ribcage and he adds, 'Don't envy you working outside.'

'I'm alright. They say it will clear this afternoon, at any rate.'

'Now tell me,' Mr Griffith says. 'How's your mum?'

'Alright.'

'You tell her I asked after her, won't you? She's a real lady, your mum. You give her my regards.'

Ted says, 'Will do,' and turns down the alley that leads to his yard. Mr Griffith always does ask after Nell, and he's only met her once. Perhaps Ted should bring her back to visit. You never know. It would be such a relief to see his mum happy, and Mr Griffith is a nice man. Nice men his mum's age are in short supply these days.

Inside the yard the ground is covered with a thin, slick mud. It's just a bit of bare earth and an outhouse, but it's the key to everything; to his future, his independence.

It's hard work but it's a bloody good idea. All the wood-paved roads are being torn up and laid down with new asphalt. Ted had been walking along Harleyford Road when he spotted the heaps of wooden blocks being pulled up, and all of them soaked in tar. They were just going to throw them away – it was practically criminal. The foreman had made a bit of fuss about the council, but when Ted replied, 'They know how many blocks there are, do they? And they're paying you enough that you can just let me walk away?' the man laughed, and Ted went and bought a barrow.

And weather like this, cold enough to bite, he can't shift the blocks quick enough. They burn like blazes and he charges nothing next to the price of a sack of coal. Every fall of the mercury has lined his pockets that little bit more.

At first he hadn't had to unload the barrow at all, just sold them right off the back of it, by the bag or bucketful. But the blocks are covered all over with little bits of stone from the road and when they went on the fires they'd spat the gravel out at people and that had caused no end of trouble.

One little boy had had a bit catch him just in the corner of his eye and there'd nearly been a brawl with the kid's dad. The stone was hot and the kid had a little blister on the edge of his eyelid, but it wasn't like he'd been blinded. You'd think people would know enough to put up a fireguard.

But Ted's got a system for cleaning the blocks off now, and his own yard to keep them in. He's really doing something. He's even started helping with his mum's rent, so that she has a bit more of his dad's pension to play with. It's not like anything Ted does for work will ever be good enough for his mum, but she's had to rein in her grand plans for his life now he's giving her money.

It takes him a while to get the fire lit under the steel tank, and it's only the tar that persuades it to take, everything is so damp from the fog. But it's worth the trouble, once it's going. His whole front grows warm, his numb fingers tingle with relief, and the fire turns the fog around him into orange swirls. When the blocks have been dipped in the water he runs a scraper over them and the stones come off without much trouble. By now his front is too warm, his back's still freezing cold, and his fingers burning with tar and hot water. He'll look like he's been down the mines by the end of the day. But he's got his thermos. It isn't too bad out there with a cup of tea.

It is as he's having his tea break that he thinks of it: Mr Griffith's man, coming to see the flat above the shop.

He finishes his tea, checks that the tank won't boil dry and wipes his hands on a bit of rag. Then he goes back out to the street, and around to Mr Griffith's.

The shop is crowded and dusty, in a comforting sort of way. It smells of good, handy things; wood shavings, motor oil, paraffin. There are stacks of tiny drawers all up one wall, each holding something different, all sorts of screws, picture hooks, fuses. There are coils of wire and fishing line hanging behind the counter. Although the shop was shut up during the war, there's a feeling of settled permanence about the place now, like a cluttered attic. It's real and solid, nothing fancy about it, the very opposite of the world the Cutters live in. It's one of the reasons Ted likes Mr Griffith so much.

The ironmonger is sitting behind his shop counter, putting boxes of screws into piles. He looks up when Ted comes in with the air of a man glad to be interrupted. The scars pull and crinkle up his cheek as he smiles.

'Alright, son? Not frozen yet?'

'No, not yet,' Ted says. 'Look here. I mean to say, Mr Griffith, how about renting the flat to me?'

Mr Griffith leans back in his chair and looks Ted over.

'Well now, how much tar would you be tracking into my place?'

Then he laughs and gets to his feet, even while Ted is stammering promises.

'Come and have a look, then.' He flips the sign on the shop door to *Closed*. 'But don't mess me about, son. I need to get someone in there sharpish. If you want it, you'll need to put your hand in your pocket.'

Ted follows him out through the back of the shop. 'Course,' he's saying, over his shoulder, 'you won't come in this way if you take the flat.' They're in a narrow hallway, smelling of damp. At the far end is a door, which Mr Griffith waves at and says, 'That's the door to the street.' Then up the stairs, past the first turn of the landing and another closed door, 'And that's my place, there.' Mr Griffith points, and up again. Finally he hands Ted a key. 'Have at it, then, lad.'

Ted steps over the threshold and Mr Griffith says, 'Come down and tell me what you think. I have to get back,' and leaves Ted all alone, closing the flat door behind him with the most satisfyingly solid click of the latch.

Ted takes off his work shoes and walks down the little hall in his socks, into the cramped sitting room. Here there are slanted ceilings and dormer windows that must usually show a view of his yard and the roofs of the houses beyond. Now there's nothing to see but the slow yellowish roll of the fog. The flat might be a balloon, flying through dirty clouds.

The chimney has been boarded up but there's an old electric bar fire and two frayed armchairs with winged backs. There's a utility side-table with a fringed lamp, and a rug that's worn right down to the warp in a crooked path across the centre, where countless feet must have walked.

Beyond this is a kitchen so small that it hasn't even a window, separated from the sitting room by a plasterboard wall. There's a sink the size of a hand basin, a table of the kind that hangs against the wall on hinges until the leg is pulled out to prop it up, and a set of two cupboards with a primus stove sitting on a square of oilcloth on the top. There's no oven. Above the sink is a wall-mounted boiler and finally, tucked into the corner, is an old tin sit-up bath.

Ted imagines himself sitting in one of the chairs, while Florrie makes his tea in the tiny kitchen. It's not much, but it's a start. It's away from their mothers. It's away from Aunt Maggie, and everything that comes with her, the petty shoplifting and the way she hangs about with spivs. Her egging Florrie on to do the same. The flat's like Mr Griffith's shop, not flashy, but real. Decent. And there's something charming about the size of the place, like a playhouse for grown-ups. He'll bring the little kit wireless over. And a clock. They should sit, in the evenings, and have the tick of a clock on the mantelpiece over the boarded-up hearth.

The bedroom door leads straight off the sitting room. Besides the bed there's just a utility wardrobe, a wicker chair and a bedside table with another lamp, this one with a cheap paper shade. But just imagine waking up here, with Florrie as his wife. *Any room would be a palace,* he thinks, and then likes the sound of that. He'll have to repeat it to Florrie, when he brings her up to see it.

He keeps trying to look at the flat through Florrie's eyes. The whole place could use a clean. But surely she'll see the romance of it, of starting small and building a life. Ted keeps hoping this, even while he thinks of Florrie's painted nails, her boxes and boxes of jewellery. But she isn't spoilt; she just likes nice things.

He stands at the bedroom window, looking down at where he knows the yard is, under the grubby sheep's wool of the fog. Then he turns and goes down to ask Mr Griffith to please, please wait while Ted finds the money.

Florrie unpins her hair as quick as she can, and fluffs the curls out. One of them is sitting oddly and she has to pin it to keep it in place. Then a bit of powder and lipstick. She looks ever so different with her lipstick on. To Florrie's mind, her face is just ordinary; all of her is ordinary. Her shoulders are too square, her face too round. She's not tall or short, she has brown hair and brown eyes and there's nothing to write home about anywhere on her. But maybe because of that, she makes up alright. A bit of a blank canvas for the paint.

'What number, please?' she murmurs to her reflection in her special telephone voice, her wireless announcer voice. 'Hold the line, caller.' The vowels feel round and satisfying, like having a mouthful of marbles. She can almost hear Dolly saying, *Yes, yes, alright. We all know you've a talent. Don't show off.*

All the Cutter women learn how to put on a posh voice to use on shop assistants and doormen and so on. But Florrie's better at it than the lot of them put together, and Dolly always chose her to do the talking when they went to the West End.

Now she wonders if her gran would approve of her getting a real job, pretending to be posh to fit in, rather than to rob. She suspects not: Dolly would say she's trying to get above her station. It was something her gran said a lot, which was odd coming from a woman who grew up poor as dirt but went about in furs, even in summer. But if anyone's trying to get above her station it's Nell, and it looks lonely, dull, and not especially convincing. Florrie's not like that. And quite as often, Dolly would say that posh people try to keep the whole world for themselves. So this is Florrie's chance to have a piece of it. She just wants a bloody chance.

She puts on her belted blue skirt and proper silk stockings, even though, cold as it is, what she really wants to wear is wool. She fishes her jet earrings out of her jewellery box. The tiny rhinestones around the jet make them a bit flash for the daytime, but she needs a bit of flash just now.

She's just fastening the second of them when she hears the staccato clipping of heels coming up the stairs, and Maggie's voice, calling her.

She goes out onto the landing just as her aunt appears at the top of the stairs.

'Where have you hid them boxes, Flo? We'll get them out from under your feet, seeing as we've got the car.'

Before my mum comes home, you mean, Florrie thinks, but she smoothes down her skirt and says, 'Ted put them up in the attic. We might need a bit of help getting them down.'

Maggie leans over the banister and shouts down, 'Harry! We need Donnie in from the car, love.'

'Right you are,' Harry says, from downstairs. There's the sound of his feet, of the front door opening and closing.

'I never told you to give them boxes to Ted. You sure he can be trusted, Florence?' Maggie says.

'I said they was things of Gran's I wanted to hang onto.'

'Good girl. Never tell a boy more than he needs to know. I'd do just the same.' Maggie jabs Florrie in the ribs with one finger. 'Oh, we're a right pair, me and you.'

Below them the front door opens again and feet stamp the doormat, Don's voice says, 'Bloody hell, it's brass monkeys out there.'

'The girls got a job for you. That'll warm you up,' they hear Harry say. 'Ha! No, son, not what you're thinking. Take that look off your face.'

Maggie prods at Florrie again.

'Come off it,' Florrie says. 'Stop.'

Don's heavy footsteps are creaking up the stairs.

'You stop, miss. Got a face as red as a smacked arse,' Maggie says, quietly. And then, louder, 'Alright, Donnie?'

'Morning, Miss Palmer.' His broad cheeks are pink from cold, his nose tipped red as a drunk's. 'Both Miss Palmers, I should say. I hear you need muscle.' He gives Maggie a wink. He doesn't look at Florrie longer than he has to.

'What are you like?' Maggie gives the throaty laugh she keeps for men, and smacks him on the arm. She has to tip her head right back to look at him. 'Did you hear him, Florrie?'

'He's awful,' Florrie says, because she has to. 'It's just some boxes want carrying down.' The landing is small and they're all standing closer than she'd like.

'Right then,' Don says, and then it's less embarrassing, because there's the ladder to move and the trapdoor to open, and Maggie says, 'I'll leave you to it,' and goes downstairs again.

Don holds the ladder and Florrie climbs up first.

'Don't worry, I ain't about to look up your dress.' He turns his head away exaggeratedly.

'I'd flaming well hope not,' Florrie says.

Don mutters something she can't quite hear, but she catches the word 'cold' and that's enough.

She's still nervous climbing the ladder, because it's hard to believe it won't slide away from the top of the trapdoor. She wishes she wasn't wearing her slippers, which don't feel steady on her feet. And then she's in, scrambling through on her knees, worrying about her stockings.

As soon as Don is in he picks up the torch standing by the trapdoor's edge and shines it about, the line of light picking out pieces of Ted's room. 'Well? What are we after?'

If it had been any of the other lads one of them would have made a joke about being alone in the dark. But Florrie just coughs and says, 'Just boxes, you know. Cardboard boxes.'

She's never seen Ted's attic before, and now she feels a rush of protective shame and wishes Don wasn't seeing it, either. There's no window, no skylight. It's just the dark, triangular space between the eaves, the roof felt glistening with damp in the torch beam.

She's had no idea that Ted has had to live so shabbily, every time she and her family have needed a place to stay. He's never breathed a word. She's sure he wouldn't like her to see it now. And how odd of Nell, with her front room kept like a museum, to let him live up here in the dark.

The camp bed is made up as neatly as a soldier's. The idea of Ted smoothing his threadbare quilt, tucking the corners in as though anyone might ever see them, seems to sum up everything she loves about him and makes her heart pull at her painfully.

The dusty light from Don's torch plays over all this and he gives a huffing little laugh, though he doesn't comment. Soon enough the beam finds the line of three boxes tucked in under the sloping roof.

Grunting, he squats and begins pulling them out towards him, passing them to Florrie. Once or twice their fingers touch, but neither of them says anything. Still, she's glad when he climbs back down and she can pass the boxes down to him, even if it means they have to look at each other.

Don takes two boxes and Florrie takes the other, following him awkwardly down the stairs, her feet searching for each step.

As they reach the hall the kitchen door opens and all three of the others, Maggie, Harry and Nell, come out.

Nell puts her hands on her hips. 'What do you think you're doing? I won't have you using this house like this, Maggie. You promised.'

Maggie doesn't look the least ashamed of herself. 'Would you believe me if I said it's some things of my mum's? No? Don't see why not. Worse than me, my mum. Oh, don't look like that, Nellie. Florrie, open one of them boxes up and give our Nell her price.'

'I should think not,' Nell says.

The box is full of smaller boxes fitted neatly together. Clean white boxes, each of them printed with a wreath of flowers and the words *Cusson's Linden Blossom Soap*.

'Don't you dare,' Nell says, but Florrie takes one of the boxes anyway, and holds it out.

'Take it, Ellen,' Maggie says. 'And don't go running to Ruby. She won't want you bothering her with nonsense when she's just home.'

Take it, Florrie thinks at Nell.

Nell puts out her hand, slowly, and Florrie puts the little box into it.

'There.' Maggie gives Nell a smile that Nell doesn't return. 'Was that so hard? Have a couple more.'

'No, indeed,' Nell says, and this time Maggie replies, 'Suit yourself.'

Don and Harry take the boxes out to the car, Harry turning to say, 'Don't be long now, Mags.'

'Miss me, will you?' she calls after him.

Nell goes back to the kitchen with the box of soap, her thin shoulders pushed back and her spine very straight.

'She'll never use that soap,' Florrie says to Maggie. 'I bet you. She'll stick it in the cupboard and we'll never see it again.'

'Got as much sense as a spoon, that one,' Maggie says. 'She loves playing the martyr. Don't pay her no mind. Now, listen, we'll be back with your mum as soon as we can be. But don't look for us until teatime at the earliest. You know how long these things take.'

'Can't I come too?'

'It's best not. Let her have a breather, get used to being out.' Maggie pulls the fur back on; she looks warm and soft and very expensive. 'Nice, ain't it?' She strokes the collar and laughs. 'Now, Flo, I don't want you bothering your mum. Let her get settled. Anything that can't wait, you tell me, not her. You follow? You tell me.'

'Yes,' Florrie says, although there are a lot of things she wouldn't tell Maggie even if there were slivers of bamboo under her fingernails.

Ruby watches the desk clerk lift a box of heavy cardboard onto the counter.

'Stand up straight, Palmer,' the screw says.

Her elbows have crept onto the countertop. She makes herself straighten up.

'One coat.' The clerk lifts it out. 'One felt hat.' It's squashed flat from its time in the box, a crease running right through the crown. It will be murder to get it back into its proper shape. 'One dress, one girdle, one pair of stockings, one pair of ladies' underthings.' His voice is absolutely steady. He lifts a paper bag from the box and opens it, tilts it to show Ruby the small red heap of her knickers. She remembers choosing red for luck and almost smiles.

Finally they let her put her signature on the paper and give her the box. She hugs it to her chest and follows the screw to the reception cell. She lets herself be shut in it.

It's not really a cell, but just a wooden cupboard built against the wall. The cupboard's walls don't reach the ceiling and its roof is wire mesh. It's so small that if she sits on the wooden bench her knees are only inches from the door. The walls are painted a grubby white, covered with the fingernail scratches of the women who've sat in it before her, waiting to go in or out of the prison. Most of them spell out women's names, *Lizzy, Patsy, Diana*, but on the right-hand wall someone has taken the time to scratch out the shape of an eye, weeping a single tear. *Watch over me*, it says beneath, in uneven letters.

There's a dull thud as the screw leans against the outside of the cupboard. 'Ready for your little jaunt to the outside, Palmer?' he says. 'Enjoy it. I shouldn't think it'll last long.'

Ruby doesn't bother to reply. She sets the box on the bench and, quickly, because it's chilly enough to make her skin creep, pulls off the grey prison dress and the scratchy wool stockings and drops them onto the floor.

'Got more of you Cutters inside than out now, don't we?' he says through the wood, in a stage whisper.

There's something horrible about him talking to her while she's undressed, even though he can't see her. She pulls on her dress as quickly as she can, the roughened skin of her fingers whispering over the soft cloth, the silky lining.

'From what I hear, they'll be rounding up the rest of you in no time. Course, there's always another lot. Can't take two steps in London without tripping over a gang of petty little thieves, all thinking they're Al Capone.' The screw raps his knuckles on the cupboard's wall. 'But never mind. The word is the Cutters are finished. What do you say to that?'

The dress isn't warm enough, but even in the dim light, it's beautiful. Dolly had chosen it. 'Navy blue is always respectable,' she'd said, holding it up. Ruby had replied, 'It'll do me as a disguise, then.'

Thinking of Dolly looking her over, checking that she'd look her best, Ruby has to close her own eyes tight. When she opens them again she's crumpled the skirt of the dress in her fists and must smooth it out, checking that she hasn't stretched the wool, before she puts her stockings on. The screw has begun to whistle.

Florrie has the house to herself. Maggie's gone to fetch Ruby, Ted's at work and Nell's gone to the shops. The house stretches around her, delicious in its emptiness. She considers having a bath – that really would be decadent, to heat the boiler in the middle of the day – but she's all done up now and it's too much trouble to have to do it all over again. Instead she goes into Nell's precious front room, kept always for best.

She feels like an invader just hearing the door swish across the rug, breathing in the smell of furniture polish and the dusty scent of the dried flower arrangement on the sideboard. The sofa and armchairs are draped in crocheted lace antimacassars, which gives them the look of old ladies, waiting. The mantelpiece and the shelves of the whatnot are mostly crowded with things of Nell's but here and there are her gran's treasures. When they came back to stay with Nell, Dolly had just swanned in, put her wax doll on the mantelpiece and flanked it with a pair of china spaniels. No one else would have dared to do it. She used to sit in here in the evenings, too, and Nell never said a word.

Behind the swagged curtains the windows are blocked with plywood, a remnant of the war. It makes Florrie feel even more of a trespasser.

She kneels in front of the gramophone, leafs through the small collection of records. She puts a record on the turntable, carefully places the needle in the groove, and Vera Lynn begins to sing. *We'll meet again, don't know where, don't know when . . .*

Florrie stands, swaying, in the middle of the carpet. Ruby loves this song. And although it's a song of goodbyes, somehow the lyrics are perfect and fitting for her mum coming back.

She's just beginning to forget the stiff and formal room, to feel the freedom in her limbs, just as she had at the club. Then she hears the front door open, and that's it. Her bit of time alone is over.

'Florrie?' Ted calls, from the hall.

Florrie calls, 'In here,' but she doesn't stop dancing.

'Just a mo, then,' he calls back.

She's dancing half for him now, but he takes an age and the record is ending by the time he appears in the doorway, his face washed and his hair combed.

He has his hands in his pockets and is shuffling about like a little boy, his cheeks faintly pinked, his Adam's apple bobbing in his throat as he swallows.

The needle has slipped into the middle of the record, swish-swish, swish-swish. She puts her hands up to pat her hair.

'What are you doing home?' She goes over, stills the needle.

'Not pleased to see me then?'

'Course I am,' she says, and now she goes to him.

He puts one hand lightly on each of her upper arms, and she has to step forward to close the gap. But the kiss itself is far less awkward, warm and sweet and already, after nearly three months, becoming familiar.

When they break away he ducks his head a bit, shy and pleased. She feels a great rush of affection, mixed, as it often is, with a sort of incredulity at herself. His shoulders are bony, the back of his neck is knobbed. He keeps his hair too short. She sometimes looks at him and thinks, *Really, Florrie? Do you mean it?* But it's just there, the wanting of him. He's so bloody good, ten times better than she'll ever be. It sometimes seems that if Ted likes her, so does decency itself.

'I thought you might like to have lunch with me.' He makes a fuss of putting the record back in its sleeve, closing the cover of the gramophone, straightening one of the antimacassars. Florrie hadn't noticed it was crooked.

The lunch is just fish paste sandwiches wrapped in brown paper, no doubt meant for his break at work. But he's brought a bottle of beer to share and Florrie finds plates while Ted uncorks the bottle. They clink glasses and she feels fond of him all over again.

Ted's got a bit of foam on his upper lip, but he licks it away before she can decide whether to mention it.

'Well,' he says. 'You'll have your mum back tonight.'

'Looks like it.'

'We'll be a bit crowded,' he says, although they won't be, not any more than they were when Dolly was alive. Florrie thinks of Ted's neat camp bed and reaches over to put her hand over his. He jumps and looks pleased.

'You've bashed up your hand,' he says, looking down at it.

There's a mark just above the rings she wears. It's just a thin red line this morning. 'It's nothing. Just a scratch.'

He wouldn't look at her half so warmly if he had any idea what sort of scratch it is. She wonders, sometimes, how much he does know. That she sometimes pinches this or that, yes. But surely not much else.

She begins to feel foolish stretching across the table, and takes her hand away. As soon as she does, Ted picks up his sandwich, so perhaps he was only waiting for her to release him.

She wants to ask him what he means to do if Ruby wants to separate them, but she can't think of any way to ask that isn't embarrassing.

Instead she says, 'I've got an interview for a little job, on Monday.'

'Do you really? What is it?'

She shakes her head. 'Tell you if I get it. Alright?'

When the sandwiches are eaten – which aren't bad, really, though the bread is dry at the edges and beginning to curl – he brushes the crumbs from his fingers and says, 'I was thinking, you know, wondering, really, whether you might want to marry me.' His face flushes a blotchy pink.

She grows very still.

'My mum,' she starts.

'Look here, mine isn't going to be over the moon. But I don't see how they can stop us.'

She thinks of how very many ways they could be stopped. And of that boy from over the river, who carelessly ran into a lead pipe.

She says, 'I need my mum's say so, though, don't I? I ain't eighteen.'

'Then I'll just have to make her see what care I mean to take of you.'

'Oh, Ted.' She reaches over and takes his hand. 'What if she won't? What if . . . ' She swallows, hard.

He shakes his head. 'I've got a trade. I can look after you. Won't you trust me? I'm sure I can talk Aunt Ruby round. We've always got on. Or . . . is it that you'd rather not? Because I'd much prefer you say so, if that's it.'

'Don't be daft.'

66

'Well, then.' He opens his jacket and pulls out a tiny bag of black cloth, closed with a drawstring.

'Oh!' She doesn't have to remind herself to smile this time.

He opens it up and pulls out a ring, holds it out to her on his palm.

She can feel her smile try to drop. It's ever so thin, just a little gold band and a whiteish stone.

'What is it?' She touches it with the tip of one finger.

'It's an opal. It's prettier if you shine a light on it.'

'It's lovely.' She looks at her fingers. This ring is going to look like a runt beside the others she wears. Ted looks at them too.

'I know it's not much,' he says. 'But I thought you'd rather I got you something fair and square. I didn't get it off a spiv.'

It's so sweet and so awful. It aches in her chest. She can just imagine the faces of the other girls if she has to show them something so piddling small. She can't bear to see them laugh at him.

'It's lovely, honest,' she says, at last.

'You can tell the truth.' Ted looks down at his big, bony hands, the tiny ring. His dear knobbed wrists, poking from the cuffs of his jacket.

'It's just . . . it don't matter where you got it,' she says, but that sounds ungrateful.

Ted shakes his head. 'The ring doesn't matter.' He puts it down on the table with a little click.

'It's a lovely ring. Didn't I say?'

'I mean, you'll marry me, won't you? That's the thing.'

'If we can get round my mum, and your mum, I'll say I will. With bells on.'

She marvels at the way he's looking at her, at his being so pleased.

'Then it doesn't have to be this ring. Any ring you like,' he says.

She looks again at the rings crowding her fingers. How much would one of them cost, from a proper jeweller? And her engagement ring should be the nicest of the lot. She can't have the other fingers showing it up.

'I don't want you scraping for it,' she begins, slowly.

'I'll find a way.'

'I can help.' *I could get a fistful of rings better than that one in five minutes flat.*

'Don't talk rot. I don't want your money. What kind of bloke do you think I am?'

She leans to put her hand on his arm. 'But I don't mean that, though, do I?'

'No girl of mine pays for her own ring.'

'Ted! Don't be dense. I mean, we can go down the shops together. I can help you. Just this once.'

She can't read his expression, but it isn't a happy one. Of course, he doesn't want her nicking stuff at the best of times. He's said so often enough. She's an idiot. She must do better. She looks again at the weedy little opal and tries to want it.

'I'm sorry,' she says. 'Forget I said that. I'll . . . I'll have this one. It's lovely.' Perhaps she can give up wearing the rest of her rings. Perhaps she'll get used to it and not mind so very much.

Now he gives her a smile, a bit of a rueful one, but a lot better than the frown.

'You know your own mind, don't you?' he says. 'I expect I was a fool to think I could get it right on my own.'

'No!'

He waves her quiet. 'We'll go together. You choose any ring you like.' He seems to mean it, although he still looks worried.

'You don't mind? Really?'

'Didn't I say? I want you to be happy. I shan't mind anything, if you're my wife.'

And now she finds she can't sit still.

'Come on,' she says, and takes his hand, tries to pull him up out of his chair.

'Hold on a minute, can't you?' He picks up the little ring, slips it into the cloth bag and tucks it back into his pocket. He pats it, as though it might have had its feelings hurt. 'Where are we going?'

'Where do you think? Down the shops, of course.'

Ted lets her lead him through the fog, though he keeps his hand over hers, in the crook of his arm. He'd been so pleased with the ring but as soon as he'd pulled it out it had looked feeble and tawdry.

Florrie's nothing like any girl he ever imagined marrying. He'd used to think her cheap, even a little frightening. You can hardly ever tell what she's thinking. But every other girl he meets seems muted by comparison, paper thin. And she's agreed to marry him. Florrie Palmer, always so cool, was almost laughing for joy at the thought of being his wife.

Now she's clinging to his arm, her hankie over her nose.

'I hate this,' she says. 'I never saw anything like it. I'd get lost in two steps without you.' He's never heard her sound nervous before.

'I won't let you get lost,' he says, and begins to feel better about the ring. He just wants to be a man. Her man.

At the bus stop he opens his coat and she leans against him to let herself be wrapped inside it. And there is something romantic about how misty everything is, as though it's just the two of them in all of London, although his feet are freezing and the insides of his nose and throat feel scratched.

Whatever ring she wants, he'll find a way to save up for it. Although there's still the rent for the flat to be found. This is shaping up to be the most expensive day of his life. But the happiest, too. What's a bit of saving, if it means a fellow gets his girl?

It's better on the bus, even if it does go so slowly that they might have beaten it by walking.

She hasn't said which shops she'd like to go to, so when the conductor comes around Ted asks for two tickets to the Brixton Road and he thinks she's pleased.

On the Brixton Road the streetlamps are lit, and all along its length there's the misty glow of shop windows. He can just make out, through the fog, the shine of the aluminium Christmas stars strung overhead. Shoppers are hurrying along, despite the weather, holding hankies over their noses and mouths. They call out to each other merrily, as though the fog were a bit of a joke. A little boy bumps, quite hard, into Ted's leg.

'Look out, mister,' the kid says. He's only about six, and is wearing a cap that's too big for him.

'For Pete's sake, Alfie, look where you're going.' His mother tugs him away. 'Say sorry to the nice man,' she says, as an afterthought.

'It's quite alright,' Ted calls after the boy as he trails away after his mother, scuffling his feet on the damp pavement.

Florrie laughs. Ted keeps a tight hold of her hand and now he leads her, and tries to think where he's going. When at last he finds a jeweller's, she stops him a couple of steps from the shop and pulls all the other rings from her fingers, working some of them back and forth to get them over her knuckles. She wraps them into her hankie, ties it in a knot and hands the little bundle to Ted.

'Put this in your pocket. Don't you dare lose it, now.'

'Roger that.' He tucks the hankie beside the little cloth bag. He's not sure why buying one ring means all the rest have to come off, but then he's never taken a girl jewellery shopping before.

The shop is a cavern of glass cabinets and lamplight. The bell over the door jingles as they come in and an old man, very dapper with a neat white moustache, looks up from behind the counter.

'Good afternoon,' he says. 'Rotten weather we're having.'

'Hello. We'd like to look at some rings, please,' Florrie says, in a clean, ice-bright voice.

Ted stares at her. He's never heard her speak like that before. He can't help but wonder where she learned it. And, for that matter, why she's so common the rest of the time.

Florrie adds, 'We're to be married, don't you know.' It's quite something to hear her say it out loud, especially in perfect Queen's English.

'Are you now?' the old gent says. 'Congratulations, I'm sure. You're a lucky chap.'

'Don't I know it,' Ted says. He feels like swinging her around and kissing her. *We're to be married.* Such a simple phrase for such a wonderful thing.

'And what sort of ring are we after?' the old man says.

'A diamond,' Florrie replies, before Ted can take a breath.

'Ah, all the girls seem to want a diamond these days,' he says, as though it were a hair ribbon. 'They do tend to run a little dear.' He looks at Ted, who shrugs. He's still got those words in his head. *We're to be married.*

'Well now,' the old man says. His face is still friendly, but Ted thinks he might be wondering where a young lad like Ted is going to get money for a diamond, and whether he's having his time wasted.

He begins fussing around behind the counter. 'Now then,' he's saying, to himself. 'Let's see.'

Ted looks at Florrie, wondering if he might be able to say something to steer her away from a diamond, but he finds he can't. Not after the opal.

There's the sound of keys in a lock, and then the old man lifts a tiny chest of drawers onto the counter, takes the tiny brass handle of the bottom drawer and pulls it open.

'Perhaps something like this?' He gives Ted a smile that might be meant to tease.

'Oh, good heavens,' Florrie says, leaning over them.

Inside the drawer, perfectly cut to fit, is a square of padded velvet cut all over with tiny slots, and in most of these sits a ring. They make the opal look like a pinhead.

'Oh, I say,' Ted says, 'I mean to say.'

The old man looks at Ted from the corner of one of his yellowed eyes. He means to see Ted squirm, doesn't expect him to buy one of these rings at all. He wishes he could, just to show the old sod, but it would take him months to save up for something like this. Perhaps years. The old man has set Ted up to look like a mug, has shown Florrie what Ted will never be able to give her.

And here she is, hovering a finger over the tray as though she's choosing a chocolate from a box.

'These are very popular.' The old man picks one up between forefinger and thumb. 'Oval cut, ballerina setting.'

Florrie takes it from him and slips it onto her finger. Twinkles run across it as she turns her hand, like water running off glass. It has a centre stone with shards of diamond set around it, radiating out in petals.

'Why's it called ballerina?' Ted asks, watching Florrie's face. She's frowning, a crease between her eyebrows, her lips pursed.

'Well now,' the man says, 'I suppose it must be because a ring like that will make a lady dance for joy.'

'Oh, I just don't know,' Florrie says. She slides the ballerina ring off her finger and puts it back in the tray, in a slot close to the edge of the velvet. Her index finger taps it twice, thoughtfully, and she looks at Ted, her eyebrows slightly raised.

'If you want it, I'll save up for it,' he says, with an effort.

'Well, perhaps I don't need anything so flashy,' she says. 'Do you have something a bit simpler?'

'Certainly, certainly.' The old man slides the drawer closed. Ted watches the diamonds disappear, swallowed by the little cabinet. The delicate brass handle swings against the wood.

'Perhaps something like this,' the old man says, pulling out the top drawer. 'Princess cut, claw setting. Just one diamond, very tasteful. Shows off the beauty of the stone.'

'Ooh.' Florrie takes a step so that she is right in front of the tray and the old man has to shift sideways so that their faces won't be too close. She leans right over to look at the jewels.

She looks over her shoulder at Ted and says, 'Come here, won't you?'

Ted moves closer too, so that he can feel Florrie, warm against his arm and shoulder. These rings look, if not cheap, at least not so very impossible.

'Oh, do help me,' Florrie says, turning her head to look at the old gent. 'Which should I try?'

'Well now.' He has to peer over her arm to see.

Against his side, Ted feels Florrie's other arm move forward and then slowly back. Under the open top drawer, and hidden by the press of their bodies, she has pulled out the bottom drawer again.

He doesn't know what to do. She isn't looking at him at all.

'No, surely not,' he says, as casually as he can. 'Do be sensible.'

The old man gives him a glance with more than a little contempt in it.

But Florrie, whose free hand is hovering over the tray of solitaires, only says, 'Well, which do you prefer then, Henry?'

Ted doesn't know who she can be talking to for a moment, and then, with a horrible little thud in his mind, realises that she's calling him by a false name.

'Perhaps something like this?' the old man is saying, his own fingers moving towards a ring.

Ted feels Florrie's arm move again as she pushes the bottom drawer closed.

'Oh, I say,' he says, loudly, and drums his fingers on the top of the cabinet. 'Are you sure you wouldn't rather something else?'

Florrie straightens up. 'You said I should have what I like, Henry darling.

Ted straightens too. 'Well, yes, but I mean to say. What's

the hurry? I'd like to save up and get you something special.' He tries to ask her, with only his eyes, to put the thing back.

Florrie laughs – a pretend one, not the laugh he loves, that he always has to work to draw out of her – and puts her hand on his arm. 'I suppose you'll only ever have to buy the one.'

'It's important to be careful,' Ted says.

'You've no romance in you,' Florrie replies. She seems to be enjoying herself.

'Oh, come now,' the old man says. 'Come, come.' The tip of his tongue runs over his dry lip.

Ted can do nothing but try to get her out of there. He can hear his voice croak oddly as he says, 'Let's not quarrel. Why don't you let me take you off for a cup of tea and we can talk it over?'

'I'm sure I have something that will suit both parties,' the old man says, hurriedly.

'No, no,' Florrie says, to Ted's relief. 'I shan't argue about tea, at any rate. We'll have a sit down and I'm sure we'll be back.'

'Very well.' The old man closes the top drawer. Then he goes behind the counter and lifts the cabinet down, bending to lock it away. Florrie takes Ted's arm and he realises how stiffly he is holding himself.

Then they're outside and within a few dozen steps the fog has hidden the shop as thoroughly as a theatre curtain dropping. Ted pulls her along as fast as he dares, watching his feet to be sure they don't trip. She is almost running to keep up, her heels clattering on the pavement.

'Slow down, can't you?' she says, but she's laughing.

'In a minute,' he says, but he slows down anyway. His whole face feels tight and set.

'It's alright,' Florrie's voice is hoarse and breathless, and back to itself. 'He won't twig till he opens up that drawer. Ted! Stop, can't you? These shoes – I'll turn my ankle.'

Ted can taste the fog right in the back of his own throat and the cold is creeping into his sinuses. The shop is lost in the murk, the pavement behind them disappearing into smudges.

He stops and pulls her near, his hand on her arm. 'Let's see it, then.'

She brings her cupped hand up between them. The ballerina ring sits on her palm, dulled by the queer light, glimmering grey.

He'd known, of course, that she had it. But it's different to see it.

'I do wish you hadn't done that.' His voice is just like his father's was, when Edward was angry. Clipped and humourless. He can't help it.

She looks startled. 'I thought you'd be glad.'

'Glad! Why would I be glad?'

'You said . . . I thought you said I should.' She bites her lip and a stain of red lipstick comes away on the bottom of her top two teeth as though she's drawn her own blood.

'Why would I say such a thing? I'd never say so. Never.'

Her face is quite blank now. 'I didn't know.'

He doesn't know where to begin. Right at the beginning, perhaps, with *Thou Shalt Not Steal*.

'I'm sorry,' she's saying now. 'I thought you wanted me to. That's all.'

Her eyelashes are clumped and spidery; he wonders if she might be trying not to cry.

'Hush,' he says. His tar blocks aren't exactly above board, and it's not like he hasn't had his fill of black-market ham,

76

living in a house with the Palmers. She doesn't know any better. He'll just have to teach her, that's all.

'Ain't it pretty, though?' She holds the ballerina ring up to him again.

'It's a cracker,' he says, 'just like you.'

A couple of women in headscarves, dragging string bags of shopping, pass by too close and he folds her fingers over it. 'But this is only for now. When I can afford it I'm getting you a proper one.'

'What's more proper than a diamond?' Perhaps she's teasing, but she still doesn't smile. And he isn't ready to be teased.

'You know what I mean. No wife of mine needs to pinch her own jewellery. I should bloody well hope not.'

'You might rather have a different sort of wife.' She slides her hands inside his coat.

He puts his arm around her waist. 'I'm going to make you a different sort of wife.'

'I'll never be as good as you.' Her voice is muffled. 'You'll find that out and go off me.'

'If I don't know you by now, it's a bad lookout for me. I'd have to be thick as anything. You must think I'm a right pudding.'

She laughs into his neck.

'And what about that voice?' he says. 'I never knew you could talk like that.'

'Learned it off the wireless,' she says. 'Thought it might help me get a job. But it might not.'

That makes him pull her even closer. He remembers doing the same thing as a kid, trying to learn how to speak well enough that the posh boys at his school would lay off him.

He can feel her body, all down the front of him. 'You lovely thing,' he says. 'You'll get your job, and I've got the yard, and you won't have to pull this sort of trick ever again.'

The taste of her lipstick lays itself over the flavour of the fog and she's warm against him, even while his shoulders creep with cold and the damp settles on the back of his neck.

The gates of Holloway close behind Ruby and there's a heavy click as an unseen hand locks the prison away. Some of the tension drains from her shoulders with it. That's it. She's out.

She stands and waits under the towering arch with its malignant stone griffins. It's too cold to relax properly, her muscles won't allow it. Her shoes seem too small, now that the ugly prison boots have let her toes spread out. None of this matters. The heavy ancient gates are behind her.

The fog is patchy, but still makes the world seem shrunken; the road stretches off into nothing, the trees and parked cars are turned to silhouettes. Then one shape begins to solidify and darken, and becomes a lady, walking towards her.

For just a moment Ruby lets herself think it might be Florrie but the figure is too short, and the next moment it becomes Maggie, the next best thing. The only other person in the world she loves with her whole heart, now her mum's gone.

Maggie's all wrapped up against the cold in a fur coat, a scarf pulled up over her mouth and nose. She looks like an elegant little bear. Her eyes are crinkled; she's smiling, under that fur.

Maggie pulls the scarf away from her mouth. 'Look at you.'

'My Magpie. You're a sight for sore eyes.'

Ruby lets herself be pulled into Maggie's embrace. Her arms close right around Ruby's back and her cheek presses against Ruby's own, just like when she was little and Ruby used to carry her about in her arms. The damp fur tickles Ruby's neck and she can smell Maggie's hair tonic, her perfume and powder. She hasn't smelled anything so nice for two years.

Maggie puts her hands on Ruby's shoulders and steps back to hold her at arm's length. 'You're skin and bone. Let's get you into the car.'

She takes Ruby's arm with one hand and with the other she unwraps the scarf from her neck and puts it around Ruby's.

Maggie talks all the time they walk. 'Ain't this weather awful? What a thing to come home to. Stinks like the grave. Here, it's this way. Harry ain't keen on driving right up to the nick. Daft, ain't he? But there we are.'

'Don't blame him,' Ruby says, although her feet are already wet and the fog seems to go right through her clothes.

Their shoes slap against the paving stones, the real world growing clearer in front of them. She doesn't look back.

And here's Harry's car, a long blue Chrysler, sleek and lovely and everything prison isn't. He gets out as they approach, holding his gloved hands out to Ruby. He looks dapper, but he's getting old. His cheeks have slid off the bones and hang on either side of his mouth.

'Ruby.' He takes both her hands. His leather gloves are queer under her fingers, too soft, almost, to bear.

'It ain't half nice of you to come and get me,' she says. She'd have thought he'd send one of his lads. She supposes it's an honour. Or perhaps it's just to please Maggie.

79

'Wanted to, didn't I. Glad to see you back. I was so sorry about your mum's passing.' She can see that he means it.

Maggie says, 'Get in, for Pete's sake. Mum wouldn't want you hanging about in the cold, God rest her soul.'

It is almost as cold inside the car as out. It's all Ruby can do not to pull her knees up to her chest; her body wants to curl into a ball. Harry lays a rug across her lap and that helps, but not enough.

'Once the engine warms up it won't be too bad,' Maggie says, climbing into the back seat beside her.

Ruby nods, her teeth gritted. 'It's worse in the cells, believe me.'

'Don't I know it,' Maggie says. 'There was a winter in Aylesbury I thought I'd lose my toes.'

Harry starts the engine and the car moves off ever so slowly, pushing a path through the fog, headlights on.

Ruby looks out of the window and London is beautiful, even if all there is to see are the silhouettes of lampposts, railings, a cardboard cigarette packet disintegrating slowly in a puddle. It's dreary and perfect and so familiar that she feels her insides swoop with gratitude.

'Is Florrie at home?'

'Course she is. She can't wait to see you.'

'Frannie come in last week,' Ruby says. 'Swears someone grassed her up.'

'Well, I'd say that's just Aunt Fran, but I'm starting to wonder. Harry's had some bother. A few of his lads been pinched.'

'You talking about me?' Harry calls back.

'I was saying, there's a grass about,' Maggie says, louder.

'Not for bloody long,' he says. 'Not once I catch wind of what bastard's talking.'

The car is slowly beginning to warm and the vibrating of the engine through the seat is comforting.

Ruby says, 'Frannie reckons someone grassed me up, and all. I've wondered about it myself, if I'm honest. The coppers got to the club that quick, they might've been waiting there.'

Maggie says, 'Having a good old knees up.'

Ruby laughs.

'But, Rue, I won't have you making yourself ill, worrying.'

'Watch it, Magpie. Don't you forget who you're talking to.'

'Oh, I know alright. The queen herself.' Maggie pokes Ruby in the ribs.

'Leave it out. Joker. What else? How are the girls?'

'Oh, you know.' Maggie puts her hand over Ruby's and lowers her voice. 'Ada and Hazel want thinking about. They're running that nightclub like it ain't half yours, now Mum's gone. Tight-fisted bitches.'

Ruby looks at the back of Harry's head to see if he's heard, but he's leaning right over the steering wheel, staring out at the road. Ada and Harry have been separated for fifteen years, but that doesn't mean he'll like to hear his ex-wife called names. And Hazel's his granddaughter. He'll like that even less.

She frowns at Maggie. *Careful.*

Maggie waves a dismissive hand and whispers, 'Honest, though. They won't let me see the cut from the club, no matter how often I say it's yours by rights. But I've been holding your cut from what the other girls make, so you'll have a bit of ready. Here, Rue, you don't know where Mum stashed the pot? I know she had a fortune kept somewhere.'

'Not a clue.'

'Oh, Lord. And you should hear the girls go on. Every one of us is scraping for pennies.'

'We'll have a meeting,' Ruby says. 'Get things straight.'

'Look here,' Maggie says, 'I'd better tell you. Half the girls have got spooked and run off. They're working the shops down in Brighton and Margate till this grass business blows over. And the ones still here are all eyeing each other up, wondering who's talking.'

'It's never one of the girls.'

'Well, I wouldn't like to think so, would you? We're all family, or as good as. More likely it's someone from the outside come in too close, heard a bit too much. Harry's moved his office, booted out everyone he don't trust. But still, the girls are too scared to do so much as pinch a hankie.'

'That bad?'

'It's a bloody great cock up, is what it is. We've all just been waiting for you to come back.'

'What am I supposed to do about it?'

'Well, I'm sure I can't say. Except you always do think of something. That's what I've been telling them all. You wait for my sister, she'll think of something.'

'I thought queening would be swanning about in furs, not thinking.' Ruby strokes the arm of Maggie's coat.

Maggie laughs. 'There's that too, I'll grant you that. And you can boss the girls about like anything. You tell them to get themselves back home, they'll come. You want some bitch's head knocked off? You just tip the wink to any one of us: we'll do it.'

'Been knocking heads, have you?' Ruby smiles at her sister. *I wonder,* she thinks. *How bad have you been?*

*

Nell has changed her clothes and cleaned the house all over again. She's just taken the cake out of the oven – it's sagged a little in the middle – when the front door opens and she hears Maggie say, 'Here we are then, safe and sound.'

Ruby, Maggie and Harry are in the hall. Ruby is taking off her coat. The shoulders of her dress hang like they've been draped over a stick, and although Nell's been expecting her cousin to have lost weight, it's a shock. Ruby isn't built to be thin, the sturdiness of her bones is all wrong for it. She looks as though someone had started building a big woman but had forgotten to apply the flesh before they stretched the skin over the frame. The tendons show in her wrists when she reaches to hang her coat on the peg. Her face is almost gaunt.

Nell steps towards her but at that moment the front door opens and in comes Florrie, who gives a little cry and rushes to her mother without even taking off her hat. Ruby puts her arms around Florrie and kisses her cheek.

'Oh, but it's a treat to see you, my girl.'

'I'm ever so glad you're back, Mum.' Florrie puts her hand to her throat. 'Oh, I could cry, I'm that glad.' Her face has mottled pink under the powder. It's nice to see the girl show a bit of feeling for once.

'Me and you both,' Ruby says, although she doesn't look a bit like she will cry. But she does look at Florrie with soft eyes.

Then Ruby turns to her and says, 'Nellie,' in a voice almost as warm as the one she kept for Florrie.

Nell says, 'Welcome home, I'm sure,' and holds her hand out.

Ruby takes it and pulls her a step nearer, says, 'It's lovely to see you, Nellie,' and kisses her on the cheek.

Over Ruby's shoulder, Nell can see Harry and Maggie watching, Harry with an amused look that makes Nell pat Ruby awkwardly on the back instead of returning the kiss.

Maggie says, 'Well, let's not hang about in the hall.'

Nell thinks, *No, why don't you go away?* But she has to say, 'Why don't you all go through to the front room and I'll get tea.'

'Ain't that kind?' Maggie says. 'What a brick you are, Nell. Never a thought for yourself.'

Ruby seems to consider this, looking them all over. Her eyes look bigger than they should in her thin face.

She says, 'I'd rather the kitchen.'

'You'll never make a lady,' Maggie says, 'Hey? She'll never make a lady, this one.'

If they'd gone into the front room Nell would have been alone in the kitchen getting the tea on, and then, once she'd brought it through, they might have expected her to go away again. Perhaps Ruby even thought of that and wants Nell to join them. She's not sure how much she wants to join in, if she's honest, but it's nice to be considered.

Florrie is feeling false and awkward, turned shy of her own mother. She wants to gaze and gaze at Ruby, but at the same time Ruby's eyes on her make her want to hide. She concentrates on keeping her face steady, and it steadies her inside, too.

The light in the kitchen is grey and soft. They all take turns agreeing that the weather is awful, and that they haven't seen such a thick fog for an age. Nell tells them that the wireless said it would have cleared up by now, and they all agree then that you can't trust a word of it. Then

84

they take turns saying how it stinks, and that they've never in their lives smelled a fog like it. Ruby, Maggie and Harry all wipe their faces with their hankies, exclaim over the dirt that comes off on the cotton. The room is still warmed by the slowly cooling oven and the air is scented with cake as well as fog.

Ruby is being too hearty, praising everything: Nell's underdone cake, the set of Florrie's hair, which is nothing special. She's like a guest who isn't quite sure she should be putting everyone to the trouble.

'What a relief to have you back,' Maggie says, for the tenth time. Florrie had forgotten how her aunt gets sometimes, around her mum. She's widening her eyes at Ruby almost like she does around blokes, and she's using her sweetest voice. It makes Florrie's muscles clench.

'Some of the girls will be round soon,' Maggie says. 'They'll be wanting to welcome you back, Rue.'

'Right you are,' Ruby says. 'The more the merrier.'

Florrie can't tell whether she's pleased or not.

Ruby smiles at her, but distractedly, spends a long moment looking at the fag packet in her hand. Nell is fussing about, although she must have fetched everything there is to be fetched. Harry has pushed his chair so far back from the table that he's almost not sitting with them at all. It would be so much simpler if he and Maggie would just leave, but he's gone out of his way and must be given tea. Only Maggie seems at ease.

'Where's Teddy?' Ruby asks, and without meaning to, Florrie's hand goes to the pocket of her skirt, touches the ballerina ring to be sure it's there.

'At work, I should think,' Nell says.

Harry is looking at Florrie with a thoughtful expression,

but she hasn't the faintest what it means.

'Got a job, has he?' Ruby says. 'That's something, then.'

'Now, Ruby,' Maggie says, and wags a finger. 'You've always said Ted's a good boy.'

'I never said I hadn't.' Ruby looks at Nell, who's turned to stare, and is holding a tea towel in both hands. 'Haven't I always said he's a good boy, Nellie?'

'He does try,' Nell says, and frowns.

Maggie says, 'Nellie, tell my Harry what your Ted's up to with them blocks. Listen to this, Harry. And Ruby, you'll like this, if you don't know. He's got a hell of a thing going on.'

'If you say so,' Nell says. 'I'd rather he got a proper job, but there's no telling him.'

'Oh, what do you know,' Maggie says. 'You, then, Florrie. I bet you know all about it.' Maggie's looking at her like a bird, eyes glittering, head tilted to one side.

'Why should I know?'

'He's your cousin, ain't he? You're thick as thieves, you two.'

'He's told me a bit,' she says, slowly.

It can't hurt, can it, for Ruby to know he's doing well for himself. She takes her hand away from her pocket and puts it on the table. Her knuckles are full of gold, but just ordinary rings she always wears. Nothing for anyone to wonder over.

Maggie says, 'It's a bloody good rig. You got a bright one there, Nellie. You want to give the boy more credit. Go on, Florrie, love. Tell Harry and Ruby what he's up to.'

It makes Florrie's stomach squirm, but it's such a relief to be allowed to say his name, to say something nice about him, that she can't stop talking once she starts. And besides,

Maggie's right: Ted does sound clever, when she says it out loud.

'Right then,' Ruby says, when the tea is drunk. She rises from her chair and the others start to get up too. She waves a hand. 'No, you stay there. You're alright. I'll just have a quick word with Harry, before he pushes off.'

Harry winks and says, 'Thought you'd never ask.'

Nell says, 'Do use the front room,' in a voice that means she'd rather they didn't.

Ruby says, 'The hall will do us. It won't take two ticks,' because she's just got back, and there's no sense in upsetting Nell the minute she walks in the door.

'You watch out for that one, Rue!' Maggie calls after them, as they leave the kitchen. 'He's a terror with the ladies.'

'Got an eye for rakes, has he?' Ruby holds out her newly thin wrist and flaps her hand. 'He might rather have the coat stand.'

She closes the door on her sister's laughter.

Harry puts his hands in his pockets and turns to face her. She's glad to see that he's lost the bored smile he'd worn in the kitchen. She's never talked business with Harry before; it was her mum's place to do that.

'Alright,' she says. 'Tell me what I need to know.'

'It ain't good,' he says. 'Lost a load of my boys, and your lot ain't looking too healthy.'

'No clue who it is, though? Have you asked whatsit? The copper my mum used to talk to?' She curses herself that she can't remember the bloke's name. But Harry, she can see, is still taking her seriously.

'That's the worst of it. He got the sack. Pushed off the

force, weren't he? That's the bit I don't like at all. So our grass knows we had him in our pocket. My guess is they was scared he'd tip us off.'

'Or it's him who was talking,' she says.

He raises his eyebrows and gives her a half smile. 'Well now, I thought of that. But there's things happened since, things he never knew about. It's someone close. I'd swear it.'

'And you? Are you lying low?'

'Pretty low, Ruby, pretty low. Got a few things going on that don't come straight back to me, but it ain't how it was.'

She shakes her head. 'I've been making plans, the last two years. I want to get back on the big earners.'

He laughs. 'Lorry jump-ups, is it? Bank jobs?'

'Wouldn't say no.' It really is perfect weather for a lorry hijack. She looks at him, trying to guess how open he might be to the idea.

But no. He's smiling at her indulgently. 'Can't say I blame you. Hang onto that. I'll be glad enough to work with you girls. Always do well with one or two of you on a job. Let's get this bit of trouble fixed first, alright? And then we'll put our heads together.'

She leans against the wall. Damn her stupid legs. She can't stand up for two minutes without her knees wanting to give. Let alone rush a lorry driver.

The irritation of this makes her snap, 'What are you going to do, sit around waiting for our grass to slip up?'

'You come up with a better idea and I'm all ears. See what you can see.'

'I blooming well mean to.'

'You do that. Nose about.' He pushes his hat back and rubs at his brow. 'It's alright for you girls; not another gang like you anywhere. You have a holiday and you don't get a load of jumped-up prats on your patch, trying to take what's yours. London's crawling with gangs of blokes. I can't just step back. I have to keep my face out there, know what I mean?'

'I do and I don't. I can't have the girls saying I've gone soft.'

He pats her arm, and she feels like a kid.

'Why not?' he says. 'The rest of them have. Ada's got her head so far down she'll step on her ears if she don't watch out.'

'That ain't how I do things.' She pushes herself back up onto her aching legs.

'Do you know, I thought you might not. You know I think the world of my Hazel. My only granddaughter. Do anything for me, Hazel would. And Ada ain't such a cunt these days. She's alright, for an ex-wife.' He gives a nasty laugh. 'But you and Maggie, you've both got nerve. Got it off your mum, God rest her. And your Florrie, she's got a bit of spark.'

She looks over her shoulder at the kitchen door, but it's still shut tight. 'Listen, that's the other thing. About my Florrie. Something I want you to do for me.'

He does listen, and he agrees much more readily than she'd been afraid he would. She'd thought he'd take a bit of persuading, with things as they are. So that's one less thing to worry about, at least.

Ted's sitting in the yard, boiling the blocks. He's trying very hard to be cheerful. It's not easy: Mr Fisher wouldn't take the opal ring back. He made Ted pawn it instead. Two pounds, three and six, that's what Ted got back, out of nearly thirteen quid. But he could hardly go haring about

London trying to flog it in this weather, and he needed the money for Mr Griffith's flat. He'll have to save up to get the ring out of pawn, just to be able to sell it. It's all a bit of a mess. And worse, he'd felt like a mug. Mr Fisher treated him like a stupid kid, and Ted had had to let him do it.

It's almost six o'clock, too late to make any money today. Beyond the fire the fog is a heavy grey; it will be full dark soon.

But, he thinks, if he gets the blocks cleaned and stacked in the barrow he can go on the knocker to sell them first thing tomorrow. And the fog's bound to have lifted by then. A fine job it would've been trying to wheel the barrow around in this weather, in any case.

The sound of knocking at the gate. A polite knock, a tapping of knuckles. He gets himself up, feeling his knees pop like an old man's, and picks his way over.

'Who is it?' he asks, through the wood.

'Harry Godden. Hurry up, son.'

Harry Godden. And too late to pretend not to be in.

Harry's hat is placed exactly on his head, his collar lying flat instead of turned up against the fog. Only the droplets gathering on his shoulders show that he isn't taking a stroll on any usual day. In the hazy light the lines on his face are softened, his edges gone, like butter just beginning to melt.

Maybe Florrie's told them all he proposed. She's said often enough that Aunt Ruby might not like that idea. What if she's sent Harry to tell Ted to forget it?

'Come in,' Ted says, stepping back.

'I'll stop here,' Harry says, although he's peering over Ted's shoulder, into the yard. 'You come out, why don't you.'

'I don't know if I can leave the yard. I've customers expecting me,' he says, although he hasn't.

'Bit late for that, ain't it? And your family wants you home. There's a little welcome-back do for Ruby. You can help me carry the booze.'

'Oh. I suppose . . . Alright.' But it doesn't sound right. Harry must have ten boys ready to carry anything he likes.

Harry looks him over. 'You got any other clobber? Or something you can sit on? Save my seats.'

Oh God, yes, Harry has leather seats in his beautiful car. 'I do have a change of clothes, you know. I don't usually, but I do today. I went to the shops. And I've just rented the flat upstairs. I suppose I could have a wash up there.' He's babbling like a fool. He takes a deep, tar-smelling breath and manages to stop.

'That's the spirit. I'll come up with you,' Harry says.

'Let me put the fire out, then.' That's twice today he's had to put it out. He might as well not have come to the yard at all.

Harry's feet clump up the stairs behind Ted like a man twice his size. His breathing is heavy, too. It makes Ted remember how old Harry's getting. It doesn't make him any less frightening. Ted has visions of a gun at the back of his neck. But he's being ridiculous.

'Nice little pad,' Harry says, when they get inside. He pokes at the coconut matting in the hallway with the toe of a shoe. The shoe's well shined, but wet with muck. 'Here, when did you get this place?'

'Not long,' Ted says, watching the matting grow damp.

He needs to take his own shoes off – they're covered in tar – but he's afraid Harry might take it as a dig at the fact that he, Harry, hasn't taken off his own. Ted stands there as if this one thing, the matter of whether or not to take his shoes off, is going to make a difference. At last he bends and pulls at the laces. He's ashamed of his socks, which have holes at the toes and darning at the heels.

He goes, in his sock feet, into the kitchen. Harry follows him, in his wet and dirty shoes.

There isn't time to light the boiler. Ted puts a kettle of water on the gas and digs about in the cupboards for a bowl. He can feel Harry watching him, but when he looks up Harry's taken out a cigarette case and is patting in his pockets for matches. He doesn't have his eyes on Ted at all.

'I'd offer you one,' Harry says, 'but you're tar all over. Don't want you turning into a firebomb.'

Ted hasn't a clue whether that was a threat or a joke. He splashes some cold water into the bowl and puts it on the little table, finds a rag and a bit of yellow soap under the sink. The only towel in the place is a pale blue, and he'd been glad to see it because he knows Florrie likes a bit of blue. He'll have to try not to make a mess of it. The kettle begins to boil and he pours the hot water into the cold in the bowl. Does Harry really mean to stand there and watch him wash?

He has to take his shirt off, because the tar has crept all around his arms and neck. He's horribly aware of how thin he is, how white and goosepimpled.

'Look here,' Harry says, as Ted begins soaping himself. 'This little thing you've got going with the tar blocks.'

Water slops onto the floor as Ted looks up.

'You've been slipping the roadworks boys a little bung, I heard.'

Ted stops, the wet rag in his hand, a trickle of water running down his chest and into his trousers.

'Them blocks belong to the council, though, see. And the council man's a pal of mine. I'll be having a word with him.' Harry says this so kindly that it sounds as though he means to talk to the council man on Ted's behalf. 'Thing is, though, son, what are you going to do when someone sees what a nice little thing you've got going and comes to take it off you?'

Ted's weedy arms move to wrap around himself and he stops them with an effort.

'I'm going to do you a favour,' Harry says. 'I'll come in with you. You need me.'

It shouldn't be a surprise but he does feel shocked, in a dull way. He's only just started. He's been such a fool, to think that he might keep his yard, to think the bastards would let him have something for himself.

'Now, son, I ain't here to stiff you. I'm here to help.'

'That's decent of you,' Ted says, although it isn't, 'but I'm used to working by myself.'

'Won't have a lot of work without me, though, will you? Not if the council fellow decides he'd rather do business with me. You don't want to set yourself up as competition, son. I'm doing you a favour. You've got the yard and I've got a lorry and a whole lot of lads to work on it. We'll shift ten times what you're doing. More.'

Imagine starting married life with a load of toughs in your back garden. This is exactly like when Walter Dawlish asked Ted for a go on his roller skates when he was seven. Ted had to hand them over, knowing he'd never get them back, and he'd smiled while he did it because he was too much of a damn coward even to show Wally that he knew what he was up to. He'd had to walk home without them, knowing what a walloping he'd take when he told his dad he'd lost them. He smiles that same, cowardly smile now and hates himself.

Harry says, 'Tell you what we can do. Tell you what. You'll be foreman. Running the yard. With one of my boys to help. And you'll take a slice of the profit. Business part-ners. How's that?'

'Foreman.'

'Too right. I wouldn't lie to you.'

'I don't know.'

'If it ain't me, you can bet it will be someone less friendly. And you'll make a lot more, with my lads giving you a hand. Don't cut off your nose to spite your face. That's my advice. You take a minute and think it over.'

Harry nods, walks back out, through the sitting room and into the hall, where he begins pacing up and down, his shoes creaking the floorboards, no doubt treading muck all over the matting.

Ted's going to have to accept. He can't think of a single thing he can do to stop Harry coming in and taking any-thing he likes.

He has to finish washing himself off but he's so afraid of making a mess of the towel that the whole thing seems to go on and on, dipping and scrubbing with the soap and rag, until the floor's soaked, the water in the bowl is black and he still isn't as clean as he should be.

He's shivering and moaning aloud at the cold. At last the kitchen door opens – Harry doesn't trouble to knock – and Ted spins about, hunching and even more goose-fleshed than before.

'Well?' Harry asks.

Ted nods. He doesn't trust himself to speak.

Harry sticks out his hand and Ted has to shake it, even

though his own is covered in tar.

'You can give us a pony now, for your cut of what we'll pay out to the council and getting the lorry running,' Harry says, just to kick him while he's down. 'And you don't worry about a thing. No shifty bastards coming on the rob, trying to get into your yard. Not now.'

A pony. Ted almost laughs, it's so far from what he can afford. 'I don't have it.'

'No? With all the business you've been getting? Well, say you bring it to me in the next couple of days. I'd say if you can manage a place of your own you can manage twenty-five quid.'

'Honest, I don't have it. I still owe rent on the yard.' And then, shamefully, before he can stop himself, Ted says, 'Sorry.'

'Oh, well, I can spot you the rest. Let's go and get that paid right now, shall we? We can just add it onto what you owe. And when you've got my money, you come and see me. We're partners now. I trust you to bring it, alright.' Harry laughs. 'Now, you look like a drowned rat. Hurry up. There ain't time for you to make yourself handsome. We'll be here all night.'

And he stands there while Ted rubs himself with the towel, and grey streaks come off on the blue cotton.

Harry looks at the floor. 'You'd better mop that up. Brand-new flat, and all.'

Ted gets down on his knees and mops up the tar water as best he can with the towel. He can feel his face wanting to pull into that weak and shameful smile while he does it.

Ruby's head is swimming. This is what comes of spending two years sober. On the wall, Nell's cat clock says it's barely six thirty, and here she is tipsy already. She isn't sure if she wants Maggie and the girls to push off or hang about for ever.

There are eight or nine women here and it feels like a crowd, because Nell's kitchen isn't what you'd call roomy. They take up all the chairs, lean up against the wall, drift out of the room to stand, cigarettes dropping ash, in the hall. And every one of them seems to be talking at once. It's like being in a room of yapping dogs, the wireless adding texture to the din. It's not so different from prison, the clamour of female voices, but the scents and colours are nothing like. Every one of the girls seems to have bathed herself in eau de toilette and there are as many flashing rhinestones and rustling skirts as you'd see at a nightclub. Ruby has been persuaded into a cardigan Ada's brought especially for her, a lovely soft black number with fur-trimmed collar and cuffs. Her fingers keep reaching to stroke at it.

Florrie has her eyes on Ruby even when she's talking to someone else. She's like a cat, watching her all the time. Maggie's talking on and on, her words as hard to grasp as fishes, slippery under the noise.

There's a little flurry at the door and the girls make way for Hazel and Val. Val's fifteen years older than her cousin Hazel, but you can tell they're both Goddens, both built like carthorses, the same dark eyes. The main difference between them today is Val's huge, pregnant belly.

Ruby stands and holds her hands out to them. She can feel herself smiling.

'Look at you two,' she says. 'Valerie, you look ready to drop. Let's get you a chair.'

'Oh, leave off. I ain't that far gone.' But Val's grinning.

Hazel says, 'She won't be told.'

Ruby laughs. 'Course she won't. What number's this one? Third?'

'Fourth. And the last, if I have any say. I told my Dennis if he comes near me without a rubber, I'll have his balls off.'

'That's telling him,' Ruby says. 'Look here, I saw your mum before I got out.'

Val grimaces. 'She got done over. She alright?'

'Right as rain. Frannie's hard as nails. Get yourselves a drink.'

Ruby sits again, grateful to have the weight off her legs. She's been given her mum's old chair, with the cushion their grandma Effie embroidered. Taking her throne. It's a strange feeling.

'Now, this is my new girl I was telling you about,' Maggie says. 'My poor little orphan. Found her living in a kiddie's home, didn't I, Cis? Filthy place, you wouldn't send a dog there. But she's going up in the world now. About to start housemaiding in a lovely big house in Kensington, ain't you?'

Ruby will have to have a word with Maggie about picking up strays, especially if there's a grass about. She gives the girl a hard look and Cissy grins. She certainly isn't shy. God knows if she'll be able to pull off behaving like a maid.

'Lovely stuff in there, I heard,' this Cissy says.

Maggie pats Cissy's cheek. 'Good girl. You tell us when you know enough. We'll slide in there smooth as butter, eh, Rue?'

'Nobody fit to beat the Palmer girls,' Ruby says.

'I'll tip you the wink alright,' Cissy says. 'Won't I just.'

Ruby gives her a tight little smile and turns away, looking about the kitchen at what girls are left.

Her girls. Everyone moans about the lack of available

men, but Ruby's never needed anything more than the Cutters. The one time she tried to leave them, in the first rush of romance with Florrie's dad, she'd felt only half a person, out on her own. Robert never had a chance, really. One day she'd looked at him eating the dinner she'd cooked, and thought, *You'll never be worth half what I'm giving up.* She'd packed her bags within the hour, been in the Golden Palm with the girls before midnight.

And now she's queen. She means to look after them, and make sure they look after each other. The rest of the world isn't going to do it; the Cutters have always had to do that for themselves.

But there aren't as many of them here as there should be. Besides herself, Florrie and Maggie, the Palmers, there are the Goddens: Ada and her granddaughter Hazel, who run the club. And the ones who are both like Frannie's daughter Val, who's taken over fencing the stuff. Val's reliable and she's got ambition, but by the look of that belly on her she might drop the kid out on the kitchen floor at any moment. Then there are three girls who've married Palmer or Godden Boys, good little hoisters, the lot of them. A good team. But they're just in it to help their men and feed their kids, they're not about to go on wage-packet snatches or housebreaks. Then there's Dolly's friend Clara, a Palmer by marriage, but she's too old to do much more than drink herself to death these days. Ruby counts, looking about. Ten Cutters left in London, and then Maggie's little friend. And most of them aren't game for anything that will bring in real money. The girls who are have buggered off, working in the seaside towns. She'll need them back, and she'll need to bring in new girls, ones she can trust, who know what they're about. Before the war there were three times as many Cutters, maybe four times. You could feel the panic in the shops when they all crowded in. They could strip a place bare; take the furs right off the window dummies, stuff their knickers full of silks, and there were so many of them the shop detectives wouldn't know where to start. And they'd had every other girls' gang in London on the run. If anyone wants to start a scrap now the Cutters could be in real trouble, with only this lot. Even Ruby herself is turned into a walking skeleton with holes in her lungs.

'Worn out, are you?' Maggie says. 'You look whacked.'

Ruby finds she has her hand to her face and is rubbing at her forehead.

Maggie raises her eyebrows and flicks her eyes down at her hand, below the table. Ruby looks, and there's Dolly's little cocaine bottle, resting on her sister's outstretched palm. It's of yellow glass, with a tiny silver spoon set into the inside of the lid, and it's a bit of a shock to see it there. Even Dolly hadn't been much for it in the last few years.

She shakes her head. Maggie shrugs and slides her hand back into her lap.

'You sure you want to be doing that?' Ruby asks. 'You know how you get.'

Maggie laughs. 'Well, what was good enough for Mum, eh? And it's all the rage again, for those in the know. You don't half fuss me, Rue. I forgot what an old hen you are.'

Nell leans over the table, picks up the ashtray and empties it into a bucket. Then she begins collecting the little paper cups from the chocolates. She has to lean past Maggie to do it.

'Have a fucking holiday.' Maggie pushes a cup of gin

into Nell's reaching hand, so hard that it slops out onto the table.

'I have a drink already,' Nell says. She gestures with the dirty plate in her other hand, back towards the dresser.

'Now you have two,' Maggie says. 'God knows you need it.'

Nell starts to speak, but Maggie is already turning back to the table. Behind her, Nell frowns at the cup in her hand. Then she just lifts it to her mouth and swallows it down, gasps.

Maggie's tapping her rings against her glass and roaring for quiet. The other voices hush by dribs and drabs, and someone turns the wireless down to a murmur. Maggie gets to her feet.

'A toast!' she shouts. Her face is blotching pink from the gin. 'To the memory of my mum, may she rest in blessed peace.'

Everyone raises a glass.

'And,' Maggie calls, 'my sister, who always has been a queen. Welcome home, Rue. May you carry on where our mum left off and keep all these bitches in line.'

There's a shifting as the discomfort goes about the room, but everyone mumbles, 'To Ruby,' and drinks.

'And last of all,' Maggie says, 'we're having a meeting. Midnight, Sunday. Right here in this very spot.'

Nell gives a surprised tut.

Maggie swings to glare at her. 'My sister's ill! She can't go trekking about London.'

'I didn't say anything,' Nell says.

'Didn't have to, did you? Face like that. Your own cousin.'

'Now hang on,' Ruby says. They shouldn't even be talking about it in front of outsiders.

'You need crowning,' Maggie says. 'And there's a hundred other things need settling.' She sits down with a little flump of her skirts.

Ruby stands, feeling her legs ache as if she's been running instead of sitting in Nell's kitchen. She meets Nell's gaze.

'A toast to my Cousin Nell,' Ruby says. 'A more generous woman I never knew.'

It's a sneaking thing to do, because Nell can hardly protest now Ruby's said that. But even so, Nell pinks a bit about the cheeks and looks pleased as everyone, even Maggie, choruses her name.

Ruby lifts her glass to the room and says, 'I'm ever so glad to see you all here. And anything you want sorted out, keep it quiet,' she looks at Maggie, 'till Sunday.'

Hazel says, 'We're all glad to see you back,' and half the women in the room call out some kind of agreement.

Ruby sits down, gratefully. The wireless is turned back up. People light up fags, turn to each other to whisper.

Maggie's jabbing her finger into the side of the young one, Cissy, making the poor thing jump.

'Here, listen to this,' she says to Ruby. 'Listen to this one sing. Got a voice straight from heaven, I promise you. You'd never know it from that face, would you? No, but listen. Go on,' she says, to the girl. 'Sing that "Five Minutes More".'

'Oh, no.' Cissy does look shy now. 'Not in front of everyone.'

'Come on then, you sod,' Maggie says. 'Ruby's only just home, it's the least you can do.' She's still smiling.

The girl shakes her head again.

Other girls are beginning to fall silent, ready for some

kind of show. Half of them are watching Maggie, but there are a lot of eyes on Ruby.

'Oh, I couldn't.' Cissy touches her cheeks as though checking to see how hot they are.

'It's Ruby's welcome home. You'll sing,' Maggie says.

Ruby, looking at the way Maggie's eyes are fixed on the girl, is too tired for it, for any of it.

She pushes her chair back. 'I'll just be a sec.' Then, to Florrie, who looks ready to jump from her own seat, 'No, you stay there. I'm alright.'

'Now see what you've done?' she hears Maggie say, behind her.

The kitchen door closing feels like an escape. She goes past the stairs and into Nell's front room and finally, thankfully, she's alone.

She feels as though she's been away for a lifetime and no time at all. Nell's house is almost unchanged.

Dolly's gold-rimmed sherry glass is still on the sideboard, where she used to able to reach it without having to bend her arthritic knees. Ruby can't help going over and touching it. It's like the urge to tongue a rotten tooth, to see how much it hurts.

Out in the hall the voices grow loud and then quiet as someone comes out of the kitchen. But these few minutes alone have been enough.

Ada knocks at the open door.

Ruby smiles at her, although she's tired of smiling now. Her face isn't used to it, after all that time away. But she's always liked Ada. And Ada's in her sixties. It's comforting to be with someone close to Dolly's age.

'Oh, Ruby,' Ada says. 'You look done in.'

'Now, is that what a lady wants to hear?'

'I don't mean it like that,' Ada lowers herself onto the armchair and sighs as though she, herself, is exhausted. 'Only we've been hanging on for you to come back.'

'I'm on the mend.' Ruby closes the door and goes to sit on the sofa. 'Your Frannie wanted me to tell you she's alright.'

Ada shakes her head. 'I know my sister. She'll be feeling it, even if she don't say. I've been all cut up over it, I don't mind telling you. If I find out who talked I'll be in there myself for murder, and gladly.'

'No clue who it is?'

'Not the faintest. Someone who's got their eye on Harry. His lads have had the worst of it.'

Ada fetches out a fag and slots it into an old-fashioned holder. She's built more like a fighter than a dancer but she sits very straight, not the least apologetic for her size. She smokes like the flapper she was, the holder in the centre of her lips, blowing out the smoke in one long, languorous breath.

'And they're calling you queen. You feeling up to it?'

Ruby shrugs. 'I'll do my best. Give us one of those.' In spite of herself, this is making Ruby feel better. It's real life.

They smoke in silence for a moment. Then Ruby says, 'I would've thought you might want the crown, or Hazel.'

'Hazel always says she don't want it. And I couldn't keep peace like your mum,' Ada says. 'But you can, I've got a feeling. You'll waltz back in and fix us all up.'

'Oh, stop.'

'I mean it. I've tried, but they're all quarrelling and looking at each other sideways.'

Ruby laughs. 'Seems more like they've all run off. Tell me honestly, Ada. You don't think it's any of ours? None of the girls have blabbed and then run off to Kent before it all gets sticky?'

Ada sighs. 'How do we know, when it comes down to it? I know what you mean, but then again, they have to make a living and it's getting hairy round here. But my bet is on one of the blokes. Someone Harry's rubbed up the wrong way. Listen, Ruby, a word about your sister.'

Well, it's not as if Ruby hasn't expected it, but she's still going to have to tread carefully. Ada's always done up so elegantly, is still a fine-looking woman. But she can't hold a candle to Maggie, twenty years younger and a terrible flirt to boot.

Ruby says, 'I know it can't be nice to watch—'

Ada looks over the top of her glasses, strict as a school teacher. 'Give me some credit. Fifteen years ago, he left me. I've seen enough girls come and go since. And what's it to me if she wants a bloke old enough to be her dad? More fool her. But she can't go on like she is. The minute she got into his bed I knew she'd get uppity.'

'Playing up, is she?'

'Been playing up since the day she was born, that one.'

Ruby sighs. 'You know how we grew up, before our mum got into the Cutters. You know it better than anyone. It's down to you she got in at all, never mind queen.'

Ada shrugs. 'She was a bloody good pal, your mum.'

'I'm just saying. It weren't a nice life.'

'We all grew up hand to mouth. That's no excuse to go mad. That fur coat your sister's swanking about in, she nicked that off a customer at the club. And we've been lucky to stay open as it is.' Ada's silent a moment, still looking Ruby over with her sharp eyes. Then, 'She's sticking that stuff up her nose, is what it is. Sends her bonkers.'

Ruby says, 'I know.' That's one thing she really will have to sort out.

'And that little girl she's got following her about. She's had the poor bitch standing on the street as bait so she can roll the blokes. I don't want to be putting into the pot to pay defence for some kid who don't know her arse from her elbow.'

'It's how it's always been done. We all chip in.'

'That's another thing. Maggie says she don't know where Dolly hid the pot, but every little thing the girls do, she's had a cut off them. Says she's keeping it for you. You make sure she hands it over.'

'Well,' Ruby says, and then doesn't know how to carry on. It's so odd to think that it's her cut now. The idea that she'll never be able to speak to her mum again. It's too big to look at.

'She was after your mum's cut of the club, but it's yours and no one else's. When you're ready, you come in and I'll show you how the place runs. Dolly never did bother much with anything except the drinking. Stuck to what she was good at.'

Ruby laughs even as she feels a rush of grief, because that was exactly what Dolly used to say.

'But most of all, Rue, it ain't safe. We've got a grass around somewhere. We don't need Maggie ruffling feathers and making a spectacle of herself. There. I've had my say.' Ada reaches for her handbag. 'I brought you some things. Just little bits and pieces to welcome you home.'

There's a book of face-powder papers and a tin of lemon drops. It was Dolly who'd loved lemon drops. The crack of the lid coming off the tin, the bit of white paper to be folded back. The lemony scent seems to go right to the corners of her eyes.

There's a tapping at the door and it opens to show Clara's face. Clara is ten years older than Ada, and it shows on her. She comes in slowly, leaning on her stick, closing the door behind her.

'You telling her?' she asks Ada.

'You know I am.'

'I did,' Clara laughs wheezily, stumping over to the sofa and lowering herself down, both hands on the stick. 'The minute I saw you disappear after Rue. How long, do you think, before Maggie tries to fetch us back?'

'Oh, now, stop! Has she been so bad as all that?' Ruby asks.

Before either of the other women can reply there's another tap at the door.

'Come in, then,' Ruby calls, and Hazel opens it a little way.

'Maggie says to ask you what you're doing hiding, and that it's a party and you're to come and hear this song.' She rolls her eyes.

'There, you see?' Ada says.

'She likes to have us all together,' Ruby says.

From the kitchen there's a crash and a scream.

Ada looks almost glad. 'You'll see how things are,' she says, again, and gets to her feet.

Clara sighs. 'I'm too old to go jumping up every second.'

Ruby gets up and offers Clara a hand out of the sofa.

'Tell her we're coming,' Ruby says.

'Right you are, dear.' Ada follows Hazel out of the room, her back very straight, as if she's trying to make as much of a contrast to Clara as she can.

Clara hangs onto Ruby's arm with one hand and her stick with the other and they begin creeping across the room together. Any moment Clara's going to start talking about Dolly, and Ruby's wondering if she can bear it.

But then, as they reach the door, Clara says, 'Listen, Ruby. Ada—'

'I know. I'll have a word with Maggie.'

'I said listen, didn't I? I've seen times like this before. There's a bit of trouble coming, as though we haven't had our share.'

'Ada did say.'

'Ada's half the problem, stirring it up, whispering on. You know how women are; she's green with envy. Here's you queen, and Maggie's walking out with Harry, and all the Godden Boys ready to jump when she says. Us Palmers are doing very well for ourselves.'

'That's daft. It's no different to when Mum was queen. And Ada says she don't want Harry, or the crown.'

Clara waves a hand. 'Not the point. If you stop and think you'll see it, Ruby. Your mum had the crown because she was always ready to get blood on her hands and Ada likes a quieter life, but her and your mum was so tight it never mattered which was queen. They came as a pair. Now the club's all Ada's got. You want things easy, you find a way to make her feel a bit special.'

'Right,' Ruby says, as they go into the hall. 'Alright. Just hang on till Sunday. So this is being queen, is it? You lot all in my ear.'

'What do you think we pay you a cut for, eh?' Clara says, and Ruby laughs.

The kitchen door opens abruptly and Nell walks past them and up the stairs, her face white and furious. She doesn't catch Ruby's eye. They hear her bedroom door close with a force that isn't quite a slam.

'Hates fuss,' Ruby says, to Clara.

'Can't say I blame her.' Clara leads Ruby into the kitchen, her step a bit quicker now.

Dolly's chair lies on its side. The girls are all on their feet. The dropping chair has pushed them up and out like ripples. Into the hush Gracie Fields is singing from the wireless, her voice turned up so that it crackles and breaks.

Only Maggie and Cissy are left by the table. The girl's crouching, her hands over her right eye, a trickle of blood just beginning to show between her fingers. Maggie looks over at Ruby and grins, her left hand cradling her right fist. She looks as though she expects Ruby to smile too.

Florrie feels the whole room grow still as Ruby opens the door and looks around at them all. Even thin as she is, she looks formidable.

Florrie thinks, *Yes. This is why Gran wanted you for queen. This is why no one put up a fuss about it.* All Ruby has to do is fix you with that stare and you feel like a kid caught doing something shameful.

Maggie, by contrast, looks ever so pleased with herself. She's still standing over Cissy. Her foot, which had drawn back to give the girl a kick, has stilled behind her so that she seems to be standing in a ballet pose.

Everyone's looking between Ruby and Maggie, waiting. And all around herself, Florrie can feel the girls leaning away from her, wary of her by association.

Cissy gets to her feet, head bowed, hands at her face.

'Let's see,' Ruby says to her.

She drops her hands and raises her head, wincing as

though this movement alone is enough to hurt. There's a gouge along the top of her cheekbone, welling with blood. There are dents in the skin, turned a deep pink, where the rest of Maggie's rings have caught her.

'You're alright,' Ruby says. 'I thought she had your eye out. My mum always said, a fistful of rings is as good as a knuckleduster. But you're alright.'

Maggie's grin has fallen, her mouth a tight line, her fist still cradled in her hand.

Ruby pulls out her chair and sits down, tops up her glass. 'Pick that chair up, Magpie.'

The moment stretches out too long. Ruby sips at her glass. No one else moves.

Beneath the shadow of the table, Florrie can see Ruby's feet slide back, getting ready to stand. She's seen Ruby and Maggie fight before, and it was terrifying.

She finds herself stumbling forward all in a rush. Heads whip round to stare at her. The girls nearest her almost fall over themselves to get away, scrambling backwards.

As she reaches her aunt, Maggie tenses as if she might leap.

Florrie stops, bends and picks up Maggie's fallen chair, rights it, pats the seat.

'Good girl,' Ruby says, without looking round from the table.

Florrie is so close to Maggie that she can see her aunt's eyelid twitching. It's the only thing moving in her face. Then she flickers into life. 'Ain't she just.' She puts her arm around Florrie's shoulders. 'Just like her mum. Just like her gran.'

The wave of relief spreads through the kitchen as Ruby laughs, and the ring of women shift and unbend, picking up glasses, beginning to move back to their seats. One of them catches at Cissy's hand and leads her off to the scullery to have her face washed.

Cissy, passing Florrie, catches her eye for a moment and flicks her gaze away. No one else seems to want to look at her much, either.

But that doesn't matter because Ruby reaches out and pats Florrie's arm.

'Always the peacemaker.'

Maggie sits, starts to slide the rings off her fingers.

Florrie fetches a bottle of vinegar and a rag from the pantry and sits beside her, to help her aunt clean the blood from the gold.

The Chrysler pulls to a halt, so smoothly it takes Ted a second to realise they've stopped at all. Despite himself, he's enjoying sitting in it. And all the drive, Harry's been telling him how much money they'll make together. It's making him feel just a bit more hopeful.

'Just need to drop in at the new spieler,' Harry says. They're outside Fisher's Pawn and Loan.

The sign on the door reads, *Closed*. Harry raises his gloved hand and raps on the glass.

Mr Fisher opens the door and gives Harry a dour but respectful nod. He only glances at Ted, and if he remembers him, he doesn't show it.

'Ted, this is Davey Fisher. A good pal, ain't you, Davey?' Harry slings an arm around Ted's shoulders. 'Ted's a pal, and all. A new chum. He turns up here, you let him in. Alright?'

Davey gives Ted a cold smile. He's lost the cocky air he had earlier, when he refused to take the ring back. He watches them pass like a tired man waiting for the last party guests to leave.

Harry strides through the racks of old clothes and shelves of bric-a-brac and Ted follows, through a hallway to the back room, from which comes a rumble of voices and the crackle of a wireless.

The room is full of blokes, and full of cigarette smoke. Around a hefty dining table men are playing cards, while others look on. Another table holds a stack of newspapers and the wireless, which is crackling out the sporting results. Here no one is sitting but only standing around, leaning over the newspapers, looking up at a blackboard mounted on the wall above, where odds have been chalked. Some of them look round and raise their hands to Harry, but most are intent on what they're doing.

'Hang on.' Harry leaves Ted by the door.

Ted puts his hands behind his back, then in his pockets. He shifts from leg to leg. Now and then he can see one of the blokes glance at him, and he looks anywhere but at their faces and waits for them to stop.

Harry doesn't come back. After a bit Ted's not sure that he hasn't been forgotten, that he shouldn't just go home. He edges back to the door, watching to see if Harry notices, but he doesn't look round.

Ted steps into the narrow hall with its cardboard boxes and shadows. It's better out here, even if he does feel a bit sheepish for hiding. He takes out his cigarette case and lights up, leans against a stack of boxes.

He's only halfway through his fag when Mr Fisher – Davey – appears from the gloom of the shop. His black jacket blends into the darkness, the white shape of his face like an eel rising from dark water.

III

'What do you mean by smoking out here?' He steps forward into the light from the spieler.

'Oh, beg pardon.' Ted looks for somewhere to put it out, but of course there isn't anywhere.

'Oh, what does it matter,' Fisher says. 'Give us one of those.'

Ted holds out the case and Davey Fisher takes a cigarette in his bony fingers.

'I suppose you're going to run to Harry and cry about that ring, are you?'

'No,' Ted says. He feels a flush of embarrassment just at the thought of it.

Mr Fisher takes a drag on the cigarette so deep that the smouldering end seems to rush towards his face. 'You think you're quite something, don't you? You wait.'

'I don't know what you mean,' Ted says. He means it to sound haughty, but it doesn't.

'Don't you? Well, I daresay you will. Once the boys get into your yard, I daresay you'll find out quick enough. Oh yes,' he says, seeing Ted's look of surprise. 'I know who you are. I know a lot of what goes on.'

'Well, bully for you,' Ted says. It's a stupid thing to say, but he hasn't another reply.

'Harry was in here just this afternoon, making plans for you.' His smile is horrible, leering. 'Do you know who I am? That's the question.'

'Look here—' Ted begins.

'I'll tell you.' Davey Fisher drops the fag end and grinds it into his own floor. 'I'm your future, that's what I am. You're looking at it. You give it a year or two, you'll find out. I was just like you are now, more fool me.'

Before he finishes speaking, the spieler door opens up and

the last bloke on earth that Ted would like to see steps out.

'You bothering the new boy, Davey?' Don says.

'Not doing a thing, Donnie,' Davey says. 'Not a thing.' He turns without looking again at Ted and goes back into his darkened shop.

'Harry says you need some gin for the ladies,' Don says to Ted. He sounds almost embarrassed. He gives a jerk of his head. 'In the boot of my motor.'

Ted follows him back through the shop. Davey Fisher is slumped at his counter, his chin in his hands, but when he sees Don and Ted he stands and comes forward to open the door for them.

'Cheer up,' Don says.

'I'll cheer up when I get to my bed,' Fisher says.

'Cheerio,' Ted says to him, as he passes. It's not a word he usually uses and he winces to hear himself. It doesn't sound manly.

Fisher gives a nod, but he's looking off into the shop, his eyes glassy.

The fog gives the night a thick, velvety quality. Don's car is parked on the corner of Ted's own street. It's a Vanguard, in much better condition than Ted's Hillman.

Don opens the boot and gropes about inside. Ted wonders whether he should strike a match, but instead he finds himself saying, 'That fellow who runs the place.'

'Miserable bastard,' Don says. 'He wants to be grateful he's still got his kneecaps.' He's bent right over, his head inside the boot. Ted has a vision of slamming it down on his head.

Don straightens up, a bottle in each hand. He hands them to Ted, closes the boot and goes back inside without saying goodbye.

Ted walks home quickly, but only because of the cold. He's not looking forward to a house full of women, not after the day he's had.

The kitchen is almost as crowded as the spieler. He holds the bottles in front of him like a shield. Their coats and handbags are everywhere. The room is filled with smoke and perfume, the table covered with half-empty glasses and full ashtrays.

One of the girls is sporting a fresh-looking cut just under her eye. One of the others has her arm about her shoulder. Ted's not about to ask. Girls are always quarrelling and making up.

'Hello,' one of the older women calls out. 'Here's a young fellow to fight over.'

'More to the point,' Maggie calls out, 'is did you bring us a bottle? I'd much rather fight over that.'

They give a great cheer as Ted holds up the bottles of gin.

Florrie is sitting at the table looking very composed, an island of quiet in all the shrieking. He'd like to go over and hang onto her, wrap his hand in her dress.

'Ain't you going to say hello to my mum?' she says.

'Course I am,' Ted says, and looks about.

It takes him a moment to spot Ruby, and then he has to be careful not to let the shock show on his face. She looks half dead. He remembers her jolly and plump.

Instead of saying hello or shaking hands, he just hands her one of the bottles, like an idiot. Ruby takes it, and then the other. She sets them on the table and stands, holding both hands out.

'Here's the big fellow.'

She's called him that ever since he was a little boy. He

kisses her cheek. Her face is so heavily powdered that he has to rub his lips.

'Welcome home.'

She winks and says, 'Get yourself a glass,' and he remembers, suddenly, sitting at this very table as a kid, and Ruby slipping extra bits of meat from her own plate onto his.

The ladies leave as soon as the gin is gone. It's almost comical, the way they drain the last drops from their glasses and begin to rise. But they all squeeze Ruby's hand, and the handshakes clink. Ruby doesn't look to see how much she's given, but only puts her hand into her pocket and says, 'Much obliged,' to each of them.

Ted follows Florrie and Ruby out into the hall to see them off.

'Don't get lost!' they call to each other, as they go.

Finally the door has closed. Ted wants very badly to have a moment alone with Florrie, and as if she can read his mind, Ruby says, 'You go up to bed, Florence,' and disappears into the kitchen.

For a moment Florrie looks as though she might be about to follow her, but Ted grabs for her hand, the hand that should have his ring on it, and strokes her fingers.

'You alright?' he asks, quietly.

'Course,' she says. Then, 'Happy.'

'Not worrying?'

She shakes her head. 'No. Yes. A bit. But we'll leave it for tonight, won't we? Let my mum get settled.'

'Of course. Just as long as you haven't changed your mind.'

She peers at him. Drinking always gives her a squinty look. But she says, 'Don't be daft.'

He strokes her ring finger and says, 'I still can't believe that voice. Why don't you talk like that all the time?'

He means it to be a compliment, but she takes her hand from his. 'Wouldn't be real, would it? What, do you wish I did?'

'No!' he says, quickly. 'No.' He thinks again of himself as a kid, trying to make his own voice nice, almost tells her what a rotten time he had of it at school. Never accepting invitations to the other boys' homes for tea because he couldn't invite them to his in return, worried they might look down their noses at his house, or worse, at his mum. But he's not drunk enough to make that sort of fool of himself.

He says, 'You're perfect as you are. Won't you give me a kiss?'

'Ted! Shush.' She looks over her shoulder at the closed kitchen door, then turns back to him, puts her fingers to her own lips, and touches them to the palm of his hand.

Then she turns and goes up the stairs. He closes his fingers tight, keeping the kiss in his fist.

Ruby is in Nell's larder, rifling through the packets and jars. Once, when she was little, Dolly had kept a stash of money buried deep in the flour bin, but Ruby's taken a wooden spoon and poked all around the inside of Nell's flour and done nothing but make a mess. Now she's running her hands along the undersides of shelves, peering into corners. She comes out of the larder and looks down the back of the dresser, gets on her knees to look under the stove.

The action of kneeling makes her dizzy. She stops on all fours on Nell's lino and waits for it to pass. And this isn't going to work. There's not a speck of dirt under Nell's stove.

Her cousin scrubs the house down to its bones – Dolly won't have hidden the pot anywhere Nell might clean.

Now Ruby's knees hurt and she's not sure she can get up.

All that time in the prison hospital, looking up at the windows crisscrossed with wire, feeling the TB burn through her. Coughing up dark clots of blood into the metal kidney dish, or, when it came upon her suddenly, her hands. She'd lain there waiting to die, thinking of all the things she wished she could say to Florrie, to her mum, to Maggie, even to Nell. Now she's just furious at what an invalid she's become, and with so much to do.

She glares down at her hands, splayed on the lino. The veins look as though she could put a finger underneath them, stretch them away and ping them back like an elastic band.

There's no time to be ill anymore. They must have that money. And her mum's pistol. She wants that, too.

Florrie's in bed, although she's not sleepy at all. She's sitting up against the headboard, waiting.

And now Ruby comes in, one hand rubbing at her temple. She looks exhausted, but she says, 'Oh, I can't tell you what a treat this is. A real bed. And is that a new dressing table?'

'I got it for you.' The dressing table does look a bit silly in the tiny room.

'It's a beauty.' Ruby's still standing just inside the door.

'That ain't all.' Florrie slips out of bed. 'Come and see this.'

'What's all this?'

The clothes don't look silly, they look perfect and new, the shop tickets still on most of them. She's hung them with care, so that the colours go nicely; navy blue hangs next to powder blue, brown beside pink.

'What's it look like? I got you some new things.'

'Oh, Florrie, you shouldn't have. These are lovely.' Ruby pulls out the sleeve of a cardigan – a soft mustard-yellow one – and rubs the cloth between her fingers. 'Quality stuff.'

'Do you really like them?'

'Well, of course I do. I'm not potty.'

'I got that one out of Selfridges. Didn't even use the knickers, just put it on over my dress and went off.' Florrie sits down on the bed and leans back on her elbows. 'Maggie went and lamped Cissy just because she wouldn't sing. Can you imagine?'

'You ain't telling me you pinched this stuff?' Ruby doesn't look thin or tired now, she looks terrifying. 'Was I gone that long? You forgotten everything I taught you?'

'No one goes by that rule anymore.' Florrie can hear the whine creeping into her own voice. And then Ruby leans forward and hits her across the face, so hard that her teeth clack together.

Florrie scrambles back onto the bed, her hand at her cheek.

Ruby has her hands on both hips. 'More fool them if they do. You want to go waltzing into a shop in stuff you've had out of it? You may as well hang a sign on your back. And what about when the coppers come sniffing around?'

Florrie's lips are humming with the slap, her cheek burning. 'They ain't been round for ages.'

'And how long do you think that state of affairs will last, now I'm home? They'll be buzzing around here like flies. You get rid of all of this.' Ruby wags her finger far too close to Florrie's face. 'And don't you look at me like that.'

This is unfair, because she wasn't trying to look like anything. This is awful. It's like Ted and the ring all over again.

'I thought you'd be glad.'

'I'd be glad to see you with a bit of common sense, my girl. Here I am, come home to a bloody mess, and my own daughter acting the fool. I won't have it. I suppose it's all gone to pot since Mum passed on. Is that it?'

Florrie doesn't reply, because of course that's it, and she's ashamed, now, that they've all grown so lax just because Dolly isn't around to tell them off.

Ruby says, in a voice very like Dolly's when she was riled, 'Where's Mum's bible?'

Florrie points, and Ruby fetches it out of the bedside table. It's the bigger of Dolly's two bibles, the one with scarlet covers and a ribbon to mark the pages. Ruby throws it down on the bed and Florrie puts a finger to it. She's not sure that Ruby's not going to just stand and watch, but after a moment she, too, leans and puts a finger to the leather.

'Let loyalty never leave me,' they say, together. 'Tie it around my neck. Or may I rot from the head down.'

'Right then,' Ruby says. 'Tell me the rules.'

'Oh, Mum.'

'Tell me. Right now.'

This is humiliating, like being singled out at school, even if there's no one but her mum here to see it. 'We don't wear what we nick,' she says, resentfully.

'Oh, now she knows. And the rest?'

'Blooming hell. We all turn up for meetings. We don't go out on a job if we've been on the drink. Um. Young ones get trained up.'

Ruby is ticking them off on her fingers. 'Too right. I'll be keeping an eye on you from now on. What else?'

'None of us talks to the coppers. We all chip in for law-yers. We don't nick off each other. If a girl with kids gets locked up, we keep an eye on them.' Florrie hesitates. She'd much rather not say the last rule out loud, but it's probably worse to leave it. 'And we don't marry outside.'

'That's right. You forgot the alibis.'

'We do that for each other, and all. Mum. I'm sorry. Honest I am.'

But Ruby looks tired again. She sits on the edge of the bed. Florrie can only see the side of her face now. Her hair is streaked with grey. Why hadn't Florrie noticed that before? The white strands are coarse cobwebs; they don't lie properly with the rest.

Florrie feels like an idiot, and more than that, it actually hurts. A pain has started up in her chest. She's spent so long in front of this wardrobe, imagining how pleased her mum will be. And all of the clothes are too big, she can see that now.

'I suppose you don't want the pyjamas I got you, then.' She tries to make it a joke, but it doesn't sound like one at all.

'My old ones will do me, love. It ain't that I don't ap-preciate it.' There. Now Ruby sounds a bit kinder, at last. 'No, you just pass me my old blue ones, if you know where they've got to. I've been thinking about my own pyjamas for two years.'

Florrie does have the old pyjamas, on one of the little shelves inside the wardrobe. She fetches them out and passes them over. Plain cotton with wooden buttons. Aus-terity pyjamas. Not special at all.

'Now, I won't ask you where you got that pair of smash-ers,' Ruby says.

Florrie's pyjamas are peach silk rayon, with trouser legs so wide that they swing like a skirt when she walks, the kind of thing that would have been impossible under rationing.

Ruby turns her back and begins to undress. 'Going to have you with me from now on. You got a lot to learn. You'll be queen after me, if you stop messing about.'

Florrie can't bring herself to reply. It's the sight of her mum's newly frail back emerging from her clothes. How do you disappoint someone, when their spine looks like a string of wooden beads under the skin? Ruby was plump when she went into prison, but now Florrie could count her bones. She'd never seemed to have bones at all, before. She'd been solid, as though you could cut her and she'd just be Ruby through and through, the same on the inside as the outside. Prison food and TB have melted her like a candle.

But once they're in bed Ruby says, 'Florrie. You're sweet to think of it all, even if you're daft with it. What did you do with Mum's things?'

'Aunt Maggie took a lot of it. I kept you some bits and pieces.' Florrie inches close and rests her cheek on the back of Ruby's neck.

'What about her handbag? Has Maggie got that?'

Florrie knows by the way she says it that she's thinking of Dolly's pistol, the little snub-nosed one she carried everywhere.

'I don't know.' She's surprised at herself, now, for not putting it somewhere safe. 'Nell might know. I should've . . . I should've thought.'

Ruby sighs a little exasperatedly. 'Well. You've had a lot on your plate.' She puts one hand over the blankets, pats vaguely at Florrie without looking. Her hand lands on

Florrie's hip, pats once, twice, and retreats back under the covers.

Florrie lies and thinks of Ted, just above them in his attic. Telling her mum about him is going to be even harder than she'd thought.

She can taste the inside of her cheek, where the flesh was mashed raw against her teeth. She smells gin, cigarette smoke and below that, something indescribable that's just her mum. She'd forgotten about that smell, all the time Ruby had been away. Now she's back it's the most familiar, unchanged thing about her. Florrie breathes it in until she begins to drift away on it and she might be a little girl again. The ache in her chest melts and spreads, turns to heaviness in her limbs.

The Third Day of the Fog:
Saturday, 6 December 1952

On Saturday the city wakes to find the fog settling like snow. A layer of filth coats the brickwork of houses, lies thick on window glass. In some parts of London visibility is said to be at zero, and all flights are cancelled, trains and buses arrive hours late. The Meteorological Office statements are understated, British to the core. *Fog, ranging from dense to very dense. Visibility low. Avoid unnecessary journeys.*

But the ambulance service is beginning to struggle, and the morning brings a fresh flurry of calls as people all over London wake to find that the poison has worked its way into their lungs. The old, the sick and the very young begin to drop, to ring up gasping for help, to be found too late.

Nell's been up for hours, cleaning as though it's the kitchen itself that has wronged her, the residue of last night's gin still coating her tongue and teeth. Now, besides a whiff of stale smoke and spilled drink, you'd never know there had been a houseful of women.

She's been rehearsing the ticking off she'll give Ruby but when her cousin does come down, Nell takes one look at

the grey of her face and finds herself fetching Ruby breakfast, almost by mistake.

She turns off the wireless and then wishes she hadn't.
The silence brings the horrible sound of Ruby's breathing,
like a child blowing through a drinking straw.

She clatters the things onto the table, just to make a bit
of noise. 'Another ghastly morning. And now the weather
man says we can expect it to last all day at least.'

Ruby's spreading marge on a slice of bread, tearing a hole
in it, rucking it up like a sheet. 'Listen, Nellie. Don't mind
Maggie. I'll get them to find another place for Sunday, if it
bothers you, us crowding in your kitchen.'

And now Ruby's reading her mind, and almost – but not
quite – apologising. It makes Nell wave a hand as though
it's all quite alright, which, of course, it isn't.

Ruby says, 'Sit down a sec, can't you?' and Nell has to do
it, although she knows now that she's really not up to any
sort of frank conversation, not so unexpectedly and with
last night's drink making a vague misery in her stomach.

'Nellie, I was meaning to say. Florrie wrote and told me
what care you took of Mum. You didn't have to do it.'

Nell puts sugar she doesn't want, and shouldn't be using
up, into her tea. 'It was my pleasure.' Although that's entirely the wrong word. There couldn't be a less appropriate
word.

'And I meant to ask,' Ruby says, 'if you've any idea where
Mum's handbag has got to.'

'No idea, I'm afraid.'

It's hidden in the cupboard under the stairs, behind the
shoes and cardboard boxes. But Nell has been meaning to
decide what to do about that. It's not a nice thing, to have
a gun about the house.

Ted whistles in his thin, tuneless way while he unpacks his suitcase in his new bedroom. His and Florrie's. Their marital bedroom. It sounds wonderfully official in his head. The tension of yesterday has lifted, and he's sure they'll be alright in their own home.

He's brought only some of his things, but it's still a thrill to hang the shirts and jackets in the wardrobe, to shake out his trousers and fold them carefully over the hangers. He's going to sleep here from now on and Florrie can join him whenever she likes. Before the wedding, if she wants to.

He's taken a few other bits, things that aren't kept for best. He's brought one of Nell's old pink towels to replace the tarry blue one. He's got a bit of tea in an old jam jar, and a fair bit of milk in the thermos.

Even though it's a womanly thing, setting up a house, he's never felt so much of a man in his life. He just wants everything to be right for when Florrie sees the place. Flowers. If he can find any that haven't suffocated in the fog, he should put some flowers out for her.

He wishes, so hard that the whistle catches in his teeth, that his dad was alive to see him making his own way. He'll get a ship in a bottle. His dad would have liked that.

He walks from room to room, marking his territory with his steps. And then he pulls on his work clothes and goes into the freezing, foggy yard, to bring in the money.

Florrie means to take Ruby somewhere with fresh air, right out of London, if she can manage it. She looks out of the window and wonders if the trains will be running. If she can give her mum a bit of a tonic Ruby might be cheered up, and Florrie might be able to summon the courage to tell her about Ted.

But she's taken ages to decide what to wear, because she doesn't want her mum asking her where she got anything. So it's her own fault when Aunt Maggie's voice comes in the hall and she has to give up her idea of a day with just her mum.

Nell is sweeping the landing with the carpet brush, and although she says, 'Morning, dear,' her voice is as clipped as if it were Florrie's fault her aunt's turned up uninvited. But she can just imagine how Nell feels. She must be wondering if Maggie's going to come round every day from now on.

Florrie says, 'Morning,' and almost runs down the stairs.

The kitchen is warmer than the rest of the house, and clean. Only the outside of the window glass is as grimy as the windows of a Tube train. The sound of Nell's furious sweeping comes clearly down through the ceiling.

Maggie says, 'Florrie! How's your head this morning?'

Florrie says, 'Better than yours, I bet,' although Maggie looks pink and pretty and not at all as tired as she deserves to.

Ruby and Maggie are sitting at the table, and someone has made tea. Someone other than Nell, because the teapot and milk jug don't match, and there's a teaspoon in the sugar bowl instead of the infuriatingly small silver one.

Ruby's cheeks are tight and loose both at once, stretched over the bones but sagging around her jaw. Every drag on her cigarette makes great hollows on either side of her mouth. Her fingers are bare of rings. She's afraid of them slipping off, she says, now her fingers are so thin. Florrie doesn't like it.

'Well, I daresay we both feel better than Cissy,' Maggie says.

Ruby says, 'For shame, Magpie. That poor little bitch,' but she's smiling, too.

Maggie waves Florrie to a chair and pulls an empty cup towards herself. She raises her eyebrows enquiringly, and Florrie nods. Maggie pours tea into it and pushes it across the table.

'Now, Ruby,' Maggie says, 'what do you fancy doing today? I thought we might go somewhere to give you a breather. The pictures, if you like.'

Florrie is filled with relief and a bit of shame. She'd half thought Maggie was here to drag them out to do something awful. 'I heard The Rex is shut for the fog,' she says. 'Nell said, yesterday. It got right in and clouded up the screen.'

'Is that right?' Maggie shakes her head. 'I never heard the like.'

'But look here,' Florrie says, 'I thought we might go somewhere out of London. Brighton, maybe.'

'Some of the girls are down in Brighton,' Maggie says. 'We could give them a hand at the shops, get some fresh air and still pick ourselves up something pretty. Go in all together and mob the place. What do you say, Rue?'

Florrie's heart sinks, because she hadn't meant anything like that. She'd been thinking of a windy walk on the beach and fish and chips.

But Ruby is shaking her head, stubbing out her fag in her saucer. 'We're going to the shops right here in London.'

'Oh, Rue, is that wise?' Maggie puts her hand on Ruby's wrist.

'But,' Florrie says, and then doesn't know how to finish. She curses herself for weakness. How hard is it to say, *Let's just stay at home?* She says, 'But,' again, but neither of the older women so much as looks at her.

Ruby shakes Maggie's hand off and crosses her arms. 'It's what we're doing. I won't have anyone say I've come home only to hide in the house. We're off out. It's what Mum would've done.'

Maggie laughs. 'In weather like this she'd have us do a smash and grab on a jeweller's, more like.'

Ruby gives her a smile, but it's one of her hard ones. 'If this fog holds, we might just do that. But first we'll nip down the shops. Have you got a fence for the stuff, with Frannie nicked?'

'Told you, Val's doing it. Got herself set up round the back of the dry cleaner's. Brand-new place, safe as houses. Can't see any grass knowing about it. Not yet.'

'There,' Ruby says. 'Knew you'd have kept your nerve. And from what I hear, you've done more than that.'

'Me? Never,' Maggie says.

'Oh, stop. I'll need your nerve. I'm bringing the Cutters back. We used to be the biggest thing going. No one could hold a candle to us.'

Florrie has to stop herself from audibly sighing. Not this tired old story, again. She could recite it in her sleep, grew up hearing it the way other girls heard fairytales. And it's not so different from a fairytale. It's rags-to-riches. Once upon a time, a hundred years ago or more, a couple of women, tired of scrubbing floors, started selling things they'd pinched at the New Cut market. And more women came and joined them, and the gang grew and grew, like a magic beanstalk, until even the men were scared of the New Cut girls, and they rode around in bloody pumpkin coaches and had all the finery you could think of.

Maggie says, 'We're still the only thing. Name me one gang of girls that's got half what we do.'

'Even so. It ain't right, scrabbling around after pennies and camping out at Nell's and all the rest. I've got plans,' Ruby says. 'Now I'm back, you check with me before you do anything big. You hear me, Magpie?'

Maggie says, 'You're a fine one to talk. I still remember that poor cow from Elephant.'

Ruby laughs. Florrie drops her eyes to her hands. She'd forgotten the way Maggie and her mum do this, tell awful stories, over and over.

Florrie was only about five. It was the first time she'd seen her mum change like that, into a monstrous stranger. And one of that girl's teeth had landed right on the toe of Florrie's patent shoe and bounced away again into the gutter.

Maggie's saying, 'If you've made your mind up. Palmer girls it is. Good times coming round again. I'd never stop you if you wanted a thing, you know that, Rue.'

'I'd like to see you try,' Ruby says, but now she's smiling back at Maggie. Their faces are far more alike when they smile.

'What we'll do,' Ruby says, 'is get Ada—'

'Not Ada,' Maggie says. 'Young Cissy, maybe.'

'I said Ada. You and her are going to sit down, sort out your quarrels and come out to the shops.'

'That old bag can't keep an eye out. Can't see her own knitting.'

'Now then, it can't be easy for her watching you go about with Harry. And we owe Ada a lot. She got our mum into the gang when we was barefoot and ragged. And stood up for her against our dad.'

'Never been allowed to forget it, though, have we? Not for a bloody minute,' Maggie says. 'And don't you call that bastard our dad. And we was never barefoot.'

'Close enough. I remember you in them cut-off wellies, with scabs all round your mouth.'

Ruby's looking at Maggie so tenderly that Florrie feels a stab of pure jealousy.

'She won't want to come,' Maggie says.

'She'll do what I ask her to, though. And I want a message sent to all the girls who've gone off out of London. They're to come back. Cutters don't run.'

'I haven't half missed you, Rue,' Maggie says.

'Am I coming too, then?' Florrie asks.

'I told you,' Ruby says. 'I want you with me from now on. Got a lot to learn.'

Thank God Ted goes to work so early; Florrie won't even have to lie about where they're off to.

She can feel the things she wants to say stretching out from her own mind to tap Ruby on the shoulder. She's waiting for Ruby to look up and say, *Come and help me in the other room a minute, love.* Her mum used to be so sharp about that kind of thing. Now, though, it's Maggie who says, 'What is it, Florrie?'

She sighs. 'Nothing.'

Now Ruby looks up. 'Out with it.'

'You're on early release. If you get nicked you won't be out in the morning. You'll be banged up for another year. More.'

'We've been through this,' her mum says, and that look of hers is there, the sharp edge of her patience.

'Oh, Rue,' says Maggie. 'She's got a point.'

'Now, listen,' Ruby starts.

Florrie says, 'I'm just saying, let's do it with bags. Me and you. Leave off the knickers.'

'That's good thinking, that is,' Maggie says. 'Go back in easy.'

Ruby frowns.

'Don't be a prat,' Maggie says. 'You're only just out, it's natural Florrie wants to be careful.'

'If you like, then.'

'Good girl,' Maggie says, though Florrie doesn't have a clue if she means her or Ruby.

'Now then,' Ruby says, 'I've been thinking over who should drive us.'

'Ivy and Delia are both off out of London,' Florrie says. 'And none of the other girls have got motors.'

'Yes, thank you, Florence, I know that,' her mum says. 'I want Ted to drive.'

Florrie's hands close, tight, on her own knees. 'Ted?'

'Ain't that what I said?'

Florrie looks from her mum to her aunt. Her mouth is so dry she can hear the edges of the words crack. 'I don't know. He's at work just now.'

Maggie waves a hand, the fag making a shining red trail through the air. 'I'm sure he can take a few minutes out of his day for us. We'll nip up the spieler and have a word with Harry, shall we? He can send one of his lads to tell Ted to come home.'

'Oh,' Florrie says, 'No, let's—'

But Ruby has folded her arms. 'I've said what's what, Florrie. He's got a car, and we know we can trust the boy. Get Teddy. You've got Harry wrapped right round your finger, looks like, Magpie.'

'Hardly,' Maggie says, but her eyes crinkle delightedly. 'Harry's taken a bit of a shine to Ted, that's all.'

Florrie's frozen up again and they're already talking

about something else. And then Maggie goes off to the spieler, still talking over her shoulder, and it's just too late, too difficult, to protest.

Nell sits at her dressing table and gets ready to go outside by not thinking about it too hard. She sings under her breath. Just 'Run, Rabbit, Run', the stupid little song she used to sing to Teddy.

She's been up here ages. It's already almost eleven, shamefully late to be getting dressed. Eventually she's going to have to brave the weather and go to the shops to see what she can get for tea.

There are voices and feet downstairs, the front door opens and closes several times. None of it has anything to do with her. She's given up control of the house, is far too tired to care that Maggie and God knows who else is back in her kitchen.

She is just fastening her gold-bar brooch onto her cardigan when Harry sticks his head in the door without knocking. 'There you are, Nellie.'

Nell sticks herself with the pin. She puts her finger to her mouth, then drops her hands to her lap. She can't start sucking her finger in front of him. One of her blasted cousins has let Harry Godden in, and not even kept him downstairs.

He stops just inside the door. 'So here's the lady's chamber.'

She tries to look stern. 'Can I help you?'

'You know, I think you could, if you liked.'

Nell shakes her head. 'You mustn't say things like that, Harry.'

'Oh, come on. Ain't you tired of your little game?' He

comes right into the room, closing the door behind him with a very definite click.

She stands. 'Don't. You mustn't be in here.'

'Silly girl. Come here.' He holds his arms out. 'What do you want? Some little treat? You want a new dress? A box of chocs?'

She stands up and tries to keep her voice steady. 'It's not a game. We really can't. You agreed.'

He shrugs. 'Changed my mind. Miss you, don't I? And I know you miss me.'

'Stop. Is Maggie downstairs? Please. You mustn't be in here.'

He's smiling at her now, and she doesn't like that at all. 'Keep your hair on, Nellie. I'll be going, if you feel like that about it. Just fetched your lad home to help the girls.'

That pulls her up short, as he knew it would. 'My Ted?'

'Do you know, the ladies wanted him to do a bit of work with them. Thought I'd nip up here and see how you felt about that.'

'Please,' she says. 'No. Not Ted.'

'Well now. Look at this. Now you want something off me, alright.'

She has her hand to her heart, can feel it pounding under the skin.

'Please. Leave him alone.'

'I could do that. I could do. I could lend the girls one of my lads instead, easy as pie. Come over here and ask me nicely.'

She closes her eyes and turns her head away.

'Suit yourself,' he says, and goes from the room, whistling. The tune is 'Run, Rabbit, Run'.

His feet walk down the stairs and seconds later, other

steps come up, heavy, creaking steps. Even thin as she is now, Ruby walks like an elephant.

Nell jerks into life. 'Ruby?'

'Just off to the shops, Nellie,' Ruby calls back.

Nell gets to her feet and goes to her bedroom door. Ruby is just opening the door to her own room. She looks around and gives Nell a quick, impatient smile.

Nell opens her mouth, but what can she say? She can hardly mention Harry. Instead, she says, 'Don't think I don't know what you're up to.'

Ruby walks into the bedroom she shares with Florrie. Nell follows her in.

'Did you hear me?' Nell says, as Ruby starts opening drawers, rummaging inside.

'Course I did.'

'You've no cause to go getting my Ted mixed up in . . . in anything.'

'Nellie, there's nothing to worry about. He's got a car, and I need to run errands. That's all.'

'And you think I don't know what you mean by that, I suppose.' The pitch of Nell's voice rises with each word.

Ruby opens the bottom drawer, then shuts it without taking anything out. She puts both hands on her bent knees, pushes herself upright wearily, as though she has better things to do. 'We're just off to the Bon Marche. Just to Brixton. Nice and near home. Alright? I've got things to buy. Buy, not pinch. He's a grown-up boy, Nell. You can't have him hanging onto your apron strings for ever.'

'Well!' Nell says.

'You want me to swear it? Eh?'

'Well. Yes,' Nell says, and finds that this is exactly what she does want.

Ruby puts her hand on her heart. 'We're running errands. Give me a bit of credit. I only just got home, I ain't up to pinching stuff, and I wouldn't have Teddy along if I was.'

Nell swallows, teetering on the edge of belief. It would be just like Harry to try to put the wind up her. He'll say anything he can think of to get his way. And surely, surely Ruby wouldn't lie about a thing like this. But she still feels a horrible, shivering tension all over her scalp.

'Even so,' she says, 'he shouldn't be driving in this weather. I don't like it. And don't blame me if you come back choking, with your lungs and this fog.'

Ruby rubs at her eyes. 'Listen, the girls gave me a bit of dough. More than I need. You take some of it and get yourself a treat.'

'No, indeed.' As if Nell can be bought off.

'Get us all a treat then. Does Ted still like a jam tart? Get us a nice tea for when we come in.' Ruby is already opening her handbag, fetching out a ten-bob note.

Nell can do nothing to stop any of them going. She will have to pace and feel queasy until they're home. She turns her back, leaves her cousin holding out her guilt money.

On the landing she hears Ted's voice in the hall below and thinks for a moment of calling to him, making him see sense. But then comes Maggie's voice, loud enough that she might be trying to be overheard.

'We'll come back here after, for the slaughter.'

'The what?' Ted's voice.

'Ain't you a green one,' Maggie says. 'You'll have to learn the lingo, sonny. For the slaughter. To see what we got.'

'Do we have to use this place?' Florrie says. 'Nell will go barmy.'

Maggie replies, 'Safer than anywhere else just now. I can

manage Nell. But let's get a move on, anyway. We don't want her throwing a fit before we're even out the door.'

Ted says, 'She's not as bad as all that, you know.'

Maggie laughs. And then, horribly, Nell hears her son join in.

She has to reach out a hand to the wall to steady herself, has to stand, taking deep breaths, before she can go back to her bedroom.

Florrie has been hoping for a moment alone with Ted. She wants to tell him that none of this was her idea, check he's alright, apologise. But Maggie's slapping him on the back, telling him that they'll make a man of him yet.

Ted looks very young, standing in the hall with his hat in his hands. Poor, dear Ted, who shouldn't be there. He looks at her and shakes his head a little helplessly, but he's laughing along with Maggie's teasing, his cheeks flushed. She can't tell if he knows what sort of driving he'll be doing.

'You don't have to do this if you've got things to do,' she says. The most she can manage. She's very aware of Maggie watching her, and it makes her voice come out stiff and formal.

'You keep quiet, thank you, Miss,' Maggie says. 'It's only right he should do a favour for family.'

'It's alright,' Ted says, almost as stiff as Florrie. 'I'd rather, than have you all on the bus in this weather.'

'We'll toughen this one up. Get some hairs on his chest. Hey?' Maggie says.

'He seems alright to me,' Florrie says.

'I don't think much of your taste, then. Soft as baby shit, this one. Oh, don't look like that, Ted, you big nancy. I'm only teasing.' Maggie goes, laughing, to the mirror and primps at her hair.

Behind Maggie's back, Florrie holds out her hand and he takes it. She squeezes his fingers and has to hope he understands some of her meaning.

Ruby puts on her hoisting knickers, voluminous things of silk with elastic at the knee. She sits for a moment on the edge of the bed, making herself breathe. Nell hasn't jinxed her, Brixton is a lucky place, and she's got the magic knickers on. Although Florrie mustn't know she's wearing them, because the girl's so set on using bags.

It was Dolly who'd been the superstitious one. She mustn't start taking on her mum's ideas just because she's taking her crown. Still, there's a tiny part of her that thinks if she'd been wearing the knickers when she did that house-break two years ago, she never would have been pinched at all.

And she has to do this. She has to be queen. She's making a start, has got Florrie under her eye now and is going to make Ada and Maggie work as a pair. It's a risk, but then, her mum always said the fastest way to heal a rift is to watch each other's backs. She's got Harry sorting out the other little thing for Florrie, so that's one more worry she can set aside for now. And she's dipped her hand into Maggie's bag and taken Dolly's cocaine bottle off her, tucked it away in her own knicker drawer.

She gets up, coughs, and stands up as straight as she can. She forces her face into a smile – it doesn't feel right but it's the best she can do – and makes herself walk downstairs.

She can feel the knickers riding up, gathering around her waist. They were baggy even before she lost the weight, but now they're swimming around her, coiling like something with tentacles.

She goes to the kitchen and leaves the ten-bob note on the table. Nell can take it or leave it, but at least Ruby will have tried.

Outside, she can barely see the car, parked just beyond the front gate. She pulls out her hankie and holds it over her nose, her lungs complaining already. Maggie is in the front passenger seat, Ada sitting in the back with Florrie wearing a dark red scarf Ruby recognises.

'My mum made that,' she says, as she climbs in.

Florrie is in the middle and Ada has to lean forward to smile at Ruby. 'It's one of my favourites. Always brought me luck.'

'It looks lovely on you. You alright? Get enough kip last night?'

Maggie has turned around in the front seat, looking at them. 'Wait,' she tells Ted, who is starting the engine. 'Ada, you get in the front. I want to sit with my sister.' Proprietorial as ever.

'I'm quite alright here,' Ada says. 'If anyone should be up front it's Ruby.'

'Old ladies in the front,' Maggie says. 'My mum would say the same.'

'Cheek,' Ada says. 'Tell her, Rue.'

Ruby says, 'Mum ain't here. And I say drive on.'

Maggie gives a little huff and turns back around, but Ada looks pleased, and Ruby remembers Clara saying, *Find a way to make her feel a bit special.*

They move off, slowly, and Ruby looks out of the window at what little she can see of London, the silhouettes of people with hats pulled low, drifting by like ghosts. The soft yellow patches of light thrown by the streetlamps.

'Ain't it awful? Have you ever seen a fog to beat it?' they keep saying, all the long, slow drive. They can't seem to help themselves. No doubt all those people groping along the streets are saying the same things to each other. A lot of them are wearing fog masks, squares of cloth with straps over the ears and around the back of the head, like groups of surgeons out for a stroll. Ruby must get one of the girls to sew her one of those.

'Oh, Selfridges,' Ada says, when at last they park on Duke Street and the misty shapes of the lighted windows show themselves. She turns to Ruby. 'I thought we was going to the Bon.'

'So did I,' Ruby says. 'I'd rather.'

'Out of all the shops in London?' Maggie says. She smirks. This is Ruby's payback for leaving Maggie in the front, where she could direct Ted without the rest of them overhearing. Maggie loves Selfridges best of all the shops.

'I wanted Bon Marche. I know how it works in there,' Ruby says. 'You want to watch yourself, Magpie.'

Maggie just grins. 'You've gone soft; you used to know how everywhere worked. It'll be fun. They've got some lovely stuff.'

'We'll go to the Bon after, shall we?' Ada says. 'I had it in my head we would.'

'We'll see,' Ruby says.

Maggie opens the door. Ted, who has come around the car to do it for her, has to jump back to avoid being hit in the shins.

And after all, Selfridges is lovely, with its high ceilings and columns, the abundance of electric light. Half London might be a bombsite and smothering in fog, but in Selfridges someone goes about buffing every smudge from the glass counters. Even during the war they had always had stock to make your fingers itch. Now, though it's only the beginning of December, there's already a display of small Christmas hampers, artfully angled to show the miniature fruitcakes, bags of nuts and jars of jam nestling on beds of shredded red paper.

'Oh, would you look at that,' Ada says. 'A couple of years ago we never dreamed of that.'

'We dreamed of it alright,' Florrie says. 'We just couldn't get it.'

'When did you ever go without?' Maggie says. 'Let's carry on, shall we? Best way I know to make our own Christmases merry.'

The shop isn't as busy as Ruby would have liked, but it's busy enough. Half the people in the place are probably hiding from the weather. There are an awful lot of grimy faces and damp coats. And the fog might work in their favour there, because the shop-girls are distracted, worrying that someone will dirty the stock.

They go up to the ladies' wear department, taking turns to hold things up to each other, carrying on in loud voices about how much this or that would suit, taking turns to be the one in the middle of the lot of them. Whichever woman is in the centre rolls a dress or a coat up on the rail and then drops it, quick as she can, into her knickers or into a bag. The trick is to roll it up tight from the bottom up, and slip it off the rail. They each have their own way of doing things. Maggie has elastic put into her waistband, and sticks things down her knickers from the front, while Ruby – when she uses the hoisting bloomers – prefers to lift her skirt and shove things up the leg.

But now she sticks to the bag, to please Florrie. And the other women bolster her nerve until she's sure that she isn't doing a thing wrong, even while she's pushing a dress into the bag. That's the trick of it: you have to believe it yourself.

She stashes away two dresses and a twinset and then they move about a bit, still talking, and let Ada have a go, all the time using their own bodies as a kind of wall from any shopwalkers who might be snooping about.

About halfway through she puts the full bag on the floor and Florrie sets down the empty one. A moment later Florrie picks up the full bag and off she goes. Ruby doesn't like Florrie taking all the risk, but the part of her that doesn't like it is deep under the layer of confidence and she can barely feel it.

And while Florrie is gone she sees the most beautiful fur wrap, golden brown, lined with satin and so thick you could lose your hand in it. She knows Florrie won't like it and that they'll do well enough with just the bags. But she also knows she can get it up her knickers, and that thought is the kind that moves her hands all by themselves. It's amazing how small even a fur will go, if you know how to roll it right. She lifts her skirt just enough and pushes it up the leg of the bloomers, wiggling until it's sitting right between her legs.

'Tidily done,' Maggie says, just loud enough for Ruby to hear.

She's flying now and fills the second bag in no time at all. As soon as Florrie gets back she's ready to fill the empty one.

'Let's get back,' Maggie says, before she can.

'I won't be a sec,' Ruby says.

'Come on,' Maggie says. 'Leave it. We'll go on somewhere else.'

And although she should probably remind Maggie of who's queen around here, she follows on anyway, out to the street. She trusts her sister to know when it's time to go.

There is always a moment, stepping out of a shop, where she feels two things at once. First that she's done nothing wrong, is just leaving a shop, like anyone might. Then there's the feeling in her shoulders, waiting for a hand to drop on her. As soon as she's walked a little way, though, that second feeling goes and she could dance. The elation of it is like nothing else.

As soon as they get back to the car Florrie clocks the way she's walking.

'Mum! What've you got?' she asks, like Ruby is the child.

Ruby climbs into the car, and once she's sitting, reaches under her skirt and pulls out the fur. It swells back into its true shape as it comes out, a golden balloon inflating.

Florrie frowns and shakes her head.

'Oh, leave off,' Ruby says. 'I got out clean, didn't I? Ain't it lovely?'

'It's a beauty,' Florrie says, 'the bee's knees. But still. The risk.'

In the driver's seat, Ted mutters something Ruby doesn't catch.

'Well, it's here now,' Ruby says. 'You have it. I don't mean for you to keep, before you start. Just this once, you wear it a bit. And then we'll move it along. You'll look a picture in it, Florrie.' It's an apology for last night's ticking off.

Florrie shakes her head again, but she lets Ruby drape it over her lap.

'You deserve something nice.' Ruby pats Florrie's fur-covered knee.

Florrie has that glassy, distant look she gets sometimes, but Ruby doesn't know whether she's glad about the fur or angry that Ruby took it, or maybe still upset about yesterday, so she just lets her be, and looks out the window at the shifting black and grey of the buildings sliding past. She remembers how she used to love the fog when she was little, the sense of the world being changed and no one being able to do a thing about it.

Ted's leaning almost into the windscreen, headlights barely cutting through the murk. The fog gathers in thick, sticky flakes which don't shift under the wiper blades. The main roads have had flares put out at the junctions, which both helps and makes him feel nervous. When they need to put flares out it's a fair bet that it's not a good day for a drive.

He'd never have imagined he'd be a driver on a shoplifting jaunt. Never. But he didn't know how to say no to Harry, and now he's driving Florrie about like an accomplice. He keeps wondering if she suggested he should drive them, if she knows him so little that she thought he'd be glad, as she had with the ring. A small part of him, though, thinks that if she's doing it at all, at least she's doing it where he can keep an eye on her. And then, of course, Ruby's promised him a fiver for the driving. It's more than he'd get selling blocks, and he does have to think of the future. But it's bitter, even so.

Ordinarily Ted loves driving, really loves it. It's really something to motor along, with most of the men in London on bicycles or their own worn-out feet. He keeps waiting for the shine to wear off but it's been eight months since Dolly gave him the car. Worth every second he spent chauffeuring the old lady about, to the doctor, to visit her hundreds of friends, to the pub. She never had him do this sort of driving, though. She'd been careful to keep him out of things. He'd liked her for that.

The Hillman's only a utility saloon, no leather trim, no quarter lights. Dolly had said there was no sense getting him anything smarter while he was still learning to drive. The Hillman's bumpers were painted white by whoever had her when London was in blackout, and chips of the paint still cling to the rust. She smells a bit like damp feet inside. But she's Ted's. People turn to look at him go. Any of the blokes on their street would give their eye teeth to have a car at all.

The four ladies are talking so loudly he can barely concentrate on the road; a fine mess they'll be in if they crash. There are an awful lot of cars out, creeping together like a line of ants. Policemen in white fog coats direct the traffic at almost every junction and crossing, walk in front of the buses with lanterns. Every time Ted drives past a policeman his stomach knots with guilt.

And now the women are arguing about whether to go home. The old one, Ada, is in the front seat now, and she wants to go to the Bon Marche.

'Oh, do you now?' Maggie calls from the back seat. 'Who are you, all of a sudden?'

He looks at Florrie in the rear-view mirror, but he can't tell what she's thinking and she doesn't speak up.

'Ruby?' Ada says. 'Tell her.'

Ruby says, 'I like the Bon.'

Ada leans and taps Ted's knee, which he doesn't like at all. 'The Bon, young man.'

'Go on, Ted,' Ruby says. 'The Bon, on Brixton Road,' and although his jaw is clenched with resentment, as bloody usual he does what he's told.

Nell is on her way to the shops, has taken the ten bob after all. She has an idea, one of those that seem to come from nowhere, that if she does get the jam tarts then Teddy will come home safely. She's not sure who she's most furious with, Ted, Harry or Ruby. Ruby lied, right to Nell's face and with her hand on her heart. They've put Ted up to something he shouldn't be doing. And he's gone along with it, when she'd expected better of him. She has the same oily feeling in her stomach that she carried all through the first part of the war, waiting for Edward to come back. And then the telegram, its stilted language like a serrated blade: *Deeply regret to inform you Airman E.J. Gibson killed on active service.*

But the anger is helping her stride on, refusing to be daunted by the fog. She stops to let a woman come past, a string of children trailing after her like ducklings, all holding hands so as not to lose each other. The one on the end, a little girl in a bobble hat, is looking about with a sort of delighted fear. She looks up at Nell as they come past and giggles, as though she's been caught doing something naughty. The woman, by contrast, looks in a terrible temper. She pulls at the hand of the oldest child and the tug travels all down the line, jerking them along.

There isn't much of a queue at the baker's, the weather keeping people at home. The woman in front of Nell is pretending to look about at the shop, but her eyes come back to Nell enough that she knows what it's about. The woman has on a patched coat and a drab headscarf in a faded green floral print, but the patches are very neat and the headscarf has been ironed. She's one of those who carries her dowdiness like a flag of respectability. If Nell were a different kind of person, she might tap the woman on the arm and say, 'Clothes are off the ration, haven't you heard? There's no need to go about looking like a dishrag any longer.'

But even so, Nell's stockings and lipstick, her eau de cologne and lovely new shoes, all of it would be murder to get hold of at a decent price these days, and Nell and the drab woman both know it.

You don't know what I put up with for these little scraps, she wants to say.

The horrible irony of it is that Nell's outfit is plain enough to draw sneers from her cousins, and her skirt has had to have a new waistband and hem in the last year. She is sometimes painfully aware that it's a bit ridiculous, this line she walks between wrongdoing and respectability. No one on either side seems to approve of her much.

Another woman comes in and says cheerily, 'Oh, this filth. Makes you sick,' to the shop in general. And although Nell responds, 'Doesn't it, though,' this woman, too, looks at her as though she thinks Nell might have been earning her money on her back.

The first woman replies, 'I saw a bird fly right into a wall this morning. Swear on my life. Flew right into the brick, it was that lost.'

And they begin telling each other how they've never seen fog like it, one woman in front of Nell and the other behind her, talking over Nell's shoulder as though she were a tree.

The baker, on the other hand, always seems pleased to see her. Today you wouldn't have thought he would have run out of anything, but he doesn't have jam tarts, only

146

currant buns. Nell buys them anyway. But they aren't a talisman. They're just buns, just flour, yeast and dried fruit. Perhaps she should go home and make jam tarts, but that's probably cheating.

She begins to walk, trying not to think about the greasy dust settling on her skin.

There is a set of lights moving towards her. In a moment it becomes the silhouette of a policeman in a cape, walking between headlight beams, and the great dark shape of a bus. He's holding his lantern aloft, guiding the bus along its route. The bus windows are shining with light, clean and safe, and she wants very badly to be aboard it.

'Excuse me,' she calls out, and he turns and peers at her. 'Where is the bus stop?'

He just holds up a hand and the bus stops. Nell runs, slipping a little on the damp pavement. She tries to thank him, but he just says, 'Quickly now,' and she climbs aboard.

Most of the other passengers give her a wry kind of smile. One man calls out, 'Isn't it filthy?' and she feels the wry smile appear on her own face.

The bus is like a capsule of air. The windows run with water inside as well as out, but the interior lamps are lit and with the fog blanking out the windows it's like being aboard a submarine.

The bus is going the wrong way, into Brixton, but if Nell has been waiting for a sign, this must be one. When the conductor comes around and asks her, 'Where to, madam?' she replies, 'The Bon Marche. Brixton Road.'

Not five minutes after Ted has let the ladies out there comes a knocking on the window and he sees a policeman's face, horribly close, peering through the dirty glass. He takes an involuntary, greasy gulp of air and rolls down his window.

'You alright there, sir?' the copper says.

'Oh,' Ted says, 'Yes. Perfectly alright.'

'Well, you can't stay here. This is loading and unloading only.'

'I won't be a tick,' Ted says. 'My wife's just nipped in the shops.'

'That's as may be, but there's no parking here. Anyone coming to load here might bump you. It's not safe. You can't guarantee they'll see you.'

'I'll keep my eyes open though, won't I?'

'You'll have to, in this weather. But you can't stay here. Move along, please. And I'd advise you to get off the roads as soon as you can. We're suggesting people abandon their cars if needs be. But do leave it in a safe place.'

Ted has no choice but to start up the engine. He can't help feeling that the bobby will be watching to see if he bumps anything. He's peering out of his wiped circle of glass, concentrating so hard that he feels the car as an extension of himself, his own stretched nerves running all the way to her bumpers.

The road is full of the shadows of people crossing, a few lumbering buses. He crawls down the Brixton Road, praying he won't hit anyone.

At the corner of Nursery Road he stops. He'll have to leave the car, find the girls and tell them where he's moved to. He looks for landmarks to help him find his way back again, and so that he can tell the ladies what to look for. There's a tobacconist's and a pillar box on the corner. It will have to do.

*

Florrie thinks she's spotted a shopwalker, walking about as though he means to buy himself a dress. She nudges her mum and Ruby looks over, wrinkles her nose in agreement and hangs back to let him go by.

They're working in pairs this time, Maggie and Ada, Ruby and Florrie, each pair acting like they don't know the others.

They take their time, waiting for him to be well away, looking about at everything, dawdling over the rails. Ruby wanders over to a rack of jumpers in crimson and white: Christmas colours.

Florrie follows, looking about. Maggie and Ada are over by the kids' things. They're still a bit tense with each other, their bodies stiff and gestures terse. They might be a mother and daughter out shopping after a quarrel. Anyone might see that much, but no one but a thief would see how carefully they're keeping an eye out, even while they hold up the little dresses for each other to admire. The shopwalker goes by them without a glance.

Ruby isn't half good. Even standing right next to her, Florrie can hardly see her at it. Before she knows it, Ruby is jabbing her in the elbow with a hard finger.

'What?' Florrie is looking all about them, without moving her head too much.

For answer, Ruby swings the bag into Florrie's leg. It's full already, that's all. She'd thought Ruby had seen something she hadn't.

They both drop their handbags on the floor, the better to admire a cardigan sewn with little golden beads in the shape of a flower over one breast. 'You'd never need a brooch, wearing that,' Florrie says. 'Oh, do you know, I've gone and left my purse in the car. I won't be a sec.'

She picks up the full bag, leaving the empty one for Ruby to fill up.

As much as she doesn't want to go into the fog alone, seen through the glass doors it's almost pretty, like murky pearls. She steps out into it and away, and no one says a thing to stop her.

Ruby bends down and picks up the empty bag. When she straightens up she's surprised and not at all pleased to see Ted. He's craning to look about the shop, although he's such a beanpole he could surely manage without stretching his neck like a rooster. He has no business leaving the car.

He sees her and stands staring across the shop. She shakes her head, as if to herself, but now the idiot is making a beeline straight for her. Then he stops and seems to think it over. He slows, wandering along, pretending to shop, but as he's already made it obvious to anyone watching that he knows her, this type of thing is going to seem more fishy than if he just came straight over. Why shouldn't they be acquainted, after all? But no, here he is, sidling along, looking everywhere but at her. She has her own, much more relaxed look about. There are a fair few shoppers and the line at the counter. But the counter girl is busy. She doesn't think anyone has clocked him. Lucky for Ted.

'What are you doing in here?' she asks.

He shakes back his cuff to look at his watch as if he's telling her the time. 'I had to move the car. Corner of Nursery Road. Keep walking up Ferndale Road from where we parked. Pillar box and a tobacconist on the corner.'

'Much obliged,' she says, and walks away from him before he can make himself any more of a prat.

*

Florrie could swear that she's standing right where they'd left the car. She's trying to stay calm but she feels hemmed in by fog, buried alive. Her whole body wants to twist around and run back; it makes her think of gas.

Surely they parked beside the grey door. But then, there might be grey doors everywhere. Perhaps she's on the wrong street altogether. The fog swirls about maddeningly and she waves a hand in front of her as though it were possible to clear it away.

At last she begins to retrace her steps. She can stash the bag somewhere, perhaps, and go back to get it later. Better than leaving her mum to wonder where she's got to, but then she'll have to find the bag again. And come to that, she has to find the Bon Marche. How can everything look so different?

When the hand falls on her elbow she almost screams. But it's Ted. Ted, who has somehow known she's lost and come to save her. She throws her arms around him, banging the bag into his back.

'Ow,' he says. 'Steady on.'

He kisses her, and she has that feeling of falling into the kiss. It only lasts a second but it is the kind of second you remember.

'What's all this?'

'I didn't know where I was.'

'You walked right past me. Lucky I saw you, really. I had to move the car. I've told your mum where to find it.'

He holds her hand all the way back to it, the two of them moving in their own little bubble.

'Here it is.' Ted opens the car door for her. She climbs in, takes everything from the holdall and packs it into a shopping bag. She doesn't take the time to look over everything, because she wants to get back. But she can see Ruby has done well. Ted gives a little whistle.

'She's an old hand, my mum.' Florrie feels an uncomfortable mixture of pride and shame. She gives him her own hand to help her back out of the car, and the shopper to put in the boot.

She takes her hand from his, kisses her fingertips and presses them to his cheek, feeling the stubble waiting under the skin. 'I'm ever so sorry you got roped in. I'm sorry I did, come to that.' She curses herself for how flat her voice sounds. It's unfair, because her chest is aching over his being dragged away from his decent job and into the muck.

He's smiling at her, though. 'Don't you worry about me. I said I'd look after you, didn't I? Better I'm here than some other bloke. And look here, we'll tell them tonight. This will be the last time you ever have to do a thing like this.'

'Well, good,' she says, but she still can't imagine how they're going to manage it.

'Don't go yet.' Ted holds her hand against his face. He's so close that he is speaking right into her mouth, his breath mixing with hers.

She kisses him again and thinks how they must look, the lovers in the fog. She wishes she could have a photograph of it.

At last she pulls her head away enough to say, 'I have to.'

'Let them carry their own stuff out. It's you taking all the risk for them.'

This is true. You don't get nicked if you've nothing on you. She almost tells him that the bags were her idea, that no one's making her, but she doesn't want him to think badly of her.

'They're expecting me,' she says, instead.

'Let me walk you back.'

'Ted, we can't. They'll go mad if they come out and you've left the car.' Oh, but she wants him to.

He lets her step sideways away from him.

'Sorry,' she says, again. And she is, about all sorts of things at once.

He calls after her, 'Careful, alright? Don't get lost. And come back quick.'

She turns and blows him a kiss, but all she can see of him is a blurry shape against the dark hump of the car.

Nell stands just inside the Bon Marche and blinks. If the bus had been a submarine, stepping into the Bon is like being ushered onto a cruise ship. Everything glitters. Ruby always calls it a lucky place: perhaps it is.

Nell spends a happy few minutes wandering between the counters, looking at the jewellery she will never afford, arranged in glass cases. She's always told herself she'd draw the line at stolen jewellery. She's had to tell Harry so several times, come to that. But now she plays a little game, choosing which pieces she might buy if she were rich.

She goes up the lovely wide stairs, behind two ladies. One of them is wearing a cream coat streaked with grime. The other's hat is drooping as though it's melting. Only imagine coming to the shop as filthy as that. Nell would rather die. But no sooner has the thought flitted into her head than she realises that the fingers of her own pigskin gloves are blackened, the hem of her coat turned grey.

As soon as she gets upstairs she has a proper look at herself in the wall mirror and puts her dirty-gloved hand to her mouth. Her hair has specks of black caught in the curls. There's dust in her lipstick.

And what is she doing here anyway? What an idiot, to come running after Ted, looking like a sack of wet washing. Well, she thinks, turning and going as smartly as she can back down, at least she's had the sense to go home before she sees the others. She hadn't really thought, until this very moment, of what a queer, sneaking thing it was to do, following them here.

But oh, no. There is Ruby. Below the glossy line of the banister, with her back to Nell. She's looking over a rack of coats, a holdall over one arm, her dark head bent.

Nell finds that she's stopped dead, her hand at her throat. A lady coming down the stairs tuts and says, 'Excuse me,' in an irritated voice.

Before she can creep back up the stairs, Ruby turns and their eyes meet. The look on Ruby's face is awful, something between rage and horror.

It's so very embarrassing to be caught that Nell just nods at her cousin, a jerky bob of the head, and instead of running back up she makes herself walk down. She doesn't look at Ruby. Once she reaches the ground floor she veers off around the hats so that they won't have to meet. The urge to turn back and grab Ruby by the shoulders, to somehow recover her pride, is awful. She forces herself on.

But now Ruby's hand falls on her arm.

'What are you doing here?' Ruby snatches her hand back from Nell as though she doesn't like to touch her.

'You needn't be like that about it,' Nell says, but the last word catches and the shame of that, too, washes over her from the head down.

'What are you up to, spying on me?'

'I've no interest in you. It's Teddy I'm worried about. And I was right to be concerned, wasn't I? I knew you were telling me fibs,' Nell says. A young couple shopping together pass close by and Nell drops her voice. 'You take me for a fool.'

Now Ruby sighs, more heavily than she need. 'Let's not have a scene. Go home, Nell.'

'I'm trying to go. You're the one making a fuss,' Nell hisses.

The lady on the hat counter has stopped, a hatbox in her hands, and is watching them.

Ruby shakes her head.

'I know what you're doing,' Nell says.

'You're off your head.' Ruby actually laughs. As though it's a joke, as though she cares nothing for what Nell knows. And then she just turns and walks away.

It is very difficult not to shout after her. But what would Nell shout? *How dare you,* perhaps. And then people really would stare.

Ruby is through the hats now, moving back down the aisle of coats. She begins to cough and has to put her bag down on the floor to cover her mouth. The cough rocks her backwards and forwards, her thin neck jerking like a bird's. She looks up, hands still to her face, and looks about her. Then she begins walking, quickly, towards the heavy doors that lead to the street.

The doorman moves to hold the door and Ruby nods to him and then she is going. But her hands are both empty; she's left the bag. She's lied to Nell's face yet again and then abandoned the evidence.

Nell's feet start forward. After all she's done for them, giving them houseroom, making the rations stretch. And this is what she gets in return. Ruby thinking so little of her, Maggie always poking fun. Even Teddy, laughing at her in the hall. *She's not as bad as all that.* That's the best her son can say of her.

She reaches the coats and bends down. Her hands are on the holdall. Well, she'll just show them. She'll take this bag out there and push it right in her cousin's lying face. *What's this, then? What do you call this?* And then she wants an apology. And for the lot of them to clear off and leave her son alone.

She hefts the bag onto her shoulder and walks, heart thumping quite unexpectedly hard, face hot. The doorman swings the door open and the murk billows in like a curtain caught in the wind.

She steps out, into the fog.

Florrie stops outside the lit windows of the Bon Marche, and puts her shoulders back. It's always more nerve-wracking going in the second time. She catches a glimpse of herself in the glass, her shape set against the fog like a paper doll on a blank page.

The shop door opens before she reaches it and Maggie comes out, walking quickly, her face very calm. She flicks her eyes at Florrie but doesn't slow. Behind Maggie she can see Ada, also on her way out.

Florrie turns too, as though she's simply forgotten something, and walks back the way she's come. She doesn't rush; she's nothing on her. Maggie walks past, then Ada, waddling a little. It's hard to go fast with your bloomers stuffed full of dresses and in four-inch heels. She can see they know where the car's been moved to, or at least that they're going the right way.

She stops and Ada frowns at her as though she thinks Florrie has stopped to speak to her. But when Florrie cranes past, back towards the shop, she hurries by.

'Come on, can't you?' Ada says as she does, but she says it as if to herself.

Both of the other women grow hazy and then disappear into the fog completely. But where's her mum?

A trio of young men pass her, their collars turned up. Then a pair of sweethearts hand in hand, fog masks over their mouths and noses. They pass in and out of Florrie's bubble of vision, getting in her way.

Finally, finally she sees Ruby. She's sure it's her mum, just by the way she walks. She starts forward to meet her—

The silhouettes of two men have appeared from what seems like nowhere, and Florrie stops cold as they grab Ruby by the arms.

People keep coming past her, hiding Ruby from sight. She catches flashes of her mum, kicking and thrashing between the two men like a cancan girl turned crazed. Florrie can't help stepping forward until she's near enough to see Ruby's mouth opening and closing as though she hasn't enough breath to scream. Florrie's jigging up and down on her own feet, unable to decide what to do.

'Florrie,' Maggie's voice says behind her, 'what are you doing, you silly bint?'

Then, the strangest thing: there's Aunt Nell, her mum's bag in her hand, and she's handing it over to one of the men, she's telling him something. The bag is full, Florrie can see that by the way it hangs. The fellow has his hand on her arm. He says something in return.

'No!' Maggie says, right by Florrie's ear. 'Oh, this is the end. I never imagined!' She grabs Florrie by the elbow, hard, her fingers digging into the muscle. 'Come on.'

Florrie says, 'Aunt Nell—'

'I'd never have believed it if I hadn't seen with my own eyes.' Maggie's pulling her away, walking so fast that Florrie can barely keep her feet. 'That grassing bitch. Her own cousin. Oh, she's going to wish she was never born. Don't you worry about that.'

Florrie can't breathe. Maggie won't let her stop.

Ted is just ahead of them, beckoning urgently.

'Mum,' she tells him. 'My mum.'

'Got nicked,' Maggie says. She pinches Florrie's arm just above the elbow. 'Hush now, Florrie. Not another word.'

Ted huffs plumes of breath out through his nose. 'Blimey.' His hand begins to reach for her but then he glances at Maggie and draws it back. 'Bloody hell.'

Florrie opens her mouth to tell him that his own mum was there, where she should never have been, where she can't have been, not really – but Maggie's saying, 'Hush, Florrie. Didn't I tell you? Not a word, now,' and Ted's turning to go back to the car, taking her arm, so that she's between him and Maggie, just like her mum is being held by those men. Ted's hand squeezes her elbow once, twice.

We're in trouble now, she keeps thinking. *We're in trouble now.* It goes round and around like a tune caught in her head, almost without meaning and entirely unbidden.

Ruby's twisting, her shoes sliding on the wet pavement. Hands are gripping her arms so tightly that the tips of the fingers seem to slide underneath her wasted muscles. She's jerking like a fish on a line, the evening bags she should never have tucked into her knickers shifting about, sliding sickeningly against her thighs. She feels her head connect horribly with the skull of one of the blokes holding her and then his fist wallops into her cheekbone and the surprise of it rockets through her and she stops thrashing, just to breathe, just to think, just to wait for the pulse of pain to finish its first hot journey through her skull. For a moment she hangs between them, strung up on their grip, and then she looks up and sees her cousin's face, Nell's arm gripped just as her own is gripped.

When the hand grabs Nell's elbow she's so surprised that she finds herself saying, 'Oh, beg pardon,' without knowing why. Then dismay at her own stupidity rises to an intensity that's enough to make her knees give out. She's stolen a bag of goods by mistake.

The hand holds her up, takes hold of her other elbow, takes the bag from her hands.

'No,' she says, 'No, please don't.'

His fingers are digging hard into the soft part of her arm, and he holds her a little way away from himself, as though she's something rotten.

'Please don't?' he says, and laughs. 'You can "please don't" the police when they get here, and see how far you get.'

Just behind him Nell can see Ruby, held by two other fellows. Ruby is looking over at Nell with an expression Nell has never seen there before; naked and wounded. One of her eyes is closed.

'Oh dear,' Nell says to her.

Ruby shakes her head. 'Shut your mouth and keep it shut.'

Nell nods, and then isn't sure if she should have.

Ruby watches Nell climb into the police van and then the copper takes her arm from the shopwalkers and pushes her inside as well. He sits himself next to her.

The police van is cold and smells of piss. And there's fog in here, too, a locked box of fog carrying her to another locked box. The evening bags press against her thighs, and she wonders, dully, if there'll be any way to fish them out before the search.

She closes her eyes so that she won't have to look at Nell's set white face, leans her head back against the side of the van and feels the vibration in the back of her skull as they start the engine. Her left cheek throbs like a drum, and her head hurts where it slammed into the detective's. The vibrations make it worse, but she doesn't move.

One day. She managed one day out. It almost would have been better to have stayed inside.

Florrie stares out of the window all the drive home, her belly a sick, sliding thing.

They pass two cars, the nose of one crinkled up, the side of the other bent inwards. Their headlamps are still casting beams across the swirling fog.

She watches the back of Ted's neck. Something about the way his ears stick out from under his cap makes her want to cry. And every time she tries to speak, Maggie tells her to hush.

Back in Nell's kitchen, she just sits down. Never mind being told to keep quiet, now she finds she can't speak. Ada puts the kettle on.

'Right,' Maggie says, her voice very calm and hard. 'We'll sort this out. I'll just bloody well say we will.'

Florrie shakes her head.

Maggie pushes her shoulder down as if Florrie were going to stand up. 'You just wait, like I tell you.'

She doesn't want to wait. She wants Maggie to spit and

snarl like she always does. She wants everyone to scream and cry or let her slap them, or something. She doesn't know. But she knows it's a bad lookout for her mum. Florrie should have been looking but she was off kissing Ted, and now the taste of it sits in her throat like vinegar.

Maggie makes Ted go back and forth from the car, fetching it all in from the boot, while she and Ada fish the rest of their hauls out of their knickers. The kitchen table begins to look like a posh jumble sale. Usually they'd all be laughing over each new piece, but today it's like a funeral.

At last it's sorted into piles, and Maggie packs it back up into the shopping bags.

'Here,' she says, beckoning Ted, 'you take these back out to the hall. And then give us a minute.'

Florrie watches Ted take the bags. Some of the things in there are things her mum got in Selfridges.

The minute the door closes behind him Maggie leans forward. 'That's got rid of him. Now, we need to have a little chat with our Cousin Nell the minute she gets home.'

Florrie can feel them waiting for her to say something. Finally, she says, 'Nell won't have meant it.'

'You don't worry about that,' Maggie says. 'I'll sort all that out.'

Ted's shuffling about in the hall.

'But look here,' Maggie says, very quiet, 'We want a word with Nellie before any of this gets back to Ted. Wouldn't you say?' She smiles, showing a lot of teeth.

'I don't know,' Florrie says.

'Then you just trust me. You just say whether you want to be there when she gets home.'

'I don't think so,' Florrie says. She wants Ruby back. She wants someone else to be in charge.

'Then you get Teddy to take you off somewhere. Keep him out the way, and leave the rest to me. Alright? Good girl.'

Florrie puts her hand to her eyes.

'And Florence,' Maggie says, 'not a bloody word to that boy. Do you hear me? For all you know, he's in this right up to his neck.'

'Oh, come on,' Ada says.

Florrie uncovers her eyes. Maggie is shaking her head and looking grim.

'She's his mum. You can't tell me he was glad Ruby was coming home. He's been moping about for days. For all you know, he cooked up that little bit of business and pushed Nellie into it. She's weak enough.'

'He never would.' Florrie is suddenly very tired. If she could just lie down, maybe she'd wake up and this wouldn't be happening.

'Well, either way, she's his mum. You leave him out of it.' Maggie puts her fingers to her lips. 'Ada, let that boy in, will you?'

Ada wrinkles her nose at being told what to do, but she does get up.

Florrie looks around and there he is, looking at her and wondering if she's alright. Her own, ordinary Ted. It's just Maggie, making up wild ideas.

'You take this girl out,' Maggie says to him. 'Cheer her up.'

He says 'Of course,' so fast and so kindly that she almost can't bear it. But she stands, and puts her green coat back on.

'Don't you want this on?' Maggie says.

It's the beautiful fur.

'Not now,' Ted says.

She lets Ted lead her off by the hand and even when he's got her into the car, she isn't sure she can keep from telling him, whatever Maggie says.

'Where are we going?' she asks, once the engine has caught and the car begins to crawl off.

'Where would you like to go?'

'I don't know. Anywhere. Not here.'

'Alright. I have an idea. Would you like to hear it?'

She doesn't say anything.

Ted drives without speaking, concentrating on the road, the headlights barely making a dent in the fog.

At last, when she doesn't ask, he tells her anyway. 'I got us a flat.' He flicks his eyes from the road for a minute to look at her.

She sighs, a deep one, the kind that seems to come from the belly. It's not like she wants to go out to dinner or dancing. But still. He's borrowed some bloke's flat. She's known he was working his way up to this, that it must come soon. She's been worrying that he might be expecting her to be a virgin, has been wondering if he is himself. Mostly, when she lets herself think about it, she's felt a trembly excitement, the kind that makes her almost queasy. But not now. Now it's the last thing she feels like. But perhaps she can get him to give her a cuddle. She needs to hang onto him, just have him hold her while she calms herself down.

He can see what she's thinking, though. 'No, I really got us a flat, didn't I? To live in. Once we're married.'

She can't find a reply.

'Well?' He sounds nervous. 'Aren't you pleased?'

She rubs at her face. 'My mum just got nicked.' *And Maggie thinks yours sent her there.*

163

'I know. I am sorry. But I'll take care of you, Florrie. You'll see.' But she can't tell if he sounds sorry or not.

Nell would never grass. She's taken them into her house, over and over again, she nursed Dolly on her deathbed. And Ted is the most decent, upright bloke Florrie knows. He might not approve of the Cutters, but he's not underhand like that.

But she saw her mum, thrashing between those two blokes like a washing line in high wind, and she saw Aunt Nell handing that bag over to the shopwalker.

She looks at the side of Ted's face peering out of the windscreen and wishes he'd park the car so she could cling to him. But somehow, when he does reach out and pat her knee, she has to stop herself pushing him away.

At the police station, Nell finds herself coming out of a terrible sort of trance. She's let herself be bundled about like a package, been searched by a pudding-faced matron, has answered question after question, had her handbag and shopping taken from her and pawed through. They took her fingerprints, which surprised her, although it shouldn't have. And now she's alone and she's not sure if that's better or worse.

The cell is like a very dreary waiting room. It's bare but for a metal toilet built into one wall and a wooden bench, shined smooth by the bottoms of all the people who have sat on it and tried not to cry before her.

She looks at the blue-black of the ink on her fingertips and thinks, *Well, this just serves me right for thinking I was anything special.* And it does stop the tears from coming. She's Dolly's niece, after all. She's Ruby and Maggie's cousin. Half her family, almost, have sat in cells like this one, with ink-stained fingers.

There's a ventilation grate set high up on the wall, a window to nowhere. But that doesn't stop her feeling as though the air might be used up any moment. Fog is drifting in through it.

Perhaps Ruby is next door, right at that moment, in a cupboard of her own, struggling to breathe.

It might not be the best moment to show Florrie the flat, but Ted wants her to see that he'll look after her. She has a whole life of her own with him, things to look forward to. Ruby has spent half her life in and out of prison. You'd have thought that Florrie would have learned to need her less, not more.

Even so, he knows, as he puts the key in the lock, that she isn't going to be as pleased as he's hoped. Watching her walk around the place is like having the veils stripped from his own eyes. It looks shabby and small. The coconut matting is grubby from Harry's shoes, the patchwork quilt is showing its age and he's left smears of tar on the kitchen floor. She looks at it all with a perfectly blank face. It's worse than if she were sneering. She walks over to the windows and looks out on the fog.

'Not much view just now,' he says. 'Not much in any case. Just my yard. And the WC is down there.' He imagines her going to the outhouse with a whole load of blokes loading or unloading a lorry. He doesn't dare tell her that part. Not yet.

Her shoulders are hunched and her brow is almost touching the glass. The reflection of her face is blurry and smudged, but he can see that she's miserable.

He wonders if he should put an arm around her or something, but then she says, 'Give me a minute, will you?'

He pats her on the shoulder and goes to the bedroom, feeling like an idiot. He should have just taken her out for tea. He's never been good around sadness. When his dad died, he and his mum had walked around smiling madly, talking about nothing in bright voices, and both of them cracking inside. He's never been taught what to do if someone doesn't want to be cheered up.

He sits on the bed and wonders how long he should leave it before he goes back in. He's trying to be sorry that Ruby's gone – he is sorry, in his own way. It's rotten for Ruby, and he hates Florrie being upset – but Florrie's said so many times that Ruby might try to stop them being together, it's hard to be miserable over it for himself. He thinks again about the yard, about Harry. But Harry did say he'd be making twice the money he is now. He'll be able to make the flat nice – he'll get Florrie anything she wants for it, as much as he can manage. She'll come around, once this shock has worn off. He waits, listening to the creak of her feet moving slowly about. Maybe, in a minute, he can go out there and tell her it'll all be alright, and this time she'll see that he means it.

Florrie is looking over the place that could become her home. The glass wants washing, inside and out, and everything needs cleaning. The kitchen floor is streaked with half circles of black, there's a bowl on the kitchen table with a filthy rag in it. She goes back to the window and looks out on the bank of dirty cloud that's fallen from the sky.

She's glad not to have Ted's eyes on her. He'd been

watching her so hard she couldn't think. Although even now, she doesn't know where to start.

She stands staring at nothing. Then she gives up. She needs him to put his arms around her. She opens the bedroom door without knocking.

He's sitting on the bed, his hands in his lap, looking a little lost.

'Let's get a cup of tea, shall we?' he asks, hopefully. 'Something to eat? It's nearly six.'

'Alright. Yes.' She tries to smile but her cheeks feel queer. She puts her hands to her eyes, instead.

She hears him stand and come towards her, feels his hesitant hands, one on each of her arms. She rests her forehead against his shoulder and takes in the familiar scents of him, Brylcreem and tar, Nell's Carlisle soap. She's had her mum ripped away from her, Maggie thinks Nell has grassed and she's not sure that Ted's sorry that Ruby's gone. Everything Florrie thought she knew about her family has dissolved under her feet. Her hypocritical hands wrap themselves into the back of his jacket and she breathes hard into his neck. She isn't going to cry.

'Steady on,' he says, quietly. 'Steady on. She'll be alright. I'll take you to visit her as soon as we can.'

He thinks she's upset about Ruby and nothing more. She begins to feel deceitful, having him hold her. She steps away, but then she can't stand how kindly he's looking at her.

He takes her to the caff down the road. She feels trembly and bruised about the heart, but she's careful, now, not to cling to him. She still can't look him in the eye but she lets him hold her hand and they walk across the road together, watching the lit windows appear out of the gloom.

As soon as they get into the caff, Ted knows this is a bad idea. The place is full of Harry Godden's boys. He's never seen a single one of them in here before, and he comes in every day, almost, for a cup of tea or a bit of lunch. Now they're sitting in groups around the oilcloth-covered tables, smoking over cups of tea and plates of bread and butter, leaning up against the counter, looking like they mean to stand there all day.

At least half of them turn to look when Ted and Florrie come in, and a few voices shout out, 'Alright, Teddy?'

They know his name. He's never spoken to most of them. Another couple say, 'Hello there, Florrie,' and he likes that even less. Florrie raises her hand to them but doesn't reply.

The whole thing puts the wind up him and he finds himself keeping a grip on Florrie like she's a life raft, even though it means them going sideways to fit between the chairs.

The waitress smiles at him and sits them down.

This is awful. Florrie's a hundred miles away, inside herself where he can't reach her. And all the time his back prickles with the effort of ignoring Harry's boys.

The waitress flicks her eyes over Florrie's hair and clothes, but twinkles and smiles at Ted. He doesn't seem to notice.

'Everyone knows you,' Florrie says, when the waitress has finally gone off with their order.

'I could say the same to you.'

But she doesn't know most of them, not really, and it's queer to see him in his own place, somewhere that has nothing to do with her. Everything about the day has thrown her.

He fetches out a cigarette.

She watches, wanting one. He sees her looking and offers the case, jigging it in his palm so that the fags jump. She takes one before he can change his mind. He thinks it's common of ladies to smoke in public. She leans forward and lets him light her.

'It's a nice place, this,' she says, although it isn't.

'Not as nice as it looks. Don't you come in here without me, Florrie. Please.'

'Alright,' she says, because he doesn't know what sort of places she's been to before now.

'You mustn't.'

'I said alright, didn't I?' Her fingers go to the largest of her rings and twist it round and around.

The tea comes, and Florrie can see the waitress thinks she's caught them quarrelling and is glad. She waits while they put sugar in their tea and then she takes the sugar bowl, and the spoon, away with her. It's that kind of place. At least the spoon isn't tied to the counter by a piece of string.

The bread and jam is alright, but the rock cakes are stale. The plate has something yellow dried on it. She picks it off with a fingernail.

Ted watches her do it. 'I know the flat's not anything much.'

'It's lovely, Ted.' But she can't make her voice sound like she means it.

'It's the best I could get.'

'It's a lovely place.' It doesn't sound any better this time, either.

Ted takes off his jacket and pulls the cloth of his shirt away from his armpits. 'I'm making a mess of this, aren't I? I meant to cheer you up.'

She looks at his dear, worried face and thinks, *Blow Maggie and her stupid ideas.* She leans over to tell him what they saw, to ask him to help her think what to do, to be Florrie and Ted again.

Then, like a bad joke, one of the wide-boys stops beside the table.

'Alright, Flo?'

'Hello.' She can't remember his name, so she can't introduce him.

'And you're Ted.' The bloke sticks his hand out and Ted shakes it. Then he takes his hand back and picks at his teeth with it. 'Going to be seeing you a lot more now, I expect.'

Ted gives him a smile that means, *Go away*.

But almost as soon as he does, another arrives to take his place, and this one is a bloke she does know: Dennis, Val's husband.

She's afraid he's going to say something dreadful in front of Ted, but he barely glances at her. Instead, he leans to mutter into Ted's ear, one hand on his shoulder. Ted looks to see if she's listening. Then he stands up and takes Dennis by the sleeve to pull him away.

She watches him go. The spivs are all looking him over in a way she doesn't like. Dennis is still talking to Ted, on and on. Every now and then Ted half turns as if to come back to her and she thinks, *Good, now we can leave.* Then Dennis says something else and Ted turns back to him and she can feel her legs, which have begun getting ready to stand, slump and go loose again. At last she gets up and goes over. They all shut up and look at her.

'Ted.' She takes his sleeve and draws him away a bit. 'Can't we go back?'

'Soon,' he says. 'I promise.'

'But why can't we just go? What on earth do you want to talk to blokes like them about?'

He looks away. 'Just business. They want to buy some blocks off me.'

'Can't it wait?'

'I'll be as quick as I can. I promise.'

'Give me your keys,' she says. 'I'll go by myself.'

'No!' he says, too fast. 'Not by yourself. Just wait. I won't be long.'

And she has to go back to her chair. The tea's gone. She doesn't want the rest of the rock cake; the more she's eaten, the more it has felt like greasy paste. She looks everywhere but at the faces of the blokes. The caff is too warm, surprising in a place with such a rickety-looking door. You could open that door with one kick. But perhaps they put a bar across it at night.

She wonders where Ruby is now, she thinks of what Aunt Maggie said, and how even if none of that's true, it's still Ted's fault that she wasn't there to watch for Ruby. Him making her late back, just in time for his mum to nip in and ruin Ruby's life. She feels a sourness rise up in her that's nothing to do with the cake.

Ted has left his jacket slung over the back of the chair and she can see the faintest bulge of his keys through the cloth.

Another man, his shirt hanging over his trousers between his braces, has come up and joined in with Ted and Dennis. She's so restless she could scream.

She stands and puts her coat on. Ted doesn't spare her a glance.

She brushes past Ted's chair and, with a stealth born of years of habit, pinches his keys from his abandoned jacket. She needn't do it like that. She could wave them about, jingling them like bells, and he'd not notice. He's still talking to his chums.

The bloke Ted's talking to is called Dennis. He's been at the yard, looking for Ted. All of them have. Harry sent them round to 'get a feel of the place', but when he wasn't there, they all piled in here to warm up. It was a bit of luck, Dennis keeps saying, that Ted came into the caff.

'We'll be running the yard, you and me,' Dennis says. 'Me and you keeping an eye on the rest of them. They're a bunch of lazy sods.'

He doesn't half go on. Ted isn't sure what Dennis wants from him. He must've said the same thing four or five times. Ted just keeps nodding, worried that if he goes back to the table, they'll try to talk to Florrie again. He doesn't want her having anything more to do with these blokes than she has to.

One of the other men comes over and starts asking him how much Ted gets for a bag of blocks, how long it takes to clean the gravel off. Ted almost starts to enjoy himself in spite of everything. They're listening to what he says, offering him their fags. It might even be better than working alone. He lets himself imagine them calling him 'boss'. Getting himself a draped jacket like Don's.

Thinking of Don makes him turn and look for Florrie, but her seat is empty. Dennis is still talking on and on.

The cell is horribly familiar, although Ruby's not sure she's ever been in this particular one before. The cold light, the uncomfortable bench, the smell of old sweat and disinfectant. All her choices taken off her at the desk.

She's been thinking, of course, of grasses. But it doesn't

seem likely. Hardly anyone knew they were going out today. It was that idiot boy, coming into the shop, acting like a prat. That's what's got her here now. But she was the one who made him drive.

And Nell. Nell is an idiot, but she's a worse one herself. It's not Nell's fault Ruby's here. It's all her own. If she'd only stuck to bags, like Florrie wanted. That bloody matron had pulled the beaded purses out of Ruby's bloomers without a flicker, like she was rearranging her kitchen shelves.

The TB is waking up, stretching its hot fingers out. She should have listened when Nell said it wasn't safe to be out with her lungs. Her cheeks are hot and her chest has that dull burn inside, and it's all so familiar she could cry, if she was the type to weep.

By the time her solicitor turns up her skin feels alien, as though she's wearing a full body suit of thin rubber.

Mr Baron is a mate of Harry's brother, or something like that. He'd usually be paid for from the pot, but since it's still lost the girls must all have chipped in to get him. He's a sallow man in a cheap suit that's damp over the shoulders from the grime outside, like filthy dandruff. He stands just inside the cell, briefcase in hand.

'This weather is murderous,' he says, by way of greeting. 'It took me an age to get here.'

Ruby ignores this. 'What are they saying?'

He sighs. 'They'll want to make an example of you if they can. They say you'll be charged with violating the terms of your early release, larceny, the incitement of Mrs Gibson to commit a criminal act, resisting arrest and the assault of a shop detective.'

'Oh, come now, I never did all that. That shopwalker lamped me.'

'Well, it's what they'll try for. They're very pleased with themselves for arresting you. They seem to think they'll have a chance to shut down the lot of you, after this. The sergeant looked ready to dance a jig.'

'What about Nellie? Mrs Gibson?'

'You must know I can't represent her as well as yourself.'

'No. Course not. But if I say I done it all, you think they'll let her go?'

Mr Baron frowns. 'That's not the way the law works. They'll not hold her long, in any case. They're as busy as I've ever seen them. This weather has them running about like chickens.'

'But they'll charge her, you think?'

'I expect so. They aren't much keen on your family. But more importantly, while I don't think we can keep you out of prison entirely, you'll certainly be looking at another couple of years if you confess at this stage. I recommend you keep silent during the interview, and let me ascertain what evidence they have.'

But he's wrong. Isn't he? Wouldn't the police give up Nell, to keep hold of Ruby? And Nell is owed something, for taking them in so many times, for nursing Dolly. It will be better for Florrie if Nell's out. She still needs a bit of mothering, and Ruby won't be there to do it.

'No choice,' she says. 'Got to try.'

And then Mr Baron leaves, and she sits and sweats.

The room they take her to is one she's sure she's been in before. Mr Baron's there already, a glass of water in front of him and a pile of papers. The sergeant is the one with the moustache that curls over his top lip.

'Calmed yourself down now, Miss Palmer?' he says, as soon as she's seated. 'And am I to congratulate you?'

Ruby just looks at him. The effort of sitting up straight is making her wearier than ever.

'The word is that you're the new queen,' he says. 'Not that you'll be doing much reigning where you're going.' He smiles, his moustache wriggling. 'Yes, we know about that.'

'Bully for you,' she says. 'Where's Nell?'

'Exactly where you'd think she is.'

'I don't want her to have a bad time. She's got nothing to do with it. And she ain't strong.'

'She was strong enough for you to use as your donkey, to do your dirty work.'

'Listen. You don't need to bother with all that. How many times have you had me in here?'

'Too many times.'

'Right. And I keep quiet, don't I?' She needs this to be quick. The constable is writing everything down and he's too slow; the sergeant keeps waiting for him to finish. The sweat has turned cold. She won't have long.

Now Mr Baron coughs. 'I recommend you continue that tradition and stay silent, Miss Palmer.' He shuffles the papers.

'Not today,' Ruby says, 'I never talk. But I'm talking now.'

'What Miss Palmer means,' Mr Baron interrupts, 'is that she might consider responding, once we have a fuller understanding of the case against her.'

Ruby leans forward, partly just to let her arms take some of the weight of her drooping body. 'No, I don't. I mean I'll talk if you let Nell go. She's just my cousin who I share a house with.'

The sergeant's moustache twitches. 'You were appre-hended with stolen goods on your person, Miss Palmer. You've broken the terms of your early release. And that's just the start. So you will understand that your cooperation isn't what one would call necessary.'

Bastard.

He purses his lips and sucks on his teeth. 'If you'd really like to help your cousin, you might like to tell me what you know about the goings on at Fisher's Pawn and Loan.'

'At where?'

'Not familiar?' the sergeant says. 'How strange. We know you're tight with Harry Godden. And now you're staying just round the corner. You can't expect me to believe that's a coincidence.'

Ruby shakes her head. 'No. I'll cooperate about . . . about me. What you say I did. I'll talk about that.'

'How about the stolen goods held at Wilson's Dry Cleaner's? Would you rather discuss that?'

So. That's it. There was a grass today, after all. Maggie said they'd never used the dry cleaner's to fence anything before. Perhaps Val, poor old pregnant Val, is being held in a cell down the hall. The idea sets her off coughing.

Mr Baron says, 'Don't say a word, Miss Palmer,' but the coughs shake her body like the leaves of a tree in a wind and she couldn't if she wanted to.

Mr Baron touches her forehead, and then whips his hand away, wiping her sweat onto his trousers.

'This lady has a temperature,' he says. 'She's in need of a doctor. Immediately.'

His words are coming from far away, and it doesn't matter anyway.

'We can send for the police surgeon, but in this weather we'll be lucky.'

'Ambulance, then. If she dies you'll be in dereliction of duty,' Mr Baron says.

176

She can hear Mr Baron insisting that they have a duty of care and they'll have to wait to interview her. *Not until she's in a fit state to understand.*

Not a chance is she going to be in a fit state until she's had time to think. She forces the coughs on, as hard as she can. It's like coughing up wire wool.

Mr Baron is threatening to call the ambulance himself, now. The copper looks as though he's being robbed; she's to be whisked away like a rolled-up pair of stockings tucked under a skirt.

Ruby begins to laugh, but it becomes a cough that doubles her over, flopping her back and then forward like a dying fish. Her pulse thuds behind her eyes as though her heart has risen into her face, and her lungs and chest strain with its absence.

She coughs up dark filth, condensed fog. And now blood spatters her cupped hands, drips onto her lap, crimson marbled with black.

Florrie is standing just outside the caff, Ted's keys in one hand. The fog is thicker than ever, dusk has fallen now, and she can't bring herself to take the few steps along the road to his flat. The windows of the caff are the only light she can see. There must be other lights, from other windows, but you'd never know it; she might be at the edge of a black ocean, the darkness like something she could drown in. She keeps thinking, *Come on, legs, move,* but they don't do more than shudder at the knees.

The door of the caff bangs open behind her.

'Oh, Christ,' Ted says. 'Blimey, Florrie. You gave me a fright. Why didn't you tell me you were going off?' A bit of rage is shivering around the edges of his relief. He's got two dark smudges down his cheeks on either side of his mouth, as though he's raked his own face with filthy hands.

She doesn't reply, but lets him lead her back to the flat, through the stifling dark. When they reach the door he pats his pockets for his keys and she hands them to him without a word. He looks at her a bit sadly, she thinks, as he takes them from her.

Upstairs he turns on the three-bar fire and sits in one of the armchairs. She stands, a little uselessly, and doesn't know what to say. For the hundredth time, she thinks of telling him what Maggie said. But everything's mixed up now, and he's been so queer, leaving her alone for those spivs, when he knows she's sick to her heart over Ruby. She watches him, and twists the rings on her fingers.

He slumps over, his elbows on his knees and his chin in his hands.

'Alright,' he says. 'I suppose I'll have to tell you. Harry came here. The other day. He's coming in with me on the blocks.'

She puts her hand to her mouth.

Ted rubs his face, his fingers finding the smudges that are already there and blending them into the skin. 'Then they were all in the caff, wanting to talk about it. They're hard to get rid of. And I was trying to keep you out of it.'

Florrie takes the two steps to the other chair and sits down with a flump. A puff of dust comes up from the cushion. She feels a little breathless. She can't believe it. And she can't believe she ever thought it would go otherwise.

'What?' He's looking at her now.

'They know. They know we've been messing about.' There's no other reason on earth for them to bring Ted in. She should have guessed it the minute her mum made him

178

drive. It's so like Ruby to just do a thing, without wasting breath over it.

He says, 'Messing about. That's a nice way to put it.'

'I'm sorry. I didn't mean that. Oh, God.' She pulls her knees up and wraps her arms around them.

'But why—'

She holds up a hand. 'Hang on a sec. Let me think.'

He's clutching the arms of the chair. He looks like a little boy, with his dirty face and his eyes fixed on her.

'You know,' she says, slowly, 'I bet they think they're doing me a favour. Giving us their blessing. Bringing you in.' She starts to laugh, although it isn't funny, not in the slightest.

'I'll just have to tell them I'd rather not,' he says, his voice unsure.

She stops laughing as suddenly as she'd begun. 'You don't get it.'

'Tell me, then.'

But it's hard, when he's looking at her with that crease between his eyebrows, like he's thinking over whether he wants to marry her after all. And she's never told him more than she has to, not about any of it.

'Well. You know, the Godden Boys – Harry's boys. They're . . . like the other half. The boys' half. All the girls are married to Godden Boys, or blokes who work with them in one way or another.'

He shakes his head impatiently. 'That's not what you want, is it?'

'Course not. Haven't I been trying to be good?' She stares into the glow of the electric fire and makes herself say the rest. 'It's just . . . my mum's . . . my mum's right in it. You know. They expect me to take after her.'

She hears him shift in his chair. 'You're nothing like her. You're ten times better than any of them.'

'Don't say that about my mum.'

'Alright. I'm sorry. You know what I mean.'

She rests her chin on the top of her knees, her eyes on the vicious orange of the bar fire. 'But you don't know what I mean. You just don't get it,' she says, again.

'Well, I can't say you're making it easy.'

She risks a look at him. He's jutting his chin, making shadows in the hollows of his dirty cheeks, sharpening the angle of his jaw.

And rising up inside her is the thought that's been twisting a corkscrew in her guts for the last three months, ever since the moment he first kissed her in Nell's hall. *You don't know me, and if you did, you wouldn't love me. I don't know if I have it in me to be decent.*

She says, 'You want to worry about yourself, Ted. You want to get away from Harry as quick as you can.' *And if I was half as good as you deserve, I'd tell you to stay well away from me, and all.*

He makes an impatient noise. 'He says I'll make twice what I've been doing by myself. He's got a lorry. And a load of blokes to help.'

She meets his eye.

'Oh, Ted,' she says, as kindly as she can. 'You prat. As if he'll stop at that.'

Ted's never seen Florrie look quite like this. She's curled in the chair, her eyes very dark. He had to screw up every last nerve to tell her about Harry, and now she's called him a prat.

A ringing sound makes him jump, and it takes him a

moment to realise that it's the doorbell.

He says, 'Wait here. Please,' and goes down the stairs fast, expecting it to be a mistake – who, after all, has any idea where he is? – but it's Don, in a camel-coloured coat, his collar up and hat low.

Ted feels a great weariness just looking at him. 'What's this?'

'Harry told me to fetch you.'

'And if I don't want to be fetched?'

Don shrugs. 'You really don't want to say no to Harry. You're coming out with me.'

'To do what?'

'Just a couple of errands. Look, it ain't my choice. I don't want you along, but Harry says you're coming, so you're coming. Don't mess about. Get your coat on.' When Ted doesn't reply he says, 'Nothing to be afraid of.'

'I'm not afraid.'

'Could have fooled me. Hurry up, can't you? I'm freezing half to death.'

'You'd better wait in the hall, then,' Ted says. 'Hang on here. I'm not saying yes.'

'You're dafter than you look if you think you can say no.'

He leaves Don standing in the hall, blowing on his fingers and stamping his feet. Ted starts up the stairs slowly, because he doesn't see why he should hurry, but then he wonders if it's making him look like a coward, and marches up.

Florrie is still sitting curled in the chair. 'Harry?'

He shakes his head. 'Don.'

She nods, unsurprised. 'Same thing, near enough. You'll have to go.'

That's what he came up to ask her, of course: *Do I*

really have to go? But now that she's said it, it seems unreal. Outrageous. 'But, well, look here. Surely I don't really have to. Who does Harry think he is? Ordering me about?'

'You know who he is.' She looks down at her stockinged feet on the edge of the chair.

He looks at them too, at the paint on her toenails showing through the silk mesh, the toes curling to grip the edge of the cushion. Her whole body looks sad. He feels a wave of tenderness so powerful that he wants to drop to his knees beside her.

He doesn't. He's not that sort of bloke. But he says, 'Look here, you're sure they know about us?'

She sighs. 'Sure.'

He takes a step nearer. 'Then I want you to put that ring on. If . . . if you still want to.'

She gets slowly to her feet, steps forward and throws herself into his arms so hard that her body thumps into his chest and he gasps for breath. Her hands grip at the shoulders of his jacket.

'Oh, blooming hell,' she says, into his neck. 'I thought you was about to give me the push.'

His arms close around her back. 'Not a chance.'

'Go out with Don. Just come back safe, and quick as you can.'

'I don't want to leave you here alone.'

She gives an unhappy laugh he doesn't like at all and grips him tighter. 'What we want don't come into it, Teddy. I bloody well wish it did.'

'I'm going to sort this whole thing out. You'll see,' he says, and kisses her. 'I said I'll look after you, and I meant it.'

*

Nell is lying on the bench, although it hurts her hip. It's taken her a long time to decide that she might as well lie down. It seems improper. But she is so dizzy, her thoughts pulling her head downwards, and it's that or tip onto the floor.

She's managed to shut her mouth and keep it shut. She'd been a little indignant that Ruby had thought she needed to be told, until they brought her into that little room and talked and talked until she felt all turned around. Some of the questions had had no right answer. Was it her bag? No? So she took it, knowing it didn't belong to her? After a while she'd just stared at the sergeant's moustache moving and thought, *Oh my goodness, I'm going to prison. I'm really going to prison.* They'd accused her of doing Ruby's dirty work. They'd said she was from a family of criminals. And they wanted her to tell them about the gang, the pawn shop and all sorts. It was astonishing and terrifying how much they seemed to know. Far more than Nell does herself.

But she's sure she said nothing that could harm anyone, except perhaps herself. By the end she'd been unable to say anything much, apart from, *No, no,* over and over, like a madwoman. And then they threw her back in here. To think, they said.

And she is thinking. She's remembering the day Ruby and Dolly first turned up, their arms full of bundles and baskets. It was early summer in 1941. Almost the last of the Blitz, although no one had any idea of that then, and the end had become unimaginable. Nell and Teddy just went on, dazed with tiredness. This was after the O'Briens' house was bombed flat, and Nell didn't like to use the shelter among all that rubble. Not then. She didn't even think of looking for it until the bombs stopped falling.

So they'd spent every night on the crowded platform of the Tube, Teddy sleeping and Nell thinking about Edward and about her life, what she had had of it, how little might be left. It sometimes seemed that the fear was all that kept her moving, the fizz of it in her limbs.

And one morning, unsteady with exhaustion, she'd opened the front door to see Ruby and Dolly on the doorstep. She hadn't seen any of the Palmers, or thought of them, for almost ten years. But how did anyone say no to family, in the Blitz?

And if she'd thought, sometimes, of her mother saying, *Watch out, or you'll end up as cheap and nasty as your cousins*, it was easy enough to push aside, in the face of black-market eggs and meat. Dolly had been so good with Teddy, too. Ted could identify which type of bomber was overhead just by the sound, and Dolly had spent hours listening to him go on and on about planes, doing impressions of the engine noise. She'd brought home bits for his collection of shrapnel, as if she were as interested as the boy was in broken pieces of bombshells and other grisly debris. He'd come out of himself, having Dolly take an interest. Nell had never bothered to ask him more than, 'What do you want that rubbish for?' She would have rathered he had a collection of stamps or buttons. She would have rathered he never knew about bombs at all, but that was a pointless wish.

And it was only the two extra women. Maggie was off in Devon, probably causing no end of trouble down there, and Florrie was evacuated to Somerset. It had been alright, really, that first time. But after that the Palmers would turn up, again and again, whenever they hadn't anywhere better to go.

And now here's Nell, lying in a cell, just as her mother would have predicted.

When the door opens it is an effort to sit up.

It's the sergeant with the awful moustache. He looks at her as though he's perfectly used to seeing bedraggled ladies lying down on benches. Perhaps he is.

'Mrs Gibson. We're charging you with larceny shop-lifting, and releasing you on your own recognisance. You'll need to attend a court hearing.'

She can't answer.

'Don't you hear me? Come along, Mrs Gibson.'

'What about my . . . What about Miss Palmer?'

'Miss Palmer will be staying with us a little longer.'

No. She thinks she might be about to start saying *No, no,* again. She swallows. 'May I see her?'

'Hardly,' he says.

'Please. Just for a moment.'

'Mrs Gibson, either you come now without making me any trouble or we reconsider sending you home.' He stands back and holds the door open.

She gets up. She is so stiff. Her bones have iced over.

'But what will happen to her?' she says, holding her damp coat closed at the throat, like a shawl.

'I should think you know that very well, already. Now run along, before I change my mind.'

But they don't let her run along. They make her sign all sorts of papers and talk at her until her head spins. At last they give her back her handbag and the shopping, the mince and currant buns.

The foyer is crowded with people, and they all look unhappy in one way or another. A pair of policemen are bringing in a young man with no shirt, his bare chest scratched and bloody, his shoulders hunched.

Someone stands from the bench by the wall, adjusting

the cuffs of her coat, and Nell realises it's Dolly's friend, Ada. Harry's ex-wife. That makes Nell want to cringe and hide all over again.

Ada's dressed very smartly, and holds herself very straight. Her eyes are red-rimmed, her nose tipped pink under its powder.

'Here you are, then. Alright?' Ada says, as if it's ordinary to meet in a police station.

Nell is too surprised to speak until they are through the heavy doors and into the street. Then she asks, 'Did you really come to fetch me?'

'Maggie said you'd be out. Now is it this way? This muck makes me feel all turned around. Come on.' Ada begins to march surprisingly quickly, for a lady her age. 'It's too cold to talk.' But she does talk anyway, on and on. Weren't the coppers busy? Like a train station in there. So many comings and goings, and it must be the weather, and she'd heard the crime rates went right up in fog, but when you see how many people they nick, don't it make you think it must balance out?

Ada seems to have the most amazing sense of direction. She barely hesitates. Nell is afraid all the time that they'll bump into something. But she's aching to get home; her stomach tells her it's long past tea time.

By the time they find the house she's so tired and cold that the shopping bag drags on her arm, although there's no real weight to it.

Ada gives her a little push to send her up the garden path, and follows along behind. Nell's hands are shaking so hard that the keys have to be jangled into the lock.

She puts the shopping down and takes off her coat and shoes. She pushes her feet into her fluffy pink slippers and closes her eyes with relief at the little bit of comfort. She very much wants to go to bed, but instead she will have to give Ada tea. And perhaps now she will be allowed to ask about Ruby.

Ada has taken off her coat and is pulling off her gloves.

'Well,' Nell says, 'Shall I get the kettle—'

There's the sound of the door to the front room opening. Turning, she sees Maggie strolling into the hall, as if it's her own house. Maggie knows Nell doesn't like people to use the front room. Behind her is a blonde girl with a scab along her cheekbone, the poor creature who took a wallop from Maggie yesterday.

Maggie puts both hands out to Nell's shoulders. Nell watches her hands come out towards her, doesn't do a thing to avoid it and then Maggie shoves and Nell's legs come out from underneath her. Her tailbone strikes the tiled floor so hard that she feels it jolt up into the base of her neck.

The girl – Cissy, her name's Cissy, she sat right in Nell's kitchen and drank with them all just the night before – laughs quietly.

Ada says, 'Oh, love a duck,' from somewhere by the front door.

A haze of fog waves in the electric light as though it's rising from Maggie herself.

'Grass.' Maggie bends down towards her, half smiling.

For a moment Nell forgets the double meaning of the word and thinks of grass, the unrealistically green grass of a children's picture book. Then her mind comes back to her. 'No!'

'Oh, yes,' Maggie says. 'And you know what we do with grasses.'

*

187

Don's leaning so far over the steering wheel that his fore-head almost touches the windscreen.

Ted stares forward. The headlamps seem to do nothing but light the fog, which moves in lazy curls, like dirty cream stiffening. The air tastes like pennies, even inside the car.

There's a terrible grinding along the side of the car and Ted hears himself gasp.

'Just the kerb.' Don turns the wheel.

But the next moment both of them jerk in their seats.

'What was that?' Ted says.

'Fuck. Fuck. Hit something.' Don is already out of the car.

Ted follows him. The something is a long, low wall, stretching off into darkness.

Don is running his hands over the side of the car, the bumper, the headlight. Ted can see that the nose has taken a dent, its left-hand corner blunted off. As much as he dislikes Don, he does feel a pang of empathy, and vows not to drive his own, precious Hillman again until the fog clears.

Don stands, rubbing at his face, and says, 'I think she's alright,' relief shaking his voice. 'But this is fucking horrible. I don't know how we ended up down here; I missed the turn, somewhere. We might've gone right over the edge.'

'The edge?'

'Into the river, bonehead.'

And it's only now that Ted realises the deep and terrible blackness to his left is the Thames. Although surely they couldn't have gone in, they'd have had to have knocked down the wall. Even so he can imagine it, the drop into dark and freezing water.

'We shouldn't be here,' Don says, again. 'I'm fucked if I know how that happened.'

'Then we're on the Albert Embankment,' Ted says, slowly.

'I know that, you berk.' Don thumps his palms on the car's roof in frustration. 'Fucking Harry. He's off his rocker, making us come out in this.'

'We could leave the car,' Ted says, wondering how he'll find the flat again if they do.

Don's shaking his head. 'Too many places to go. Got to risk it. I'll be alright once we're away from the river. Do me a favour, walk in front of the car?'

'What? No!'

'Don't be soft. Go on. Just till we get to Black Prince Road and we can turn off.'

Ted puts his hand on the side of the car to steady himself. It's powdery and soft with grime. And then he nods and walks around to the nose.

Behind him, Don starts up the engine.

At the sound, he feels the start of true panic; Don could run him down in a heartbeat, flip his legs out from underneath him. The backs of his knees feel queer with waiting for it.

The aching void of the river on his left. To the right, grey shapes keep coming out of the fog, dark patches that suddenly become post boxes and parked cars, looming towards him as though it's they that move, rather than the car.

He keeps walking. He doesn't know how far it is to Black Prince Road, and is only half sure they're going the right way. He knows that he should turn and check Don isn't waving at him which way to go, but he feels certain the car will run into his legs the moment he does.

But now the fog in front of him is spreading out, turning a flatter grey, and after a moment he sees the pillars of

Lambeth Bridge. So they were going the wrong way. But he knows where he is now. Don will know where they are. He waves his left hand behind him, meaning, *Stop. Please stop.* He's still too afraid to turn his head. And then, like an idiot, he stops walking.

Don's bumper hits his calves. It's more surprise than anything that makes Ted cry out. It doesn't hurt. It's only that he's been waiting for the car to hit his legs and all the time telling himself that it won't, and then it does. It nudges him forward, and then, thank God, it does stop. He can feel how heavy and pitiless it is.

When he climbs in, shaking right inside himself, Don's face is as ashen as Ted's feels.

The car starts up and crawls away.

Don says, peering right into the windscreen again, 'You know, you've got more guts than I gave you credit for. I might have squashed you flat.'

Nell pushes herself backwards with her slippered feet, her bruised tailbone jolting over the joins between the tiles. Then she scrambles up. Nobody stops her.

Maggie is on one side, too close, still smiling. Ada is barring the way to the front door, and Cissy is nearest to Nell, blocking the way to the kitchen. Wildly, Nell shoves at Cissy's shoulder, and somehow she's done it, is running to the kitchen, her slippers flipping against the soles of her feet and the women's shoes clacking like hooves behind her.

She means to slam the door but they are there before the latch clicks, pushing hard enough that Nell herself stumbles back. She finds herself clawing at the edge of the table as if it could save her. The red and white oilcloth slides under her hand, the butter dish and salt cellar come rushing towards her and all of it falls to the floor with a slither and a dull crash. Nell manages to keep her feet, but only just.

'What do you want?' Her voice is a kettle's first whistle, high and breathy.

'Grab her,' Maggie says.

'Now, hold on there,' Ada says. 'No need for that.'

Nell darts around the table. Her thigh smacks into the corner but she hardly notices. The table is between her and the women now.

With horrible ease the women move so that there is no way to get past without running straight at one of them. Nell is in the corner, between the stove and the window, is in the corner, like an animal. She sinks to her knees.

They come in closer. Cissy grabs Nell's upper arms.

'Now,' Maggie says, and there is a flash of silver in the corner of Nell's vision.

The pain comes across her face, thin pain, a hot wire.

'Just a taste,' Cissy says.

'You didn't have to stripe her,' Ada says, but Nell can't be sure if she's talking to her or Maggie.

'Please!' Nell hears herself shriek, and now her head whips from side to side. She can feel the blood, the soft warm spill of it down her cheek, her neck, running along her collar. 'I never did!'

'Look at me,' Maggie says, crouching in front of her. 'I knew you was low. I've seen you making eyes at my Harry. I suppose you've been telling them everything you can about him.'

'I didn't,' Nell says. 'I haven't.'

'This is a bit much, even for you. You can start by paying us back for the cost of what was in that bag you handed over,' Maggie says. 'Give us a little something for Ruby, to help her time go by a bit easier.'

Nell can hear the words but she can't see anymore; everything is black dots. Her head is somewhere up there but her mind is falling. She has no breath to speak and nothing sensible to say. *No,* she thinks, *no.*

'Come on now,' Maggie says, from far away. 'Don't faint on me yet.'

'I'll give you money,' Nell says. 'Please.'

'That would be a start,' Maggie says.

'Let me get it,' Nell says, and the hands finally let go of her arms.

The women move back just enough to let her scramble to her feet. Moving is to discover a hundred pains. Her hip and shoulder, her tailbone. She's twisted her ankle somehow, her cheek burns from jaw to eye. She stumbles into the hall, Maggie right at her back. She can feel the malignant closeness of the knife.

She opens the cupboard under the stairs, Maggie looming above her as she crouches. The cupboard is dark and she has to do it all by feel but here, on the floor at the back, is a cardboard box. She lifts off the lid, gropes underneath the folded clothes inside. Dolly's crocodile bag. She pulls it close, shielding it with her body. She opens it, her fingers questing around the change purse and powder compact, the smooth shape of Dolly's little bible. And yes. Thank heaven. The pistol is a snub-nosed thing, small but heavy. All she knows about guns is which end to hold and which to point, but perhaps that's enough. She loops the handles of the bag over one wrist and keeps her other hand inside it, feels her knees creak as she rises and turns.

Maggie is right behind her, looking short and merry and

not at all like someone with fresh blood on her hands.

'Let's have it, then,' she says. 'How much have you got?'

Nell's mouth is dry, shrivelling up. She pulls the pistol free, letting the bag drop back to swing from her elbow. She has to have both hands on the pistol to keep it steady. She points it straight at Maggie's face.

'Well, well.' Maggie's still smirking, but her eyes narrow. 'Set on getting into trouble, ain't you?'

'Stay away from me.'

Cissy is already backing away down the hall, towards the front door.

'Careful,' Ada says. 'Careful, Nell.'

Maggie moves and for one awful moment Nell thinks she might be about to grab at her, but then she just holds up her hands – one of them still holding the knife – in mock surrender. Then Nell is edging past her and backing into the kitchen. She closes the door.

'What do you think you're going to do now, Ellen?' Maggie calls from the hall.

'Now, stop!' Ada sounds furious. There's the murmuring of a whispered quarrel.

Nell keeps checking behind her, but the kitchen door is still closed when she gets to the scullery, and the next second she is in the garden. The sun's gone down heavily, smothered by fog.

She finds the loose bit of the fence and squeezes through, every muscle strung tight as a wire. Her footsteps across the rubble have never seemed so loud.

As she reaches the bottom of the steps to the shelter, she hears them in her garden, Cissy's voice: 'Cooee, Nellie! You don't want to hide out here in the cold, dearie!'

She stops. Footsteps clack around the garden. No doubt

they are trampling what's left of her vegetable patch.

At last Maggie calls, 'Well? Ain't you got her?'

Cissy calls back, 'Nothing. She's hopped it over the wall.'

'I should just think she has.' Ada sounds glad.

Cissy says something else and there's a bit of mean laughter, and then she hears the snap of her own back door closing. She waits for what seems an age, but there's nothing else and at last she opens the shelter door with clumsy, numb fingers.

Her legs are trembling like a whippet's. She sinks down onto the narrow bunk in the dark and puts her head in her hands. The right one touches something wet and painful, and of course, oh goodness, her face is bleeding.

And it's so cold. She pulls the blankets from the top bunk and gets into the lower one, all the blankets on top of her. She has to keep one arm out, so that she can have the pistol ready.

Imagine if she had stayed at home today, waved them all off without a word and spent the day baking the bloody jam tarts.

On the damp mattress she stays very still and listens. Her breath is very loud in her ears. Even when her muscles begin to feel like they are setting for ever, stiff and painful, she doesn't move more than the slightest rise and fall of her ribcage.

Ted follows Don into the snooker hall. The place is dim, most of the light coming from the lamps that hang low over the tables, the green of the baize bright and the rest of the room in shadow. There's no music, just the sound of low voices and the solid clicks of the balls hitting each other. The players are dark figures with brightly lit hands.

As Don and Ted pass, heads turn, nod, murmur, 'Evening, boys.'

It's the queerest feeling. Ted's worried about Florrie and it does seem ominous, Harry making him follow Don about. But. Even so. Every place they've walked into – two snooker halls, a pub and a cafe – has been like this. Blokes who might give Ted a barge of the shoulder on the street are nodding respectfully at him, offering him drinks. Don is introducing him by name – 'This is Ted,' with a clap on the shoulder or the back – but half the time he doesn't bother to introduce the other fellow in return. It's like Ted is the important one. He can feel himself stand up taller with every repetition of his name.

They go straight to the bar, where they're each given a beer. There's no mention of paying for it. Instead, the barman takes an envelope of what must be money from the pocket of his apron and gives it to Don, who tucks it inside his jacket, exactly as he has in every other place.

Don's talking to the barman. Ted watches the nearest snooker game and tries to make it clear, by the angle of his body, that he's not trying to eavesdrop.

'Hello, there.' A woman has appeared next to him at the bar. She has a neat cap of rather boyish dark hair and she's almost as tall as Ted.

'Hello,' he says.

'Hazel. I was at yours yesterday.'

Her hand is cold but she's got a firm grip.

She leans her back against the bar, plays with the stick in her drink. 'My grandad got you running about all over the place, has he? Where are you off to next?'

Her being Harry's granddaughter ties his tongue. And she's a bit like a schoolteacher, kind but authoritative. He just shrugs and tries not to look embarrassed at his own ignorance.

She gives him a sideways look. 'You'll be alright. Granddad needs blokes who've got reason to be loyal.' She winks.

So Florrie was right. They do know. He feels his cheeks warm.

She pats his arm and goes off, winding around the snooker tables.

'Was that Hazel?'

Ted turns to see Don, buttoning up his coat.

'She's alright, Hazel. Always liked her,' Don says. 'Ready?' And he starts across the club towards the door without waiting for Ted to reply.

Ted does up his own coat as he follows, feeling a bit silly for trailing after Don like a girl. Don is already stepping outside, not looking back or holding the door.

Ted readies himself for the cold and takes a last breath of the warm, smoky air of the club. As he steps outside, he almost collides with a little man trying to come in.

'Watch it,' the bloke says. And then, 'Hey!' as Don's big hand lands on his shoulder.

'Look who it is,' Don says. 'I've been looking for you, Bernie.'

He takes the bloke by the upper arm and pulls him a couple of steps to the side, out of the way of the door.

'Oh, hello there, Donnie,' Bernie says. He's tiny, a shrunken gnome of a man, on his way to old age. He gives Ted a nervous smile. 'Sorry about that. Didn't mean to bump you.'

'That's alright,' Ted says. 'Weather like this,' but the man looks even more nervous, if anything. Don's still got Bernie by the arm, his free hand clenched in a fist.

'Listen, Donnie,' he's saying, 'tomorrow. Honest. I nearly got shut down, was what it was. Got a tip-off they were going to raid my place, had to do a bunk. But I'll come to the spieler with it. Just give us a couple of days.' He wipes his nose with the back of his free hand.

'Hang on now,' Ted says, but neither of them is listening.

Any second Don's going to smack this little fellow, who's half his size and thirty years his elder, and Ted's going to have to decide whether he dares do anything about it.

And then something much worse happens: Don reaches into his pocket and pulls out a bit of lead piping. And he hands it to Ted.

Don says, almost apologetically, 'Harry told me. He said, make sure that boy gets his hands dirty.'

'No,' Ted says, but he stands there holding the pipe. It's smooth and very heavy in his hand.

Don has both the little bloke's arms twisted behind him. Ted would have expected the fellow to struggle, but he seems to sag in Don's grip.

'Don't be a fucking nancy,' Don says. 'Wallop him. Do his knee.'

Now the bloke's craning to see Don over his own shoulder. 'Donnie, come on. Be fair. I'll bring his money. Listen, listen, here's a thing. What if I heard a little something about this grass of yours?' He sounds like he might be about to cry. It's awful. Undignified. Pitiful.

Don gives him a shake. 'And you didn't come straight to Harry with it? If that's true, you're going to bleeding well wish you did.'

'Well now, well now, it ain't much though, see? I just heard it was a girl. Some bird got a grudge.'

'Don't give me that,' Don says. 'No name? Come on.'

'I got it off a bent copper. He didn't say a name. He's a flatfoot, might not know himself. Come on, Donnie, don't that help?' A drop of moisture has appeared at the end of Bernie's nose.

Ted says, 'For God's sake,' to Don, to the street in general.

'You're full of it,' Don says to Bernie. 'I never heard a true word come out of your mouth. Hurry up, Ted. Fucking hell.'

There's no way, not a chance, that Ted's going to hit this little old man, but he doesn't know what he should do instead. He looks about wildly, as if help might come.

And there's someone watching. A misty figure, leaning against the wall to his left. And now he's afraid all over again. It could be the police. Harry. Anyone.

It detaches itself and becomes Hazel. She walks up and looks them over, completely unruffled, her hands in her coat pockets.

'Ted ain't up to it, Donnie. Look at him. He's ready to piss himself.' She gives him another wink.

Ted doesn't know what to say. It's true, he's not up to it and he doesn't want to be. But it sounds insulting, all the same.

'He has to be up to it,' Don says. 'He don't have a choice.'

'Don't be daft. Course he does,' Hazel says. 'Honest, Donnie, Ted ain't the type.' She holds out her hand and Ted puts the bit of pipe into it.

Bernie looks at her now, as though she might be about to hit him with it. 'Just give us a couple of days. Alright?'

She's already putting the pipe into her pocket.

'Don't you talk to Hazel,' Don says, and finally lets go of

the man's arms. 'Go on. Fuck off out of here quick, before I change my mind.'

'You're a pal,' Bernie says.

'No, I ain't. But I won't break your legs in front of a lady,' Don says. 'Give over that hat. Ted here could do with a new tile.'

The old man takes it off his head and gives it to Don with a twitching smile that reminds Ted horribly of the one he'd felt on his own face, when Harry was watching him wash.

Then Bernie goes off, not into the snooker club after all, but down the road, into the fog. They hear his feet patter out of sight, almost a run.

'What the fuck did you do that for?' Don asks Hazel.

She shrugs. 'It weren't a nice picture.'

'And what am I supposed to tell Harry?' Don's chest is heaving, his cheeks mottled with anger or cold.

'Don't tell him a thing. Ted ain't about to blab, are you, Ted?'

'God, no,' Ted says.

'There you are, then,' Hazel says. 'What my granddad don't know won't hurt him.'

Don is starting to deflate, rocking back on his heels, flexing his hands. 'And I suppose you heard what he said about the grass?'

'I heard him. I don't expect there's much in it. But I'll ask the girls. Alright? Forget it, Don. Poor old Ted's had enough. Look at his face.'

Ted wonders what his face looks like. But now Hazel's going back inside, calling out that they should come in the club later, and he hasn't even thanked her.

Back in the car, Don tosses the hat onto Ted's lap. It's a

good one of heavy felt with a ribbon band.

'Too small,' Ted says. There's no way he wants that poor bloke's hat.

'Chuck it on the back seat, then,' Don says. 'But you want to smarten up. You can't go round looking like that.'

'Oh, shut up,' Ted says.

He feels a bit sick at the way he was letting himself swank about, being introduced to people. They must all have been looking at him and thinking he was a big, stupid bully, like Don.

Don looks away and rubs at his brow. 'Have you got a cig?'

Ted lights one for each of them, hands Don his without looking at him. Don smokes in silence and then says, 'I'm going to the Palm. Hazel's place.' He looks over at Ted and hesitates. 'You sure you don't want to come?'

'Take me back home, can't you?'

'Got your own flat,' Don says, starting the engine. 'How did you manage that?'

Ted says, 'Where do you live, then?' He doesn't feel like telling Don anything he doesn't already know.

'With my old man,' Don says. 'John Ruskin Street. Ain't like my own place, but it ain't bad.'

Ted finds he doesn't want to imagine where Don lives, or hear about his dad. He'd rather not think of him as a real person at all.

'Look here,' Don says, peering out at the fog. 'Don't you breathe a word to Harry.'

Ted doesn't reply.

'Because you should've given that weasel a wallop. I should've made you do it.'

'You're a real gent,' Ted says. 'Just to steal his hat.'

'You know,' Don says, 'you want to come down off your high horse a bit. You'll learn.'

Ted turns and looks out of the window and stares out at the fog curtaining London. He thinks again about the swollen, buoyed-up feeling he had, walking about like a big man. Even now, while he's hating Don, while he's wondering how to tell Harry to shove it, he can still feel a leftover scrap of the thrill. He thinks of Florrie's sad little laugh, and wonders if this is how she feels all the time. This queer mixture of excitement and shame, of power and powerlessness. He wonders how she can stand it.

The Fourth Day of the Fog:
Sunday, 7 December 1952

On Sunday the fog seems a settled, permanent thing. The roads are littered with abandoned cars. The milkmen have stopped doing their rounds, and grocers are beginning to run short of goods as deliveries are cancelled. The police, the ambulance drivers, the doctors and nurses, all are working double shifts. The hospitals are full and the morgues are filling. The fog is so thick that the meteorological instruments meant to measure smoke levels in the air have stopped registering. No one at the Meteorological Office, nor the Ministry of Health, reports the full extent of what they know, or suspect they know, to the newspapers – even if it could be measured, there's no sense creating a panic.

Ruby's slept poorly. The ward has been full of sounds all night, the hospital groaning at the seams, and everyone in it coughing in a harsh chorus. They've had to put both men and women in the ward here, because there aren't enough beds to do otherwise. That's how many people the fog has done over. And they're having to wait for a private room to come free, so that Ruby can be locked into it; in the meantime they've put a policewoman at the door to the ward. When Ruby raises her head she can see the bitch pacing back and forth, her shadow falling over the glass in the door.

The coughs are like being bombed inside. They shake her frame, her bones rattle like windows. And all through this shifting, awful night, the idea of her one wasted day out has nagged at her worse than if she'd never been out at all. If she hadn't been so busy making grand plans, she might have been able to find out who the grass is. She should have put that first, instead of worrying that people would think she'd gone soft.

She keeps thinking that if she were well, if her mind would work properly, she could untangle this whole mess. The face of the grass is hovering somewhere at the back of her mind, obscured.

She's got Harry to agree to help with Ted. That's one thing. She had so many letters from the girls while she was in prison, letting her know that Florrie seemed to have her eye on the boy. Thank God they were watching out. If anyone can teach Ted how to stand up and be a real man for Florrie, Harry can.

But if only she'd found the grass, or found the pot. Done something more to help Florrie and Maggie, to keep them safe. She squeezes her eyes shut tight and tries to squeeze her heart shut with them.

When they were little and sharing a bed, Maggie wouldn't sleep without wrapping Ruby's hair around her fist. She was afraid that Ruby would disappear in the night, like Dolly so often did. But Ruby would never have done that, wouldn't leave her now, if she had any choice.

And then Florrie. When she was born, and the midwife put her, newly wiped clean of Ruby's blood, onto her chest, she'd smelled of meat, but in the best way, like something you'd want to eat. Ruby's own flesh, made new.

It was a difficult birth and she'd been in bed a full week, with Florrie sleeping beside her in a drawer from the dresser. Ruby was so weak that Dolly had had to do most of the work, washing and changing the baby, walking her about with Florrie's tiny soft head on her shoulder.

Dolly was better about it than Ruby would ever have expected, and even Maggie brought her magazines and little things for the baby. Still, Ruby didn't want anyone else to look after her girl. She missed Florrie every second that she wasn't with her. Even when Florrie's tiny mouth was joined to Ruby's breast, she'd missed her. Florrie was a part of her that had been ripped out; Ruby wanted to wrap her body around her again, cradle her as she'd been doing, inside her, where she was safe. She'd only her own arms to hold Florrie in, and it wasn't enough. Florrie was her heart, grown arms and legs.

'I'm your mum,' she'd kept whispering. 'I'm Ruby, I'm your mum.'

She'd never felt hope like it, so desperate that it spilled over into hopelessness. *Oh, God. Let her be happy. Let me be able to keep her safe.* But no life would be good enough for such a perfect baby girl. Not in the world they lived in. So she'd done what she had to do for Florrie, just as she had for Maggie: she'd taught the both of them to use their fists and their wits, and to take what they could from a world that never wants to give. And that might be it, now, the last of what she has to offer them. But they're good girls, the both of them, and won't let themselves be walked on, whether they stay out or end up in the nick along with Ruby.

She should get up, try to get herself past the policewoman and out of here, but she can't keep her eyes open. Her treacherous body wants to lie still, doesn't care that it will be going back to prison. And there's no point in fighting it now.

Ted, slumped in the armchair, opens his eyes at seven thirty, although he's been just under the surface of a cramped, shivering wakefulness all night.

Florrie was asleep when he got back to the flat, and though he very badly wanted to crawl into bed beside her, he wasn't sure he should. They've never slept in the same bed before. If she'd only been awake he could have asked her permission, but instead he took the chair. Now his whole body is uncomfortable and he shakes himself like a dog.

He doesn't like to think of what state his mum must have been in last night, alone in the house. He should have thought to leave a note.

He writes one for Florrie, on the back of his receipt for the yard's rent. He's never written her a note before, and it's harder than it should be. At last he writes, *Nipped home. Will bring breakfast back. Don't worry about anything. T,* and hopes that will be good enough.

Stepping outside is like a release and it's good to move, even if it is beginning to feel as though the fog will never lift. He pulls his head into his shoulders like a tortoise, and walks without thinking.

At home, the light is on in the hall and he feels a twist of guilt go through him. A light for himself and Florrie to come in by. He takes off his shoes and goes up the stairs as quietly as he can.

He's so sure of finding Nell asleep that when her bed shows itself flat and empty, he stands blinking his sore eyes as though any moment it might resolve itself into the shape of Nell beneath the covers.

'Mum?'

Of course there's no reply. He goes back down the stairs.

'Mum?' His voice has that hollow, lonely quality. Where can she have gone, at this hour and in this weather?

In the kitchen the chairs are standing crookedly. The oilcloth has come off the table, the ashtray fallen, spreading a starburst of ash.

And blood. It can't be anything else. Soft circles the size of pennies, a dot-to-dot zigzagging right into the scullery. The back door has a glass panel in it with a white lace curtain. On its frilled edge is a smear of red.

Ted backs away from it, shaking his head without meaning to.

'Mum!' The panic in his voice scares him almost as badly as the blood.

He clenches his fists. He has to be calm. Her name is just waiting in his mouth but he can't let himself call again. He goes back out to the hall. The cupboard under the stairs is ajar, there are more blood drops here, and he can't think why he hadn't noticed them before. His throat turns to bitter heat and he's sick in his own mouth, but he swallows it back down.

He opens the cupboard quickly, half expecting her body to tumble out, but nothing happens. He picks up the torch from the shelf inside and shines it over the coats and shoes, the boxes of miscellaneous things. There's nothing there.

He moves his palms through the air in front of him, as though he's pushing down an invisible object. Someone was bleeding in the house, but that doesn't mean his mum is hurt. Much more likely one of the girls. And Nell, who might so easily have been upset, has gone off somewhere to get away from the fuss.

He goes back through the kitchen, turning his head from the drops, and takes the handle of the back door carefully, trying not to touch the blood. Whoever was bleeding went out this way.

He shines the torch around the back garden, the fog undulating in the beam. The washing line comes looming out at him, but no Nell, nor anybody else.

Then, for good measure, he squeezes through the hidden gap in the fence. His shoulder scrapes the corrugated iron, cold droplets soaking his face and hands, running down the back of his collar.

He edges carefully forward, shining the torch over the rubble. Every step crunches and seems to send other sounds out from the sides of it, skittering gravel, rustlings. He can't tell if all the sounds are his own.

He knows the bombsite well, played a hundred grubby games in here as a kid. Over there was the old shelter, now buried deep under blackberry bushes. And just beyond this rise, this piece of jagged wall, is the thin place, the place that isn't safe to tread.

He edges as close to it as he dares, runs the torch over it, but nothing has broken, no hole has opened up.

He can feel his skin prickling all over, feeling like the torch makes him a target, the way it would have in blackout. The fog seems to be coming from underneath the rubble, like the ghost of the bombsmoke.

'Hello?' The silence is even more silent, after that. Just his own breathing, the clouds of his breath catching in the torchlight, his own kind of fog.

There's someone outside. Nell wakes knowing it, rigid as a doll, her whole being in her straining ears.

She draws the pistol from under her pillow. And then, for what seems a long time, she stays perfectly still in the dark. She has visions of someone standing just outside the door, as motionless as she is, like one of those staring contests in which you try not to blink first.

Back inside, Ted can't help retracing the steps he's already taken. In the hall her string bag, the one she takes shopping, is slumped by the front door, brown paper packages peering through the webbing. That hadn't been there before, had it? Hope flares in his chest and he calls out Nell's name again, eagerly, like a boy coming come from school. The shout disappears into the dark of the house.

He bends and opens the bag. The package on the bottom is soggy, sitting in a little pool of pinkish water. It's clearly been there for ages. And of course, it would have been behind the front door when he opened it to come in.

On top is a bag of currant buns, stale and hard to the touch. He eats one anyway, feeling it stick in his throat, feeling his stomach wake up, unsure for a moment whether he's starving or queasy.

It's impossible to think in this house. He has to get out, and then he has to think.

Nell has made herself get up and stop being silly. She examines herself in the little bit of mirror: the wound is a black streak across her face. She moves her jaw up and down and the cut cracks in reply, fresh blood leaping to the surface in fat globs. She has nothing clean to dab at it with. At last she uses the sheet, sitting on the edge of the bed, pressing it firmly against the wound. The pressure lessens the pain, although there is something awful about the slow turning of her own blood into jelly. She almost certainly needs stitches.

There are sticking plasters in the tin, only the little ones left. She sticks them over the cut like big fat stitches side by side, feeling them pull at the skin when she blinks. Perhaps she will have a scar across her face like one of the drawings of pirates Teddy used to do.

Poor Teddy, who must have come home to find her gone. She wonders if Maggie had been there to meet him, and what she might have told him.

The temptation to stay in the shelter is almost overwhelming, but she can't do that. And she needn't brave her own house, where Maggie might still be waiting. Her watch says it's almost nine in the morning: she'll try to find Ted at the yard where he cleans his wooden blocks.

She's only been to the yard once before, but she does know the street it's on. The chemist there sometimes sold her tiny bottles of olive oil, when you could still get it, for Teddy's earaches. It's quite a walk, though, daunting in this weather. And she hasn't a coat or shoes. She'll be going for ages along wet streets in her fluffy slippers.

There's the tin of condensed milk tucked away on one of the little shelves, the creamy white of the paper wrapper, the jolly red of the writing. It's only here because she's been saving it for a treat, is pure selfishness to drink it all herself. But even as she thinks this, she takes up the tin opener and, stabbing at it, trying not to think of how easily Maggie had punctured the tin of tomatoes, manages to make two holes at its rim. She pours the liquid straight into her mouth.

She pulls the handbag onto her lap and looks through it. The first thing she sees is Dolly's little bible, puts her finger to its spine, touches the gold lettering. Then there's an old tin of throat pastilles, which might help against the fog, keys to Nell's own house tied with a piece of ribbon, and Dolly's purse. Eight shillings and sixpence. She tucks it all back, and goes out into the smothering cold.

She finds her way over the rubble and out through the other hole in the fence, the one that leads onto the street. She looks up at her house. There's not a light showing anywhere on it. She thinks for a moment of going in to fetch a coat and shoes, but she just can't risk it. The very thought makes her heart lurch.

But even on her own, familiar street everything looks wrong. This is a terrible fog, an impossible-seeming fog. The walls and lampposts loom up and disappear as she passes, the road seems longer than it should. She's never going to be able to find Ted's yard, and if she turns too many corners she might not be able to find her way home, either. Already her toes are beginning to freeze inside her slippers.

When she reaches the end of her road she sees a faint light and realises it must be the pawn shop. Harry might well be in there. And however bad things are between them, she knows he does care for her; it's because he cares that he's been so awful. He has a car, a fleet of cars. He could take her to Ted. He could talk to Maggie for her.

The door has glass set into it, grime gathering on it in flakes like soft iron filings. Through it she can make out the shapes of men, the faint red points of cigarettes.

She stops, one hand on the door. But if Maggie herself is in there—

She sees one of the men lift his head, and his hand waves to another to open the door for her. Through the grimy glass he seems to float towards her and then he is looking down on her and saying, 'It's Sunday. We're shut,' and then, 'Bloody hell, love, what happened to you?'

Sunday, of course, how stupid of her. Teddy won't be at his yard at all. He could be anywhere.

'I've made a mistake,' Nell says, but he just reaches out and takes her by the elbow.

'In you come.'

Coming into the light makes her feel dazed. The young spiv lets go of her.

Behind him, Harry stands up. His suit is as clean as if he'd just stepped out of a tailor's. His eyes are all concern, but there's the edge of a smile at the corners of his mouth.

'Will you look what the cat dragged in.' He comes towards her with his hands stretched out.

Even if Maggie herself isn't here, she might already have told Harry lies about Nell. She thinks of how often she tempted Maggie's wrath by getting involved with him, driven by loneliness and boredom and, at first, the respite from caring for Dolly. She's lost count of the times, over the last year or so, that she's let herself be persuaded to meet him in shabby hotels. But she's never been really afraid of Maggie before. She's been an idiot.

She puts her filthy hands into his big, clean ones because she can't see how to avoid it. He looks her up and down, makes a face as he notices her damp slippers.

'I'm sorry to bother you,' she says. She sounds quite

dignified. She hears it, and it helps.

'You're bleeding,' the young man says.

'Clear off, boys,' Harry tells him, without taking his eyes from Nell's.

'No,' Nell says, 'no, I'm quite alright. I'm looking for Ted.'

But the young men are disappearing into the back room, and she's alone with him. She takes her hands from Harry's, and then isn't sure what to do with them. She clasps them on the handle of the handbag, feels the weight of it. The pistol is making that weight.

There's a rush of voices and the crackle of a wireless as the boys open and close a door somewhere unseen.

'Are you having a party?' Nell says, without listening to herself.

'Nellie.' Harry puts his hand up, strokes her cheek. Just that soft touch makes her wince. 'You want to tell me what happened to your face?'

'It was an accident,' she says. 'I was careless. My own fault.' It's the truth, in a way.

He moves his thumb across her cheek again, a little more firmly this time. A flash of pain.

'You're right about that,' he says. 'Didn't I tell you not to mess me about? You don't listen. Now look at you.'

The fear is as sudden and sharp as the pain under his pressing thumb, and she can feel herself shaking her head. His pouched eyes are just as soft and kind as when they first met. It's more frightening than if he were snarling.

He drops his hand from her face and takes her by the wrist. She still has hold of the handbag in both hands, but now, held by him, it's too much like being handcuffed. She lets go with the hand he doesn't have hold of, the handbag swinging back to her side.

'Do you know,' he says, 'I had Maggie in here with a story that didn't half make me laugh.'

'No,' she says. His fingers are very tight. She can feel the bones of her wrist shift as he moves his grip.

'Told her she weren't thinking straight,' he says. 'Told her you don't know enough to be our grass. So you don't need to worry about that anymore. Alright?' He shakes her wrist, her hand flopping uselessly. 'Alright? You can say thank you now.'

'Thank you.' Her voice is very small.

'But here's the thing.' He steps even closer, close enough to kiss her. She can smell his breath, cigars and something meaty. 'Thing is, I don't think it would take much to change her mind back again. Not too much at all. And if I decide I need to have that little word with her, well, let's just say you'll be thinking back on this scratch she gave you as a bloody dream compared to what you'll get. Ain't that true?'

She can't speak. There isn't anything to say, except, perhaps, please. But that wouldn't do a thing.

He's smiling down at her, an indulgent, fatherly sort of smile. 'So now let's have no more of your games. We'll just go back to how it was, and we'll both be happy. Alright? That's my good girl.'

Now he does kiss her. She keeps her lips closed tight but she doesn't push him away, even while the weight of the pistol is pulling her free hand down. One of his hands goes again to the cut on her cheek and strokes the skin there.

He releases her and steps back, licks his lips. She looks away, wanting to rub her wrist, where his fingers dug in. She won't do it. And she won't cry.

'Now,' he says, looking her up and down. 'Let's get you out of these wet things.'

'No – please, no—' She takes a step back.

He steps towards her, closing the gap.

'You want to calm your nerves, Nellie. I don't mean that. Although that ain't a bad idea, now you mention it. But alright, alright, I'm only teasing.' He laughs and a drop of his spit lands on her lip. 'We'll make it special, our first time back together. You'll see, I ain't so bad at all. Treat you right. And speaking of that –' He gestures at a box at the base of a rack of men's suits. 'There's a load of ladies' shoes in that box. Dig yourself out a pair.'

'Oh, I couldn't,' she says, automatically. She is rubbing her wrist after all. She hadn't meant to do it.

'Didn't I say, Nellie? You need to behave.' And he's lost the pretend softness now. 'Get out of those slippers, like I tell you.'

She bends and shuffles quickly through them. Some of the shoes are squashed out of shape and the whole box smells musty, the scents of other people's feet all jumbled together. But there's a pair of black heels with an ankle strap that are about her size. She puts them on. They have little cut-outs in the leather, which will let in the damp.

'There, don't I look after you?' Harry says.

She looks up to see him holding a ladies' coat, a red wool number with a fur collar. He reaches out with his other hand to help her up.

'Here we are.' He holds the coat out for her to put her arms into it. It's a little too big. It's the sort of thing Nell would privately sniff at, is for someone much faster and cheaper.

'Well?' he says.

Nell manages to say, 'It's very nice.'

'And warm, too. Warmer than you treat me. But look, you're bleeding again,' he says, as though it weren't his own

215

thumb that had pressed the cut apart. 'I'll get one of the boys to take you to the hospital. It's only ten minutes' walk. You never know, you might see Ruby.'

'She's been nicked,' she says, distractedly. The word *nicked* is clumsy in her mouth.

'Let her out, I heard. Took her to hospital. Her chest is playing up.'

Nell feels unsteady. One hand gropes in the air for something to catch herself on and he takes it.

'Yep, she's there, alright.' He strokes her fingers. 'And here's the other funny thing. This really is funny, you'll like this. It was your Ruby asked me to bring Ted in and look after him. Ain't that a bleeding hoot? Imagine what I thought, when she asked me to do that. And he's walking out with Florrie. Love's young dream.' He laughs. 'I should think she'll eat him alive.'

'No,' Nell says, faintly.

'Now, shush. It's alright, I like the boy. I think I'll keep him around. Got a lot to teach him. You and me and Ted. A little family.'

For a moment she really does think of the pistol. She stares at the deep crease between his eyebrows and im-agines a dark and bloody hole.

He calls, 'Oi, Phil!' and after a moment, one of the young spivs appears at the back of the shop.

'Take Mrs Gibson to the hospital. She needs her face stitched up. Get your hat.' Then, turning to Nell, 'Not going to give me a smile?'

It makes the cut on her face sting to do it.

Florrie is wiping the worst of the muck off her coat in the little kitchen of the flat. She's made it damp; she should have tried a brush first. Every movement of her hand makes the ballerina ring glitter in the overhead light. Her mind feels as limp as her coat, washed out inside.

She'd woken, in the thick, serious dark of the middle of the night, alone in the bed, a barb of fear in her heart: Ted wasn't back.

She'd got up and gone out to the sitting room to find him asleep in the chair, and then the fear had turned, as it does at that hour, and burrowed deeper: he couldn't bear to share the bed with her. She told him too much about her real life and then he went out and saw some of it for himself. Or perhaps someone – maybe Don, Don has reason enough to hurt her – has told him something he hadn't liked to hear. And she's been trying so hard to be someone he could love.

She'd stood in the dark and listened to him breathe, and then she'd gone back to the bed and lay awake, cold right to her bones and absolutely certain that she'd lost him.

And then she woke again, and the flat was empty. The tendrils of the night have stayed with her all morning.

Ted's note is on the table next to her, the edges grown damp where the rag has dripped. She wishes he'd written 'love' or something like it. There's *I'll bring breakfast back*. But that might mean, *I'll bring breakfast back and we can break it off over tea and toast*.

And when he does come, though she whirls around to greet him, dropping the rag, trying to smile even while her heart thuds, he just stands in the kitchen doorway, looking at her with a grave face.

He's still in his coat and wearing his flat cap. He's taken off his shoes. His feet look knobbly and vulnerable in their socks, with the rest of him still dressed for outside.

'My mum wasn't at home,' he says.

She feels, very suddenly, as though she might be sick. Oh God. This is it. Maggie's chased Nell off and it's going to put the lid on any remaining chance they had. She wonders if she's going to beg him.

'Is that right?' she asks, finally. She sounds much calmer than she feels.

'She wasn't home. I've spent all blasted morning looking for her.'

She's going to have to tell him. She just needs to think how. It's not like she really knows anything about what Maggie said to Nell, but she does know enough to guess. She puts her hands on the table edge to still her trembling fingers.

'Go and sit down,' she says. 'I'll bring tea through. I've put the kettle on.'

'I don't want tea.' He rubs his face. His lower lids are a furious red from the fog.

'Alright.'

'Do you know where my mum is?'

He's never spoken to her so coldly before. She's going to lose him. She'll have no one. Except Maggie. And that looks lonelier, perhaps, than having no one at all. It looks like Cissy's life.

Behind her, the kettle is beginning to boil. She turns to take it off the gas, but he reaches out for her hand, and she closes her fingers over his, a little desperately.

'Ted—'

'Florrie.' He's gripping her hand in return. 'Where's my mum? What happened at my mum's?'

She wants to tell him but her throat's closing again. The kettle's whistle is rising like a siren.

'Please!' He has to raise his voice to make himself heard

over the kettle. He's glaring at her as though he's forgotten he ever loved her at all.

She shakes her head. 'I don't know what you're on about.' She's a coward. Such a bloody shameful coward. If only he wasn't looking at her like that, she could tell him.

He drops her hand and walks out of the kitchen.

She takes the screaming kettle from the stove. Only when she hears the bedroom door open and close again does she say, 'Ted, wait,' but she doesn't call it very loudly, and he doesn't come back.

She's steeling herself to follow after him when she hears the Cutters' knock at the flat door, and a voice calls, 'Cooee, anyone about? Florrie?'

This is absolutely the last thing she needs. She comes, forcing her back straight, to the kitchen door. Ada and Val are standing in the hall, both looking as though they're on their way to a luncheon party.

'Bloody hell,' Florrie says, 'how did you know where I am? I'm not even sure myself.'

'Bumped into your Ted, didn't we?' Ada says. 'On our way to call on you at Nell's.'

She feels dazed. 'But he was by himself just now.' Your Ted. So they really do know. Unless she just means your cousin, Ted. And perhaps that's all he's going to be, now.

Ada says, 'He told us to wait in the hall. Said he wanted a word with you. Well, I let him have a minute, then we thought we'd pop up here. Can you imagine? Left us down there. And here's Val with swollen ankles, about to drop a baby any second.'

Val takes off her hat. 'Be fair, Auntie Ada. We did push ourselves on him. I don't think he was keen on having us along.'

Ada's peering in at what can be seen of the sitting room. 'Oh, Ted's alright. You could do worse.'

Florrie feels her face warm. She says, 'Sit down. Tea's brewing,' and almost runs back into the little kitchen. She can hear Ada chuckling, Val shushing her.

She busies herself getting cups, the thermos of milk, and makes herself calm. She'll give them tea and then she'll talk to Ted. They won't stay long. Please God, they won't. She just has to get through one cup of tea without cracking up.

When she does come back in with the tray, she feels almost like herself. The bedroom door is still firmly closed, and Ada and Val are sitting in the armchairs, looking quite at home.

'Now, look, love,' Ada says, when they've all got cups and Florrie is sitting on the floor, next to the three-bar fire. 'We wanted to tell you that Maggie's going to find out what can be done for your mum, and you're not to worry.'

Florrie nods and stares at Ada's buttoned shoes. There won't be anything to be done. Her mum is probably on her way back to the prison by now, if she isn't there already.

'Bloody miracle Val didn't get nicked,' Ada says. 'They raided the dry cleaner's, did you hear?'

'No,' Florrie says, but it's hard to summon up much interest just at this moment.

'Hazel asked me to give her a hand at the club,' Val says. 'Ain't that luck? I'll have to buy her a drink. All the lads at the dry cleaner's got nicked, and all the stuff you lot got at the shops is gone for evidence.'

'Not a good day,' Ada says. 'But look, love, you don't worry about that.'

'And don't bother about the meeting tonight,' Val says.

Florrie looks up. 'I forgot. You ain't telling me that's still on.'

'Course not.'

'But look, love,' Ada says, 'we want you to stop here, alright? Just wait here, and we'll get you news as soon as we can.'

'I'd rather go home,' she says, and wonders if she still has one.

'You stop here. We want to know where you are. Best not go home just now,' Ada says, and Florrie knows it can't mean anything good. Then Ada leans forward, points a gloved finger and adds, 'You promise me, Florence.'

Florrie looks at the bedroom door. 'Where's Nell?' she mouths, silently, to Ada.

'Oh, lord,' Ada says, in her usual voice, too loud. 'I don't know. We'll see what we can do about that, as well. I told your fellow I wouldn't have thought she'd meant to grass.'

Florrie has to put her teacup down on the rug to stop herself from spilling it.

'You never said that to Ted?' she whispers. 'Tell me you never said that to Ted.'

Ted is on his knees, listening at the bedroom door, which is a pitiful thing to be doing. He keeps telling himself to get up. It's desperate, painful hope keeping him here, that Florrie will be able to explain, that he'll hear something that will make it all alright. The hope keeps bobbing up, a body that won't stay drowned.

And he's just heard one of the women say what he's been waiting to hear. But he doesn't hear Florrie's reply at all.

One of the other women says, 'Don't you worry about your fellow. He'll get over it.'

Florrie's voice says, 'I don't know about that.'

'Bleeding hell, Auntie Ada, keep your voice down, can't you?' the other says.

'I'm just saying, Nell's a bit simple. Not all there.' The first woman's trying to be quiet now, and Ted has to lean right into the door to catch it. 'But Maggie goes too far, don't she? Every bloody time. No need to cut the poor cow's face.'

Ted has scrambled to his feet. He takes an unsteady step backwards and sits down, hard, on the edge of the bed. The hope finally sinks, sending up little bubbles of pure, uncomplicated rage, and it's almost a relief.

Thankfully, Harry's young friend leaves Nell at the door of the hospital. She stands in her hateful new coat, staring up at the building, barely noticing the people pushing past her to come in or out. She's trying to form a coherent thought beyond the drumming of, *Help me, help me!*

All that time with Harry, she'd felt she was playing a game, playing at having an affair. She hadn't even liked him that much; it was just something to do, to keep her from going entirely mad. She'd thought she could stop if she liked. Oh, she'd known he was stronger than her, but she'd thought she was cleverer than he was, as though that might be enough to give her some control. It's just how she'd felt about the Palmers. Like trying to keep a lion on a lead. And it turns out that she's not cleverer than anyone, has been an unbelievable fool. She's a frightened, bleeding idiot with no idea what to do next, and she's freezing cold to boot.

But here's the hospital. It's an old workhouse, grim but familiar. All through the first part of the war she'd come here as part of her work for the Women's Voluntary Service, to push a tea trolley or read the Bible to patients. And perhaps she really should go inside. She has nowhere else.

She steps from the muffled blankness of the fog into chaos. The fog has driven people in here by the hundreds, the noise immense and formless, rumbling like the beating of bird wings. The entrance hall is heaving, and everyone in it gasping, wheezing, coughing into handkerchiefs. Nurses, walking as briskly as space allows, are waving away the voices calling out to them, *You must wait your turn, wait your turn.*

The hospital Nell knew was clean and orderly, everything labelled, beds made so neatly the nurses might have used a ruler. Now the floor is covered with dirty footprints. The fog has come in with the crowds, and hangs like a lowered ceiling above them, the electric lights flickering sadly through it.

She feels the cut on her face wake up and grow wet. The doors open behind her and she moves to let through an old man carrying a tiny girl. The girl's mouth opens and closes soundlessly.

Ducking her head, Nell joins the queue. She stares at the back of the elderly lady in front of her, a damp patch across her shoulders and down the middle of her back, like the shadow of a crucifix.

At last a nurse comes down the queue, taking down names. A whisper comes back along the line that she's finding the most urgent cases.

'Oh well,' the lady with the damp-streaked back says to her husband, 'you can bet your life that won't be us. We'll be waiting even longer now. At least this queue's moving.' Her husband nods without looking at her. 'The last one didn't move,' she says, to Nell this time. One of the lady's eyes is bright red, quite horrible to look at, like a peeled tomato.

'Oh dear,' Nell says. She feels incapable of speaking to strangers.

'This fog is poison. Have you heard?'

'Don't start that again,' her husband says, showing teeth streaked with black, as though he's been eating the fog.

'Look at them all,' the lady hisses at him, gesturing around at the rows and rows of people wheezing and coughing. She turns back to Nell. 'You see it, don't you? Poison.'

'I couldn't say,' Nell says, and the old lady glares at her and turns to face forward again.

The queue does move, slowly dripping them towards the desks. And by the time Nell reaches the front, she knows, in a queer, distant way, what she wants to do next.

The young man at the desk is bespectacled and weary. 'How can I help?'

'My cousin is here,' Nell says. 'Ruby Palmer.'

'What was she admitted for?' He pulls a ledger towards him.

'I'm not sure. TB, perhaps.'

'Respiratory complaint?'

'Yes, I should think so.'

'Your cousin isn't alone there.' He thumbs through the pages. At last he stops, his finger on a pencilled name. 'Miss Ruby Palmer?'

'That's right.'

He looks up. 'No visitors permitted, I'm afraid.'

'But whyever not?'

'Madam, there could be a host of reasons. It's not for me to say. If that's all, please do step aside. We're terribly busy, as you can see.'

'Can you tell me where she is, at least?' Nell asks, but even as she does, she knows it's hopeless. No help here.

'I should think not,' he says, in a voice that implies she's asked him to do something dreadful, take off his trousers, perhaps. 'Can I help you with anything else?' As though he can't see the cut across her face.

'I need stitches, I think.'

'Take a number and wait. Superficial cuts are low priority just now.'

But now the nurse with the clipboard is beside her, saying, 'Mrs Gibson, well I'll be! It's been a long time. You haven't changed a bit.'

'Oh, hello. How are you?' Nell can't remember the nurse's name, would never have placed her. There had been so many nurses. There must have been so many WVS tea ladies, come to that.

The man at the desk says, 'Do you mind having your chat elsewhere? There's a queue.'

The nurse gives him a bright, false smile and pulls Nell aside. She drops her voice. 'Are you having that cut seen to? I thought you must be. We're awfully busy, but if you wait ten minutes I can get to it. Come this way, will you?'

Nell can feel the whole queue staring resentfully after her as she goes.

But it's wonderful, to have someone examine her with such care, to clean and powder and stitch and snip, to look intently at her poor face and ask if she's comfortable. The contrast of it against the last few days wells up in her throat and it's all she can do not to weep.

Ruby is flat on her back, turned to a log in embers, a burning lump.

'Now don't you move,' the nurse had said. 'You must ask for help if you need the WC. No sitting up. No talking. And no deep breaths.'

When she coughs, and she can't help but cough, something hot and foul surges up and dribbles itself into the metal dish placed on her chest, just below her chin. It is blood, of course, boiling with illness. Her lungs are slowly drowning in it.

She closes her eyes and lets the fever roll through her.

'There you are,' a voice comes from above her. 'It was murder to find you. They'll shoo me off again any minute, I bet.'

Ruby opens her eyes. A damp fur collar, the underside of Maggie's chin, the lines in her neck, her nostrils.

'Oh, Rue, you look at death's door.' Maggie bends so that Ruby can see her face.

'I'm alright.' Ruby's voice is wet and spidery. 'Just an act. Got out of the police station.'

Maggie shakes her head. 'Oh, someone's going to pay for this. I told you there's a grass.'

'Hush. Copper.'

'Don't I know it. I told her I was visiting my husband. But Rue, look at you.' Maggie bites her lower lip and puckers her chin, just like she used to when she was a little girl and something frightened her.

'Did Nell get out?' Ruby manages.

'Don't you worry about that. You just get well.' Maggie pats her arm.

'Tell me.'

'Oh, for God's sake. She got bail and Ada walked her home.'

'And Val?'

Maggie drops her voice. 'Well now, that was a bit of luck. Hazel needed her at the club, so Val weren't about. Some of Harry's lads got nicked, but don't you worry about that. Let's just get you well. There anything you need?'

'New lungs.'

'I'd give you my lungs in a second, if they'd let me,' Maggie says.

Ruby jerks her chin to say, I know. On her chest, below her line of sight, the dish shifts, the blood in it making a soft lapping sound.

Maggie's eyes drop to it and move quickly back to Ruby's face. 'They say this fog's poison, did you know? I thought it was a lot of rubbish but there's people coughing themselves stupid all over the place in here.'

'I'm alright, Magpie.'

'You better be. I don't know what we'd do without you.'

'You'll have to, one way or another.'

'Don't you fucking dare.' Maggie shakes her head vigorously, although she must know it's true.

'Florrie,' Ruby manages to say. Any moment the coughs are going to come. She doesn't want to start convulsing in front of Maggie.

'Harry's looking after Ted. So we'll see. I know you think he ain't up to it, but he can learn. That's if she don't change her mind about him.'

'Look after her.'

'She'll be my number two,' Maggie says. 'There's a meeting tonight. You remember about that?'

Ruby's afraid to nod again, lest she send the dish slopping onto the floor. She raises her eyebrows instead.

'Well. I'm going to make sure they know you're still queen.' Maggie's biting her lip again.

Ruby reaches out and takes her sister's hand. Maggie squeezes her fingers gently and with her other, smoothes a lock of hair behind Ruby's ear.

'Just let me tell them they're to mind what I say. Just nod. Or shake my hand.'

Ruby tries to speak and finds her throat is full of fluid. She swallows, painfully.

'Oh, Rue,' Maggie says. 'I don't want any other bitch trying to take what's yours while you're down. They'll behave if you give me your blessing. Let me look after things for you. Till you get home.'

As if Ruby has a chance of going home.

'Ada won't have it,' she manages, in a half-whisper.

Maggie shrugs. 'Then she'll find out what happens, won't she?'

'It'll be a fucking war.' The words come out ragged.

'Now, Rue, don't get worked up. It ain't that bad. Ada don't want Harry, and she couldn't have him if she did.'

'Not the point.'

'It is, though. He's with me, and half the girl's husbands are with him. They're all coming home as soon as the weather clears, just like you said. The girls will do whatever you say.'

'Magpie – don't get yourself—' Something bubbles up between her lips and she chokes herself to a halt. 'Got a grass,' she says, at last.

Maggie's nose wrinkles, but only for a moment, a flicker of a crease across it. She bites her lip again.

'I can watch out for myself. Do you know,' her fingers stroke circles over the top of Ruby's, 'I had an idea, on the way here, that I might get in bed in your place. Give you my coat or something. I thought you might just walk out of here.'

Ruby gives a stinging wet huff of a laugh.

Maggie gives a sad half smile. 'Silly, now I see you. You really got to rest, Rue.' She gives a little start. 'Whoops, here we go. She's clocked me.'

'Excuse me,' a voice calls, 'Miss Palmer's not to have visitors.' Swift footsteps begin to clack towards them.

'Cheerio for now then.' Maggie stretches her hand out. 'I'll be back as soon as ever I can be, copper or no copper. Will you shake hands with me before I leave? That I can look after things for you?'

It's probably a terrible idea. Ada won't like it, and that might be just the start. If things get sticky Ruby won't be able to help, not past bits of coded advice in prison letters, and she'll be lucky if she lives long enough to do that. But now she's trying to take in every detail of Maggie's face and she can't say no. She has to leave her sister with something.

'Just till you get home,' Maggie says.

She shakes the hand holding Maggie's, sending the liquid in the dish slopping gently again. Squeezes her sister's fingers.

Nell's face is numb on one side. It makes her feel off balance. The nurse cleaned her face and neck; she's been stitched and dusted with antiseptic powder.

The entrance hall is as busy as ever, the lady with the reddened eye still sitting on one of the chairs. Her husband has found a newspaper and is determinedly trying to read it, even while his wife seems to be muttering to him. *London Fogbound, Traffic Chaos,* the headline reads. As if anyone needs to be told.

She has to find somewhere quiet, somewhere she can think. She turns her shoulders sideways to squeeze past a pair of women, one wiping the other's face with a hankie. Then, excusing herself, past a shabby, exhausted-looking woman holding a yellow-faced baby in a shawl. It's looking out over its mother's shoulder, its eyes huge and pink-rimmed. One bony little arm hangs limply outside the fold of the shawl. She looks away from the poor creature.

Across the hall and picking her way through the crowds, her fur coat slung over one arm, is Maggie.

She spots Nell at just the moment that Nell sees her. Maggie's face splits into a horrible smile. *You*, she mouths, and points one gloved finger.

She begins picking her way towards Nell, stepping over the people's legs as though they were fallen branches.

Nell turns and plunges into the queue. She goes straight through and out the other side, excusing herself all the way, towards the blessed gloom of the back stairs.

Florrie closes the door behind Ada and Val and takes a deep breath. She's going to go into the bedroom and tell Ted everything she knows, and if he leaves her after that – when he leaves her – at least she will have been honest. It hurts already. But that's alright, because she's ready for it. She'll keep steady.

But there's a sound behind her and it's him, before she's ready, after all.

'Ted,' she says, a bit stupidly.

'Don't talk to me.' He bends and begins putting his shoes on, yanking at the laces.

'I have to though, don't I—'

He pulls his coat on. 'I said don't bloody well talk to me.'

His hands are balled into fists. His eyes squeeze closed and then open again.

'Please.' She reaches out a hand, the one with the ballerina ring on it. Lightly touches a finger to his lapel, afraid to touch him but wanting to so, so much.

'I really thought you were different,' he says, without meeting her eyes. 'But I've got your number now. You're just the same as the rest of your family.'

She drops her hand. It's the thing she's always been afraid of, that she knew, one day, she'd hear him say.

He turns and walks out of the front door without looking back.

Ted's arms are humming with the urge to hit something, legs striding on, feet coming down heavily, as though to crush something underfoot. It's easier to be angry than afraid.

He'll have to go to see Harry. It's all he can think of. He walks all the way to the spieler, stamping the pavement to death.

He bangs on the door, making the 'closed' sign judder on its string. A figure comes through the dark towards him and turns into Don, wearing a roll-neck jumper that makes his neck look even shorter than usual. He seems to take an age finding the key and opening the door, while Ted bounces on his toes like a fighter about to go into the ring.

'I need to see Harry.' He almost wants Don to try to stop him, he's that angry.

'You want to ask nicely,' Don says, but he steps back to let Ted come past.

Ted follows Don through the shop and into the hall he waited in before. There are even more boxes now, stacked almost to the ceiling. Some of them are the boxes Florrie asked Ted to store in his attic. Things of Dolly's, she'd said: another lie.

'Wait here a sec.' Don goes into the spieler, closing the door on him.

Ted swings his arms, drums his fingers on the cardboard boxes.

At last the door opens and Harry comes out, followed by Don and another bloke Ted doesn't know.

'Not here,' Harry says, before Ted can speak.

The men push past Ted, Don saying, 'Come on, can't you,' as he does. Ted is so full of pent-up feeling that his legs feel springy and elastic on the stairs.

There's a room at the half landing, and here there are more cardboard boxes and other people's abandoned furniture. A sofa, a glass-fronted drinks cabinet, stacks of chairs, an old-fashioned desk. Harry walks over and sits behind it, his fingers steepled like a headmaster waiting for a recalcitrant boy.

The bloke Ted doesn't know goes straight over to the sofa and slumps there in a bored sort of way, but Don stays right at Ted's side, just inside the door.

'Ted,' Harry says, 'wouldn't you know I just sent a couple of lads out to look for you. Come and have a seat.'

Ted can feel his hands opening and closing; fists, release, fists, release.

'Didn't I just ask you to sit down?' Harry says.

Ted can feel his own pulse thrumming in his neck.

'Don,' Harry says, 'give this little sod a wallop.'

Don's fist loops towards Ted and he thinks, *Oh no you don't*, but then Don does, and Ted's head jerks back on his neck and he can barely keep his feet. His cheekbone takes the brunt of it but his left eye flares with light and a dull pain spreads right down the side of his face.

'Come on,' Harry's voice says. 'Don't just let him bash you up, son. Fight back.'

Then Ted's swinging at Don without looking to see where the blows will land, missing Don entirely half the time, his breath coming fast and ragged. His eyes are hot, he can't move his fists fast enough, he has the lapel of Don's jacket in his hand but the bugger won't stay still, won't fight properly, has his arm around Ted's neck. He can do nothing but hit at Don's back; he's trapped in a twisted position. Someone is laughing. His feet catch in the carpet, the bend of Don's elbow thudding into Ted's throat as it takes his weight.

'That'll do,' Harry says, and Don lets go.

Ted puts his hands on his knees and bends over. The patterns in the carpet swim.

'Better now?' Harry says.

The air is coming easier now. Then he swings his fist, his whole body behind it like a kite string, right at Don's temple.

Don skips backwards and there's a weight on Ted's back and the floor comes up to smack against him.

He lies for a moment. The carpet is dusty. His face is pushing against it, sore and heavy. There's a hand on the side of his head, a knee on his shoulder. The other fellow was the weight thumping into his back and now both he and Don are crushing Ted into the floor.

'No, son,' Harry says. 'That's enough now. Behave.'

The weight lifts off him. He gets up slowly and just the act of standing makes his head swoop. From the corner of his eye he can see Don and the other bloke standing by the sofa, and then Harry must give a wave because they both sit down.

'Ready to have a chat now?' Harry asks.

Ted walks over to one of the wooden chairs in front of Harry's desk, without looking at Don and the other bloke. But Harry jerks his head at one of them and there's the creak of the sofa, the clink of glass. Don walks over and puts a glass in front of Harry and holds another out to Ted, who takes it as though Don wasn't just pushing his face into the floor.

'There we are, son.' Harry takes a drink, grimaces. 'Rough stuff. But it's hard times.'

Don is still standing there, holding the bottle like a butler.

'What was that about?' Ted's nose is tender, the septum stinging with every word. He puts his fingers up to it, but it doesn't feel broken. The gin burns the inside of his cheek, where it's been mashed against his teeth.

Harry leans back in his chair. 'You had steam coming out of your nose, didn't you? Thought we'd better let you blow it off. Alright, Donnie? Any harm done?'

'Nah.' Don puts his hands up to smooth his hair. One side of his face is mottled red and white. 'Hits like a girl.'

'Now then,' Harry says, 'don't start him off again. You want to say thank you to Don, Ted.'

'What the flaming hell for?'

'Didn't I just tell you? You wanted a dust up, Don obliged. Did you a favour. Shake hands.'

Don reaches out his hand and Ted has to shake it. His own grubby hand looks thin and childish in Don's. Don gives him a nod and Ted, wearily, nods back. Finally Don retreats back to the sofa.

234

'There we are,' Harry says. 'Why don't you tell us what you're all worked up about?'

He isn't worked up anymore. The gin is turning the inside of his chest warm and soft, and he's so tired. It really does feel as though the steam has blown out of him.

'My mum,' he starts, but he doesn't know how to finish.

'Yes, I thought that would be it. How is she now? Feeling a bit better?'

Ted sits up straight, the gin sloshing in his glass.

'Ah, you didn't know? We've had your mum here,' Harry says. 'No, hold your horses, she's alright.'

Ted's on his feet without knowing that he meant to stand.

'Sit down, son. Sit down. I wouldn't lie to you. Not about your mum.'

He makes himself sit again, but the humming in his legs is back. 'I think Maggie – I think she's saying something about my mum that's not true.'

Harry rubs the soft, pouched skin underneath his eyes. 'Maggie gets all sorts of ideas into her head. I talked her out of that one. It's blown over. Alright?'

'She cut her. I heard – I heard she cut my mum.'

'A scratch. A little stripe. All girls fuss with each other, even your mum. One of my boys took her to a doctor to be on the safe side. But she's alright. She seemed happy enough now it's all sorted. Understand me? Let it go, now.'

'Yes,' Ted says, but a bit resentfully. 'I want to see her.'

'And so you will. Course you will. But not just now. She's not home just now.'

'Where is she?' His face hurts. He hasn't been to sleep properly for ages.

'How should I know? Gone off to the beauty parlour

or something. She'll be wanting to treat herself, now everything's settled again. She won't thank you for bothering her. Later I'll send one of the lads over to hers, tell her you're alright. Maybe I'll drop in and see her myself.'

Harry's right. His mum won't like to see him until she's pulled herself back together. She has her pride. But even so.

'I want to see her,' Ted says, dully. He's so tired now that he feels pinned to the chair.

'I can see you ain't listening, son. Let me make this clear for you. Your mum was in a bit of bother, and I sorted that out. For you, see? You're one of mine, now. As long as you're with me, you never have to worry about your mum, or about anything else. But you do have to do what I say. You don't do what I say, well, then you do have something to worry about. Listening now? Follow me?'

'Yes.'

'Right then. Give your mum a bit of peace. Leave her be. Go and look after our yard. Clean your blocks. And come back here later. There's people I want you to meet.'

Ted says, 'Yes,' again, because it's hard to say anything else when Harry's looking at him like this, fatherly and frightening, both at once.

'We take care of our own,' Harry says. 'Now. Where's my money? Not got it yet? Even more reason to go and get your blocks ready, then. Off you go.'

Ruby has her eyes closed, stuck in a circle of worries, chasing each other around and around. What will happen if Ada can't be persuaded, if Maggie won't behave, if the girls are forced to take sides? And the men are bound to be drawn in, if there's trouble inside the gang. They're all family, all married or related in one way or another. They already have the grass and the coppers trying to take them apart from the outside and other gangs just waiting to step in and take whatever they can. If they can't stick together—

But the only thing left is to try not to think about it, and try not to die. And she isn't sure that she can manage either one.

'Wakey, wakey, Miss Palmer,' a voice says.

Ruby opens her eyes to see a nurse holding a wheeled pole, from which dangles an oxygen tank and a rubber mask with curled leather straps.

'Up you come.' She heaves Ruby up against the pillows. 'Oh, there's nothing to you, is there?'

Ruby opens her mouth to say, what a cheek, but just drawing breath brings the cough on and she needs to double up, she can't breathe, but the nurse is pulling her hands away from her face and strapping the mask around her head and then the oxygen comes creeping through Ruby's throat, pushing it open, spreading through her like water. She can feel the blood and mucus in her lungs bubbling, shifting aside to let it pass. She breathes deeply, more deeply, perhaps, than she has in years. The oxygen is overwhelming and clean and—

And she knows who the grass is. She really thinks she does. But oh, God above. This is going to make the biggest mess of all.

Nell hurries up the stairs, waiting for her own echoing footsteps to be joined by the sound of Maggie's feet behind her. When she reaches the first floor she stops, but the stairs are quiet, the only sound the rumbling murmur of the entrance hall below.

There are three gurneys just a bit further down the

corridor, parked in single file against the wall. Their occupants are lying still, the sheets drawn over their faces. She flinches away from the sight of them.

But here's the door of the WC. She goes to it quickly and sits on the seat of one of two toilets, head in her hands, dizzy from the narrowness of her escape.

She goes through the options remaining to her. She could go back to the shelter and – what? Die there, probably. It might be alright for a night, but no one could live in it, not really, not in winter. And what would become of Ted? She could go home, snatch up everything she can find to sell and run away from London. She could go to Ted and beg him to leave with her. That idea makes a sour, humiliated taste rise in her throat. He'll never look at her the same way again, once he knows she's been carrying on with Harry. She could go to the police. But that thought is most frightening of all. If they can't help her – if they won't – she'll be dead. Ted will be alone, and they might do anything to him.

There's nothing else. Unless – unless Ruby can talk to Maggie for her. If Ruby could just get Maggie off Nell's back, she could take the final option: go home, grit her teeth and let Harry do whatever he likes, until she can find a way out. It's not a nice choice, is shameful and painful. But it's the best of a terrible bunch. It buys her time, and Teddy needn't know a thing about it.

Nell knows the hospital. She'll just have to find Ruby, whatever the man on the desk says.

Right, she thinks. *I shan't be a baby.*

The corridors are just stretches of dull parquet flooring, the old familiar scents of Dettol, carbolic soap and kaolin. She peeps through the glass panel set into the doors. So many patients. So many oxygen tanks dangling from poles.

Behind the fifth door is a ward just like all the others, but beside one of the beds, a uniformed figure.

Nell jerks her face quickly back from the glass.

A policewoman. Nell hadn't thought of that, she'd thought Ruby's being in hospital somehow cancelled out her arrest. Silly. More than silly. Stupid.

Florrie's been sitting and staring at nothing. Ted's left her. Her mum's gone. Aunt Nell's got a cut across her face, which is at least partly Florrie's fault. And she can't think of a thing to do but sit and feel her stomach ache.

She went to borstal for six weeks when she was fifteen, has been kept in a police cell overnight twice since then. Before she was evacuated, she sat with Ruby and Dolly on the Tube station platforms during air raids waiting for the ceiling to cave in and bury them. And she's still never felt as trapped and powerless as she does at this moment.

Someone knocks on the door.

She lets out a squeak, swallows it, grows still.

'Who is it?'

'Mr Griffith. From downstairs.'

She hasn't the faintest idea who Mr Griffith might be.

Hurriedly, she smoothes down her skirt, wipes her eyes and pats at her hair. The door judders in its frame and finally pops open.

Mr Griffith is huge and scarred, with broad shoulders and stubbled chin, and is peering at her worriedly. 'You alright, my dear?'

'Fine, thanks,' she says, a bit more abruptly than she means to.

'You're the fiancée, are you?'

'Yes,' she says, although it might not be true, anymore. 'Florrie Palmer.'

Mr Griffith shakes her hand and gives her really quite a sweet smile. 'Well. Lovely to meet you, my dear. I brought you up some things.'

It's a paper bag of bread rolls, a tin of fruit cocktail, a package of powdered egg.

'You didn't have to do that,' she says.

He looks embarrassed, shifts from leg to leg. 'Well, you know. The wireless said the shops are running short, and I have things in. So I just thought. Not easy at the best of times, is it? Starting a home. And with this weather. Got to look after each other, don't we?'

This is so kind that she doesn't know what to say. Thinks, for a moment, that if she opens her mouth to thank him, she might spill out everything that's gone wrong. He's got that sort of face.

But he's already digging in a pocket. 'And I've got a set of keys for you.' He hands them to her. They have a brass fob with the words *Snore Hall* engraved in a curling script. He sees her looking and says, 'It's supposed to be funny, I think.'

'I see,' she says. 'Well. Thanks.' Now she has the feeling she's going to laugh, though not at *Snore Hall*. But perhaps she's going to cry. She might be going mad.

'Not a bother,' he says, and thank God he's going off down the stairs, before she can crack up entirely.

She eats a bread roll, almost absent-mindedly. It must be past lunch time now, and Ted never did bring breakfast back. It's absurd how much better the roll makes her feel. Or perhaps it was Mr Griffith. *Got to look after each other, don't we?*

Right. She'll find Maggie, make it alright for Nell, and perhaps that will bring Ted back to her. She feels more determined than desperate now. But she made her coat damp, sponging it. And it's freezing outside. Stupid. She hurries into the bedroom to look for something else to put on.

The wardrobe has double doors, and half is empty, she supposes, for her to fill. Behind the other door are all Ted's things. And here is his good woollen overcoat.

Wearing a bloke's togs is hardly a new idea, and she has a feeling that she'll be braver in the fog, got up like a man.

Ted's a tall bloke and she has to roll the trousers up to stop them trailing. But her shoulders do fit his coat properly. Quickly, and without letting herself think about what Ted will think of her if he comes back now, she pulls his flat cap from the shelf and tucks her hair inside it. His shoes slide about on her feet but she rolls a pair of socks and stuffs them down into the toes.

Shame she's not got a pencil to draw on a moustache. She'll have to hold her hankie over her face, but half London is doing that just now.

Then she runs for her handbag, the shoes threatening to slide off her heels at the back, and fetches out her purse. A ten-bob note and a twopenny piece. She stuffs the money, and her *Snore Hall* keys, into the trouser pocket.

Downstairs, the door closes behind her with a solid clunk. She's not sure where she is, and the fog is already terrifying. Doesn't matter. Don't think about the fog, or Maggie, or Ted's face. Keep walking.

Most of the shops are closed but the caffs and pubs are lit. Misted up windows, steam inside and fog outside.

She passes a couple smoking, him having trouble with

the lighter, her laughing and calling him a silly sod. Two flat-footed coppers with a lantern. She keeps her head down as she passes them, though she needn't; they're looking at the road, calling out to a bloke on a bicycle that he'd better walk it if he hasn't better lights.

When she sees a telephone box, a little refuge in the fog, she goes inside, finds the twopenny piece and dials the operator.

'What number, please, caller?' comes the lovely clear voice. It seems a very long time ago that she sat on the stairs, holding the letter from the telephone office. It might almost have happened to a different girl entirely.

'I'd like to be connected to Fisher's Pawn and Loan, please.' Florrie's own telephone voice comes rolling out. 'Kennington Lane.'

'One moment please, caller.'

The phone rings for what seems like ages. Finally it's picked up and a voice says, 'Hang on a minute,' and there's a clonk as it's put down again.

Faintly she can hear voices, although she can't make out the words. Then there's a loud, impatient breath, and the voice says, 'Yes?'

'Mr Fisher? It's Florrie Palmer. I don't suppose my Aunt Maggie's there, is she?'

'No, she ain't. And I've said before, I ain't her secretary.'

Behind him, very faintly, she can hear two men, the rise and fall of their voices. One of them is Ted, she's sure of it. Just the sound of him there, out of reach and thinking ill of her, is like a physical pain.

She hesitates, gripping the receiver, trying to make out what he's saying, strung between wanting desperately to talk to him and not knowing what to say.

And then there's the click of the receiver going down. No goodbye.

She goes back out, keeps walking. There's something horrible about her toes bashing against the rolled-up socks. They're so cold she can feel it and not feel it. She'll have to find Maggie, somehow, in all London and in this weather. She hangs on, as hard as she can, to the determined feeling, so that she won't have to think of Ted, of how he'd looked when he said she was just like the rest of her family.

At last, a taxi rank, the drivers all standing beside their cabs, stamping against the cold.

'Will one of you take me to Soho?' She makes her voice as low as she can.

'In this weather, pal? It'll cost you. We'll be going at a snail's pace. You're better off walking to the Tube.'

'If they're still running,' one of the others says. 'I heard they had fog in the tunnels.'

'I'll pay,' Florrie says.

But one of them has stepped closer, is peering at her. 'Here,' he says. 'I thought you were a bloke.'

'I'll pay,' she says again.

But he's shaking his head, his mouth pulling up on one side in disgust. 'Hop it,' he says, suddenly. 'Hop it, before I get the old bill on you.'

Nell is sitting on a bench in the corridor, just around the corner from Ruby's ward. She's cadged a cigarette from a woman walking by, although she hardly ever smokes and has never used the word 'cadge' before in her life.

She's in a hospital full of other people who are having their own terrible days. She's angry on behalf of all of them, and with all of them. She can't think of a person alive she isn't furious with. She's been pushed around by everyone, for ever, has let it happen. But they've pushed her into a corner now.

She stubs the cigarette out on the floor. Then she pulls Dolly's handbag onto her lap and reaches inside it. The pistol and the bible. God and the devil.

Ruby's allowed to sit up to eat her lunch. All along the ward, people are propped up against pillows, hunched over their trays, with a great clinking of spoons against china.

There's no sign of the fever, though each breath needs to be pulled through a thick, liquid lump in her chest. But she can't eat the soup. It's full of bits of turnip and carrot, and her throat's become the eye of a bloody needle.

To her left is a bed just like her own, where sits a bent old lady, spooning her soup with shaking hands. When Ruby turns her head the other way, to the right, she can see how long the ward is, the rows of black iron beds. It gives her a creeping feeling of doom. It is easier to look down at her soup, the yellowy skin of her own arms.

She hears the ward door open, but doesn't raise her head until she hears the sister say, 'Mrs Gibson has come to read the Bible to you.'

Nell is standing beside the first bed, looking down at the tiny old lady. She has a cut across her face, neatly stitched with black thread. Dolly's crocodile bag is over her arm.

Ruby begins coughing, explosive coughs, solid bubbles that burst in the mouth. She watches over her hands, through watering eyes.

Nell doesn't look at Ruby, but sits on the stool on the far side of the old lady's bed and fetches out a bible.

Ruby waves one of the nurses over with a frantic hand. 'Please, will I be allowed to have Bible reading?'

'Well, of course you will.' The nurse is holding a piece of rubber tubing and a bowl, and isn't in the mood to chat.

'Can I really?'

The nurse is already walking away. 'It's the Bible,' she says, over her shoulder. 'It's for everyone.'

Ruby tries not to watch but her eyes keep drifting over to Nell all by themselves. Nell, by contrast, doesn't seem to look at Ruby at all. When finally she does close the bible, stand and come over to Ruby's bed, she looks at her brightly, like a stranger.

'How are you feeling?' she asks Ruby. 'Should you like a Bible reading?'

It's Dolly's bible. Ruby can see the bite mark on the cover, made by Florrie's baby teeth.

She nods. She has a feeling that if she speaks she's going to start coughing again.

Nell pulls up the stool and begins to flip through the pages. Her fingers are trembling ever so slightly.

'Your face,' Ruby says. A cough is sitting in her throat and she stops, breathes, feels it settle.

Nell looks up. 'Ruby, I would never grass. Never.'

'Course not. What—'

'It was an accident.' Nell looks intently at her and then flicks her eyes back down to the bible.

Ruby starts coughing again, and curses herself. 'What? What was? What did you tell them?' she asks, in between coughs.

'I didn't tell them anything!' Nell hisses, to her hands.

'What . . . ' The coughs are trailing off, into little gasps. 'What are you on about then?'

245

'It was an accident that we . . . that I took your bag. I didn't think.'

Finally Ruby stops coughing long enough to take a drink of the stale water in the tin cup beside her bed. It helps.

'I know that. What's that got to do with anything? What happened to your face?' But even as she asks, she knows the answer. 'Oh, no,' she whispers.

Oh, Maggie. You idiot. Making a mess again, and Ruby not even there to help pick up the pieces.

Nell still doesn't look up from the page. 'They were waiting in the house. I . . . I ran away. And poor Ted. Oh, God. You can't let Harry! Ted mustn't—' She sounds as though she might scream at any minute.

'Read to me,' Ruby says. 'I need to think.'

Nell hesitates, then nods and begins, 'I write unto you, little children, because your sins are forgiven you . . . '

Ruby looks at Dolly's bible in Nell's pale and freckled hands. She looks at Nell's face, so much like Maggie's. Nell's voice drifts in and out of her ears. She looks at Dolly's handbag. Her heart starts thumping, hard enough that her eyes blur and she's afraid she'll start choking again.

'Come here,' she whispers, urgently.

Nell stops reading. 'What?'

'Come here, Nellie. Come close so I can whisper.'

Nell draws her stool in. Ruby takes her hand, pulls her near and says, very low, 'What I want you to do, Nellie, is trust me.'

Her fingers are in Dolly's handbag, are fumbling around the cloth lining, the shape of what might be Dolly's purse, and then—

'Beg pardon?' Nell says.

She has it. Her fingers hook under the ridge of the pistol's barrel. And there. It's out.

She lets go of Nell, shifts slightly onto her side, thrusts the pistol quickly under her pillow and puts both hands innocently on top of the blankets.

'Go, Nellie. Push off.'

Nell shakes her head. 'You haven't said what I should do! You don't understand—'

'Right then,' the policewoman says, loud enough and close enough that they both jump. She has come to the foot of the bed without either of them noticing.

Nell draws herself up unnaturally straight. Ruby feels her hands close tightly on the sheet, just to have something to hold onto.

But the policewoman nods at Nell. 'Not giving you any trouble, is she?'

'Oh, no. She's good as gold. God's word, you know. A great comfort.' Nell's face is white and set, but her voice is pretty close to her usual one.

'Couldn't agree more,' the policewoman says. 'Even so, that's enough now.'

'I should like to finish the reading,' Nell says, a little more desperately.

'She's had her share.'

'Wouldn't you rather get home? With this weather and all.' Ruby tries, with her eyes, to tell Nell to do what she says.

Nell just glares back. 'I'm sure I'd rather do God's work. I shan't go anywhere. I'm sure I'll see you again on my rounds.'

'We'll see,' the policewoman says.

Nell has to go to the next bed. 'Should you like a Bible

247

reading?' she asks the woman there, quite as angrily.

'I don't mind,' the woman says, in a tired, wispy voice. 'If you like.'

'Right you are.' Nell plonks herself down and begins ruffling the pages.

The policewoman steps right up to Ruby's bed. 'Repenting, are you?'

'You ain't allowed on the ward.'

The policewoman waves this away. 'I came to tell you we've got your private room. They're getting it ready now. Aren't you the lucky one? Quite the princess.' She laughs. 'But you know, if you're awake enough to have Bible study, perhaps we should just move you to the police station.'

Ruby turns her face away. She can hear the low rise and fall of Nell's voice, reading aloud. She slides her hand underneath the pillow, just enough to let her fingertips brush the smooth, squat nose of the pistol.

Nell concentrates on the Bible verses, her voice rolling out as though her thoughts aren't scrabbling about, wild and confused.

A voice in her mind is whispering, who does she think she is, dashing around pretending to be a Bible lady, behaving like a character in the pictures? Well, she feels silly enough now.

She moves down the row of beds, reading to anyone who asks, and trying not to look at Ruby. She has to have one more try at talking to her cousin. She doesn't know what else to do.

She is almost at the end of the ward, where the wide windows show only blank grey, when she opens her bag for the throat pastilles and realises that the pistol is gone.

The elderly man in the bed nearest her is looking at her expectantly.

She sits, somewhat dazedly, and begins to read without asking him if he would like her to. She doesn't listen to a word she's saying, only lets her mouth run on.

'Who shall separate us from the love of Christ? Shall trouble or hardship or persecution or famine or nakedness or danger or the sword?'

Ted finds his way back to the flat by letting his feet do most of the thinking. His hankie is over his mouth and nose, although it's so stiff with grime that he might be pressing solidified fog to his face.

He's relieved when he finds the alley. On the other side of it is the door to the flat, and Florrie is inside. He wants, very badly, to see a way clear to untangling the mess they're in.

Just take charge, Teddy, Edward says, in his mind. *This can all be straightened out.* Imaginary Edward is always saying things like that. Ted wishes he were better at taking the advice.

He hears footsteps behind him. Instinctively, he stops and turns, but there's nothing to be seen but the swirl of yellow-grey.

The footsteps come closer. The shape of a shortish bloke in a coat and hat. Ted steps back before the fellow draws close enough to clock him. You never know what type of character will be out in weather like this.

The bloke passes Ted's alley, and then the footsteps stop. There's the jingling and clonks of someone trying different keys in an unfamiliar lock. Ted creeps forward, and listens to the sound of a stranger trying to get into the door that leads to his flat.

Florrie hurries through the flat, into the bedroom and starts to strip off. She's managed nothing she set out to do. Ted is still furious, Nell might still be in trouble, Ruby is gone, Harry is trying to take Ted and turn him into something he isn't, and she can do nothing about any of it. And now she's got Ted's coat and hat damp and dirty and she'll have to think of a way to explain that. She thinks of his face when he held out the opal ring, before everything.

And then all the sobs she's been holding in just burst out of her mouth and she sits on the bed half-dressed and bawling her eyes out like an idiot.

Ted has followed the bloke up the stairs, creeping behind him in the dark, all the way into the flat.

He can't work out how this fellow came to have a key. Can't help wondering, painfully, if Florrie might have found a way to get it to him.

There's no sign of the bloke in the sitting room. But then, from the bedroom, a muffled and watery voice.

'Stop it.' It's Florrie. 'Just stop, for God's sake.' The last word rises into a moan.

And nothing that's come before matters.

He runs the few steps to the bedroom and wrenches the door open. It rockets inwards, and Florrie screams as it slams against the wall.

She's beside the bed, fumbling her skirt up her legs. Her makeup is smudged, her eyes huge and wet.

'Where is he?'

She just looks at him, blinking.

'Who are you talking about?'

'I saw him!' He crosses to the wardrobe, pulls it open,

pushes his hand through the line of hanging clothes, turns in a frantic circle, staring into the empty corners of the room.

Behind him, Florrie starts to laugh.

He wheels around. She has her hands to her mouth, her laughter hitching on her breath.

'It was me,' she says, through her hands.

'What? What was you?'

She points to the wicker chair, where his green worsted trousers and wool overcoat are slung over the back of it. 'I was wearing your things.' She's still laughing, rocking back and forth, gasping.

He stares from the chair to Florrie.

'Jesus Christ.' He puts his hand to his heart. 'I thought someone was . . . was hurting you.'

She shakes her head, looks at him over the top of her hands. Her eyes are watering, and the tail end of the laughter is closer now to sobs.

'Stop, can't you?' He takes a step back from her.

She gasps once, twice more, and drops her head.

'Tell me again,' he says.

'I thought – my coat was damp, and it's safer for a girl in the fog if she's got up like a bloke.' She's talking to her lap, hands clasped, her voice hoarse. 'I thought I might sort it out.'

'What do you mean, sort it out?'

She looks up. Her eyes smeared with black, her expression the blank one he knows so well. 'Make Aunt Maggie see, you know. That Aunt Nell never. That she never would.'

There's a moment now, Ted looking at her, Florrie gazing back. And then he's pulled her to her feet and into his arms. She smells of fog and perfume and just a whiff of his own aftershave, where it must have rubbed off on her from the collar of his coat. Her hands curl against him, fingers hanging onto the cloth of his shirt.

'But you're scared of the fog,' he says, into her hair. It's scratchy with hairspray and grime, but he buries his face in it anyway.

'No, I ain't,' she says, against his chest. 'Alright, I am a bit. But I didn't care.'

He can't speak, so he holds her tighter still.

'You come flying in here to save me,' she says.

He gives a shaky laugh. 'And you were going to talk to Maggie for me.'

'I still will. Where did you go?'

'I went to see Harry.' It's uncomfortable, saying it out loud, and to her, but it is the truth. 'He said it's blown over.'

'Blooming hell,' she says, into his shoulder. Then she grows still and her hands close tighter on his shirt. 'Ted.' She doesn't lift her head.

'Yes.'

'When you said I'm like the rest of the family.'

'I was talking rot. Don't listen to me.'

'You wasn't though. Not really,' and she says something else, something he can't make out. She's turned her face right into his shoulder. He feels her lips move against his shirt, whispering.

He wants to say, *Don't tell me. Just never tell me,* and he wants to beg her to tell him everything. He wants to tell her what a mess he's in with Harry, and he's afraid of how weak he will sound when he does. But the things they haven't told each other have nearly ruined everything.

'I suppose,' he says, slowly, 'we might both need to be honest.'

'What've you got to be honest about?' She's looking at him now, tilting her chin up.

'I'm a bit ashamed to tell you.'

'You think you are? You want to try being me for half a minute.'

She's got her cool look on again. It's going to be very hard to tell her how foolish he's been, while she looks at him like that.

Even so, he says, 'Should we, I don't know. Should we sit down?'

'Do you really want to hear it?'

'Do you want to tell me?'

She breaks away from him, takes his hand. She looks as though she might speak, but then she leads him the few steps to the bed.

She sits and begins, clumsily, to undo the buttons of her blouse. He hovers, watching, awkward limbs and thumping heart, not sure she can really be doing what he thinks she is.

One button, and then another. Her clavicle a gentle line above the smooth skin of her chest. Another button. The curve of her breasts above her brassiere.

'Come on, then,' she says, without looking up. 'If you're going to find out what I'm like I want you in a good mood for it.'

He's been holding his breath and now it comes out in a disappointed rush. He sits beside her, puts his own hand up and stops the movement of hers.

'No. That can't be why.'

She looks at his hand over hers. Her fingers are still at the opening of her blouse; he's almost touching her breast, can feel the heat of her just under his fingertips.

'Course not,' she says. 'I didn't mean it.'

Disappointment again. He takes his hand away. She wraps her arms around herself, closing her blouse, looking away at nothing, at the empty corner of the room.

She says, 'I meant, you know. I do want to. I want to be with you.' And then, so quietly he almost doesn't catch it, 'While you still think you might love me.'

The slump of her shoulders is so sad. He never has known what to do, around sad women. He pats her, awkwardly, on the back.

'Is it going to be as bad as all that?' His voice is too cheery. It doesn't sound real.

She shrugs. Something about her air of defeat makes him put his hand to her chin and turn her towards him. He can see her now, behind the blank face. He's always thought that look of hers so impenetrable, but now it seems the thinnest sheet of ice, that he could shatter it with a fingertip. He's afraid of what will happen when it does.

He kisses her, and it's inside his own chest that he feels something crack and thaw.

Ruby, lying on her back, can feel the lump of the pistol digging into the base of her skull. She can hear Nell reading aloud, even under the other sounds on the ward. And there's the shadow of the policewoman ticking back and forth outside the window in the door.

She's trying to decide what to do. But what is there besides shooting the woman? It's hard to kill someone with a little pistol like Dolly's. *It's just to slow them down*, Dolly used to say. Ruby's mind is so thick and slow. *Just to slow them down.*

It might be impossible to get out once they lock her into a private room, and they might find the pistol when they move her. But she can't do anything here, not in front of all these people and certainly not in front of Nell.

She eases the gun out from under the pillow and tucks it into her knickers.

Now she's up, feeling slow and unsteady. She finds her slippers under the bed, stands shivering in her hospital nightie. They've taken her clothes off to God knows where.

'You shouldn't be out of bed. Go back and lie down.' The ward sister is at the end of Ruby's bed, hands on hips.

'I need the lav.'

'I shall bring you a pan. You're not to stand up.'

'I'm up now. I won't be a minute. This ward is full of men,' Ruby says, a desperate hiss. She moves forward, to push the woman if she must.

The ward sister sighs, says, 'Wait, please,' comes back with a dressing gown, and helps her into it.

The sister takes Ruby's arm on the way to the door and she finds that she needs it. She can barely walk. This is going to be impossible. But there's no choice, not really.

The sister opens the door and says to the corridor, 'Miss Palmer is just going to the lavatory.'

'Very well,' says a weary voice. The copper takes Ruby's arm, strong fingers above her elbow. 'I suppose you think this is a neat little trick you're pulling, but it's quite useless, you know. The moment you're allowed up I'm to bring you back to the police station. It's of no concern to me whether that's sooner or later. We're all on double shifts, and if I'm honest, you're giving me a reason to stay in here out of the cold. So you carry on with your little charade. What you hope to achieve by it, I can't imagine.'

Ruby doesn't reply. She concentrates on walking, on the

cold metal of the pistol pressing against her buttocks. She hadn't meant to use the WC at all, but all of a sudden she's afraid she will wet herself.

The copper follows her into the ladies' room. That's good. And she lets Ruby go into a cubicle alone. Just the action of sitting down on the toilet seat makes her dizzy. She holds the pistol in her weak, shaky hands while she uses the toilet, pulls up her knickers, sits again. She wants to lie down so badly, but instead she's going to have to do this stupid, reckless thing.

She leans and knocks six times on the inside of the cubicle door, the Cutter knock.

The policewoman pulls open the door. 'What's this? If you—'

Still sitting, Ruby fires. Her hand jerks, pulls at her shoulder muscles. The crack of the shot ringing through her head. And it's too late now.

The policewoman's mouth opens in surprise. Her left leg is pushed out from underneath her, a spray of blood puffs from below the knee. She folds to the floor, her arms flying up in surprise or surrender. There's the thump of her landing and a ringing in Ruby's ears.

There is one long, strange second in which nothing seems to happen. The copper looks up at Ruby. Her eyes are very wide, glazed with shock. Ruby, sitting on the toilet, stares back, the gun warm in her hand.

Then she forces herself to her feet.

The copper gets halfway up and falls again, landing on her knees and crumpling forward. And this time, as she hits the tiled floor, she screams. The sound sends a jolt of pure fear through Ruby's heart.

The copper's head is almost at Ruby's feet, the parting

in her gingery hair very straight. Her legs are splayed out through the cubicle door.

Now Ruby curses herself for an amateurish fool. She's trapped herself in the toilet, no way out but over the policewoman. She begins to edge past. Only three or four steps and she'll be free to run.

Fingers close around her ankle.

The copper has rolled onto her side and is looking up at Ruby. She's panting, her brow beading with sweat.

'No,' the copper gasps. 'Not a chance.'

Ruby lifts her free foot, the one the policewoman hasn't got hold of, and kicks her in the chin.

The hand lets go. The copper's head falls back.

Ruby gives a desperate, stumbling skip away and then another one over the copper's legs, her heart beating too hard, her breath refusing to draw properly. She's almost at the door, almost free, when her vision shrinks, the world seems to tip and she feels her own knees thump into the tile.

The moment Nell saw Ruby leave the ward, she stuffed the bible back into her bag and followed. When she'd realised that Ruby and the policewoman were going to the lavatory, she'd stopped, embarrassed, and hovered about, unsure what to do. And then there had come the sound. She wasn't sure at first that it was gunfire. It certainly wasn't the ack-ack they'd been used to in the war. Then someone screamed.

And now she's pulling open the door of the ladies' room.

The first thing she sees is Ruby on her hands and knees, the pistol in one fist against the floor, her hair hanging in strings around her lowered head. Behind her, the policewoman lies half in and half out of the toilet cubicle, her eyes slitted, showing the whites. But she's breathing; her chest rises, hitches, falls, rises again. Blood is pulsing up from her leg in steady swells, pooling onto the floor. Through the woman's torn stocking Nell gets a glimpse of flesh, horribly like minced meat. The foot is juddering about, twitching on its ankle.

Ruby raises her head, gasps out, 'Nellie. Thank God. Help me.'

Nell slams the door shut on her cousin's upturned, desperate face.

She doesn't mean to. It's the shock.

But now, behind her, a voice says, 'For Pete's sake, William.'

Three people. A woman, pushing an old lady in a wheelchair with one hand. With the other she leads a red-faced, weeping child by the wrist. She looks at Nell. 'He's had an accident. And him a big boy of five.'

'Oh dear,' Nell says.

'See?' The woman says to the boy. 'See how you shame me?'

Nell stands in front of the door. 'I wouldn't go in there! Trust me. You'd rather not. Don't!' Her voice cracks; she sounds half-mad.

The woman frowns. 'I can hardly go into the gents. And he can't be trusted alone.'

'I'll make sure no one comes in after you,' Nell says. Through the door she can hear a thump, a groan.

But now the little boy is sobbing in earnest.

'Oh, for heaven's sake. Behave, William!' The woman is flustered now. She bends over the lady in the wheelchair. 'I won't be a moment, Mother.'

The little old lady doesn't move or respond. And thank

God, the woman and her wailing boy are going into the men's WC.

Nell opens the door again. Ruby is on her feet, her face grey and her mouth hanging open like an idiot. She shakes her head at Nell, though heaven knows what she means by it. Nell pulls her, quite roughly, out into the corridor, and Ruby stumbles after, her breath harsh and wheezy.

'Can't walk. Buggered,' is all she says.

Ahead, distantly, Nell can see the doors that lead to the lifts. If they can just get to the basement and the service door out of the building—

The old lady is watching them silently with hooded, sunken eyes. Nell bends, murmurs, 'Sorry,' and takes her under her spindly arms.

'Oh!' the old lady whispers, but she puts her arms around Nell's neck obediently and Nell lifts her out. It's a little like lifting a bird, the sense of fragile bones just below the blankets. She smells of sweat and lavender. There is nowhere to put her but straight down on the floor.

'I'm ever so sorry,' Nell says. She lowers the old lady as quickly and gently as she can and leaves her propped against the wall.

The moment she gets Ruby into the wheelchair she begins to push as fast as she can, her arms straining, her shoes clacking like gunfire on the parquet floor.

Ted has his arm around Florrie's shoulders. It's almost nice to know that the fog is outside closing them in, while they lie under the patchwork quilt, with the bedside lamp on.

He'd kept asking, all the time they made love, whether it was alright, whether she was comfortable. At last she'd put her fingers to his lips to stop him speaking.

But he's talking now, he's telling her everything. A piece of chivalry, so that she won't have to be the first to feel vulnerable. He's told her about his debt to Harry, his blocks, his trip out to collect protection money with Don, sometimes stumbling over the words. The nearness of her skin is making him awkward, distracted, grateful. He hasn't been able to look at her. He stares at the ceiling, at a spider's web of cracks across the paint.

When he finishes, he asks the ceiling, 'Well? What do you think of me?'

'I think you ain't the first, is all,' she says. 'I know how Harry goes about things.'

'I blooming well wish I'd known. I feel like such a fool.'

'Don't. Please don't.'

She raises her head from his arm and he risks a look at her. She looks just the same as usual.

'Well, I do,' he says. 'So that's who you'll be marrying. A bloody fool.'

'I can't wait.' She leans her head back against his arm.

Thank God. He squeezes her shoulders. 'Your turn.'

Her hair rubs against his arm as she shakes her head. 'Oh lord.'

'Honest, you can't feel more of an idiot than I do.'

She wiggles away from him and lies down on her side, facing him.

Ted slides down too. Then he pulls the quilt over their heads, so that they're lying in a cave of cloth. The light from the lamp comes warm through the colours of the patchwork.

'Does that help?' he asks her.

'You know,' she says, 'it's lucky they did make you come in.'

'Is it?'

He can't make out her face, but her voice sounds as though she might be smiling. 'Because we never tell outsiders this stuff. But no one can tell me off for it now.'

He puts out a tentative hand and rests it on her naked hip. He can't think of another time in his life when he's felt so lucky to be close to another person. Her fingers find his chest, stroke a circle there. He tries not to wonder if she thinks he's too thin.

She says, 'I'll tell you a story, alright?'

'About what?'

'About the Cutters.'

'I do hate that name,' he says, before he can think it through.

Her hand stops. Perhaps she, too, is thinking of his mum's poor face.

Then, hesitant, 'It ain't as bad as how it sounds. It's just they used to sell their bits and pieces down the New Cut Market.'

He puts his hand up and takes hers. 'Alright. Tell me the story. I do want to hear it.' He really does. It seems to him that this, confessing together in darkness, is the true beginning of their marriage. She takes a breath and lets it out again, and it rushes, soft, over his face.

'Alright. So . . . '

'Once upon a time.'

'Yes. Once upon a time, there was my grandad. Mickey Palmer. Gran – Dolly – was really poor when she met him. She thought she'd struck gold. Did your gran ever tell you what it was like when they were little?'

Ted says, 'No.' Grandmother Lillian never said a single

thing about her personal life in all the time he knew her. She wasn't the sort.

'Well. Alright. Mine used to talk about the workhouse. Dolly and Lily and their mum was always in and out of it, always half starved. So Dolly went off with Mickey Palmer, and she had everything you could think of. Her whole family was against it. He did bank jobs. Safe cracking. But you can just imagine, can't you? What it must have been like. All that money and flash.'

She pauses and he squeezes her fingers to say, *Go on.* It's growing warm and muggy under the quilt, but he's afraid to lift it in case she stops talking.

'Well,' Florrie says, 'he turned out . . . not too nice, after all. They don't like to talk about it. But my mum said once that she'd sit at the top of the stairs when she was little, with baby Maggie, and just wait to hear him come in. She'd know what mood he was in by his voice, or something. And then she'd know if she had to run and hide. Anyway. They did run off, properly, in the end. Dolly ran off and took my mum and Maggie with her. Still with me?'

'Course I am,' he says.

'Ada – you know Ada – she was married to Harry, then. She found Dolly, and she helped her . . . stand up to my granddad. And then he weren't, well, he weren't around to bother them.'

She goes quiet. He feels a rush of the same hungry, ugly interest he feels when the papers report a murder. And that is what she's talking about. Isn't she?

He looks at what little he can see of her, the curve of her neck silhouetted against a crimson square of patchwork, the softer shadow of her curls.

He says, tentatively, 'Do you mean—?'

But Florrie says, 'If you must know, I think my granddad was really not nice at all. To my mum and Maggie. You know. You must know what I mean.'

'Oh. Blimey.' He blinks. He has the feeling he must tread very carefully, that at any moment she might stop talking.

'I think so. Because the blokes got as riled up as the girls. They don't often get between a fellow and his wife, but anyway. Mickey was gone after that. And Ada helped Gran. She brought her into the Cutters. Her and my mum and Maggie.'

She moves nearer, creeps her hands over his ribs.

'So the Cutters were sort of . . . they wasn't what they used to be. They'd been around for a hundred years, but they'd sort of stopped bothering so much. Relying on the men a bit more. Then here's my gran, without a husband. And she was, well, you knew her.'

'I'm beginning to wonder if I did.' She'd been kind to him, when he was little. She'd bought him his car, too. But Ted couldn't help being a bit afraid of her. She was the sort of woman who was bigger than herself, who stretched out her personality and filled the whole house.

'Well. She was hard as nails. She'd take on any bloke. She got all the girls behind her, showed them what they could do. No one could hold a candle to her, course they made her queen. She made them swear to all the rules, all the Cutter rules that had sort of been forgotten. She was ever so strict.' She sounds proud.

He's never heard her talk like this, not a hint of it. He thinks of how she'd said, *while you still think you might love me*, and it's dawning on him that this isn't just a story, or even a confession. It's an opening door, and beyond it is something he's been trying not to look at. He almost stops her, but the pull to know is as strong as the fear of what will follow.

'There weren't a gang like the Cutters in all London. Not women. They got up to a lot more than pinching clothes. They'd break open warehouses and pack up everything in the place. Then the blokes would come with a lorry and help carry it. Clean the place out. And wage snatches: get a job, maybe in a factory, just till the wage packets come in. Mob the office, have it all. Lorry jump-ups. That's where you stop a full lorry—'

'I can imagine.' He's thinking about how often she's used the word 'they'. Wondering if it's the right word at all. 'Look here,' he says, and he can hear the strain in his own voice, 'do I need to know all this?'

'This is who I am though, do you follow? How I grew up. It was like a religion with them. That's why it ain't that easy to get them to let me walk away from it. When the king died, you know, and the Princess Elizabeth was made queen, I looked at her picture and I thought, I know what that's like.'

'It's hardly the same.'

'Ain't it, though? She didn't get a say. Raised to it. No chance at an ordinary life.'

'But you want to be ordinary.' He feels a little desperate now.

She sighs. 'You know I do. But I never have been yet. I never had a choice, Ted.'

It's the only thing to cling to. She didn't have a choice. And he knows what that's like, has just been through it, after all, with Harry.

He tries, very hard, to soften his tone. 'Look here. Let's

leave it, shall we? I mean to say, you needn't tell me any more.'

She rolls onto her stomach, her face on her arms. The quilt billows and settles.

'I'm sorry,' he says. 'I said the wrong thing, did I?' But he still sounds tense; he is tense. There's a fluttering muscle underneath his left eye.

'It don't matter,' she says, very quietly.

'What matters is that you want to change. To be decent. It's enough for me. I promise, it really is.' There. He's managed a bit of tenderness.

But she's drawn all her limbs in, away from him. 'Forget I said anything. Just . . . leave me alone, will you?'

And there's nothing he can do, then, but get up and pull his clothes on. She's a motionless shape under the quilt. He stands for a moment, wondering if he should put his hand to her shoulder. When she does shift he takes a step back towards the bed, but it's just her hands that move. She pulls the top edge of the quilt even tighter over her head, wrapping herself like a shroud.

Ruby is slumped over in the wheelchair, not quite asleep, but not awake either. All her energy is needed just to breathe. The cold is relentless, creeping to her bones.

The chair stops.

'Come on. You'll have to get out now.' Nell takes her arm and pulls her up. 'In here.'

It's the bombsite next to Nell's house, the hole in the fence. Ruby lets herself be guided through it and waits while Nell heaves the chair through after them, grunting and puffing.

'We can't be here,' Ruby says, but her voice is a whisper, and Nell doesn't reply.

Nell must leave the chair because they're walking now, stumbling across rubble, and then they're going down steps, and into darkness. It smells like a shed, of dust and damp and wood.

When a lamp flares with a warm and comforting light, Ruby sees it's an Anderson shelter, one she'd never known was there. It's just as poky and ragged looking as they'd all been, but it's a tiny hidey hole.

'It's probably better to strip off than be in wet things,' Nell is saying, taking off Ruby's dressing gown. Then, 'No, the nightie's not too bad. Just the hem and sleeves. Let's just get you in bed.' Nell helps her into a bunk and covers her with a heavy layer of blankets.

'How long has this place been here?' Ruby asks, stupidly.

Nell's bringing out a gas mask. 'It's under brambles,' she says, as though that explains anything. 'Now hush. This might help against the fog.'

Ruby lets herself be strapped into the gas mask, just as she had let herself be strapped into the oxygen.

The smell of rubber and the amplified sound of Ruby's own breathing, unpleasant during the war, is soothing now. The eye pieces shrink her field of vision and she has to turn her head to watch Nell lighting tealights and putting them under upturned flower pots on the little table to warm the place, lighting a primus stove and a paraffin heater, filling a battered kettle from an earthenware jug.

When it's boiled Nell pours the water into two hot-water bottles and lays one at Ruby's feet and one on her chest. Her feet are juddering with shivers against the warm rubber. She thinks of the policewoman's foot twitching in its pool of blood.

'Stop,' Nell says, putting her hand on Ruby's quivering

legs like a healer laying on hands. And miraculously, her legs do stop and lie still. The warmth is beginning to form a skin around her. Only her insides are cold. The smell of the paraffin, the weight of the blankets, the way the gas mask makes everything seem far away, all of it pushes her down into the bunk. And all the time she's drifting off she can feel Nell's hand, this new, surprising Nell, patting her shins.

Florrie has pulled herself together. She takes the loneliness that's trying to frost over her insides and crushes it as hard as she can. She's no more alone than she's always been; she shouldn't have hoped he'd understand. If he did, he'd be a different bloke. She doesn't half wish she'd kept her mouth shut, though.

She comes out of the bedroom, fully dressed, to find Ted in the kitchen, peering into the thermos flask. He's in his shirt and braces but has left off his collar and tie. He looks up when she comes in, and she can see by the way he looks at her that he's not sure, now, how to talk to her at all.

'There's not a lot of milk left,' is all he says. He shakes the flask.

'Never mind. Ain't you cold without your jacket?'

He gives her an embarrassed smile and says, 'I left the rest of my things in the bedroom.'

She says, 'Let me make the tea then, and you get yourself dressed.'

He goes past her quickly, and she busies herself, making up the powdered egg and slicing rolls, determined to be as ordinary as she can. The awkwardness stays, though, even when they're seated in the armchairs with their supper and a cup of tea. The only sounds are their chewing and the clink of cup on saucer. Ted keeps rubbing at his face. He's sitting with his legs at a funny angle, knees together and bent to the side, a bit like a lady. Then he shifts, spreads his knees, closes them. She makes herself smile at him, but it's a stiff one, and the one Ted returns her is worried, a little sheepish.

They're in what's supposed to be their marital home and it just shouldn't be like this.

'Listen.' Her voice is brisk, a bit like Nell's. 'I've been thinking. What we need to do is get you out of Harry's debt.'

He puts his teacup down and straightens up. 'Let's, if you've got thirty odd quid lying about.' He laughs, and then says, 'I'm messing about. I wouldn't take your money.'

'No, but honest, I've got a load of things he might take. That fur wrap my mum got, for one. And some other stuff, up in my room.' It's not like Ruby will be here to wear any of it now.

He shakes his head. 'I couldn't.'

'It ain't just for you. I'll get him a bundle of stuff, and we'll tell him we want you out of it. And we'll talk to Maggie about your mum.' She doesn't say, *Not that any of them listen to me.* And anyway, that's not quite right. It's more that she never speaks up.

He says, slowly, 'He'll still be in on my blocks, though, won't he? He's not going to just wave me off and say no hard feelings.'

'Can't you do something else for work?'

He looks miserable. 'Give it to him, you mean? I built it up.'

'Wouldn't it be worth it, to get ourselves out?'

'I suppose so,' he says, but he looks sadder than ever.

'Would it get us out? Do you think it would? What about you?'

'Let's just see what we can do,' she says. 'Got to try.'

They look at each other and she can see her own rising hopelessness in his face, she feels how very young they both are. And Maggie and Harry are scary enough even when you're doing what they ask.

Ted says, 'He did ask me to come to the spieler tonight, you know.'

'You never said! Let's go now.'

'I don't want you in there. It's not a nice place.'

But she's already standing, putting down her teacup on the little table. 'Come on. We can talk it over on the way.'

Ted hesitates. 'Do you really think we need go now? The weather's worse than ever.'

She feels restless, anxious to go before she loses her last screwed up bit of nerve. 'It's past eleven already. Let's just go. The last thing we want is him browned off with you.'

Ted rubs at his brow with a bunched fist. He takes a deep breath. 'Right. Alright.'

Florrie picks up her coat from its peg. It's hardly damp at all, now.

Ted says, 'You look like my girl again. Not in my hat and coat this time,' and they both laugh, nervously.

Stepping out of the front door and into the fog is like plunging into a swimming pool, the slap of the cold, the sting in her eyes. It's so dark.

'I don't dare drive,' he says. 'Will you be alright walking?'

She clutches his arm. 'I'm alright if you know the way.'

The streets are quiet. Not silent, London is never silent, but all the sounds are far off, muffled. A train passes by, somewhere distantly above and to the right of them, and it seems like a stage play, as though someone's pouring gravel down a pipe and only pretending to be a train.

Florrie begins to feel detached, the way she does when she's out with Maggie. Perhaps Harry will let Ted go easily, and perhaps he won't. And Maggie might hold onto Florrie tighter than ever, now Ruby's gone. Perhaps Nell will be furious with Florrie for not standing up for her. But even though she's walking towards it all, she's not afraid. She's not anything. Everything but herself and Ted, the dark and their own footsteps, seems a million miles off. Whatever kind of scene is waiting to crash down upon their heads is clouded and distanced by the depth of the fog.

After a bit he says, 'Do you know what Aunt Dolly said when she gave me the car?'

Florrie has to lift her chin up and out of her collar to speak, she's hunched so tightly against the cold. 'I bet she said, "Now you're a chauffeur, young man," or something.'

'She said I could keep the car. On condition I left you alone.'

She draws in a gasp and has to cough into the bend of her arm. He stops walking and waits while she regains her breath.

When she can speak she says, 'But that was before . . . anything. I never had a clue you thought about me.'

'Aunt Dolly knew more than you did, then.'

'She was sharp as anything,' she says, to cover up her embarrassment. He puts his arms around her, the warmth of him and the cold of the fog.

She whispers, up towards his ear, 'Don't you listen to my gran. You'd bloody well better not leave me alone.'

'Not for a minute,' he says, and pulls her closer. 'I'll not lose you now.'

The Fifth Day of the Fog:
Monday, 8 December 1952

Far above the fogbound city, the anticyclone at last begins to move, although it will take hours for anyone on the ground to notice. The day will begin as grey and choked as the previous three, and will clear by inches. For thousands of people it will clear too late, and for many others, the lifting of the fog only marks the beginning of long and lingering illness. Nonetheless, as Sunday ticks into Monday, the winds of change are finally beginning to blow over London.

Ruby wakes in a lamp-lit place, her mouth dry and tasting of sour rubber. She puts her hands up to rub at her eyes and they meet the cold glass of the gas mask's eyepieces. Sitting up, her head smacks into the bunk above. The jarring pain goes through the back of her head and down her spine, her surprised cry echoes inside the mask. She falls back onto the thin pillows.

Then there are gentle hands helping her sit up, the push and release of the mask's buckles and Nell is lifting the blasted thing off her face. It pulls on her skin as it's peeled away. The damp air floods her chest and sets her off coughing.

'What time is it?' Ruby asks, when she can speak.

'Just after midnight.' Nell touches Ruby's brow with cold fingers. 'I was hoping you'd sleep through.'

'Glad I never. Help me up. Got to get back over to yours.'

'I'm making soup,' Nell says, as if Ruby hasn't spoken.

'Did you hear me?'

'For the love of God, Ruby, of course I heard you. But I don't know how you imagine you're going anywhere. You can barely sit up.'

This is true. She's not sure she can manage a spoon, let alone anything she might have to do later. She can smell the soup warming now, homelike and comforting.

'Nellie,' she says, 'the girls will be at yours for that meeting.'

'Not still, surely!' Nell turns, wooden spoon in her hand and eyes wide. 'I'm sure I heard someone knocking at my front door while you were asleep. It must have been the police, don't you think? And they could come back at any moment. You mustn't think of it.'

Ruby can't tell Nellie that she needs to get over there and sort out the matter of the grass. She can already guess what sort of tight-mouthed reaction her cousin would have over that. Or would she? It will clear Nell's name, after all. She can't think straight. There's an exhausting urgency running through her limbs. She says, 'Look, Nellie, if I can just get over there they'll help me. You don't want to be mixed up in this. They'll sort me out. Maggie. And the rest. You've done enough.'

'And just suppose there are things I want sorted out?'

'Even more reason, ain't it?'

'Eat this. And then perhaps we'll discuss it.' Nell puts an enamel bowl of soup into Ruby's hands.

'I'm late already. It's a midnight meeting.'

'Just eat it,' Nell's voice is bright and sharp as coloured glass.

It's tinned oxtail soup. Ruby leaves the spoon on the bedspread, lifts the bowl in both hands and tastes it with the tip of her tongue. It's too hot, but so good that it takes an effort not to bolt it and scald her throat.

Nell sits at the little table. The shelter being so small, she's almost as close as if she were sitting beside Ruby on the bunk. She spoons her soup neatly, front to back, like she's at a dinner party, the lantern light making her faded hair bright again. She's humming as she eats, very quietly.

Ruby puts the bowl down and touches the comforting curve of the pistol, weighing down the blankets in her lap.

Ted can see the shape of the pawn shop's sign hanging over the door, the faint glow from the windows.

Florrie's seen it too. She says, 'You'd better go in without me.'

'I'm hardly going to leave you outside.'

Although he doesn't like the idea of her coming in. The place is full of blokes, and none of them nice people.

She says, 'No, listen here. You go to the spieler, and I'll go back to your mum's. Get a bag of stuff ready to give Harry. I can go by myself from here.'

He starts to protest, but she says, 'Honest, Ted, go now. Harry will be wondering where you've got to. And you ask if he'll see me. He don't like things sprung on him, unexpected. Go and find out what he wants off you, and then come and get me if he says so. I'll get some things together, look in on Auntie Nell.'

'She'll be in bed. It's past midnight.'

'Well, I won't bother her if she is. I'll just creep in and get some things. You get Harry's say so. I'll be waiting for you. It's the right way round.'

He wants to see his mum. Enough, almost, to wake her up. And he still doesn't like the sure way Florrie's speaking, as if she knows all about how Harry likes things done.

'Shan't I walk you?' he asks, a little pitifully.

She steps in front of him and winds her arms about his neck.

'No time. Go on, now. I know you want to, that's enough for me. I know you're a gent. I'll say I do,' she says, and he has to be satisfied with that.

Florrie feels strangely dreamlike, stepping from the fog into Nell's hall, with its familiar tiles and shabby carpet runner, her own slippers by the doormat. She climbs the stairs quickly, two at a time, trying not to make a creak in case Nell's asleep, wondering what she'll say if Nell's awake.

But Nell's room is empty, dark and silent.

This is very bad. She goes to her own room, biting her lip, trying not to panic. Alright. She'll get the stuff for Harry, and then she'll think what can be done to find Aunt Nell.

And now all the clothes she collected for Ruby come out of the wardrobe and are rolled back up, as tight and neat as they were when they came from the shop, tucked into her knickers. She fits them into a bag, pressing them down, pushing as she forces her own feelings not to rise. The worry over Nell, grief over Ruby, and with each new thing she takes from the wardrobe, a whiff of humiliation,

as if the world might be laughing at her for having collected these things at all, for having let herself hope she
might have her mum back. Push with both hands. Give it
all to Harry. And if she can't help her mum or Nell, she can
help Ted, and maybe, hopefully – dear God, please – herself
along with him.

She is just about to change her own clothes when she
hears the front door. Ted back, already. She picks up the bag
and hurries to the stairs so fast, so sure it is Ted, that when
it isn't she stops halfway down and just stares.

The hall is full of women. Maggie is shrugging off the
fox fur, the red-gold of it rippling in the overhead light.
Ada's unwinding Dolly's scarf from about her throat,
Hazel's taking off her neat little hat. Val's letting Cissy help
her off with her coat, her hands flying back to her pregnant
stomach as soon as they're free from the sleeves, as though
it will fall if she doesn't hold it up.

'Hello,' Florrie says, and they all look up.

Maggie grins and calls over the heads of the other
women, 'Look at the state of you. You look like you've been
run over by a cart.'

But Florrie's looking at Ada and Hazel, at the way their
faces flicker at the sight of her and then break into careful
smiles.

'Why, Florrie, dear,' Ada says. 'You came.'

Yes, she thinks, *and you and Val told me not to.*

'How did you get in?' Florrie asks.

Maggie laughs. 'Borrowed Nellie's keys, didn't I? She's
run off and left them lying about.'

Val doesn't seem surprised to see Florrie. Or does she?
Her smile is a stiff one. Cissy, the little bitch, only laughs as
though it's a great joke to see Florrie so dishevelled.

She's suddenly very tired, and very cold. Colder than she'd felt outside.

Maggie has her hands on her hips. She's all done up in indigo velvet. The ink of her tattoos is almost the same shade; she might have done it on purpose. 'Come on, can't you? It's past midnight already.'

'And whose fault is that?' Ada mutters, stripping off her gloves. She holds the index finger of each between her teeth to do it.

'Keep your hair on,' Hazel says. She hangs her coat on the post at the bottom of the banister.

Florrie comes down the stairs. She's walking very quietly, as though they might not already have seen her. She feels queer. Dizzy. Very slightly sick. The tips of her fingers are tingling.

In the kitchen, Maggie is back in Dolly's chair.

'Going somewhere, Florence?'

'What?' Florrie looks down at the bag, still in her hand. 'No.'

'Come over here, then. I want you by me.'

Draped over the back of the chair opposite, where Florrie usually sits, is the beautiful fur wrap, the last present her mum gave her. Maggie grabs her wrist and pulls her arm so that Florrie has to bend close.

She whispers, very fast and low, 'I said I want you next to me. You stick to me like glue.' She gives a wide, slightly frightening smile, and pats the seat of the stool next to her.

'I just want the fur,' Florrie says, and Maggie says, 'Quick, then.'

But Ada's picking it up, turning it over in her hands. She says, 'Quality,' and holds it out across the table, a flopping golden brown spill.

It's so lovely, so obviously expensive and new, that Flor-rie knows she shouldn't put it on, but she's doing it anyway, her grubby shoulders raising up with the pleasure of it. It smells of the shops, of light, of something animal. It falls to the middle of her back, encases her upper arms.

Hazel, Ada and Val have taken the other chairs, leaving Cissy to stand.

Florrie sits on the stool. 'Auntie Maggie.' The fur bushes against her jaw as she speaks.

'Not now,' Maggie says, also keeping her voice very low. 'Hush for now.' Then, much louder, 'Ain't this nice, all of us getting together.' She's using her dangerously cheerful voice.

'And don't you look a picture,' Florrie says. If Maggie wants to pretend everything is ordinary, perhaps it's safer to join in.

'Shame I can't say the same for you.' Maggie plucks at the damp cuff of Florrie's sleeve, where it protrudes from the beautiful fur. 'Didn't I say? You look like you've been knocked over by a cart. I hope you've got on clean knickers.'

'What?' Florrie's watching Ada and Hazel across the table. Ada is sitting very straight, her head tilted sideways to listen to Hazel, who is murmuring something that makes Ada shake her head. Ada has her big hands clasped, the light glittering off her rings and the bracelet on her right wrist.

'Make sure you've got clean knickers, in case you get run over by a cart. That's what Mum always said,' Maggie says.

The women here are the big bananas of the gang, what's left of them. Maggie, who's always been the muscle. Ada and Hazel, who run the club. Val, who's taking over the fencing of the stuff. And, inexplicably, Cissy.

Maggie turns around, to where Cissy leans against the sideboard behind them. 'What's there to drink? Cissy, find us the booze.'

Florrie watches as Cissy tries to ask Val, who doesn't even meet her eye, but just shakes her head like a horse clearing away flies.

Ada says something, and Hazel laughs. Then she sees Cissy watching, and gives the girl a look that makes Cissy turn around quickly.

Maggie looks exasperated and amused as the girl comes back. 'They thought you was after it yourself, you ninny. You should've said it was for me and Florrie.'

Cissy tosses her head as though she doesn't care, but she can't stop a little sigh escaping her nose.

'Alright,' Maggie calls. 'Who's got the gin?'

Hazel fishes a half bottle of gin from her handbag and holds it up.

'Well, alright then,' Maggie says. 'Cissy, get the glasses.'

'And then get out,' Hazel says. She jerks her thumb. 'Old girls only.'

Cissy says, 'I've been in for nearly a year!'

'So you say. And a year's nothing. Go on, hop it. Sling your hook.'

'Maggie,' Cissy says, 'tell them!'

'Well now,' Maggie raises her chin and looks dead into Hazel's eyes. 'Look who's giving herself airs.'

'You keep a pet if you like,' Hazel says. 'But it's real Cutters only tonight. You'll have to make it wait outside.'

No one speaks. Florrie can hear the cheerful, oblivious tick of Nell's cat clock, swinging its tail.

Hazel says, 'Someone's been grassing, and for all we know it's her.'

'I never would!' Cissy looks as though she might cry. 'Cheek!'

'Where's the other girls?' Florrie asks. The question has been sitting behind her teeth from the moment she came down the stairs.

'Well now,' Ada says, 'we thought we'd go round and tell them not to bother.'

Maggie gives one of her bright and terrible smiles. 'And you didn't breathe a word to me about that, did you?'

'Couldn't find you, could we?'

'And here was me, at home, all the time,' Maggie says.

'Oh, well, hard enough getting anywhere in this weather,' Ada says, as if they're making chitchat. 'Why don't you and Cissy go off to your room, Florrie? Or nip out to the spieler for a bit?'

'Don't you fucking move, either of you.' Maggie is still smiling.

Cissy has her hand to her brow like a girl in the pictures. 'No, no, I'm sure I won't stay.'

'Shut up, Cissy,' Maggie says.

Florrie opens her mouth, though she's not sure what she means to say. Half of her wants to get as far away from whatever this is as fast as she can, and the other half is desperate to know what's going on, to hear about her mum. But Ted will be turning up any minute—

'Don't you breathe a fucking word either, Florence,' Maggie says, so forcefully that Florrie's shoulders curl under the fur, like an animal protecting its underside. She finds herself staring at a corner of the floor, at what looks like drops of dried blood. On Nell's floor, that she always keeps scrubbed.

'Oh, for the love of God,' Val says. 'Let's not have a row

before we start.' She looks hard at Hazel, and then at Ada.

Hazel begins, 'But—' but Ada says, 'Fine. If that's the way you want it.'

Under the table, Florrie feels Maggie's hand squeeze her leg, and has to stop herself giving a jump. She can't be sure, but she thinks her aunt murmurs, 'Stick to me like glue, now,' under her breath.

'Right then.' Nell puts down her soup spoon. She's been steeling her nerve as she eats. She's going to be honest about everything, and she's going to make Ruby help her.

But then she looks over and gets a little shock: Ruby's gone a pasty white, her face shiny with sweat. She's drooping over the soup bowl, her hands clenched on the blankets. She raises her eyes, but not her head, and gives Nell a sort of smile.

Irrationally, unfairly, Nell feels annoyed. How dare Ruby be too ill to help? How dare she?

She goes to the bunk and leans to take the bowl from Ruby's lap. It's still half full. Then, with a quick, jerky swipe, she snatches up the pistol, too.

Ruby's thin hand closes on her wrist. 'Nellie,' she wheezes, her voice full of fluid.

'Let me go,' Nell says. 'I need to talk to you. Wake up.'

'Give me that back.' But Ruby's fingers have slid from Nell's wrist, her hand dropping back to the blankets like a dead thing.

Nell goes back to her stool, and puts the pistol on the table, where both of them can see it. 'There we are. Now. I need you to help me.'

Ruby closes her eyes. 'Nellie, this ain't the time. I got things to do.'

'You're to tell Harry to leave Ted alone.'

'You don't know he wants to be left alone.' Ruby's voice is so low as to be barely audible.

'I don't care!' Nell's own voice is shrill, and seems to vibrate off the corrugated walls. 'You're to tell Harry.'

'Alright,' Ruby whispers. 'If you like.'

'And,' Nell says, 'you're to tell Maggie I didn't grass. That I never would. That I helped you.'

'I was always going to. That all? Give me back the shooter.'

'No, it's not all. I need,' she swallows, hard, 'I need you to ask Harry to leave me alone. As well as Ted.'

Ruby opens one eye a crack. 'Why wouldn't he?'

Nell looks at her with as much pride as she can gather from the shreds of what's left. 'I may have made a mistake. I was, well. I was lonely, I suppose. But now I want him to leave me alone.'

'Bloody hell, Nellie, you're a dark horse.' Ruby laughs, coughs, puts her hands to her mouth and speaks through her fingers. 'You'd better hope Maggie—'

'You're not to breathe a word to her. You owe me.'

'Don't I know it.' Ruby rubs her fingers across her lips. 'But bloody hell. You and Maggie and Ada. There are other blokes in London, you know.'

'I've tried to tell him. He won't listen. He's—' Nell tries to say, *He's frightening me,* but she can't do it. She says, 'Give me your word you'll talk to him,' instead. To hide her embarrassment – no, not embarrassment, but thick and sickening shame – she concentrates on the waxy, stretched texture of the skin on Ruby's face, the hints of bones in her thin neck. The way her chest rises and falls unevenly.

Nell thinks, although she's known it already, must have

known it, *You're dying. Right in front of me.*

Ruby says, 'Look, Nell, I don't know how much I can help you with that one.'

'You can! I know you can. He'll listen to you.' She wants to say, *And you might not have much time to do it in,* but she just – just – manages to stop herself.

'I don't know that he will.'

'But you'll try.'

'Yes. I'll try. Or may I rot from the head down.'

Nell says, 'You look as though you might be doing that already,' and then wishes she hadn't.

Ruby is struggling to sit up. 'Ain't you a charmer? Give me that thing back before you hurt yourself. And help me up. Don't fucking argue with me now. I ain't staying in this hole in the ground—' she coughs, chest heaving.

'Alright,' Nell says. 'Well, if we must. Alright.' She stands up. 'I'm ready. Come along.'

'You don't come,' Ruby chokes out.

'No, indeed,' Nell says. 'No, I'll just wait here, while everyone else in the world has some sort of party in my own house. I should just think I am coming. Have you lost your mind, as well as your breath?' She holds out her hand.

Ruby takes it and shifts to the edge of the bunk, bending awkwardly so as not to hit her head. Nell's annoyance is gone, driven off by the feeling of Ruby's hand in hers, so damp it threatens to slide from her grip.

'I don't know who you think I am, asking me to stay here,' Nell says, not really listening to herself.

Ruby is swaying on her feet, her breath like marbles rattling in her chest.

Nell strips off the red coat and holds it out. The cold rushes to lick at her, right through her clothes. 'Let's get this on you. I won't have you shaming me in that dressing gown.'

Ruby grins at her. Her teeth are streaked with blood.

But once the coat is on she sinks to the edge of the bunk and sits hunched over, her head hanging on her neck and her hands in her lap. 'I'm alright. Just give me a minute. And the gun.'

Nell puts it in her lap and watches the thin fingers close over it.

She stands, wondering what she will do if Ruby dies here, feeling the darkness and fog outside bearing down on top of them. She thinks again of submarines, the depth and pressure of the sea.

Florrie is remembering Ted saying, *You're just the same as the rest of your family.* It hurt her at the time, but now it makes her feel better. Palmers don't get shaken up over nothing. She picks up her gin and the action of drinking, the steady hand to mouth, is calming.

'Right,' Maggie's saying, 'let's get on with whatever this is. Anyone bring a bible?'

Everyone shifts and shakes their heads.

'Swear it anyway,' Maggie says. 'Some of you could do with being reminded.'

'Do we need to go through all this?' Hazel asks, but the women have already begun chanting, 'Let loyalty never leave me. Tie it around my neck,' and even Hazel joins in the last part: 'Or may I rot from the head down.' Cissy's voice lags behind, stumbling over it.

Florrie has a sudden memory of being very young, women's voices in unison. Of not knowing the words, opening and closing her mouth silently, the way she did during church hymns. And of Dolly next to her, holding her hand.

'Well, then,' Ada says, as soon as the oath is finished. 'I hope you'll all excuse me speaking up. I know it ain't my place. But then, whose is it, just now?'

Without looking, Florrie feels Maggie grow very still beside her.

'And I think it's time we know what we're about a bit more,' Ada says. 'Decide what's what.'

'And who are you to say?' Maggie says.

'Steady,' Hazel says.

'I'm your elder, just for a start,' Ada says. 'Now, like I say.' She takes a deep breath. 'Well. It was a shock for all of us, losing Dolly.'

'God rest her soul,' Val murmurs.

'We've all been cut up over it. But we have to think how to go on without her. There's too many people saying the Cutters are finished. We've got to come back fighting.'

'You've pushed my sister aside very quick,' Maggie says.

Hazel puts a hand on Ada's arm, to stop her. 'If we could have her, we would. You know that.'

A chorus of agreement.

'And,' Maggie says, 'if you knew what she wants us to do?'

'Well, how can we?' Ada says.

'Saw her yesterday, didn't I?'

'What?' Florrie whips around to look at her aunt.

'That's right,' Maggie says, with the air of someone laying down an ace. 'She's in hospital. A bit of a cough. Now, now,' she says, as Florrie draws a sharp breath. 'She says she's playing it up, if you must know, to get out of going straight to the nick. Kidding them along.'

'Ain't that just like Ruby,' Val says.

'I want to see her.' Florrie doesn't care that she sounds like a kid. Her mum's in hospital. And Maggie went without her.

'Well now, it's not quite as simple as that. They've got a copper at the door. But we'll think of something,' Maggie says. 'Tomorrow. Let's get this little bit of business done now.'

Florrie tries to lean back but she's on a stool and only sways. She puts her elbows on the table instead. The rest of the women are all talking at once. She's not sure whether it's good news or bad. It's only that she's been imagining Ruby in prison, all this time.

When she comes back to herself, Maggie is saying, 'I'll look after things. Just till Ruby comes home.'

Ada says, 'Now, hang on. Why should you look after the crown? Why not my Hazel?'

Hazel says, 'For God's sake, Gran. Haven't I said fifty times, I don't want it?'

'We'll need a vote,' Val puts in.

'Leave me out of it.' Hazel raises her voice. 'I'm happy running the club. I've got enough on my plate. I don't know why we need a queen at all, if it's going to make trouble like this.'

Ada says, 'Oh, you young ones. You don't know how it is. We have to have a queen. Who's going to deal with the bent coppers and sort out quarrels? Who's going to hold the pot? It's not having a queen that makes the trouble.'

'That's another thing,' Val says. 'We ain't seen hide nor hair of that pot. We all chip in. It's all of our dough.'

'I ain't got it,' Maggie says. 'My mum went and hid it.'

'That's true,' Florrie says, wondering if it is. For all she knows, Maggie's had it all along.

'We had to get that solicitor out of our own bloody pockets,' Val says. 'I don't mind it for Ruby, but for that Nell!'

'Don't be daft, Nell didn't get a solicitor. And I chipped in, didn't I?' Maggie says. 'You all know this is because Ada don't want to give out a share of the nightclub, don't you?'

'Nerve!' Ada says. 'Ruby can have your mum's share of the club, what little there is of it. You can have a taste, if your sister says. But you ain't having a hand in the running of it. Over my dead body.'

'Your dead body,' Maggie says, 'sounds good to me. Well, if it ain't that, it's because you don't like to see Harry and me together.'

Ada just waves a hand. 'Good luck to you with that one. He never does stay long. Now. Enough. We're having a vote.'

Maggie leans back as if she's relaxed, and gives Ada the smile that bares most of her teeth. She says, 'Who died and made you queen?'

'That ain't funny,' Ada says.

'Too fucking right it ain't funny. Look at you. You're past it.'

'We're having a vote,' Ada says. 'Any of us could hold the crown, just for a bit.'

Maggie doesn't shift her gaze from Ada. 'This is why you kept the others out, is it? You call this a fair vote? You know full well they'd never have you. No chance.'

The room falls silent. Even through her thoughts of Ruby, Florrie feels herself grow still. Someone mutters, 'It's you got no chance,' so quietly that Florrie can't tell if Maggie hears it, nor who's spoken.

Ada says, 'God's honest truth? Too right we kept them

out. We tried to keep Florrie out, and all.'

'Is that right?' Maggie's smile pulls even wider.

'We wanted to make you see sense without having a scene, didn't we?' Ada says. 'We've all had it up to here with you—'

It's so fast that even Florrie, who's half expecting something, cries out in surprise. One moment Maggie's leaning back in Dolly's chair and the next her glass is flying in a glittering arc across the table, turning in the air, droplets of gin trailing behind.

Ada's head whips to the side, her glasses clattering onto the lino.

Florrie puts her hand to her heart. A little late, Cissy screams. Hazel jumps to her feet.

'There now.' Maggie's on her feet too, both hands on the table. 'That's what you get.'

Ada has her hand to her cheek like a girl checking the heat of a blush.

'Here, Gran.' Hazel fetches Ada's glasses from under the table. She puts a shaking hand on Ada's shoulder, her face blazing as furiously red as her gran's cheek.

Maggie says, 'Who wants a taste?'

'I'm alright.' Ada's eye is streaming with tears.

'My mum made Ruby queen,' Maggie says. 'She said it before she died. And Ruby wants me looking after things. So you can all lump it.'

'Not if we won't have you. That ain't how it works,' Val says. Her face, in contrast to Ada's and Hazel's, has turned a sick sort of yellow.

'It's how it is,' Maggie replies, cool as anything. She puts her hand on Florrie's shoulder, just like Hazel has her hand on Ada's.

Ada looks at Maggie, one eye hard and cold and the other red and watering.

'I did give you a chance to make this easy,' she says.

Unlike the last time Ted was there, the spieler's half empty. Harry has raised a finger to Ted to say, *Wait*, and is talking to a trio of old blokes in suits over by the wireless, which is booming out the sort of big band swing that Dolly used to like.

Ted's been given a glass of real whisky, which he's not sure he likes much, and a cigar, which he doesn't like at all, and now he's standing against the wall with Don and that Dennis, the bloke from the caff with the red face.

'Ted's walking out with Florrie Palmer,' Don tells him.

'Is that right?' Dennis says.

'Got engaged, didn't you?' Don gives Ted a look he can't quite read.

Ted jerks his head in a nod that probably makes him look stupid and sets the whisky in his glass sloshing. He thinks of Florrie, who must be wondering how long he's going to be. He wonders if she's making up with Nell right this minute, and how his mum might be feeling now.

'Welcome to the family.' Dennis makes Ted shake his warm, clammy hand. 'My missus was a Palmer. Valerie. Frannie's daughter.'

Ted doesn't know enough of the girls' names to comment on that so he says, 'Rightyho,' and then wonders if that's a soft choice of word.

Now Dennis is gesturing around the room. 'Them two, playing cards, they're Goddens. Married to Delia and Wendy. But that one talking to Harry, him with the blue hat, he's my father-in-law. Married to Frannie, who just got nicked. He's your Florrie's great uncle. Ain't he?'

Ted shrugs.

Dennis says, 'Must be. Yeah. Mickey Palmer's brother. Course, you never met Mickey.'

Ted looks quickly at Mickey Palmer's brother, and then away again, quickly. The man is old, shrunken. But Ted feels an uncomfortable tightness across his shoulders, as though his jacket is suddenly too small. He thinks of Florrie saying, *The blokes got as riled up as the girls, and Mickey was gone after that.*

Don says, 'Course he never,' in a voice Ted thinks might be meant to shut Dennis up.

But Dennis says, 'Now then. Frannie's my mother-in-law, for my sins. And she's Florrie's great aunt, and my Val's her . . . what is it, second cousin once removed, or something. What does that make me and you, Ted?'

Ted shrugs. *It makes us nothing much*, is what he wants to say. But of course he doesn't. He doesn't tell Dennis that he's already Florrie's second cousin, either. But it gives him a queer feeling. Half the blokes in here are already his family, in one way or another. And half the Cutters. He's never really thought about it before.

Dennis seems to be enjoying himself. He leans in and puts a hand on Ted's shoulder. 'More to the point, Frannie is Harry's ex-sister-in-law. What does that make you to Harry? Eh?'

'It makes him Ted's boss,' Don says. 'Do shut up.'

Dennis finally takes his hand from Ted's shoulder. He says, 'Now, that's a good thing. There's two types of blokes get married to Cutter girls. There's the ones who never say boo to their wives, live off the girl's money. Useless bastards.'

'Jesus, Dennis, keep your voice down,' Don says.

Dennis shrugs. 'They know who they are. But you, Ted, I heard you're a man on the up. You're like me. And let me tell you, what you want to do is put your foot down early. Show her who's boss.'

Ted gives him a strained smile and takes a swallow of the whisky, which isn't so bad now he's getting used to it.

He wishes he could show Dennis who's boss. The man is unbearable. To change the subject he turns to Don and asks, 'Did you drive here?' and Don, thankfully, says, 'Thought I was going to smash her up. Bloody lucky I got here in one piece.'

And Don's off now, talking on and on about his car. Ted can tell that Don doesn't know half as much about cars as he, Ted, does, and everything Ted knows he's had to teach himself. But he also knows that Don's car is ten times nicer than his own, and it weighs him down and stops him joining in. He drinks the whisky instead.

There was a time, when he was five or six, when Teddy decided to run away from home. He'd been spanked, or something. He'd packed his lead soldiers and his pyjamas into a bag and gone into the kitchen for provisions. His mum was at the stove, and even though he was in disgrace, she'd given him the crust of the bread with a bit of jam, with no idea that he'd be taking it away with him and never coming back. He'd looked at her and thought how she'd miss him, and been glad.

But Edward had been reading the paper, and when he'd looked up and said, 'Be back in for tea if you don't want another wallop,' Ted had a vertiginous feeling, like looking over a cliff edge. Edward hadn't guessed he was running away. No one would stop him. He was going to let Ted go. Of course, he'd only got to the end of the road and sat on the kerb, and then he'd gone home and Nell had given him a slap across the head for making her worry and for being late in to tea.

He has that same feeling now, that he's going to have to hold himself back from the cliff edge, that no one will do it for him. That these people will try to push him over.

He looks about at the whole poisonous lot of them. Harry, who's nothing but a thug. Dennis, who thinks he's going to work in Ted's yard. Mickey Palmer's brother, who might be a murderer. Even if Ted has to give up the yard, he's not going to end up like Don or Dennis, or worse, like Davey Fisher. He could ask Mr Griffith for a job, maybe, learn how to run a shop.

Finally Harry comes and puts an arm around Ted's shoulder. 'You follow me. I want you to meet some old pals.'

And although Ted doesn't especially want to hear what Harry has to say, has only come to try to disentangle himself from the man, there's something satisfying about the looks on Dennis and Don's faces as they're left standing by the wall.

'Family of yours, you might say,' Harry says, as they squeeze past the card table.

The three dapper old fellows look Ted over as though they're planning to buy him, their eyes bright and interested.

'Here he is, then.' Harry picks up a bottle and splashes more whisky into Ted's cup.

'So you're the bloke put a ring on Florrie Palmer's finger, are you?' Mickey Palmer's brother says. He doesn't offer his hand or give his name.

Another says, 'Don't seem the type, does he? No offence meant, son.'

'We'll look after him.' Harry's arm gives Ted's shoulder a shake.

'He might need it, and all.' The bloke laughs, showing yellow-brown stumps of teeth. 'Looks flat as a pancake.'

'He'll learn,' Harry says.

'I always say, best way to learn is on the job,' says the last of the three, a skeletal old bloke in an expensive-looking suit.

Ted knows they're taking the mick, but his mouth twitches into an idiotic smile.

Harry says, 'Ted knows he'd better do right by her, don't you Ted?'

Ted lowers his voice and says, 'She wanted me to ask if you'd let her come. Have a word with you,' although he'd rather not in front of these old men. But he wants to get out of here.

'Did she, now?'

'She's waiting at my mum's. I could go and get her.'

The old blokes are watching, too closely for Ted's liking.

Harry says, 'Hold your horses. I want you to talk to these fellows. Got some good ideas for your yard.' He tightens the arm around Ted's shoulders. 'Business partners, now.'

'I don't know.'

'No?'

Ted lowers his voice even further. 'I don't . . . I might not want to do the blocks thing anymore. You . . . maybe you should have it. I might get a different rig.'

'Oh, well, ain't that generous? That's very kind. And I want you to be happy,' Harry says, in his usual voice. He gives Ted another shake. 'You find something else that takes your fancy and I'll come in with you. Choose whatever you like. We're going to do very well together, you and me.'

Florrie is on her feet only because the rest of them are. Ada, Hazel and Val are moving towards Maggie. But Florrie is beside her aunt so they're coming towards her, too. Only Cissy, on Maggie's other side, is hanging back.

'Oh, now.' Maggie takes a step back. She's almost against the sideboard now. 'My mum would never want this.'

Hazel pushes a chair out of her way. 'Oh, and she'd want you chucking glasses at old ladies, would she?'

Suddenly every one of them seems to be holding something shining. Ada has a slim silver knife, and Val, although she still has one arm under her belly, is holding a much larger one, with a serrated blade. Hazel has a piece of lead pipe, just like Maggie's preserver.

'Florrie,' Maggie says, and Florrie feels dread drop into her belly at the sound of her own name.

Maggie pulls her closer so that they're standing shoulder to shoulder, the solid wooden bulk of the sideboard and the big iron stove at their backs.

'And you, Cissy. Come here,' Maggie says.

Cissy's face is white to the lips.

'I said come here, you stupid little bitch.'

Cissy takes the two steps to Maggie's side. She looks ready to vomit.

The table fills most of the kitchen and they're coming around the sides of it. Hazel pushes it back against the dresser, opening up the space, and now they're stepping in front. It's like a dream, the girls turned hateful and strange and coming towards them with knives. Florrie turns from face to face, looking for anyone who might look just a little bit soft or reasonable. But Hazel, with whom she's always wanted to be friends, is flushed and furious. Val, who used to babysit for Florrie, who would dress her up like a doll and curl her hair, is very close now, her expression that of a woman who has to do something unpleasant but which can't be helped. And Ada looks positively gleeful. Ada, who brought Dolly into the gang, who had cried at Dolly's funeral and not even tried to hide it.

There's a glint in the corner of Florrie's eye and she knows, without even looking, that Maggie's pulled out her own knife.

This isn't Florrie's fight. Surely it isn't. But her knuckles tighten on her gin glass.

'You're with me,' Maggie hisses to her. And then, before Florrie can reply, she calls out, 'Three on three.'

'Oh hell,' Cissy whimpers.

'Let Florrie speak for herself,' Val says.

'She's my fucking niece!' Maggie waves the knife through the air, a zigzagging streak. 'And you think Ruby's going to stand for this? You've got another think coming. You're all fucking dead. All of you. Cissy, you fucking coward, you stick next to me.'

Ada says, 'Just simmer down, Maggie, and this will all stop. Nice and easy.'

'You come here with shivs,' Maggie says. 'I call that very nice. Friendly.'

Hazel says, 'Course we brought something. We know what you're like. And here you go and throw glasses at old ladies.'

Ada holds up her free hand, the one not holding the knife. Her cheek is so swollen there might be an apple under the skin. 'You need to behave. We won't have you for queen, not for a minute. You calm yourself down, and this all stops. Don't make us go the other way.'

'You'll find out what the other way is alright.' There's a tremor in Maggie's voice. Florrie's never heard her aunt sound afraid before.

Any moment Maggie is going to start cutting people. She'll lunge and she won't care who it is. And they'll kill her, won't they? They'll all leap on Maggie and someone will cut her throat, and no one will be able to say who did it.

She thinks, *This is why they wanted the rest of us out of it. This is a murder.*

And is she, Florrie, going to let this happen, as she lets everything else happen? Never speaking up, mutely obeying—

For just a moment, she wishes desperately that she'd never found out the meeting was on, just as they'd hoped she wouldn't. She imagines diving under the table, trying to get out. They'll let her, probably, if she does. She takes a deep breath. She has to say something. She has to. For once in her bloody life.

'Stop.'

'You stop,' Ada says.

I would if I could, she thinks, desperately. *I would if I could.*

Ted is waiting for Harry, yet again. But at least he's managed to ask Harry to see Florrie. 'Alright, alright, just hang on,' Harry said, and pointed Ted back over to the wall. 'Be with you in a tick.' But that's probably a yes. Ted wonders if all Harry's boys spend this much time standing about doing nothing. He remembers watching Don and the others, before any of this, and thinking they must have exciting, glamorous lives.

Harry's still in conversation with the old blokes, pouring

one of the fellows a drink from a crystal decanter, waving a hand, exuding warmth. Dennis has gone off to play a hand of cards, and now Don, for no reason that Ted can understand, is talking on and on at him. Ted is barely replying, but Don doesn't seem to notice.

'What I'm going to get is a Sapphire,' Don says. 'What do you think of that? You wait, next year. Brand new. Black, I want, or blue.' He fishes out a cigarette case and offers it to Ted, who shakes his head.

Don's got the cigarette held between his teeth like a cowboy, the smoke making him squint. It makes him look a bit of a prat. 'Look who it is.' He's staring over Ted's shoulder.

Ted turns. It's Bernie, the gnomic old man from outside the snooker hall. He's wearing a new hat, a nice one in camel felt. He sees them and comes straight over, digging in the inside pocket of his coat. 'Got it, Donnie. Got it for you, like I said.'

Don holds out his hand, takes the little pile of notes and shuffles through them quickly. 'Alright, then.'

Bernie winks. He doesn't seem the least crushed by the horrible encounter in the fog. 'Didn't I say? Man of my word. And did you tell Harry my bit of news, then? What did he think of that, eh?'

From behind Don's shoulder, Harry's voice. 'What's this?'

Ted jerks in surprise, blinks.

The little man laughs. 'Caught you unawares, didn't he?' Then, to Harry, 'Brought your money.'

Harry takes it from Don's hand, without looking to see how much is there. 'What bit of news is this, Bernie?'

'Saw Donnie in the street, didn't I? Told him I heard your

grass was a bird. But he'll have told you that.' He watches Don's face, and laughs again. 'Or perhaps he never did.'

Don's trying to explain himself, his voice like a swagger. Bernie is leaning against the wall and watching as though it's a play, a cig in one hand and his new hat in the other. He looks ready to cheer Harry on.

Even though there's nothing funny about it, Ted feels his face pull into that shameful, cowardly smile.

'Right,' Harry says, when Don's finished. The calm in his voice is terrible. 'Later, we'll have a little chinwag, shall we, about what I do with lads who keep me in the dark.' He looks at Ted, as well as at Don.

Don's still got his swaggering look, but the corner of his mouth twitches unhappily.

'But now,' Harry says, 'the both of you come with me.'

Ted tries to say, *Where?* And, *No*, and *But you said I could fetch Florrie.* He shifts from foot to foot.

As if he can read Ted's mind, Harry says, 'Don't tell me you didn't know the girls are all at yours. Oh, yes. Didn't your bird say? Well, there's a little taste of your own medicine. Get your coats on.'

And Ted and Don have to trail after him, while Bernie chuckles to himself, turning his new hat over in his hand. Don whispers, 'Fuck, fuck, fuck,' to Ted, as they pass into the hall. But Ted hasn't any attention to spare for him, nor for Bernie, nor even, really, for Harry, who's looking over his shoulder and saying, 'Chop chop, boys.'

He's wondering if Florrie knew the girls were there, if that's why she didn't want him to walk her home. He's wondering, for what feels like the hundredth time, if he knows her after all. And whether his mum's alright, if Maggie is there—

On the street he speeds up, overtaking Don and then Harry, hardly hearing when Harry says, 'Don't you fucking run from me, sonny.' He's desperate now to get things straight, for this horrible time, this whole filthy fogbound weekend, to come clear. To see what's bloody well in front of him.

Florrie can feel the iron knobs on the stove digging into the small of her back. She keeps turning her head to look first at one woman's face, then at another. Her eyes are the most open, perhaps, that they've ever been.

'Stop!' she says again. It's the only thing to say.

'Let them come,' Maggie says, beside her. There's a shifting glimmer in the corner of Florrie's eye as Maggie moves the blade to point first at one woman, then another. 'Come on, you bastards. I dare you.'

Val's close enough that if she swings her knife, Florrie will have to block it or be cut.

Any second, it will begin.

Cissy is looking at Florrie as if she might be able to do anything about it, desperate and pleading.

Florrie tries to say, *Please. For God's sake, please.*

And then she tips right over the edge and it's impossible to be any more afraid.

Instead of *Please,* she says, 'I said stop.' She puts her free hand up in front of her like a copper halting traffic. 'The lot of you. Stop just where you are.'

And, for a wonder, they do stop, caught by surprise, every eye on her, hanging in the moment. Ada frowns. Val has a mean little smile. Hazel raises an eyebrow. *Oh, really?* she seems to say. *Now what are you going to do?*

Florrie takes a breath. 'Cissy,' she says, 'Grab hold of Maggie for me.'

She doesn't wait to see what Cissy will do. She reaches out her own hand and takes Maggie's wrist, the one holding the knife. She can feel her aunt's pulse fluttering under her fingers. One beat, two. Their eyes meet.

Then Maggie twists, her skin moving inside Florrie's grip so fast that it burns. But Cissy is lunging, has hold of Maggie's other arm, her eyes huge with terror.

Florrie shouts, 'Help us, then!' to the room, to the world.

And the other women are here in a rush of sound; chairs clattering to the floor, a terrible crash of falling china, and Maggie is forced to her knees, the women holding her arms out from her body like Christ on the cross. She has her head bowed, breathing harshly, half her hair hanging over her face, the knife in one captured hand.

Then she begins to scrabble and she's nothing like Christ, she's a wild, kicking thing. The knife twirls uselessly in the air.

They move with her, the lot of them swaying together. Cissy is still in there, hanging onto Maggie's arm, looking like she can't believe what she's doing.

'Down,' Hazel says, and together, they push Maggie onto her stomach on Nell's blue lino. Maggie howls. It's a guttural sound, pure fury.

'Sorry,' Florrie says, stupidly. But the word is lost.

And now they're sitting on her, like men wrestling a crocodile. Val is on her shoulders, Ada on her lower back. Hazel has her by the legs. Cissy backs away, and clutches at the edge of the table as though she might fall.

Florrie stands up slowly. She rubs her hands on her skirt.

Even with three women on her back, Val leaning forward

to pin her arms, Maggie quivers and shifts beneath them. And even now, she hasn't let go of the knife.

Ada has her one open eye on Florrie. The other is squeezed shut, still running with tears.

She's waiting to see what I do, Florrie thinks. But they all are.

She puts her foot on the wrist of Maggie's knife hand and pins it to the ground, she's careful to use the toe of her shoe, rather than the pointed heel. She can feel the sliding of Maggie's skin across the bones.

'Drop it, can't you?' she says. 'Please.'

'Showing your colours, you little backstabber.' Maggie's voice is slurred by the pressing of her cheek against the floor. 'And Cissy. You little traitor bitches. You wait.'

One more twist of Florrie's shoe and the knife finally slides from Maggie's hand.

Florrie picks it up carefully, snaps it shut. 'I'm looking out for you.'

'She is, as well,' Hazel says.

'Don't you hurt her,' Florrie says.

The calm seems to be drifting out of her grasp. Her legs are beginning to tremble. Sooner or later, Maggie will get back up, and then what? She imagines, again, just leaving them all there and running away.

Maggie spits across the floor, towards Florrie's feet.

'This is all very well,' Val says, 'but what's the idea now? We can't get up off her, can we? She'll go barmy.' Her arms are tense with the effort of pushing Maggie's arms down.

Florrie feels her bladder squeeze and threaten to let go. She puts the knife on the kitchen table and sits down, right on the floor.

Maggie's lipstick is smudged right onto her chin, and

saliva has gathered in foamy flecks at the corners of her mouth. 'You'd just fucking better let me up, Florence.'

But she can't. They'll have to stay here for ever, or die.

Ted can hear Harry and Don lumbering along behind him, but he doesn't wait. He lets the garden gate bang shut, and fumbles his key into the lock with clumsy fingers. His only concession to their following is to leave the front door ajar.

There's a light on in the kitchen, and he goes straight there without taking his shoes off, which is strictly against his mum's rules for anyone but guests.

The first thing he sees is that the table is pressed up against the dresser, his mum's good dishes lie in pieces on the floor. And just beyond it, a strange tableau: Maggie on her stomach, head turned sideways and lipstick smudged across her cheek. Three women on her back. The one on her shoulders, pinning her arms, is hugely pregnant. Sitting on Maggie's bottom is an older lady with a battered face, and crouching, one hand on each of Maggie's ankles, is that Hazel, who helped him outside the snooker hall. A much younger blonde girl is by the window, pressed against it as though she might be hoping to slide through the glass and disappear.

But it's Florrie who draws his gaze, who fixes him to the spot. She's sitting on the floor, her legs crossed, her neck and back as straight as a dancer's. She has on the golden fur wrap over her coat, her neck is dirty, and she's right under the hanging light, so that the tips of the fur, her arms and hands and the fuzz around her curls, are all made bright.

She's drawn the gaze of the women, too. As Ted watches, the pregnant one asks her, 'What now, then?'

Florrie has that look of hers, but more, much more; it's

distilled, past cool and into imperious. She says, 'No one else gets hurt.'

He feels a shot of pride so unexpected that it's almost painful. She's in charge. She's so obviously in charge, here. She's come in like his mum's saviour and pushed Maggie onto her belly.

He hasn't known her. He really hasn't. This is what she was trying to tell him, that she's nothing like he thought. She's nothing like anyone.

Maggie spots him first. Her eyes roll up to meet his. 'Here's the big fellow. Tell your girlfriend to stop messing about.'

Florrie sees him, gives a little start, and her look grows wary.

Ted shakes his head. 'Fiancée.' It's a stupid thing to say, but it's what comes out.

Florrie blinks. And then she smiles.

The blonde girl puts her hands to her mouth and gives a shrill laugh.

Maggie says, 'You fucking prat.'

He hears the creak and pop of the garden gate. 'Harry's here.'

It's like a starter's pistol; they all move at once. Florrie is getting to her feet, the women on Maggie's back are scrambling off her. Ted looks towards the kitchen door – he can hear Harry and Don in the hall, the click of the front door closing. And as he looks back, he sees Maggie give a great jerk, her right leg shooting out like a piston. Her heeled shoe kicks Hazel full in the jaw. The sound of the stiff sole landing is like a slap. And Hazel screams.

'Will you look at this,' Harry says, from the kitchen door.

There's a moment's silence, broken only by the blonde

girl's nervous laugh. And then Maggie's own cackle. Even as she scrambles to her feet, she's laughing so hard she has to steady herself on the sideboard.

'What was that?' Nell puts her hand to her heart.

Ruby shakes her head.

They stand still, both listening hard, but the scream doesn't come again.

Ruby's eyes are very big and dark in her thin face. One of her hands is still hanging onto the top bunk, just to stay upright. The other is holding closed the fur collar of the red coat.

'Florrie,' Ruby says.

'You don't know that.'

Ruby, who had barely been able to stand only a moment ago, is striding to the door, the pistol in her hand.

'I'm flaming well going to find out,' she says. 'Are you coming?'

Florrie is holding both of Ted's hands. They're in his mum's ruined kitchen and all about them is chaos, but it seems distant, nothing to do with her. He's looking down at her with eyes as soft and shy as when he held out the opal ring.

She's only vaguely aware of the sound of Ada and Maggie fighting in the hall, the grunts and scuffling feet. No one has lifted a finger to stop them. Harry and Don are out there now, watching, and occasionally one of them calls out, 'Get her,' or 'Come on now.'

Cissy is watching from the kitchen door, bobbing on her toes, as though she might join in or run away at any moment.

By the stove, Val is bending over Hazel, who crouches,

hands to her face, a slow string of blood creeping down her wrist.

And Florrie is holding Ted's hands.

There's a thud from the hall: the women thumping into the wall.

Ted says, 'Shouldn't we do something?'

Past him, and over Cissy's shoulder, she gets a glimpse of Maggie, pressed suffocatingly into Ada's huge bosom. Her fists are pounding into Ada's back.

She says, 'We have to let them fight it out, or it'll never end,' and then, a little defensively, 'It's what Gran would say.'

Ted shakes his head. 'You're quite something, Florrie Palmer.'

'Don't think I'm heartless.' But she can see what he thinks of her. It gives her a fierce, hot feeling, makes her want to whoop, or dance, or hit something. It makes her want to ask, *Really?* again and again.

But then he says, 'My mum must be scared witless, though. Is she still in bed? She can't be asleep.'

And like a hypnotist's snap of the fingers, her bit of joy, the feeling of being outside it all, is gone.

She almost says, *I don't know*, but she can't do that, not again. She says, 'She ain't here.'

Ted's eyes go from soft, through confused, and into desperate. He squeezes her hand, too tightly.

He says, 'Oh, God. I can't stand any more of this. It's the middle of the bloody night. Please don't tell me she's not here.'

'I'll help find her. I promise. Ted, look at me. I promise.'

Florrie can hear Hazel whimpering, feels the floor judder under her feet as the women crash about in the hall.

Ted says, 'Help me get these bloody people out of her house. Please. I'm about to lose my mind.'

'Yes. Course.' She lets go of his hands and says, 'Val? Can you get Hazel home? Everyone's got to push off.'

Val straightens up, hands at her back. 'I think she's really bashed up. She won't let me look at it.'

Florrie goes over to where Hazel sits on the floor, hands to her face. 'Come on, Hazel. Don't mess about. Let's see.' She touches Hazel's wrist with the tip of one finger.

Hazel drops her hands. The whole of her chin is streaked with blood and the side of her mouth is askew, drawn down like the victim of a stroke. She gives a monstrous, slurring moan.

'Broken jaw,' Ted says, faintly.

Val draws a sharp breath.

'Could be. Blooming hell,' Florrie says.

Hazel has started trying to talk, in the round slobbering way of someone trying to make herself understood around a dentist's fingers. It's quite horrible to listen to. 'Fucking kill Maggie.'

Cissy has turned to look and widens her eyes at Florrie, as though she thinks Florrie's going to do something. But she is going to have to do something.

'Hospital,' Florrie says, to Val. 'She can't stay here.' She's trying not to let the horror show in her voice but she goes too far and now she does sound heartless.

Hazel begins getting to her feet, her blood-streaked jaw working oddly, as though she might be chewing cud. Val heaves her up, one hand under her elbow.

Hazel tries to shake her off. 'No.' She sounds drunk. Strings of blood stretch between her lips when she opens her mouth. 'Kill Maggie.'

Florrie steps in front of her. 'Can't let you do that. You're off to hospital.'

They hear Harry say, 'That's enough now, girls,' out in the hall.

Ted says, 'Thank God. Everyone out.'

He chivvies Cissy, and then Val and Hazel out into the hall. Even from behind, Florrie can tell he's about to throw a fit. His shoulders heave, cords stand out in his neck.

She follows him, feeling desperate, guilty. Even though she didn't invite any of these people in, didn't know any of this would happen, it feels like her fault.

Past the tight scrum ahead of her, she sees that Ada and Maggie have come apart. Maggie has a trickle of blood from one nostril. Her collar is torn and a set of three scratches run down the side of her mouth and onto her neck as though she's been clawed by a bear. Ada's swollen eye is running with water. Her hair is as bad as Maggie's, half pulled out of its pins and sticking up in all directions. Maggie holds up her fist. An ugly clump of hair, dark but for its grey roots, flops back and forth in her hand.

Don is pressed against the wall at the foot of the stairs, looking a little sickened. Harry, standing a couple of steps up, out of the way, has a horrible half smile.

'Evens,' Maggie says, to Ada. She grins, showing a new gap in her teeth.

Ada glares, chest heaving.

'Now stop,' Florrie calls. 'Stop!'

Harry says, 'Fair's fair.'

But Hazel has slipped free of Val and is staggering down the hall. She stops in front of Maggie, and a plume of blood and spit flies from her broken mouth and lands on Maggie's own jaw.

Maggie laughs, even as spitty blood runs a path down her neck and into her collar.

'Stop!' Florrie calls again, as if Maggie will listen to her.

Ahead of her, Ted is gesturing at Cissy and Val, shooing them down the hall towards the other women. 'All of you! Out. And I want to know where my mum is. Now.' He sounds as though he's talking through gritted teeth.

Harry pushes his hat up on his head. 'Look who grew a pair of bollocks. But we're here for a reason, sonny.'

Don says, 'Steady on,' but Florrie can't tell if he's talking to Harry or Ted.

Now Ted's voice is cracking, wild. 'Everyone out of my mum's house!'

'Thank you, Teddy,' Nell says, behind them.

Florrie turns so fast she almost loses her balance. She puts out her hand to steady herself, finds Cissy's shoulder and hangs on.

Nell's framed in the kitchen doorway, a swoop of black stitches over her pale cheek, her face strained.

And behind her, Ruby. Ruby, looking like she might have crawled her way out of a grave. There's a smear of something pale down her cheek, her hair straggles dark about her neck. She has on a filthy nightie and a red coat Florrie's never seen before. She holds out her hand. Her palm is bleeding. And in her other hand, by her side, she has Dolly's snub-nosed pistol.

Ruby blinks at the light, the faces turned to stare at her, the little hall packed with people. She starts to walk. Everyone shuffles about, squeezing out of her way. She's glad they do: this sort of momentum is hard to stop, like running downhill.

She doesn't slow when Florrie puts out a hand, touching her sleeve as she goes by, nor when Val asks, 'What the bloody hell? Nell, what's the idea?'

'Don't you dare speak to me,' Nell says, just behind Ruby. 'You should all be ashamed.'

Ruby doesn't turn. Every bit of her strength is needed to carry her onwards. She feels Nell push forward to take her arm again, and is glad.

She passes Ted, leaning out of her way and gaping like an idiot, Cissy, flattened against the banisters, wringing her hands. Harry on the stairs, looking almost amused, Don below him, ham-faced and frowning.

She reaches the knot of women at the front door. Hazel, her jaw swelling up on one side like the elephant man, her mouth and chin a mess of blood. Maggie and Ada, their faces scraped up and their hair half pulled out.

Maggie puts her fingers to her bleeding lip. 'Rue,' she says. 'What the fuck are you playing at?' She's lost a tooth, is almost snarling.

But Ruby knows her sister: just like when Maggie was little, when she'd wake up afraid that everyone had left her in the night, her relief at seeing Ruby comes out as fury.

Then Maggie points a finger at Nell. 'And this bitch.'

'Hang on, Magpie. Nellie never grassed. I'd have had no chance without her.'

Nell lets go of Ruby's arm and points her own finger back at Maggie. 'There! You horrible, bloody . . . Palmer.'

'Button it, Nell,' Ruby says.

Maggie rubs at her lip again, smearing blood onto her chin. 'I never thought she did. Just took my chance to spoil her face.' She grins. 'Tell me you never deserved what you got, Nell.'

'If I did you've paid me back,' Nell says.

'Well now, that depends if you'll be keeping your hands off my Harry.'

'Tell him to keep his hands off me!' Nell's voice is so high that it disappears on the last word.

Harry laughs.

Ada says, 'Oh, for the love of God.'

'Enough,' Ruby says.

She lifts the pistol. She has to use both hands to keep it steady, her vision pulsing with exhaustion and the congealed fury of days. She points it at Ada's elderly, swollen face.

'Out of the way, Magpie. Here's your grass.'

A moment of stillness.

Then Maggie says, 'No!' but she sounds delighted. She moves the two steps to the bottom of the stairs and squeezes next to Don, away from Ada.

Hazel has her hands to her bleeding mouth.

Ada puts her big hands on her hips and looks at Ruby over her eyeglasses. 'Ruby Palmer, have you gone mad?'

'I've woken up, is what I've done.' The shaking of Ruby's hands is travelling all the way through her arms. Her shoulders strain with the effort of keeping them steady.

'Don't you point that at my aunt!' Val shouts, from further down the hall.

Behind Ruby there's a scuffling sound, the thump of something hitting the wall and then Val's furious, strangled cry, 'Get off, Florrie! And you, you little bastard.'

'I can't.' Florrie's voice. 'Let my mum talk. Cissy, you'd better hang on.'

'I'm trying, ain't I?' Cissy's panting. 'She don't half wiggle.'

Nell says, 'Ruby, for God's sake!'

And now Hazel has produced a knife, her mouth a skewed snarl. 'My gran,' she spits at Ruby. 'You get off my gran.'

'No!' Florrie and Ted shout together, from behind Ruby.

Maggie is inching forward again, edging around the stair post, is almost at Hazel's side, her hands hovering in front of her like a woman waiting to catch a ball.

Ruby says, 'All of you stay where you are.'

Ada says, 'Hazel, put that thing away. Now.'

Hazel doesn't move.

And then everyone is trying to say something at once, a rising thunder of voices.

Harry's cuts across it all. 'Shut it!' he bellows, and they do. And then, to Ruby, 'Explain.'

Ruby keeps her eyes, and the pistol, on Ada's swollen face.

'We always said what a fucking miracle you kept the club, seeing as how I got nicked there.' Her voice is ragged around the edges. 'But it weren't that. And the coppers was there that quick, they might've been waiting.'

Ada's voice is very calm, as though she's talking to a child. 'You ain't thinking straight, Rue.'

Hazel is staring from one to the other of them, blood dripping with every movement of her head.

Ruby says, 'No wonder you was cut up over Frannie. You never meant her to get pinched, just the blokes she was with. Harry's lads. Ever since he took up with my sister, his boys have been getting nicked left, right and centre.'

'No,' Ada says, a little less gently now.

'Oh, oh! You underhand bitch!' Maggie has her hands to her cheeks.

Ruby can feel the coughs pushing up towards her throat. All in a rush, she says, 'And then I thought how quick the coppers come to the Bon, weather like that. You told them where we was. Then we go to Selfridges instead—' But now she is coughing, swaying on her feet. She can't let go of the pistol to cover her mouth. Her own blood-tinted spit spatters her hands on the juddering gun.

'No!' Ada stamps her foot like a little girl. 'You know me! Ruby, for the love of God.'

'Yes!' Maggie steps over next to Ruby and Nell steps back, just as fast.

Maggie says, 'You were the one insisted on the Bon after! Oh, you fucking cow. You meant it to be me who got nicked. I'd bet anything.'

Ruby's coughs are tailing off, reaching the end of their ragged rhythm.

'And,' Ruby manages to say, her words catching on the sandpaper of her throat, 'no one knew about the fence at the dry cleaner's. But then it turns out the coppers do. And then you make sure your Val's out of the way. Another miracle.'

'You're barmy!' Ada says. 'I'd die first.'

'And so you will,' Maggie calls. 'Do it, Rue.'

'Not in my house!' Nell shrieks.

'Explain, then!' Ruby shouts.

'You know,' Harry says to Ada, 'I'd like to hear this.' He's turned to face her, has put his hand in his pocket.

Ada has grown still. She puts her hand to her throat. She frowns.

Then, very slowly, she says, 'Oh, Hazel. Say you never.'

Hazel's misshapen jaw twitches, but she doesn't speak.

'Hazel!' Ada's pleading now.

Maggie draws in a breath. 'You fucking filthy Goddens. Do them both, Rue. Do it.'

Harry says, 'Never Hazel. Never.'

Hazel's eyes follow Ruby's shaking hand, pointing the pistol at Ada's good eye. Her broken mouth opens, closes. Fresh blood spills from her bottom lip.

'My own granddaughter,' Ada says, very quietly. 'You sent them to the Bon. Not enough to give up Ruby, but your own grandmother?'

Hazel's words are slow and as swollen as her mouth. 'They promised you'd be alright. And I kept Val away.'

Ada puts her hands to her face.

Ruby swings to point the pistol at Hazel, hands shaking so hard now that the gun wavers crazily in the air.

Harry puts his hand to his chest. 'You little cunt,' he says, faintly. 'After all I've done for you.'

Hazel turns to him, half wild. 'You never do anything that don't help yourself! You think you're king of the world, you selfish old fuck.' Blood sprays from her mouth with every word. 'I'm not allowed to do one single thing you don't agree to! You say what I wear, what I do, who I see—'

'Let me, Rue.' Maggie puts her own hands over Ruby's, gently pries the pistol from Ruby's fingers. Ruby lets her take it.

Maggie aims at Hazel, a grin spreading over her face. 'Stay back, Harry. This is my treat. What do you say, Rue? Right in the eye?'

Harry says, 'Wait just a minute. Wait.' His face is the grey of a very old man.

'I saved the club! They'd have closed us down!' Hazel's hands are up, one holding the knife but the other palm out, *halt*. 'They said they'd nick us both, Gran! And you don't know what they're like. They said, they said—'

A knock on the front door, a heavy, businesslike fist. Everyone jumps.

A deep and carrying voice calls, 'Police! Open up!'

Ted has been standing at the back of the hall, constantly on the verge of doing something, but unable to decide what the something should be. Now, he meets Florrie's gaze and the inertia breaks.

Without needing to speak, they both rush forward, pushing past Cissy, who's trying to go the other way. Ted grabs Nell's elbow at exactly the moment that Florrie takes Ruby's.

'Oh!' Nell's eyes are wide and wild.

'Ruby Palmer! Open up or we'll force entry.'

'Go!' Maggie hisses at Ruby. She thrusts the pistol at Don, who looks at it, stupidly.

Reflexively, Ted reaches out and takes the filthy thing from his hand. Don holds his palms up, grateful to be rid of it.

He hears Florrie say to Ruby, 'We have to go. Now,' and doesn't need to say it himself. He just tugs his mum's arm and she lets him lead her back towards the kitchen.

Florrie is trying to pull Ruby into the kitchen, but her mum's hanging back and is surprisingly strong. Ahead of them, Nell and Ted are already in the kitchen and Cissy is beckoning frantically from the scullery door, using her whole hand, like a woman waving down a taxi. Now Don and Harry shove their way past, bumping into the kitchen table, saving themselves without even looking around for the others.

Behind them, Florrie hears the coppers shout, 'We can hear you inside. Last chance, Mrs Palmer. We're coming in.'

Maggie shouts, 'Alright! I'm coming out!'

But Ruby, damn her, is craning back to look. Desperate, Florrie hisses, 'She's giving you time. Fucking take it!'

And at last Ruby is moving. Ted appears from nowhere and is ushering them on, his face as tense and strained as Florrie feels. They're moving in a block through the tiny scullery, a shuffling scrum, the only sounds their feet and breath, everyone in each other's way.

Just as they reach the back door they hear the front door open and a man's voice. 'Ruby Palmer?'

'That's right,' Maggie says, faintly. 'It's your lucky fucking day.'

Ted is picking his way across the bombsite, looping around the edge, where he knows the ground is safest, moving slowly, feeling with his feet. So many pieces of brick, just waiting to slip away from a misplaced step. Somewhere ahead Don and Harry are making heavy weather of it, far too much noise. Almost every other step they take, something rattles or clatters.

But there's no sound behind him. Where are Florrie and his mum, where's Aunt Ruby? He stops still, listening. Nothing from behind him. Ahead and to the side Don swears under his breath, and there's the heavy rasp of Harry's breathing.

He's straining so hard for the sound of Nell and Florrie, strung so tightly between going forward and back, that it takes him a moment to understand the significance.

Harry and Don are ahead and to the side. Going right across the middle of the bombsite. For Ted's whole childhood he'd had it drilled into him by Nell: never go near the remains of the house. He's known it like a legend, a lesson, an irrefutable fact. But Don and Harry have never been told.

He begins to move that way, still careful, still slow. He's following Don and Harry's lumbering footsteps, eyes straining for the jagged edge of the wall, for anything standing blacker than the fog, through darkness as thick as paint.

Now he's close enough to the sound of their feet that he dares to hiss, 'Stop! Wait!'

And as if he's made it happen, like an avalanche started by a whisper, there's a creak, a gasp, a horrible double thud – *duh-DUM* – and the rushing slide and patter of stones.

'Jesus!' Don's voice moans from just ahead.

Ted struggles over the rubble, expecting with every step to feel his feet begin to sink, the ground to split beneath him.

'Harry,' Don says. 'Mate. You alright?'

There's no reply but the swishing fall of gravel and dust.

Ted whispers, 'Don! Where are you?'

'Here. Fuck. I'm here.'

Finally, when Ted's almost close enough to touch him, he makes out the patch of deeper darkness that is Don. It has its arms held stiffly out from its sides, like a man who's only just realised he's walking a tightrope.

Florrie has the damp fence against her back, and beside her, warm against her arm, is her mum. These are the things she's sure of. She thinks there are others, standing just as still and silent, beyond Ruby, but she can't tell who they are. Across the bombsite are the footsteps of whoever has decided to keep going. And then, behind them, in the garden, the creak of the outhouse door opening and a copper's voice says, 'You. Come out here. Don't make me come in and fetch you.'

Val's voice replies, 'Do you mind? I'm on the lavvie.'

'Out.'

A shuffling, the closing of the outhouse door.

'Get off me! I'm pregnant.' And then, 'Alright, alright. Watch where you're grabbing me, can't you?'

Then the glow of what must be a torch beam flickering past the crack in the fence.

'There's no one else in the garden, sir,' the copper calls.

She can't hear the reply, but there's the familiar rusty swing of hinges as the back door shuts.

She can hear Ruby's breath hitching, and knows her mum is trying hard not to cough.

Hang on, she wills her. *Hang on just a minute more.*

Ted is standing in the dark, praying to a god he's not sure he believes in. Prayers without words, unspecified prayers. Next to him, Don breathes the word, *Fuck*, over and over, and somewhere below their feet, Harry is silent. Out on the road, Ted hears the coppers calling to each other, Maggie's voice saying something cheery that he can't make out, car doors slamming. Then a patch of yellow light across the sky, and an engine turning over, revving, moving away.

Thank you, God, Ted thinks. Then, whispering, 'Can you see him?'

'I can't see a fucking thing.' Don's voice is thick and frightened.

'Come this way a bit. Careful,' Ted says. 'Harry?' No reply.

'Fuck,' Don says. 'Fuck.' He hasn't moved.

316

'Alright. Hang on,' Ted tells him. 'Just stay put.'

'Where are you going?'

'I'm getting a torch.'

He starts back over the rubble, towards the house. He leaves Don there, still whispering to himself.

Florrie can hear someone coming towards her over the rubble and she knows, just by the careful movement of the feet, that it's Ted. She doesn't spend even a second wondering if it's a copper. He's come to get her.

'Here,' she whispers. 'Here,' and then he's taking her hand in the dark, kissing her palm, which is probably filthy. 'Thank God,' he says.

He pulls her by the hand, and she reaches out and tugs her mum's arm. There's the shuffle and scrape of a few pairs of feet following, as she follows Ted through the gap in the fence, into Nell's garden. He holds the fence panels apart for the others to get through. Florrie feels her way, touching her foot to the line of bricks along the vegetable patch, towards the misty yellow square of the scullery window, and finally, through the back door and into the house. And here they come after her, squeezing past the old scullery sink and into the kitchen. Ruby, Nell, Cissy, Ted. He closes the back door behind him.

'Where are the others?' Cissy asks.

Florrie shrugs. 'Don't worry about them now. We've got to go. Ted, what do you say to the flat? Is it safe there, do you think?'

'I don't see why not. Better than here. Hang on for me. I won't be a minute.'

He disappears into the hall and comes back holding a torch.

'Where are you going?'

'I left Don on the bombsite. Hang on.'

'Stay away from the middle,' Nell calls after him.

'I know, Mum,' he says, over his shoulder.

'Can't stop here,' Ruby says. She's swaying on her feet.

'I know,' Florrie says. 'Ted will be back in a minute. We'll scarper. Hang on.'

Ruby shakes her head and staggers forward, catches herself on the back of Dolly's chair. The cushion slides off, hits Cissy in the leg. The girl squeaks as if it hurt.

But Florrie has no attention for her. She's at her mum's side in two steps. Ruby has both hands on the back of Dolly's chair, her head hanging. She looks like a woman trying to push something heavy across the floor. Her thin shoulders heave.

It's quicker going over the rubble with a torch. Ted finds Don standing just where he left him, hands jammed into his armpits.

'He ain't made a sound,' Don says, before Ted can ask. 'Not a fucking sound.'

Ted goes carefully past Don and then, in fairy steps, towards the hole. A couple of feet from its edge, the ground creaks and his left foot sinks with a soft splintering.

Very slowly, he leans forward, shining the torch into the depths.

'Harry?'

The hole is jagged, black and silent. The fog dips down to fill it. If he looks hard, he can see the shapes of things. Broken beams, the lines in the brickwork.

'Harry.'

Underfoot something shifts. Ted wrenches up his foot,

almost losing his shoe, and scrambles away from the edge, the sickening sound of gravel pattering down behind him.

He shines the torch to check the ground. He's standing on a heap of stones beside one end of a beam, a long and very solid bit of wood. It stretches away, into the hole. He crouches, which makes him feel safer. The beam has fallen in one piece, one end by Ted's feet, the other resting far below. The angle isn't impossibly steep.

'If it holds,' he says.

'What?' Don says. 'Is it going to go? Is the rest of it going to go?'

'I can see how to climb down.' Even as he says it, he's not sure he means it.

'You'll break your neck.'

Ted prods the beam with the toe of his boot. 'I'm more worried about slipping off it. It's pretty damp. Maybe we should go to the phone box. Ring up for an ambulance.'

'Harry?' Don says. 'Harry? Please, mate.'

It's hearing Don so afraid that makes Ted move. He strips off his jacket, drops it onto the rubble and, heart singing in his ears, climbs onto the beam. He sits, feet out in front of him, knees bent up. He sticks the torch between his teeth and begins to shuffle down feet first, both hands on the wood.

'Jesus Christ,' Don says, behind him.

Ted says, around the torch in his teeth, 'You're a soft bastard, aren't you?' but he doesn't know if Don hears him and he daren't look round.

After he's gone a couple of feet he stops and puts one hand flat as firmly as he can on the damp beam. He tries not to notice how spongy the wood is beneath his hand.

Then he takes the torch from his mouth.

There is a shape, down below. It's difficult to tell, but it could be Harry, if his head were tipped back and his arm twisted. Ted follows the shape of shoulders down. The dull shine of what might be shirt buttons, the curve of a ribcage. And there, that glint of gold. A tiepin. The torso is perfectly motionless. Only the fog moves in the torch beam.

'I can see him.'

'Is he alright?'

'I don't know.' Ted says. 'I don't think so.'

Again, he plays the torch over Harry's shape. A ridge that might be the underside of Harry's jaw, but if it is then Harry's neck is not where any neck should be.

'I think he's dead.' He almost laughs, at the horror and impossibility of it.

'He can't be. Shit. Bloody hellfire.'

'Will you shut up for a minute?' Ted says.

He inches forward. Beneath him the beam shifts downwards with a terrifying clonk. It stops as suddenly as it had started, caught on something.

'Fuck,' Don says, again.

Ted's breath is coming in wheezes around the torch. He has pins and needles in his lips. He clenches his hand around the edge of the beam, feeling his fingers sink into the rotting wood.

He begins inching his way back up. It's much, much harder going backwards. The beam is tilted and slippery.

He jolts downwards again.

He flips himself over onto his hands and knees. His shoes won't grip, they slide and scrabble. His eyes are watering.

'Careful.' Don sounds almost as frightened as Ted. 'Slow down!'

Ted crawls as fast and desperately as a drowning man swimming for the surface.

Don reaches out a hand. Letting go of the beam long enough to grab it feels like the greatest risk of all. He might pull Don over. Their combined weight might bring the ground beneath Don down. But his own hand is reaching out now and Don's fingers are on his wrist, and with one desperate lunge he's on his feet and up onto the rubble.

Without a word the two of them stagger, as fast as they can, away from the hole, back towards the house.

Nell is sweeping the floor. The kitchen looks as though it might have been bombed. The furniture is all pulled about, fog has crept in. There's blood all over her lino, great patches, and a looping trail of drops. No doubt it's all over the hall as well.

Ruby is being fussed over by Florrie, and that horrible little Cissy is standing about saying unhelpful things.

The cat clock says it's twenty past three in the morning. She could just go straight up to bed and pretend it's a usual night. No one should have to clean the kitchen at this hour. But she can't do that until Ted comes in, and she has the feeling that if she stops sweeping she might crack up, start ranting and raving, or weep. Much easier to move the brush, watch the pieces of her mother's best china fall into the clinker bucket with the dust.

Ted and his friend come in, and she looks at him just long enough to make sure he's alright. He isn't, of course. He has the smile he uses when he's pretending. But she isn't alright either, so she looks back down at her broom.

Ted and Florrie heave Ruby to her feet and they go past

her, out of the kitchen, a ragged little train. None of them says goodbye.

From the hall, Florrie calls, 'Come on, Aunt Nell. We've got to go.'

This makes her give a little jump.

'Oh, no, I should think you'll do well enough without me,' she calls back, although now she's alone in the kitchen she finds that she's dreading being left here with the blood and the mess, and the not knowing who might come knocking at the door, or what they'll be looking for.

'For God's sake, Mum,' Ted calls. 'Hurry up.'

Nell goes to the kitchen door and looks at the five of them. Ruby is sagging between Ted and his friend. Florrie's holding the bag that Nell picked up in the shop, the very same. Either that or one just like it. And Cissy, for some reason, has Dolly's embroidered cushion held to her chest like a teddy bear.

'Quick,' Florrie says. 'The coppers might be here any minute. It won't take them long to work out Auntie Maggie ain't Mum.'

Nell turns the kitchen light off and leaves the whole mess behind.

They go in Don's car. Florrie sits on Ted's lap, in the back, with Nell and Cissy. Ruby is in the front, next to Don. The drive goes on and on, but Florrie can't see anything much, she has no say in anything that happens and no room left in her head to be afraid. And Ted's arms are around her. By the time they get out of the car the adrenaline has worn off entirely and when Ted says, 'Go on up without me, can you? I won't be long,' she's too tired even to ask where he's going. She just nods, and fishes out her *Snore Hall* keys.

322

It's very dark in the hall, but the feel of the air is immediately different. It's like having a hood taken off her face. Cissy helps her get Ruby up the stairs, one arm slung around each of their necks.

'I can walk. Don't fuss.' Ruby says this even as Florrie can hear the patting of her wavering feet searching for each step. Nell comes up behind, carrying the bag and telling them, in a hoarse whisper, to be careful.

Cissy supports Ruby while Florrie gropes the key into the door of the flat.

'Who's got a shilling for the meter?' she asks, as soon as they're in. A coin is pressed into her hand.

The electric light blinks the little hall into life and the dark goes back to the shadows.

Florrie takes her own shoes off and the damp slippers from her mum's feet. Ruby's toes are white and frozen looking.

'Let's get you to bed.' She slings Ruby's arm about her neck again.

'Leave off,' Ruby says, but Florrie just sighs and opens the door to the sitting room.

As they step inside Florrie feels as though she's finally home. It's all so untouched by everything that happened at Nell's. There are the chairs, the three-bar fire, the worn rug. The empty teacups she and Ted used.

'Get the heater on, will you?' she asks Cissy, and leads Ruby slowly into the bedroom. Her shoulders ache. Her mum's breath hitches.

Nell follows them without asking, and Florrie sits Ruby down on the side of the bed. Her mum sits hunched over, rubbing her hands together.

'Let's get you undressed,' Florrie says.

Ruby shakes her head. 'Too tired.'

Nell says, 'Don't be ridiculous,' and Florrie feels a wash of gratitude for how matter of fact Nell sounds.

Nell tugs the cuff of the coat over Ruby's hand. 'Come on, now, help me get this off. You're not a rag doll.'

As soon as the coat is taken from her, Ruby regains enough movement to shift herself up the bed and lie down. Florrie pulls the quilt up over her thin shoulder and says to Nell, 'You sleep in with her.' It's a wrench to offer it.

'It's good of you.' Nell's face is almost as drawn as Ruby's, and across her cheek the skin around the stitches has flushed an angry pink.

On impulse, Florrie crouches beside the bag and pulls out the peach silk rayon pyjamas.

'Here.'

Nell blinks. 'Well. Good heavens.' She shakes them out, the silk rippling in the light from the bedside lamp.

Florrie's careful not to look at Nell as she undresses.

Ruby seems very small under the faded patchwork of Ted's old quilt. Florrie aches for her mum to wake up enough to say some loving word she can hang onto. Or perhaps she only wants to crawl in beside her.

Without opening her eyes, Ruby says, 'You get some rest and all, Florrie.'

'Night then,' Florrie says.

There's no reply, only the steadily deepening wheeze of Ruby sliding towards sleep.

Then her mum mutters, 'Magpie. Poor Mags.' She sounds as if she's talking to herself.

'Oh, for God's sake,' Nell says, coming around to the other side of the bed and climbing in beside Ruby.

Florrie only says, 'Me and Cissy will sleep on the floor.'

'You'll freeze,' Nell says.

'Don't worry about us.'

Nell gives an exhausted huff into the pillow and pulls the quilt up over her nose. Then she reaches one silky arm from under the quilt and turns off the bedside lamp. It's a kinder, softer sort of dark than the darkness in the street.

Ted lets Don go into the phone box ahead of him. His nerves are still jangling; he seems to feel them in all his joints, right up his spine.

It's a tight squeeze, and Ted's shoulder is pressed against Don's even when he turns himself sideways.

'You ring,' Don says.

'Soft prat,' Ted says, although he is just as afraid. 'Alright. I'll do it. What do I say?'

'Just, I don't know, just say you heard a crash on the bombsite. Just tell them to look.'

'They might not see him,' Ted says.

'They'll see the hole, if they're looking. Tell them you heard it cave in.'

Ted picks up the receiver and dials.

A woman's tinny voice: 'Nine-nine-nine, what's your emergency, caller?'

'Uh.' Ted clears his throat.

'Police, fire or ambulance?'

He slams the receiver down so hard that Don jumps and swears.

Ted takes him by the sleeve. 'Jesus Christ. I left my jacket by the hole. I took it off to climb down. It's got that pistol in the pocket.'

'Bloody, bloody hell,' Don says. 'It's got both our finger-prints on it.'

'And Aunt Ruby's. And Aunt Maggie's.'

'They could do us for murder.'

'But it wasn't.'

Don shakes his head. 'They might say we pushed him. Or anything. Out on the bombsite with a gun, I don't fancy explaining that. Do you?'

Ted's own fingers close convulsively into fists, open, squeeze closed again. He pushes open the door of the phone box, and the moment he's away from the light, he feels better.

'Now what?' Don says, behind him. 'What do we do now?'

Ted says the only thing he can think of. 'We could go and tell Florrie.' He half expects Don to sneer or call him henpecked, but he looks relieved.

'She don't like me much,' he says. 'But I can't think what else to do. Lead the way.'

When Florrie comes back to the sitting room, Cissy is in one of the faded armchairs, staring at the electric fire. The room is already warming, filled with the smell of burning dust.

She gestures vaguely at the bedroom. 'I let them keep the blankets.' She can hear the defiance at the edges of her voice.

Cissy shrugs. 'We've got coats. I've kipped on the floor enough times before now. Are we waiting up for the blokes? I've got another shilling. We can keep the fire on for a bit.'

'I'm waiting up. You don't have to.'

'Oh, no, I will.'

'Let me get in the warm, then.' Florrie doesn't bother dragging the other armchair, but sits on the floor, right in the orange glow. She wraps her arms around her knees.

Cissy has her own arms wrapped around Dolly's cushion, hugging it to her chest. 'You know, I'm a bit nervy of your aunt.'

'Me too,' Florrie says. 'But that was a tight spot. All of them, coming at us. I nearly pissed my knickers.'

'I don't mean Maggie. Well, I do, I suppose. She'll be hopping, I should think. But I mean the other one. I held her arms when Maggie striped her face. Here, you don't think she'll try and get me in my sleep?'

Florrie stares at her own feet on the rug. She wiggles her toes. 'Not Nell. You just say sorry in the morning. Lay it on thick. She'll come round.'

'I am sorry now. It wouldn't be a fib.'

'You shouldn't let Maggie push you about so much,' Florrie says, although she's hardly one to talk.

'She's hard to say no to though, ain't she?' Cissy rubs her eyes. 'And she's been kinder to me than anyone.'

'Maggie? Not really?'

'I weren't in a good way when I met her. I'd run off from the kids' home and I was bunking up with a bloke who was,' Cissy hesitates, 'a bit mean. She let me stay at hers. She's been like a mum, sort of.'

'And I thought I had bad luck. Where's your mum?'

Cissy shakes her head fast, like a shiver.

Florrie looks back at her feet. She can hear Cissy sniffing, quietly. She stays just where she is, her front warm and her feet cold, and wonders what can have happened to a person that Maggie seems like a good bet for a mum.

'Here,' she says, when Cissy grows quiet. 'What are you dragging my gran's cushion about for?'

'I was going to wait till Ruby was up to say,' Cissy says.

'Tell me now,' Florrie says, more sternly than she means to.

Cissy gives her a watery smile. 'Alright. When I was in the kids' home I had this rabbit.'

'What's rabbits got to do with anything?'

'Not a real rabbit. A soft toy one. And one day he gets ripped along his side. Don't look at me like that, I'm getting to it. So the matron lets me have a darning needle and a bit of wool and I sew him up. So you know, it weren't always a nice place. If you got anything nice, a bit of money or sweets or anything, you could bet a bigger kid would have it off you quick as blinking.'

'So?'

'So, I'd hide stuff in my rabbit. Snip the wool, shove it in, sew him back up. There was always wool for darning. Our stockings was all darned to death.'

'Alright,' Florrie says.

Cissy grins. 'Well. The cushion gets knocked off your gran's chair and it whacks me in the ankle. Heavy, ain't it? Hurts a bit. So I pick it up. And, well. It don't half look like Blue Rabbit. And I knew you was all going bananas over the pot being missing. So I just thought. In case.'

She dumps the cushion at Florrie's feet. It makes a gentle thud as it lands.

Florrie runs her hands over the tiny bumps of the embroidery, the faces of the black and white puppies, forever staring out of their basket. She turns it over, feeling the weight of it, the slight strain in her wrists. The underside is less faded than the top. Across its middle is a row of darning stitches in dark red wool, the same wool as the scarf Dolly had made for Ada.

She can't believe she's been so dense as not to realise. It makes her miss her gran, and want to wake her mum. It makes her hold her breath.

'Here.' Cissy holds out something. The dull shine of a blade.

'Where did you get that?'

'It's Maggie's.' Cissy blushes. 'I thought, after you stamped on her arm like that—'

'I never stamped.'

'I thought I'd better grab it, is what I mean. Keep it safe.'

Florrie hesitates a moment before taking it. 'Ought we?' But then, 'Bring the lamp closer, will you?'

The red wool springs apart with only a little tug and it's a small matter, then, to pull the stitches from their places. The cushion cover splits to show a mass of cotton batting. Florrie prods it with her fingers.

'Well?' Cissy breathes, leaning closer.

For answer, Florrie pulls back the batting and there's a piece of thick green felt, lumpy to the touch. She eases it from its place. Sewn onto the felt with wool of all different colours are gold sovereigns, shining like rows of brass buttons. She lifts the felt and it unfolds to show more sovereigns sewn to the other side, follows it with her fingers to where it folds again. Underneath, shards of light on a background of green. Rings, some of them diamond, the glittering coil of a bracelet. These, too, have been sewn in place. Underneath the felt, packed into the batting, is paper money in bundles, each wound around with more wool.

'Will you look at that,' Cissy says. 'Do you think your mum knows?'

'If she don't, she will,' Florrie says.

'Just think of it,' Cissy says. 'Sitting on a gold mine.'

'Sitting on the pot,' Florrie says, and they both laugh, their hands to their mouths. Then, as the sound of keys comes in the lock, she lays the cushion on the floor and sits on it herself.

Ted is momentarily surprised to see Florrie and Cissy looking so giggly and girlish, so much like friends. But it's nothing to his relief at finding Florrie still awake.

There's just a moment of awkwardness, when she sees Don behind him, and Ted wonders if she's going to boot Don out. But then she says, 'Thanks for driving us,' in an ice-cold voice.

'Not a problem.' Don gives her a curt little nod.

Cissy giggles. 'Ain't this friendly?'

'Shut up, Cissy,' Florrie says.

Unabashed, Cissy scoots off the chair and sits on the floor next to her, and although Ted shouldn't let her do that – Cissy's a guest in his house – he finds himself sitting down, heavily, in her place. The armchair is warm. Don takes the other.

'Tell me,' Florrie says. And he does.

By the time he's finished, Cissy has her hands over her eyes. But Florrie is quiet, thoughtful.

'Well,' she says at last. 'No rush. He won't know the difference if it's now or later.'

Cissy giggles, nervously, into her hands.

Florrie says, 'So what I'd do is get some kip and go back in the morning. Get your jacket, and then you can ring up.'

'Really?' Ted feels a rush of exhausted gratitude. So simple. Go to sleep and go back in the morning. Although he can't think of anything he wants to do less than go climbing about on the bombsite again. But that's tomorrow, an age away.

He looks at Don, who nods in a hopeless sort of way.

'Our mums are in the bed,' Florrie says. 'Me and Cissy can sleep on the floor in there.'

Ted doesn't want her to go anywhere, but she puts her hand on his knee and says, 'I want to be where I can hear my mum if she needs anything,' and he has to let her go. They kiss goodnight, awkward because of Don and Cissy watching, and then the girls go into the bedroom.

Ted leans back and rubs his eyes.

The bedroom door clicks open again and Ted turns, expecting to see Florrie, but it's his mum. She's wearing a pair of shiny pink pyjamas.

She says, 'Oh, there you are, Teddy,' as if she was just waiting for him to come home from work.

Don starts to get to his feet but Nell says, 'Oh, don't get up. I'm just. Well. I just wanted a glass of water.'

'I'll get it.' Ted pushes himself up with both hands on the arms.

She follows him into the little kitchen.

He fills a teacup with water. Some of it slops out onto the edge of the sink. His hands are shaking. He has so many things he wants to ask her, to say, but he already knows he won't. 'There isn't a glass,' is what he says.

'Beggars can't be choosers.' She takes the teacup. 'It's a shame there's no window in here. But it's more than many have.'

'Yes.' He feels on the verge of tears.

She points to the water, slowly dripping from the sink's edge, onto the floor. 'You want to catch that. This lino is cracked; you don't want puddles getting under it.'

'No,' he says. 'No, of course not.'

'Get me a cloth,' she says, and he knows that she knows. That's the thing about his mum. They don't need heart-to-hearts.

'I can manage.' He gestures vaguely at the kitchen. 'You get some rest.'

She says, 'You're a good boy,' pats him once on the arm, almost a slap, and goes back to the bedroom.

He wipes up the water, not because he cares one way or another about the lino, but because she told him to. Then he goes back into the sitting room, flops into the armchair and feels exhaustion come up through his body like a wave. God knows what the time is. It must be almost dawn.

'Here.' Don is handing him a bottle. It's very cold to the touch. Whisky again.

'Had it in the car. It's Harry's,' Don says. 'But he won't be wanting it now.'

He gives a shaky laugh, and Ted can't help joining in, even though it's not funny at all.

The whisky spreads through him until only his hands and feet are cold. He and Don pass it back and forth in silence.

Don says, 'He was a right bastard, you know.'

'I thought you were his mate.' Ted feels numb and clouded from the booze and the whole, horrible night.

'I worked for him, that's all. And I didn't want to do that. Not really. You don't know how lucky you are.' Don passes the bottle back.

'I don't feel lucky.' Ted's chest is so warm now that the whisky has stopped burning.

'Believe me, you're a jammy git.' Don's voice is growing thick with the drink. 'He had some plans that you weren't going to like at all. And me. My dad owes him money.

Owed. I suppose that's over now. Bit late to make much difference now.'

'What do you mean?'

Don shakes his head. 'Not right in himself. But maybe he'll get a bit better, without Harry breathing over him. You never know.'

Ted hadn't been asking about Don's dad, he'd wanted to know what plans Harry had had. He passes him the bottle back, in case it helps. Then he says, 'A lot of things will be different, I suppose.'

'You never know. But it might just be more of the same. They're all bastards. The lot of them. We'll see.'

Every time Ted closes his eyes his head seems to fall, and keep falling. He's not drunk, exactly, but it seems like he's been awake for days.

'Need to go to sleep.'

'You want me to go?' Don says. But he sounds half asleep himself.

Ted tries to say, no, don't be daft. But the words just don't come out of his mouth.

He hears himself say, 'You're a pal, Don. You know that?'

Don mumbles, 'You nancy.'

And then Ted falls down a soft dark well inside himself, and into sleep.

Florrie wakes to the press of her hip against the floor, the pale line of light from the crack in the curtains, the dark bulk of the wardrobe. Her coat is spread over her like an uneven blanket.

The shape of Nell, sitting up in bed.

Florrie sits up too, and wraps her arms around herself against the cold. 'Morning.' Her mouth is very dry.

Nell hesitates, then whispers back, 'It must be. At last.'

'Are you . . . are you alright?'

'Quite alright, thank you for asking.'

Florrie gets to her feet, retrieves the coat from the floor, pulls it on as though it were a dressing gown, hugs it closed. Cissy is still asleep on the floor, curled like a prawn, her coat drawn up over her head.

Ruby is hogging the middle of the bed, flat on her back, her mouth open. Nell is at the far edge, the quilt pulled up to her chest.

Florrie watches the rise and fall of her mum's ribs, the miracle of her continued breaths.

She wants to thank Nell for giving her mum back to her. But her throat is constricted and at last, very low, she just says, 'I'm sorry, you know.' She doesn't say what for. The list is miles long.

Nell shakes her head, irritably. 'I'm sure I don't know why. Make yourself useful and get us all tea, if you have such a thing.'

So she does that.

The sitting room is filled with the faintest of dim yellow mornings. It's the very start of Monday, and in another life she would have been dressing for her interview, worrying, no doubt, about things that don't matter a bit.

The room smells of men. Cigars and feet and night breath. Ted and Don are asleep in the armchairs, each with their coats spread over them. Ted's turned himself sideways, his head resting on the chair's upholstered arm, his hands up by his cheek like a kid's. His legs are bent, a strip of hairy ankle showing between trouser cuff and sock. His big bony feet point their toes almost elegantly. Don is sitting upright, his head tipped back and his hat over his face, like a man asleep on a train.

She steps over Don's legs and goes to the kitchen, closing the door carefully.

She's trying not to wake the others, so of course everything she does makes a noise. The tap creaks and then gushes. She clonks the top of the kettle against the tap and the bottom against the stove. Even the striking of the match seems noisier than usual, the drag and the pop of it.

And for the first time she's thinking about Hazel. How trapped she must have felt, to do what she did. If it's hard to be ordered about by Ruby and Maggie, it sounds like it was ten times worse under Harry's thumb. Florrie's not sure what she hopes will happen to Hazel now, but she's sure that whatever it will be, she doesn't want to watch it happen.

From the sitting room there comes the sound of bodies shifting, of yawns and a quiet groan, as the sleepers begin to rouse.

Ruby is sitting up in bed. Faint grey light comes through the curtains, making the room seem all the plainer. Cissy is sitting on the floor, rubbing her neck and yawning. The pain on Ruby's chest, the crouching cat with its claws ready to rip at her lungs, seems to have gone for now, but something else has taken its place. It's a feeling that she's dwindling away, that she's more than tired or weak. That she's using the last scraps of her own time.

Florrie brings a tray of tea, puts it on the bedside table and sits with a little flump, making Ruby bounce where she lies. 'How are you feeling, Mum?'

'Me?' Ruby says. 'I'm right as rain.' Her throat feels full of sand.

Florrie puts her hands up to her eyes. 'Thank God. Though I haven't got a clue what we're going to do now.'

'Let's turn this light on, for a start.' Cissy's been standing and watching, Ruby sees now, and when she comes around and turns on the bedside lamp the whole room grows yellow tinged and warmer looking.

'Thanks, love,' Ruby whispers.

Florrie gets up and goes to the foot of the bed. She bends over and comes back up holding Dolly's cushion in both hands. 'Had my head on it all night.' She puts it into Ruby's lap, turns it over, and parts the fabric.

Ruby runs her hands over the cotton batting, the rings, the bundles of paper money. 'My clever girl.' She closes her eyes with sheer relief. They want to stay closed; her eyelids peel apart, reluctant and sticky.

Cissy says, 'I found it,' and then claps her hand over her mouth.

'She did, and all,' Florrie says.

Ruby's cheeks crackle and stretch as she smiles. 'Two clever girls, then. You help me sit up and Florrie can put it behind me.' She holds her hands out to Cissy.

Moving makes something shift and rumble in her chest.

Ruby wonders if either of them helped themselves to any of it last night. She'll never know, if they have. But she thinks Florrie wouldn't, and Cissy is frowning and biting her lip, so openly anxious that Ruby thinks she probably hasn't either.

'What's going to happen to Hazel?' Florrie asks.

Florrie must mean, *Are you going to kill her*, but Ruby says, 'If the coppers nicked her I daresay they won't keep her too long, nor the rest of them. Might all be out already.'

'Not Auntie Maggie,' Florrie says.

'Well now, we don't know. Wait and see.'

Cissy looks more worried than ever, and Ruby can just see Florrie's readying herself to ask another question she won't want to answer. She says, 'It's good to see you pals. Florrie will need a good pal, if she ever takes the crown.'

The two girls look at each other.

'No fear,' Florrie says. 'Not me. I couldn't do it.'

Cissy rolls her eyes. 'She don't have a clue. She could do it now, I shouldn't wonder. All the girls our age are scared to say boo to her. Even the older ones was, last night.'

Florrie has a tiny crease between her eyebrows that could mean anything.

'Well,' Ruby says, at last. 'One thing at a time. Seventeen's too young for queening.' Although there may not be much choice. It occurs to her that Florrie might very well be left to deal with the pot, keeping it safe, dividing what should be divided. And there are a lot of other things she'll need to tell the girl.

She says, 'I need to see my solicitor. Mr Baron. Someone's got to ring him up.'

She waits to see if Florrie will have Cissy go out to the phone box, or if she'll scurry off herself.

Florrie says, 'Cissy, do you mind?' and the girl goes from the room without a word. So that's alright. Good girl.

'Look at you, like a queen already,' Ruby says. She wonders if she should take Florrie's hand.

'Mum.' Florrie's voice is as hard and flat as the one she just used to order Cissy. 'You know what else seventeen's too young for? It's too young to get married without your mum's say so.'

'Can't see me waltzing up to the register office to give permission. Can you? You might have to wait.'

But Florrie might not have to wait, if Ruby's lungs carry her off. Do orphans need permission to marry? She doesn't know. But she finds she's glad Florrie will have Teddy by her, even if he is a bit wet.

'But you don't say no,' Florrie says.

'I don't say no.'

'And . . . what if I want an ordinary job? Go a bit straight? What then?'

Ruby has to think about this. If she's honest, it's the last thing on earth she expected the girl to say, and she's not sure she's pleased. Her first instinct is to ask what sort of job Florrie thinks a girl like her will manage to get. But she can't bring herself to do it. Then she thinks, let her find out for herself what it's like in a factory or scrubbing dishes. And the Cutters are a mess. The circle of family loyalty she's always relied on is shaky and uncertain now. She doesn't know what will happen, and God knows she'd like to see her girl safe. Might be best if she's out of things for a bit.

At last she says, 'Got a lot I need to teach you. Even so.'

'Alright.'

'And you know, the government only ever wants to help the rich stay rich and the poor stay poor.'

'Oh, Mum.' Florrie looks impatient now.

She pats Florrie's knee. 'Well, then. If you find a job you can stomach, why not?'

Florrie looks down at Ruby's hand. 'Just like that? You ain't telling me it's that easy.'

'You want to be glad, my girl.'

'I am glad.' But she doesn't crack a smile.

'Never know it looking at you,' Ruby says.

Florrie lets out an exasperated sigh. 'For God's sake. I am glad. This is just my face.'

Ruby's laugh makes the inside of her throat feel raw. 'Pass me that tea. I'm dry as a bone. That's my good girl.'

Ted and Don are in the little kitchen. They've already agreed that they'll go back to the bombsite the moment they finish their tea. But the women are all in the bedroom getting themselves dressed, and Ted doesn't want to go without telling Florrie, and perhaps his mum, that he's off out. So he's lingering over his cup. Don's taking his time as well, both of them swilling the liquid about, peering into it like fortune tellers, blowing on it even though it's growing cool. And if he's honest, it's not just that he's waiting for Florrie, it's the bombsite itself. It's Harry, lying out there. It's the fog.

And now Florrie does come in, wearing clothes Ted's never seen before.

He whistles. 'You look a picture.'

'Listen,' Florrie says. 'You remember I told you I had a little interview? It's later this morning.'

Ted feels a rush of tenderness. 'You must go.' Good God, his voice is cracking. It's the lack of sleep. He glances quickly to see if Don's noticed what a soft prat he's being, but Don's dusting off his trousers and straightening the cuffs, ostentatiously looking anywhere but at Ted and Florrie.

'What's the job?' Ted sounds more like himself now.

She says, 'It's a telephonist job, if you must know,' and he marvels at his new ability to read her face, under its shell.

'You mustn't be nervous,' he says. 'You'd be ever so good at that. You've got a voice and a half on you when you want to.'

'Oh, don't,' she says. 'You'll jinx me,' and puts her arms around his waist.

She lets him go pretty quickly, though. Don has begun to whistle to himself.

She says, 'But you know, I was going to go with you to see about Harry.'

'Oh, no, I wouldn't let you come.'

She raises her eyebrows, 'Let me, now?' and jabs him in the chest. But not hard.

He says, 'Unless you really wanted.'

She laughs, then. 'But never mind that. Your mum wants to go.'

Ted stares. Don, too, has straightened up and turned to look.

Florrie says, 'It weren't your fault. And I had to tell my mum.'

Ted remembers, suddenly, his own mum shouting at Maggie last night. *You tell him to keep his hands off me.* With everything that had happened it had slipped away from him until now.

'But . . . ' he says. 'Well. What's she want to come for?'

'She said, and she don't half have a point, that it ain't her jacket, and she's the one of us least likely to get into trouble. It's next door to her own house. She wants to keep you safe.'

Don says, 'Well, you know, that's not bad thinking.'

Florrie doesn't acknowledge that he's spoken at all.

Ted is shaking his head, but he can't find anything to say that makes sense. 'No,' he says.

Florrie shakes her head right back at him, almost smiling. 'You can tell her, then. You know how she gets. Looked ready to throw a fit. Right up on her high horse.' She puts her hand on his arm. 'And my mum said to me, private, you know, that we none of us give Nell enough credit and it

340

might be time we start.'

'Right,' Ted says. 'Did she? Right. Blimey.'

Ruby is up and dressed in one of the things Florrie nicked, a dress suit in tweedy rose pink. The colour makes her face look pale and washed out, but it hardly matters now. She aches all over, like an old lady.

Nell knocks on the bedroom door, and Ruby says, 'Come in,' as if it were her own room.

Nell has scrubbed up too, and is in a dress suit of brown and white chequered wool. Another thing Florrie pulled from the bag.

'Mr Baron is here.'

'Weren't he quick,' Ruby says. 'Can you ask him if he'll come in here?' Ted and Don are in the living room, and she doesn't feel like having an audience.

Nell says something to someone Ruby can't see, and Mr Baron's voice replies, 'I've been in stranger places.'

He comes past Nell, and into the bedroom. Ruby waves him over to the little wicker chair with one exhausted hand.

'Do you know,' he says, as he sits down, 'I do believe the weather may be starting to clear.'

'You got here quick,' Ruby says again.

'I rang the office after seeing the other Miss Palmer at the police station,' he says, 'and got your message. I thought I should get this out of the way. You'll understand that I won't be coming again.'

Ruby shrugs. 'Fair enough.'

Nell is still hovering at the door. For just a moment, Ruby considers asking her to leave them in peace, but she finds she can't.

'Come in, if you're coming, Nellie.'

Nell steps into the room, closes the door and stands with her hands clasped in front of her.

'You do know I shouldn't be here at all.' Mr Baron looks meaningfully at Ruby, who leans and hands him a folded sheaf of paper money, taken from the cushion.

'That stiffen your spine?'

He puts his hand in his pocket. 'It helps, certainly.'

Ruby can hear herself breathing like a blocked drain. She wants to lie down again.

'Let's hear it,' she says. 'Don't save my feelings. Give it to me straight.'

'They've charged Miss Palmer with burglary, I'm afraid, as well as wasting police time.'

'Which Miss Palmer?' Nell says.

'Oh, do excuse me. Margaret.'

'What burglary?' Nell's voice is higher than it should be. 'Not my house?'

But he's waving a hand. 'An old charge. Apparently they've been looking for her for some time.'

'Oh, no.' Ruby puts her hand to her cheek. *Oh, Magpie.*

'She seems in good spirits,' he says. 'She asked me to tell you that from now on you're not to say she never does anything for you.' He coughs and looks embarrassed. 'And she said I should instruct you all that when she does get out, it will be her turn to be made a fuss of. She says she hopes you'll all fall over yourselves to worship at her feet, as you have over the other Miss Palmer. Her words, not mine.'

And now Ruby is laughing, in spite of herself. It hurts to do it.

'What about Ruby?' Nell asks. 'The other Miss Palmer?'

'Well, what do you want me to say?'

Ruby says, 'She wants you to tell her it's all forgotten, is what it is, Mr Baron. That's what Nellie's after.'

'I'm not as naive as all that,' Nell says. 'I just wonder if it's as bad as you think it is.'

'It couldn't be much worse,' Mr Baron says. 'Although I haven't spoken to the police about it. It's nothing to do with me at all.'

'If they do catch you up, it'll be worth your time to keep quiet, Mr Baron,' Ruby says.

Mr Baron says, 'I've been representing your family for years, Miss Palmer. You must know by now that I can be trusted. Even in unconventional circumstances.'

'I'd bloody well hope so,' Ruby says. He'll charge an unconventional price, and all.

Nell looks a little desperate. 'It wouldn't be better if she turned herself in? Be easier on her?'

'Mrs Gibson, even if that were true, and I'm not at all sure it is, the shortest sentence Miss Palmer could expect—'

'Is too fucking long,' Ruby interrupts. 'No. I'll stay out as long as I can, thank you very much.' She raises her eyebrows at Nell, because really, her cousin should know better than that by now.

'Now, as for you, Mrs Gibson.' He shifts in his chair. 'I'm afraid it's a certainty that the police will want to speak to you about the goings on in your house. There's no reason for you to be overly concerned about that, but I think it's best that you do present yourself at the station. I'd advise that you have legal counsel. Shall I recommend a man?'

'Yes,' Nell says.

'Not overly concerned,' Ruby says. 'They don't want her for nothing else? You sure about that?'

'As I said, I haven't spoken to the police. But I should think it's unlikely.' He turns and looks at Nell sternly. 'You are still charged with shoplifting, Mrs Gibson. Let's not forget that. It would be unwise not to attend your court date.'

'Will your man be able to get her off?' Ruby's leaning forward, both hands on her knees.

'I can't make promises,' Mr Baron says. 'But it's a first offence.'

Ruby feels a little weight shift from her shoulders. That's one thing, then. It would be too much to have Nell in real trouble, after everything.

'Well. I'll be off,' Mr Baron says. He shakes Ruby's hand, quickly, as though he's not sure he should be touching her. She can't blame him. 'Mrs Gibson can bring me word, if you need to find me.'

'Right you are,' Ruby says. 'Much obliged.' And she is. She finds, in fact, that she feels better than she has done for days.

Nell follows Mr Baron down the stairs.

'Mr Baron? If I were to go with Ruby, just for now, would you be able to keep me informed, so that I don't miss court? I'm hoping I can persuade her to go somewhere for—'

He holds up a hand. 'Don't tell me where you're going.'

'Oh. I'm sorry.' Nell feels chastened. 'I was only going to say, somewhere for her health. I just thought. Well. You already know where we are.'

'And I would rather not know. Don't even hint at it to anyone who doesn't absolutely need to know. You're going to have a devil of a time as it is. And Mrs Gibson, I must advise you not to travel with Miss Palmer. If you return to your house and carry on as normal, you might escape this whole business relatively unscathed.'

He shakes her hand as quickly as he had Ruby's.

She closes the door behind him and turns to go back upstairs, but as she passes the door to the back of the shop, it opens and Mr Griffith looks out.

'Mrs Gibson!' Mr Griffith's scarred face breaks into a smile. 'Nice to see you again.' He shakes her hand. His is huge and very warm.

Oh, Jesus lord. He might have heard everything Mr Baron just said. Stairs always do make sound carry, don't they?

'Your visitor gone?' he says. 'I thought I heard the door.'

'Yes. He's just off. He's . . . well, he talks a lot of rubbish. Always teasing.'

Mr Griffith looks confused. 'Is he?'

'Oh, yes. Awful.'

'I just,' he says, 'wondered if you were getting on alright.'

'Quite, thank you.' Nell feels utterly at sea.

'Good. Good. Well, you know where I am, if there's anything you need. Pop in any time you like. A visit from a lady like you wouldn't half brighten my day.' He gives her a shy smile and retreats back into his shop.

Nell stands and looks at the closed door. The man was flirting with her. The strangeness of it, of someone coming over all shy and courteous, after these days and days of fear and horror. It makes her feel like laughing.

And now Ted and Don are coming down after her, in the thundering, heavy-footed way boys do.

'Ready, Mum?' Ted is holding her coat.

'I suppose so,' she says, grim again.

But as she follows the boys out she lets herself feel a glimmer of relief; *may escape relatively unscathed*. Only imagine escaping relatively unscathed.

But it isn't that simple. Nothing ever is. Even if she does go home and pretend nothing's different, what will Ruby do? What will Ted do, if Ruby dies in his flat? That would be awful, impossible to explain. And when Maggie comes out, what then?

Outside, the fog is thinner than it has been. Nell concentrates on ordinary things. Don's hand on the wheel, Ted drumming his finger on the window, the warp and weft of her own skirt, the sound of the engine. She doesn't think about where they're going.

Don pulls up a few houses down from the bombsite.

'Mum,' Ted says. 'Are you sure I shouldn't go?'

Nell opens the door, without waiting for one of the boys to do it for her. 'Don't be ridiculous.'

She gets out. She feels as though she's swimming through the fog, her legs moving all by themselves.

The bombsite looks different in daylight, with the fog less dense. Smaller, more mundane. But also, as she comes up the rise and sees the gaping black space, dangerous. The ragged edges of the hole look hungry, toothlike.

She goes closer, listening with her whole body for the sound of creaking below. She finds the coat, much closer to the hole than she'd have thought, and picks it up gingerly, covering her fingers with her sleeve. For some reason she can't explain, she doesn't want to touch it.

She stands, undecided. She can't go closer to the hole, knows she mustn't. But she'd feel so much better if she could just see him there. See, with her own eyes, that he's gone for ever. She takes a tiny tentative step, shines Ted's torch into the hole. Blackness.

A shifting sound.

She freezes.

Very faintly, a moan. A hopeless sound from the darkness below.

Nell stands, her eyes on the pit, the broken edges. She doesn't move. She doesn't call out.

Another shifting. And the moan again.

She gathers up a mouthful of saliva and spits. It glitters gently in the torch beam, a falling star, and disappears silently into the hole.

There are birds singing, somewhere in the terrace of back gardens. She turns round, and slowly, to give herself time to decide what to say, she begins to pick her way back to the car, to her son, to the rest of her life.

Florrie's managed to buy bread, but she never does do the food shopping and can't think what else she can get without a ration book. She should have asked Nell. But perhaps bread will do for now.

Cissy is waiting just where she said she would, on the bus-stop bench, opposite the Telephone Exchange.

'Don't you look smart,' she says, before Florrie can ask. 'And here.' She digs in her handbag.

'Thanks,' Florrie says. She's got on a grey dress she'd nicked for Ruby. It fits her alright, though the skirt had needed a pin around the waist.

She takes the envelope from Cissy's hand. 'Any trouble?'

'Easy as you like. Took him ten minutes, that quick. And I did the other. Have a look.'

Florrie opens the envelope and unfolds the two papers inside. She's no idea what a Matriculation Exemption looks like, but it's got a fancy typeface and her name written in the blank, in ink. The paper is thick and an expensive shade of cream. The other is a sheet of typed foolscap.

'Did it myself,' Cissy says. 'Is it alright, do you think?'

The reference calls Florence Palmer 'a good-natured, hardworking and decent girl'. The paper is headed, *Hillview School for Girls, Tonbridge.* The signature is looping and unreadable.

'Tonbridge?'

'It's in Kent,' Cissy says. 'It's a real school, where I went when I got evacuated. I mean, I never went there. I just walked past it all the time. D'you think it will do?'

'Let's find out.' Florrie folds it back into the envelope. 'Here, thanks for doing that. You're a pal.'

Cissy shrugs. 'It was your money. Well, your mum's, anyway.' But she looks pleased.

'And it was enough?'

'I talked him round.' Cissy giggles in the silly way she does, but Florrie doesn't seem to mind it this morning.

'Here,' Cissy says, 'where's your ring? They don't do the marriage bar, do they?'

Florrie looks down at her bare hand. 'I don't know. But I bet they'd rather have a single girl. I can put it back on after.'

Secretly, she's got this idea that she might want to get back the opal, if it can be done. Maybe have it reset into something a bit more flashy, but still. It's the ring she should have, the only one that means anything.

She says, 'Look here, do you want to wait? I can't say how long I'll be.'

'Course I'll hang on for you.' Cissy looks delighted to be asked to sit and freeze.

'And do I really look alright?'

'You'll have their eye out. But smile, won't you? You don't want to put the wind up them. You want to look like a nice girl.'

Florrie hitches a smile onto her face.

Cissy giggles again. 'I've seen worse. Go on. Don't want to be late.'

Florrie takes a deep breath and walks across the road. The door to the Telephone Exchange opens easily. There's a flight of stairs directly ahead of her, and from above there is the clatter of typewriters, the ringing of bells. Voices are saying brisk things, feet are walking smartly across the floorboards above her head.

She puts her hand up to check her hat is sitting well. One last look in her compact mirror. Her exhaustion shows in her eyes, but she only has to keep it at bay for a little while more and then she can go back to the flat and sleep and sleep.

And, she can't help thinking, even if they won't take her on, she might be able to see if there's a back door, find out what day the wages come, what office they go to before they're handed around. Perhaps she can persuade someone to show her over the place. But she thinks it in a habitual, uninterested way. She doesn't mean it. Almost certainly not.

'Hello,' she murmurs to herself, in her best voice. 'Florence Palmer to see Mr Johnson.'

She mounts the stairs, her heels clicking against the wood. As she climbs, her shoes and ankles are striped by a patch of misty light, cast by the pane of glass over the front door. It's not much, as light goes, pale yellow and thin, but it's a start, and an ending. The fog is beginning to lift.

Author's Note

Five Days of Fog is a fiction, but the Great Smog was real, and we know of at least one organised gang of female shop-lifters, about which more in a moment.

In 1952 London was well used to smog, but in December of that year an anticyclone pushed down all the filth in the air; the industrial smoke from the factories, the fumes of motor vehicles and the smoke from millions of coal fires, and held it over London for four and a half days. In parts of London it was said to be so thick that pedestrians couldn't see their own feet. It went through clothes and blackened skin; it crept down chimneys and invaded houses. And it was poisonous. A government report at the time put the death toll at 4,000, but it's since been suggested that the number might be as high as 12,000 with an additional 100,000 people's respiratory health affected. The Great Smog spawned new legislation in the form of the Clean Air Act of 1956, and was the beginning of the end of the residential coal fire. For *Five Days of Fog* I read a lot of anecdotal accounts and journalism of the time but I also drew ideas from *London Fog: The Biography*, by Christine L. Corton, and *Killer Smog: The World's Worst Air Pollution Disaster*, by William Wise.

The Cutters are my own creation, but are loosely based on the Forty Thieves, later called the Forty Elephants, a gang of female shoplifters from Elephant and Castle who operated from the 1890s possibly until as late as the 1960s. They were certainly still being referred to in police reports after World War Two.

Like the Cutters, the Forty Elephants had gang rules and meetings, chipped into a 'pot' to pay solicitors' fees and referred to their leader as the queen. The Forty Elephants were prolific shoplifters but they would also turn their hand to housebreaking, street robbery and wage-packet snatches. They were notoriously violent, and seem to have been as ready to attack men as they were other women. The idea of 'rolling' – posing as a prostitute in order to rob clients – was drawn from Lorraine Gamman's book, *Gone Shopping: The Story of Shirley Pitts*, although Pitts seems to have had male associates do the actual robbing. The Forty Elephants also had a male counterpart gang, the Elephant Boys, from which I derived the idea of the Godden Boys' tangled association with the Cutters.

I was inspired to have the Cutter women dress as men by Brian MacDonald's *Alice Diamond and the Forty Elephants* – in which, among many other fascinating things, can be found a list of the gang rules – which describes Elsie Carey, who led gangs of housebreakers while dressed as a man in the 1930s, and by Margo MacDonald's play *The Elephant Girls*, in which the female protagonist dresses as a man to act as minder for the other women.

Shirley Pitts, who lived from 1934 to 1992, is often described as the last queen of the Forty Elephants. I couldn't find evidence that she ever referred to herself as a member, although she does admit to having been trained in the art of shoplifting by Alice Diamond, who certainly was queen from about 1915. In her book *Borstal Girl*, Eileen MacKenney refers to Pitts' mother, Nell, as having been a member of the gang, although Gamman's *Gone Shopping* paints a picture of Nell as a dependent, somewhat helpless alcoholic. Alice Diamond died in 1952, just like Dolly Palmer.

Shirley Pitts also gave me the idea of having Florrie learn to speak 'nicely' by listening to the wireless – Alice Diamond forbade Pitts to open her mouth in the shops until she could lose the cockney from her voice.

Maggie Palmer was inspired by Alice Diamond's associate Maggie Hughes, who, like my Maggie, had tattoos, a baby face and a wild temper. But, according to legend, it was Alice Diamond who started a fight at the Kit Kat Club in 1927, provoking the band leader to play 'Lady be Good', which idea I liked so much I included it as happening to Maggie in my novel.

The idea of Ruby's early release through TB also came from *Gone Shopping*: Pitts' father obtained an early release for the same reason. He also ran an illegal printing press, as one of Harry's friends does in my novel.

Ted's tar blocks were real, too: Billy Webb's book, *Running with the Krays: My Life in London's Gangland*, describes a yard and block cleaning system just like Ted's. Webb also describes persuading a less powerful associate to run an illegal spieler from his home.

The Green Gate, mentioned briefly, were a gang of the late nineteenth century, based in Hoxton, and named after the pub in which they congregated. I resurrected them for the purpose of the novel, partly because I liked the name, and partly because they were well known for antagonising the male gangs south of the river.

Finally, the character of Nell, though she grew into her own person as I wrote, was originally inspired by my grandmother, Cora, who grew up in poverty and whose father and grandfather were by all accounts quite frightening men and not above breaking the law. Cora strove relentlessly to make a safer, more 'respectable' life for herself, and eventually became a teacher. She was a real survivor and an admirable person but, like Nell, was rigidly attached to her ideas about propriety and wasn't always able to express warmth or vulnerability. Her influence crept into the other characters, too. Ruby's memory of sitting nervously at the top of the stairs waiting for her father to come home, for instance, came from her, as well as Ted's fears about bringing friends from school home for tea. I have dedicated the book in part to her memory.

Acknowledgements

I am immensely grateful for the help and support of Karolina Sutton at Curtis Brown, Lettice Franklin at W&N and Arzu Tahsin, formerly of W&N.

Thanks are also due to the friends and family who agreed to act as readers, especially Caroline New and Norman Freeman, who spent countless evenings talking over ideas with me and read multiple drafts. Jessica Winkler, Sarah Freeman, Chris Beschi and Helen Palmer all gave astute feedback and encouragement. Jen Williams was invaluable in plotting the early shape of the story.

I'm also indebted to Debbie Freeman, whose feelings about her son I used as the basis for Ruby's flashback to Florrie's birth, and Anna Sopwith, who provided gruesome details about the experience of breaking her jaw.

Amy Underdown was kind enough to answer my questions about solicitors. Alan Moss of History by the Yard and Martin Stallion of the Police History Society were both incredibly helpful and patient in answering my questions about 1950s policing. Any inaccuracies remaining in the text are my own.